BIANCA

Also by Robert Elegant

FICTION

China and the West:
White Sun, Red Star (1921–1952)
Manchu (1624–1652)
Mandarin (1854–1875)
Dynasty (1900–1970)
A Kind of Treason
The Seeking

NONFICTION

China's Red Leaders
The Dragon's Seed
The Centre of the World
Mao's Great Revolution
Mao versus Chiang
The Great Cities: Hong Kong
Pacific Destiny: Inside Asia Today

BIANCA

A Novel of Venice

ROBERT ELEGANT

ST. MARTIN'S PRESS
NEW YORK

for
ED VICTOR
Who thought of it
and also for
Ann and Robert Tuchman
who made it possible

www.stmartins.com

ISBN 0-312-26127-6

First published in Great Britain by
Sinclair-Stevenson Limited

First U.S. Edition: August 2000

10 9 8 7 6 5 4 3 2 1

PROLOGUE

THE *Dove* fluttered timidly out of the harbour of Livorno, her white sails flapping in the variable winds. Eager for a quick passage eastward to Bari around the heel of the Italian boot, her captain ignored the misgivings aroused by the overcast skies and the mist offshore.

The guardships of the Order of St Stephen, founded a few decades earlier by Duke Cosimo of Tuscany, the captain assured himself, had swept the Ligurian Sea clear of predators. The Genoese merchant ship, laden with Florentine silk and woollen goods, was safe from attack by freebooters, whether Arab or English. The weather was deteriorating, but he had rounded the hook of Livorno and steered southward towards the isle of Elba so many times that he knew these waters as well as his wife knew her extensive and gaudy wardrobe. No reason to fear either man or nature today.

As the *Dove* turned her bulbous stern to Livorno, her bowsprit cleft a patch of fog, and in two minutes the entire vessel was swallowed. Ten minutes later, the little ship emerged into an ampitheatre of clear air beneath a vivid sky unflecked by cloud. The mist was scudding northward before a strong wind from the south. Obviously relieved, the captain set the *Dove* on a south-by-south-west course.

'Wind could be better,' he observed to the tall man in worn jerkin and breeches standing beside him at the rail. 'But what can you expect at this time of year?'

'Don't rightly know!' The accent was indefinable, offering no hint of his origins. 'Know nothin' 'bout the sea. Landsman myself. Farmer before . . .'

The captain waited, curious about his last-minute passenger. But the strong jaw snapped shut, and the landlubber said no more.

The captain was not altogether easy in his mind about the villainous-looking man with the slate-grey eyes who appeared to be in

(1)

his mid-forties. Travel-stained and weary, he had come aboard to buy passage only half an hour before the *Dove* sailed. He was accompanied by a blonde woman of fragile, aristocratic beauty, who was at least twenty years younger. Was she, the captain wondered, daughter, wife, or mistress?

The mismatched pair had a conspiratorial air about them. Why did they glance over their shoulders at the guardships even after the *Dove* had cast off the ropes that bound her to the dock? Why did they insist that their meagre belongings, even two casks of rough country wine, should not be locked securely in the hold, but crammed into their tiny cabin?

Fugitives from someone's justice, were they? Or they might be eloping. But the woman looked too aloof and the man too unkempt, as well as too old, for such romantic tomfoolery. More likely to be fleeing the vengeance of a swindled merchant, rather than a wronged husband. As likely, they were being pursued for burglary or murder; he had the look of a man accustomed to violence. And she? Most likely the fallen daughter of some worthy family, brought low by misplaced ardour and the clap!

Yet what did it matter? They had paid well for their passage, very well indeed. Eight gold ducats would buy the captain's wife six silk dresses or keep her serving maid for two years. They had paid the exorbitant fare without protest, immediately arousing the captain's suspicion. Well, the *Dove* would be rid of them within a week.

Glowing with pleasure at his windfall, the captain was expansive. He expounded the mysteries of the winds and the tides to his passenger, who, although clearly no fool, could not quite grasp the principles.

'Now, my good sir, when the wind is from the south, as now, I must sail across it, back and forth eastward and westward many times, to work my way southward. Each time my little *Dove* gains a few hundred yards or so. And soon . . .'

The captain broke off to peer around the horizon. Yes, damn it, his instinct was right. The wind was rising, and mist was rolling up from the south. Worse, they were sailing towards a dense fogbank only three miles to the west. He heard the wailing of horns and the dismal tolling of bells from ships warning of their approach as they groped through the fog.

'At least, there's no danger from pirates or privateers,' he told his enigmatic passenger. 'On a filthy day like this, even the goddamned English will be too busy worrying about their own necks to . . .'

'Vessel to starboard. Due north,' the lookout shouted from the main mast. 'Just coming out of the mist. Two or three miles distant. Heading westward.'

'Keep a better watch!' the captain called. 'Night's coming on. You'll need to be doubly alert.'

He turned to his attentive listener and explained: 'She's sailing parallel to our own course, probably bound south, too. But it's hard going. We have to fight for every inch of southing.'

'Capt'n!' The lookout hailed again. 'Looks like a war-galley.'

'No help for it.' The captain discarded his greatcoat and shivered in the chill December late afternoon. 'Have to see for myself.'

Remarkably agile for a middle-aged man with a wobbling pot-belly and pendulous cheeks spattered with red grog-blossoms, he shinnied up the mainmast. His long arms and legs scrabbling in the rope rigging, he looked like a giant black spider scuttling across its web.

Three minutes later, the captain came down even faster, sliding on the stays that supported the mast. He resumed his greatcoat, spat meditatively into the tumbled wake, and finally spoke, soft-voiced but vehement.

'Cursed Venetians! A war-galley no less! Venice, that nation of robbers and braggarts. At least we're not at war with 'em, not this year. But they always make trouble.'

'Trouble?' the passenger asked. 'What do you mean?'

'Just to show off . . . show Venice rules the seas. From Gibraltar to Constantinople, they claim. Since the Battle of Lepanto, they've been impossible . . . I'd almost rather she was a Turk or a Barbary pirate. Only the English privateers are worse.'

As he blustered on to himself, he was calculating rapidly. The passenger heard snatches of sentences: 'Too far for him, I reckon. Not against the wind. *We* could just make it, though . . . Better play safe, peace or no peace.'

Cupping his hands, the captain shouted: 'Make sail! Set all plain sail . . . and all kites. Helmsman, steer due west. Make for the fogbank.'

The *Dove* leaned over and surged forward when the helmsman pushed the long tiller to the right.

Happy to impress, the captain told the landlubber: 'Just for safety's sake. No need to worry, but I'd as soon he don't catch us. We're on a broad reach, you see. Our best point of sailing.'

When his passenger looked blank, the mariner drew a diagram on the wooden deck with a moistened forefinger: 'Now this long line's the wind, blowing due north. This short line here's us, like the top of a T. So the wind takes us on our side, and my little *Dove* goes her fastest. Way up north here's the galley. Wind's blowing in his face, you see. So he can't sail south fast enough to catch us, not even using his oars. Before he can come up to us, we'll be right inside the fog. Then he'll never find us. Thank God night's falling.'

'Galley's putting out oars,' the lookout reported. 'They're thrashing away like fury.'

'Take a good look, my friend,' the captain advised. 'First time you see a Venetian war-galley at full stretch is something to remember.'

The passenger watched with fierce concentration. The Venetian warship was magnificent, at once awe-inspiring and sinister. Her upper works shone gold, and the silver armour of her men-at-arms flashed in the sunlight. Thirty long sweeps on each side swung together to assist the sails set on her two stubby masts.

'The ultimate fighting-machine: three to four hundred men crammed aboard, 'bout 190 foot long, but no more'n seventeen across.' The Genoese captain gave grudging admiration to his city's hereditary enemy. 'A bitch to handle, but, by God, she's fast! You know, they make 'em by eye, never use a plan in the Great Arsenal. Cursed Venice still rules an empire. She's still the richest city in Europe, after nigh seven hundred years.'

'I know,' the passenger said softly. 'That is, I've heard.'

His gaze was fixed on the flags streaming in the wind of the galley's passage. On the foremast flew the ensigns of her squadron and her captain. On the mainmast a crimson banner with long swallow tails standing stiff in the breeze displayed a golden lion with golden wings, wielding a sword in its right paw.

'It seems she wants to say something to us.' The passenger pointed to the signal flags hoisted on the mast.

The captain shaded his eyes and squinted at the galley. 'Bloody be-damned hell! She's making: *Halt and heave to! I wish to speak with you.*'

He pondered for an instant, assessing distances with his eye and muttering: 'She's faster'n I thought. But we can make it. I *don't* wish to speak with you.'

He shouted to the mate: 'Run up everything you've got. I want to see your scarf, the cook's apron, and your wife's shift set and drawing wind.'

Many small sails were hurriedly set on the stays and extended out-board on long poles. The passenger thought he felt the *Dove* move a little faster through the whitecaps, which now were turning into storm

(4)

waves. The captain scowled and measured the angle between the two ships, using his thumb as a marker.

'Well, we should make it. Just!' he told his passenger and shouted to the helmsman: 'Bring her up a shade. Closer to the wind, but don't lose way. Steady now!'

The *Dove*'s rounded prow pointed a fraction to the south, marginally increasing the distance between the two vessels.

'That's better,' the captain declared. 'Let the damned bitch of a galley row her heart out. Arrogant bastard, her captain. But he's got guts. Doesn't worry about the guardships of St Stephen. He's a real Venetian, proud as the devil. But he's not catching my *Dove*, not today.'

The fogbank was perceptibly closer, as if itself drawing nearer in sympathy with the captain who feared the Venetian war-galley would loot his cargo. He was leaning forward, his clenched fists flung behind him, urging his ship on.

Having studied the galley intently, the passenger suddenly lost interest. He slid down the ladder from the high poop to the midships deck, where the blonde woman stood nervously clutching a stay. He smiled and leaned over and spoke softly. Her tense posture eased, as if the landlubber had somewhere found nautical wisdom that reassured her. More relaxed, they watched the galley together.

A puff of black smoke blossomed at her prow. Ten seconds later they heard the sharp report of a cannon.

The captain stood rigid, his eyes searching the roiled water between his ship and the galley. He smiled in triumph when a water spout marked the shot's fall two hundred yards north of the *Dove*. The galley was wasting powder and shot by firing her light cannon at an extreme range. Only another four minutes and the *Dove* would reach the shelter of the fogbank, where the galley would never find her.

Two more cannon-balls fell short, although ranging nearer. The last splashed eighty yards from the *Dove*. But that was margin enough with the fogbank only three minutes away.

'Ease her!' the captain roared. 'Let her fall off. I want her top speed.'

The helmsman moved the tiller minutely, and the water seething along the ship's sides burbled in a higher tone. The *Dove* surged towards the shelter of the fogbank as if aware of her peril.

A fourth puff of black smoke rose from the galley's prow, markedly larger and darker than its forerunners. The cannon's report, when it reached the *Dove*, was louder and deeper. An instant later, the ball plowed across the poop, hurling up a fountain of jagged splinters.

The helmsman crumpled without uttering a sound. He slumped face down on the deck, felled by the six-inch splinter that protruded beneath his left shoulder-blade.

Unguided, the *Dove* began swinging her nose into the wind, and her speed dropped sharply. The mate sprang to the tiller and wrestled the ship back on course. But she had lost two ship-lengths, and the galley was drawing close. Yet the captain grinned, derisively and triumphantly.

'Double-charge of powder!' he swore. 'Hell and be damned, they must want us bad. She could blow herself up, shake herself to pieces, using so much powder in a light gun. But, my Venetian friends, you've lost.'

The *Dove* was already wreathed by wispy grey tendrils as the fog reached out to embrace her. In a minute, no more, she would be totally enveloped – and safe.

A long shape glided out of the fog hardly twenty yards from the *Dove*, barring her way. Again the sailors saw the swallow-tail flag bearing the golden lion of Venice. The blonde woman clutched the arm of her companion.

The captain's grin turned to a grimace of horror, and he threw up his hands. There was no need for him to give any order, no point. Upon sighting the second galley, the mate had moved the tiller to bring the bow into the wind and halt the *Dove*'s movement.

While the new galley lowered a launch with brisk naval efficiency, the *Dove* rocked in the trough of the waves. The first galley drew up on her other side to quash any thought of escape. Three ghostly vessels wallowed fog-wreathed on the rising waves.

The oarsmen of the launch backed water as two officers clambered up the *Dove*'s rope-ladder. The rotund captain stepped forward, loud protests on his lips.

'Outrage!' he sputtered. 'A peaceful trading vessel on her lawful business fired upon. My helmsman killed . . . my ship damaged. You'll hear about this day's work! Your captain will rue it. I've got friends in Venice, important friends, even on the Council of Ten.'

'We are on the business of the Council of Ten, Captain,' the older officer said. 'Make whatever protests you wish – later. For now, stand out of my way. I seek two fugitives, a man and a woman, criminals to deliver to the justice of the Council of Ten.'

The captain said not another word. Even the bumptious Genoese was awed by the power of the Council of Ten, which dominated both the courts and the espionage services of the Most Serene Republic of Venice. Disdaining vain concealment, the passenger stepped forward.

'You want me, Lieutenant?' he asked, resigned.

'You and the lady . . . the woman. You're to come with me. With your baggage.'

Thankful to be getting off so easily, the captain sent two sailors to bundle the fugitives' belongings into the Venetian launch. A jute-sack, a valise of cheap carpeting, a willow-withe basket, and two rough-hewn casks of wine.

Stoically, the criminal helped his female accomplice down the rope-ladder to the launch that would carry them into captivity. Uncaring, the rowers looked stolidly at their feet. The woman appeared stunned. Only when the casks of wine were lowered on ropes did she show emotion, watching anxiously.

Formal in a steel helmet with a crimson crest and a mirror-polished breastplate above crimson trunk-hose, the galley's captain waited at the head of the gangway. Lowering that wooden walkway, so much easier for the woman than a rope-ladder, was a remarkable courtesy. As his captives' feet touched the deck, the captain removed his helmet and bowed.

'My Lord Commodore, Your Ladyship, welcome aboard,' he said. 'Thank God I found you quickly. A bit tricky so close to the port, but I was told you wanted no delay.'

'Precisely!'

'My cabin is at your disposal, as well as the stern saloon.'

'Thanks, Aurelio,' the middle-aged man nodded casually. 'Now, first, above all, get these casks into the cabin. You men, handle them gently. Very gently!'

The lady went ahead, her eye on the seamen who carried the wine-casks as if they were egg-crates. The man addressed as commodore asked in the clipped accents of Venice: 'Aurelio, how many ships've you stopped?'

'Six yesterday and seven today, sir. Most gave no trouble. Before this Genoese rascal turned up, we only had to fire one shot across a bow. Even with the damned fog . . .'

'Well done,' the commodore commended him. 'I'll deal with any political fuss. Now, let's pray all else is well.'

They entered the cabin that stretched across the stern, which, nowhere more than twelve feet wide, nonetheless appeared spacious. The lady was kneeling beside the casks, which were gushing wine into basins. When the flow stopped, she turned a bolt and removed the top of one cask to reveal a smaller cask inside. Reaching into the opening, she turned a second bolt and lifted the top off the inner cask.

Smiling in relief, the lady took from the inner cask an infant swaddled in blue silk. Quickly assuring herself that the boy was unscathed, she handed him to the commodore, who shrugged in ostentatious resignation. Kneeling still, she manipulated the second cask, from which she took an infant swaddled in red silk.

'The air tubes worked perfectly, Marco,' she said. 'I'm sorry I doubted you. Both are unharmed. Both Francesco and Francesca are very well indeed.'

Cradling the boy, the commodore turned to the galley captain and asked: 'How long to Venice?'

'With present winds, my Lord, a week to ten days.'

'Make haste, Aurelio. Make all reasonable haste. But do not give the lady and the babies a rough passage.'

CHAPTER I

'YOU'D marry me to a Turk to promote your schemes,' Bianca charged. 'I won't . . .'

'I couldn't,' her father replied. 'What sane Turk would marry you? Even if he had a hundred wives, your tongue would still drive him mad.' He added hotly: 'You know what I *will* do if you keep on defying me?'

'Tell me,' she challenged, her bravado hiding her fear. 'I know you want me to tremble.'

'Do you know what the old Venetian nobles did? They'd wall up a defiant daughter in a black cellar, wall her up with bricks. They'd keep her there, only a slit to pass in food, till she came to her senses. It didn't take long.'

'You couldn't do it!' she countered softly. 'Not nowadays!'

'Don't be certain of that. In this house I am king. But I won't keep you here, even in the cellar. I'll send you to the nuns. The Carmelites're enclosed, totally cut off from the world. They'll lock you in a tiny cell with only a wooden cross on the wall and a lumpy straw pallet on the stone floor. We'll see how you like that! Wearing sackcloth, never speaking to anyone, only praying to God for mercy.'

Her green eyes widened in recognition of the reality of the threat, but she responded with the calm learned from repeated encounters: 'Don't be ridiculous. You need me in the world outside. I know you've got to marry me off well. Only a wealthy son-in-law can save your business.'

'You'll marry who . . . and when . . . I say. You won't marry at all if I choose. But, Bianca, why make it so hard for yourself, for me? You know you'll do as I say in the end.'

Abruptly, his mood altered. The black-furred hand raised to cuff her fell now, and his fingers gripped her bare shoulder. He did not shake her, as she expected, but ran his hand down her side in a parody of affection. Feeling the heat of his palm through her thin shift, she hid her revulsion.

Placing both hands on her shoulders, he shook her gently, almost playfully, and demanded: 'Why can't you be a good, dutiful daughter, Bianca *mia*? Why do you always defy me? I've never given you reason.'

'No, Father,' she responded perfunctorily, pulling on her robe. 'Never.'

His often-repeated complaint was not worth a quarrel. She would save her energy, although he had, in truth, given her many reasons to resist his will. If she did not, she would be smothered by his demands and his self-serving schemes for her future. These clashes drained her emotionally, but she could not give in. If she did, he would use her as he pleased, regardless of what that meant to her life.

And why did he have to come into her bedroom while she was dressing, even if Rosanna Lomanin, whom she called Zia, Auntie, was with her? The crabbed woman of forty-eight, who was half governess and half lady's maid, made no difference. At the age of sixteen, Bianca was too old for any man to enter her bedroom, even her father, particularly her father.

Bartolomeo Capello, she warned herself, *is trying to charm you. Watch out!*

Bianca habitually thought of him by his full name. She had not called him Daddy for years, and she would not call him Father, not to herself. She had to keep a distance between them in her own mind. Accordingly, she thought of him as Bartolomeo Capello, nobleman of Venice, fifty-two years old, dark and burly, with a long white scar on his left cheek, which a Turk's scimitar had slashed a decade earlier. After years of abuse and bullying, she thought of him first not as her father, but as the violent former captain of a war-galley and present ship-owner now falling on hard times.

She almost preferred him in a rage to this edged silkiness. He could hurt when he slapped her with his calloused palm, but she knew where she stood. She never let him see that he hurt her, for she was no longer afraid of him – had not been for three years. With Bartolomeo Capello for a father, she'd had to grow up quickly.

Oddly, *he* was now a little afraid. Nowadays she could often outface him. That was why he resorted to threats – and why she had to take his threats seriously. He could no longer bully her with words alone, and he would not bruise her so badly that all Venice knew of his brutality. He was afraid of running down his few remaining assets, among which she was the foremost. Like most Venetian nobleman, he was, above all, a merchant. He believed himself a shrewd trader, and only a fool would damage his own merchandise. But she would not be the first Venetian noblewoman to be locked up in a convent to force her obedience.

Bianca wondered when he would stop toying with her – and say exactly what he wanted. He had stormed into her bedroom four minutes earlier and snatched from her hands the long silver gown she was to wear as a lady-in-waiting on the Royal bucentaur, the magnificent ship of the Doge, the reigning Duke of Venice.

'Not that dress!' he had observed. 'You're not going to wear it!'

Looking at her half-naked body with the speculative gleam in his eyes she had seen too often recently, he had grabbed the gown with both hands, as if to tear it in half. Instead, he had flung it to the tile floor, where it lay crumpled, bereft of all its gaiety.

Bianca bit the inside of her lip, determined that she would not cry. Although a silver gown that glistened when she walked was beautiful, it was hardly vital. Yet she loved that gown, which had been worn only twice by her mother's younger sister before it was recut for her.

Aunt Sophia was wonderful, although it could be embarrassing when she grew sentimental over her motherless niece. Bianca could barely remember her mother, who had died of a fever when she herself was only three. She could only remember soft hands smelling faintly of almonds and a soft voice sometimes raised in anger at her father.

Nowadays, Bartolomeo Capello stormed at her, calling her self-willed and a hoyden. He detested her independence, and he despised her fondness for study, which he swore was unfeminine. Above all, he wanted to break her spirit. He swore her stubbornness was like that of a sour crone, rather than a young gentlewoman. When very angry, he swore she was just like her mother, whom he had loved despite her obstinacy.

'You're not to wear that dress today.' His voice was tense, his violent temper just under control. 'Not today or ever. I don't need charity from your mother's rich family. The Morosinis can keep their hand-me-downs.'

'She has nothing else to wear, Ser Bartolomeo.' Zia Rosa steeled herself to interrupt. 'And she has to look beautiful for the Doge's Marriage to the Sea.'

'You needn't worry!' he rejoined. 'She's not going.'

'Not going, Ser Bartolomeo?' The timid governess was roused to indignation. 'How many young ladies are chosen to attend the Doge on the greatest day of the year? Who knows who'll notice her – or what could come of it?'

'She not going,' he replied. 'That's all.'

'Why?' Bianca demanded. 'How can you forbid me to . . .'

'Who gave you the right to question me? I said no!'

'But lady-in-waiting to the Dogaressa herself. The honour to the family, to the Capellos of Sant' Aponal . . .'

Bartolomeo replied coldly: 'I don't want you parading our poverty in a hand-me-down dress. I don't want everyone to know the Morosinis' influence got you the honour.' His anger flared again. 'I . . . we . . . don't need your mother's rich relations patronising us as if we were nobodies. Bucentaur or not, you'll still be a noblewoman of Venice.'

'Am I never to get out? Am I supposed to stay forever in this hovel . . .'

She knew her mistake as she spoke, and his explosion came within seconds: 'Hovel is it? The palazzo where your ancestors . . .'

Yet he could still surprise her. Instead of raging, he added shortly: 'Anyway, you won't stay forever. I told you I had plans for you.'

Although determined to remain calm, Bianca erupted. The volcanic Capello temper was not a male monopoly.

'Other plans?' she demanded hotly. 'And may I ask what those plans might be?'

'Not now. I'll tell you when the time comes.'

'It's my future . . . my life! And you won't . . .'

Rosanna Lomanin was once again an uneasy spectator to a clash between father and daughter. The child was growing up, the child whom she loved as a mother would, but had never given a full measure of a mother's love or protection. Rosanna was deathly afraid of losing her place in the household, which was her only refuge, if she dared stand up to Bartolomeo Capello.

Chastened by her guilt, the governess watched with her plump hands clenched on her round belly. Her little black eyes, gleaming raisins in her dough-white face, darted back and forth from Bartolomeo to Bianca.

Their fiery temperaments were so alike. Although the girl was not cruel, she could be just as obdurate as her father. She was, of course, at a great disadvantage, as was any woman against any man of equal rank. She was virtually her father's possession, utterly dependent on him until he married her off – and she became dependent on another man. But Bianca was fighting as hard as if she could really hope to win the unequal battle.

Their heads thrust forward combatively, father and daughter hurled words at each other. Alike in temperament, they were superficially different in appearance: gnarled autumn and bright spring.

The soot-black hair that hung over Bartolomeo's ears was streaked with grey and thinning on top so that he resembled a tonsured monk. The pale scar that bisected his left cheek accentuated the strong arch of his nose and its flaring nostrils. His mouth was wide, but his lips had been drawn taut by time.

Yet he was not an ugly man, far from it. His forehead was nobly domed, and Rosanna Lomanin was captivated by his large green eyes, which were youthful, candid, and, somehow, innocent, as if untouched by his volcanic temper or his violent past. Although hot-headed and domineering, he had not been so harsh before the last merchant ship that flew his flag was taken by Arab pirates six months earlier.

Almost the identical eyes now glared from his daughter's oval face. Also deep green, Bianca's were set farther apart, slightly canted, above all softer and vulnerable.

Bianca's courage faltered for an instant, and her full lower lip trembled very slightly. Her thick lashes curtained her eyes, and her eyebrows drew together. They were a shade darker than her hair, which flamed red-gold in the morning light. Venetian ladies spent hours in the sun, their hair drenched with unguents, then spread to dry on broad-brimmed hats without crowns. The colour they coveted, called Titian after the greatest living painter, was Bianca's already at birth.

Bartolomeo Capello was distracted from his purpose. The first time he saw Bianca's mother among the holiday throngs at the bull-baiting in the Campo San Polo, Pellegrina Morosini's hair had glowed with the same fire in the afternoon sun. He was momentarily abashed at his own harshness. Yet he could not relent, for his daughter was virtually his last negotiable asset.

The dark face and the bright face seemed to Zia Rosa's unhappy eye like an angry god and goddess glaring at each other in an allegorical painting. The family resemblance went beyond their green eyes: the delicate arch of her nose reflected the bold arch of his, and their high, narrow foreheads were alike.

Her skin was, however, fair, having been protected since birth from the Mediterranean sun that had burnt his olive complexion. Her high cheekbones and large eyes gave Bianca an air of expectation and wonder. She had a way of widening her eyes when she was moved that in turn moved others. But there were now dark bruises beneath her eyes.

Notwithstanding, Zia Rosa thought Bianca looked beautiful, but, as always, too sensual, too open. Her features were truly too marked for conventional beauty, too striking for an age that favoured docile ladies with blunt, rather sheeplike faces.

'Won't you tell me,' she pleaded again, 'what you're planning for me?'

'No reason I should explain myself to you.' Bartolomeo recovered his purpose. 'But I will tell you why you can't go on the bucentaur today – whatever you wear. You've got to learn one thing above all: *When you do marry, it'll be a man I choose*. I won't have you parading yourself among the ladies-in-waiting today. And I won't have you flirting with Florentine scum like that Buonaventura. Not ever.'

'Father, I never . . . I only said good day to him, just once. Otherwise, I never . . .'

Bianca's anger at the unjust accusation choked her, and her words stumbled. Knowing herself innocent, she gave an impression of guilt.

Wryly triumphant at that apparent confirmation of his suspicions, Bartolomeo added: 'You can also forget about going to the gala for my cousin Damiano's new palazzo tonight. Anyway, you're much too often with his son Marco. Not only the Florentine, but your own cousin.'

His self-righteousness becoming fury, he raged out of control: 'You just can't leave the men alone, can you, Bianca? You've got the soul of a slut, so unlike your mother. Maybe you'll learn from being cooped up on the greatest day of the year. Maybe, just maybe, you won't end up in the gutter.'

'I don't believe it!' Bianca was furious at that new attack. 'You *can't* mean what you're saying. It's too ridiculous! How you can think . . .'

'And, for God's sake, put some clothes on.' He cut her off. 'You're always flaunting yourself. It's disgusting. Even with your own father . . .'

The front door slammed, and Zia Rosa called a loud farewell. Bartolomeo's heavy tread reverberated on the Crooked Bridge that arched over the narrow Sant' Aponal Canal. The thud of his heels on the flagstones of the alley receded and died away. He was now, Bianca knew, striding past the thirteenth-century Church of Sant' Aponal, which had given its name to the district. He would, she assumed, just this once ignore the courtesans who hung out of the windows overlooking the church square.

Imposing in the black ceremonial robe of a nobleman, Bartolomeo would hail a public gondola on the Grand Canal, for the Capellos of Sant' Aponal no longer kept their own gondola. Before he sold it, even that battered craft had looked pretentious before their modest house. His position was, however, untouched by his new poverty – for the moment, at least. He was, regardless, a patrician of Venice, his name inscribed in the *Golden Book of Noble Families* among some two thousand men who ruled the city by hereditary right.

The crimson sun rising out of the east gilded the spires and domes of Venice, turning the Grand Canal to molten gold. The tall palazzos on its banks shimmered in that mirror like enchanted castles, their faded rust, ochre, and lime façades undulating whenever a gondola passed. The silver reflections of their windows, pointed Gothic or rounded Romanesque, shattered into bright fragments each time an oar broke the surface of the water. At the centre of the city born of the sea, the graceful arch of the Rialto Bridge glowed honey pale.

Bartolomeo Capello's destination lay the other way: the Piazza of Venice, the grandest square in Europe. In its centre the red-brick belltower thrust high into a sky that seemed to mirror the vivid blue of the Adriatic Sea, and the five bulbous domes of the Cathedral of St Mark shone luminous grey. Bartolomeo would join the entourage of noblemen who escorted the Doge to the Mole of St Mark's, where the land that gave the Venetians shelter met the sea that gave them wealth and glory. The Doge, the elected ruler of the city-empire, would then embark on his gold-and-crimson barge of state, the Royal bucentaur, for his symbolic Marriage to the Sea.

Furious at being deprived at her part in the solemn ritual, Bianca stalked down the stone stairs, her heels clicking a staccato protest. The drab counting-room was deserted, the two remaining clerks off for the holiday. She slammed her fists down on the ink-stained leather top of Bartolomeo Capello's writing-table. Snatching up a sheaf of documents, she began to tear them.

When the paper resisted, she stopped and smiled grimly. Why tear them, after all? She was bound to be holding some of the long-unpaid bills and dunning letters that tormented Bartolomeo Capello. Besides, there was another way, a better way. Still quivering with indignation, she slammed the heavy door behind her and clicked up the narrow stairs.

No matter how justified she might be, she could not ignore her father's flat prohibition. She could not put on the silver dress and take her place among the ladies-in-waiting to the Dogaressa. She could not defy him in this, as she had in the past defied him on lesser issues – and would cheerfully again.

If she did, his rage would erupt the moment he saw her, and the scene that followed would be a humiliation the city would never forget. Then, he would assuredly carry through his threat to lock her up under the harsh discipline of the Carmelites. The stern laws of Venice gave him every right to punish her severely for public disobedience – and to keep her confined until she gave in.

A private party, no matter how grand, was a different matter. Bartolomeo Capello would probably beat her for attending the celebration of the opening of Ca' Capello, Cousin Damanio's magnificent new palazzo on the Grand Canal, but that was a trifling risk to run. She knew, though, that she could not wear her Aunt Sophia's silver dress.

Puffing up the narrow staircase fifteen minutes later, Zia Rosa sensed that something was amiss. She was, she realised, startled by the silence in the palazzo. Bianca should have been raging, perhaps sobbing out her anger on her bed, perhaps appealing to the Blessed Virgin for justice. But there was only silence.

Zia Rosa found her charge in the big parlour on the second floor. Bianca was humming a favourite song, 'Our Lion of Venice', while turning over the dresses that lay, well protected against moths and mildew, in her mother's big wedding chest.

Bartolomeo had never been able to bring himself to give those dresses away. His daughter was, this once, grateful to him.

CHAPTER II

HIS eyes narrowed against the glare of the morning sun, Captain Marco Capello looked for his cousin Bianca on the deck of the great ship. But he was too far away to distinguish the faces swaying like white peonies above the bright flowerbed of the noblewomen's festive gowns.

His galley was anchored with her squadron off St George's Island, while the Doge's bucentaur was just putting off from the Mole of St Mark's half a mile away. A yellow haze shimmered on the royal vessel where gold leaf lay thick on her immense figurehead and along her sides. Urged by roaring cannon and pealing bells, forty oars a side churned the aquamarine water. But the stately vessel moved at her own pace, matching the solemn rhythm of the hymns chanted on her deck.

Lifting off his gleaming steel helmet, Marco wiped his sweaty face with his sleeve. He shaded his eyes with the palm of his hand, peered hopefully at the ship – and glimpsed her face above her silver gown. The next instant he saw that the wench's hair was darker than Bianca's flaming red-gold and her features were coarse. Ignoring a stab of disappointment, he continued his search.

The golden radiance enveloping the bucentaur made her seem a vessel of pure light floating above the placid lagoon. The refracted light distorted her outlines, and the great belltower in the Piazza of St Mark's behind was bent sharply. In the Piazzetta, between the Cathedral and the Mole, two slender white columns also bent: on one, an image of St Theodore; on the other, the winged lion of St Mark the Evangelist, the city's patron. No criminal or traitor hung between the columns on this festive day.

To the right, the pale mass of the Doge's Palace also seemed to float in the cinnamon-spiced spring air, its pointed arches reaching towards

Heaven. To the left, the New Mint was still under construction after five decades; never wholly content with the present, the city was yet reluctant to change. Away to the left, beyond the façades of pale ochre and faded crimson, opened the broad mouth of the city's chief artery, the Canalazzo, which visitors called the Grand Canal.

All this was today merely a backdrop for the gold-and-crimson vessel that was re-enacting the role she had played for five hundred and sixty-three years. Bucentaur she was called from the Greek: *bu* for bull and *centaur* for a creature half beast and half man, for the figurehead of the first bucentaur had been a man's head and torso on a bull's body.

Most Venetians, however, called her *la maesta nave*, the ship of majesty, for she carried the Doge, the ruler of the city that ruled half the Mediterranean. His title meant no more than Duke; his fellow noblemen elected him for his lifetime; and he was closely accountable to the Senate, made up of those noblemen. Nonetheless, the Doge was more powerful than most kings. Only the Pope in Rome and the Emperor in Vienna rivalled his power – and them, too, he ignored when they presumed to command him.

As the bucentaur approached the anchored war-galleys, Marco Capello unsheathed his Toledo steel cutlass in salute. Bianca, he concluded disconsolately, was not aboard, having perhaps been forbidden by her choleric father.

Beset by misfortune, Bartolomeo Capello was a trial not only for his daughter, but for all the family. Marco let his elders worry about the damage to their name done by Bartolomeo's erratic behaviour. He was concerned only for Bianca, who, he feared, might act recklessly, perhaps self-destructively, if pressed harder by her brutal father.

Marco felt almost parental responsibility for Bianca. Four years older, twenty to her sixteen, he had played the elder brother to the motherless girl. He might have fallen in love with her were such love not forbidden by Holy Church because of their close ties of blood.

Yet he sometimes wondered if he were not in love with her. He could not allow himself to think of marrying Bianca, even though they could win a dispensation from the Patriarch of Venice. His branch of the Capellos was prosperous, but their principle was to bring new wealth into the family, not to endow each other. The greatest obstacle was, however, the difficulty of engaging her attention, much less her affection, for more than an hour or two.

Well, she was only sixteen, a year short of the age of marriage for a patrician lady. What girl of sixteen was not flighty?

Yet you could not really call Bianca flighty. Her hard upbringing had given her a seriousness, a sense of purpose, that would have graced some ladies twice her age. Clearly, her purposes did not include her Cousin Marco, except as a friend, counsellor, and, if need be, champion.

Eighty crimson oars fluttering white foam, the bucentaur drove through the black smoke from the salutes of the galleys' cannon. As he followed the great vessel with his eyes, Marco knew he cut a heroic figure in his mirror-bright breastplate, puffed scarlet trunks, and the green hose that showed off his muscular calves. He was justly proud of being captain of the *Galley of the Angels*, at twenty the youngest captain in the Venetian fleet.

He returned his cutlass to its gold-chased scabbard, gave the order to weigh anchor, and listened to the festive tumult from the shore.

In the Piazza, trumpets, mandolins and drums were weaving melodies to the obligato of firecrackers. The common people cavorted on the mosaic pavement to airs by Scarlatti, skirts swirling high as women pirouetted across the carpet of confetti and flower-petals that covered the vast square. For two weeks, all Venice would feast and drink, sing and sport, gamble, gawk at mountebanks, and make love with unlikely partners in unlikely places. The Marriage to the Sea was the start of the most uninhibited party of the year in a city renowned for extravagant parties.

Marco marvelled at what he saw: tanned Persians in flower-pot hats, yellow Mongols crowned with black fur, Egyptians in red fezzes, even a pale Japanese princeling in a short royal-blue coat with a broad sash. All the nationalities of Europe were there. Even stateless Jews were welcome to live in the district called the Ghetto, the Foundry, where forges had once echoed. To divert her guests, Venice offered the largest corps of prostitutes in the civilised world.

The lagoon had for centuries been the West's chief seaport, although it covered less than two hundred square miles and was never inhabited by even two hundred thousand souls. Richest and most advanced of the states of Europe, Venice had shaped its trade and finance, its literature and art, its science, technology, and manufacturing. She was today, as in the past, Europe's channel to the wealth of the Orient – and Europe's shield against the expansion of the Orient.

That grandeur was now gravely threatened. Having captured Constantinople a century earlier, the Turkish Empire was now challenging Venice herself. Every generation, it seemed, had to fight its own wars against aggressive Islam.

Marco Capello marvelled at the panorama that encapsulated his city's glory, power, and wealth. After High Mass in the cathedral, noblemen and noblewomen, as well as prosperous burghers and their wives, had boarded a flotilla of gondolas, wherries and barges, to escort the Royal bucentaur across a lagoon strewn with blossoms. All those craft carried revellers and musicians; all flew bright pennants; all were laden with food and wine.

When the bucentaur drew near the *porto di Lido*, where the lagoon opened to the Adriatic Sea, a stately barge flying green-and-blue banners with bold white crosses drew alongside. It carried the Cardinal-Archbishop, the Patriarch of Venice, who was the spiritual heir of St Mark the Evangelist.

The barge circled the bucentaur thrice. Each time, the Patriarch pronounced his benediction, ending: 'We worthily entreat Thee, oh Lord, to grant that this sea be tranquil and quiet for our men and for all others who sail upon it. Oh hear us, Lord!'

While hymns of supplication and praise were sung, the Patriarch flourished an olive branch heavy with holy water. The Doge nodded, and the Patriarch poured holy water into the salt sea. Then Venetians forgot for a moment the reverses they had recently suffered, as well as the peril that threatened them from the aggressive Moslems and, almost equally, from their Christian allies.

Marco Capello swore to himself that he would make his name in the coming war against the Turks. Far better to lose all, even his life, than to fail in courage.

He knew he looked the part, having escaped the excessively regular features that made his father Damiano look like a handsome but rather insipid hero in a classical painting. His face was ruddy from exposure to wind and rain. His wiry black hair was cut short, just fringing his broad forehead and neck. The previous year he had grown a short beard that hid his strongly rounded chin. Since the beard itched unmercifully and made him look like a young satyr, he had shaved it off. But his steady grey eyes, the humped bridge of his nose, and his height of five foot eleven were appropriate for a fighting man.

Captain Marco Capello again unsheathed his cutlass in salute when Gioralamo Priuli, the eighty-third Doge of the Most Serene Republic of Venice, majestic in a gold-embroidered crimson robe with an ermine cape, strode to the bucentaur's prow where the golden figurehead of Justice wielded her golden sword. Like his forerunners for half a millennium, the Doge reaffirmed the sacred union between the Sea and the City, which was itself as much a creature of the water as of the land. Raising his arm high, he threw his gold ring into the sea.

'We espouse thee, O Sea,' he declaimed triumphantly. 'We espouse thee as a sign of true and perpetual dominion.'

EVENING: ASCENSION DAY, MAY 11, 1564
VENICE: CA' CAPELLO ON THE GRAND CANAL

'They're mad for art, these Capellos, obsessed with pictures and music. You'd think they were new rich!'

The venomous words filtered through the pouting lips of the noblewoman's mask. Pink and blue swirls concealed her face, but her cerise gown showed the white-powdered slopes of her bosom as far as her rouged nipples.

'They're not really *old* nobility, of course,' said the man with the pale-blue eyes. 'Only been in the *Golden Book* for three centuries.'

'It's absurd, this music. A castrato singing "Jason's Lament"! Mourning the death of *his* sons at Medea's, their mother's, hand.'

'I know who Medea was, my dear!'

Through windows open to the spring breeze, customers in the shops on the Rialto Bridge heard the limpid soprano soaring over the viola and the harp. But the five hundred guests of Damiano Capello, crowded into the great portego of his rebuilt palazzo, could barely hear their own words for the general din and the clatter of plates in the hands of the hired waiters who assisted Damiano's fifty-six house servants. Yet, from time to time, a sentence rang out.

'That ceiling's the best thing Tintoretto's ever done,' a male voice declared. 'Just look at those goddesses! Glorious breasts . . . and what buttocks!'

'Perfection! Even the golden apple in Paris's hand . . .' The female voice replying was extinguished by the noise.

A feminine laugh tinkled, and Marco Capello turned expectantly. Finding it came from a dark, black-haired, middle-aged woman, he moved away disappointed.

The empty portego had looked immense when he returned from the Marriage to the Sea. Crammed with guests, it now seemed small. But it was large enough to hide the face he sought.

Marco studied Tintoretto's latest work with fascination. Three goddesses candidly displayed their charms so that Paris, the Trojan prince, could choose the fairest. Even their private parts were lovingly depicted behind the transparent veils perfunctorily painted to placate the prudish.

Marco looked again for his cousin Bianca, who so much hated to miss a party. He had looked for her on the bucentaur and in the Piazza. He had not gone to the Palazzo Capello in Sant' Aponal. He did not fear Bartolomeo, but he did fear bringing Bartolomeo's wrath down on Bianca.

The great men of Venice were assembled for the opening of Ca' Capello: senators and ministers, admirals and directors of the great Arsenal, justices and state inquisitors in ceremonial scarlet robes trimmed with gold and ermine. Foreign ambassadors and merchants were brilliant in parti-coloured silks with sleeves slashed to show canary linings. Scientists and artists stood out in dark academic robes. But Tintoretto with his little grey beard and Titian with his benign smile were richly attired, grandees in their own right in the art-crazed city.

After the Habsburg Emperor sacked Rome four decades earlier, Venice had become a haven for thinkers and creators. Her publishers were the most enterprising, and her universities were eager for new ideas. The vast wealth accumulated through centuries of trade and banking was lavished on paintings, sculpture, and splendid edifices, private or public.

The noblemen were outshone by their ladies. Their gowns were low-cut, and their wide skirts, which swept the marble floor, were boldly dyed: scarlet, tangerine, lemon yellow. Necklaces of Red Sea pearls cascaded around smooth white throats. Diamond clasps secured egret feathers soaring from high-piled coiffures. Rubies, sapphires and emeralds glittered in bracelets and tiaras.

Gusts of attar of roses contended with zephyrs of orange blossom and gales of musk. Also with other odours: sweat long-dried on rich fabrics and the underlying reek of mould. The fragrance of basil, rosemary, and sage from the kitchens below almost overcame the stale odour of unwashed bodies.

The great hall shimmered, all the bright colours melting and whirling like a frenzied kaleidoscope. Marco had never been seasick, not even when his galley rolled and bucked in a storm, but now he was nauseated, almost overcome by the stench, the heat, and the din.

He searched for escape. At the far end of the portego, big windows opened onto the balcony overlooking the Canal. Marco heard the pure voice of the castrato singing Cassini's paean to his 'beloved beauty', but he could not squeeze through the throng. Behind him, a small door stood open to the breeze. He slipped onto the narrow balcony overlooking the rear courtyard.

Although the air was heavy, he recovered rapidly. Suddenly he heard the murmur of voices behind the wicker screen that partitioned the long balcony. He moved his head slightly to peer through a crack between the strands.

His cousin Bianca was standing with her back to the courtyard, her hands grasping the balustrade. He could not see to whom she was talking so animatedly. But he did not want to move and, perhaps, alarm her by making a noise. Not wishing her to catch him out as an unwilling eavesdropper, he became a deliberate eavesdropper.

The red sun descending in the west threw a rainbow aura around Bianca. Her flame-red hair, wound in a braid around her head, glowed like a halo. Her lips, just glossed with rouge, smiled lazily. She chuckled softly.

A canary-yellow overskirt flared from her narrow waist in an inverted vee, its panels looped back to show her sky-blue underskirt. Like a mirror image, her blue bodice, embroidered with tiny golden galleys, opened to show the inner curves of her breasts.

Marco was spellbound, though he disliked the daring style. Respectable ladies had taken it from the courtesans, who were ordered by the Senate to show their breasts – in the hope of winning over the many young men who preferred their own sex. Despite that immodesty, Bianca was lovely silhouetted against the setting sun. Her unseen partner guffawed.

'So you just slipped out?' The accent was not Venetian. 'And when the old man discovers . . .'

'Maybe a slap or two. I'm used to that.' She shrugged. 'He won't lock me up with the Carmelites for going to a cousin's party.'

'You know just how his mind works, don't you?'

'How else can I stop from getting beaten black and blue? But this plan of his . . .'

'What plan is that?'

'I don't really know. That's the worst of it. Probably wants to marry me off to some fool with an old name and a rich father.' She paused. 'I couldn't bear it, Pietro. I couldn't . . .'

Marco started, missing the first words of the man's reply: '. . . could always, you know. Not the worst thing in the world.'

Bianca smiled and mused in a low voice: 'It would be exciting, very. To get away from Venice and to see something of the world.'

'Then why not?' he pressed. 'Why don't we . . .'

Her eyes glowed. Then she laughed and replied without rancour: 'Frying pan to fire, a penniless Florentine adventurer . . . I am fond of you, Pietro. But we'd be caught before we got twenty miles. *You* sound like the romantic girl, not I. You know I'm fond of you. But no more foolish talk.'

Marco disliked the man's voice. It was too smooth – golden and greasy as second-rate olive oil. Now, though, it sounded a little gritty.

'Just to give you a way out. No more!' he said stiffly. 'And I'm certainly not penniless. The Buonaventuras are highly respected in Florence, and we're winning back our estates. Do you think the Salviati Bank employs penniless adventurers?'

'I'm sorry, Pietro. You're so good to me – and I tease you. I was only teasing, but I'm glad you're not proposing.'

'No, I'm not. Not now.'

Marco clenched his fists when the man stepped from the shadow at the back of the balcony. He was six inches taller than Bianca's slender five foot four, and he swaggered in a green velvet doublet and scarlet hose. But the sunlight showed the doublet's frayed cuffs and hose worn thin at the knees. Yet, Marco conceded bitterly, a naïve young girl could easily be carried away by the foreigner's false glamour.

He knew Pietro Buonaventura, the junior clerk at the Salviati Bank of Florence, whose branch was near the Palazzo Capello in Sant' Aponal. A year or so older than himself, Buonaventura was at twenty-one well practised in deceit and vice. But, then, so were most Florentines.

Yet the rascal would be attractive to an infatuated sixteen-year-old. His dark eyes were framed by sleek blond hair that curled above his shoulders. His mouth, full and self-indulgent, moulded and red as a painted cherub's, could appear sensual to a very young woman. The Florentine had a devil-may-care air, and his skin was tinted pale gold by the sun. The answer to every maiden's prayer, he clearly thought himself.

'May I hope that you are free for this dance, my Lady?'

Buonaventura bowed formally, sweeping his plumed red-velvet cap across his chest in self-parody of a dashing cavalier.

'Perhaps, Signore.' She laughed and opened her arms. 'But we must really dance, not stay out here. We've already been far too long. Pietro, I wonder. My father . . .'

'How better show our innocence . . . nothing to hide . . . than dancing together before all your relations?'

'Well . . . Oh, why not? I suppose it'll be all right.'

Marco wanted to shout a warning, but could not reveal his presence. It would not be all right at all, their dancing together in view of half the nobility of Venice. It would, at the least, mark her as careless, or, worse, as reckless and headstrong.

This Buonaventura was not even a Venetian. He was certainly not a patrician. Noblewomen of Venice married only noblemen of Venice or, if so instructed, foreign kings or princes.

The Florentine took Bianca in his arms as if to dance on the balcony. He lowered his head and pressed those full, red lips to her throat. Bianca finally pushed him away, her palms flat on his chest.

But, Marco wondered, was that rejection a little slow? Was she a little reluctant to let him go?

CHAPTER III

BIANCA smiled hard at her own reflection. Although her features were splintered by the spiderweb cracks of the old looking-glass, she could see that her smile was forced and her high forehead was knotted with strain. She smoothed the momentary wrinkles away with her fingertips, but could not so easily remedy her red-rimmed eyes. She had been weeping too much.

They were tears of anger, not tears of submission. While Bartolomeo Capello thought she was lying in despair on her hard bed, she had been making up her mind what she must do and how she would do it. The storms were now over, and her resolution was hardened. She must act soon, act swiftly and coolly.

She had not seen the storm coming, for she had allowed her vigilance to lapse. He had put her off guard by his lenience after the reception at Ca' Capello.

Fortunately, she had not danced with reckless Pietro Buonaventura, but had discreetly left him on the balcony. Under her Aunt Sophia's tolerant but watchful eye, she had spent the evening with Marco and his three sisters. He had been in a foul temper, addressing hardly a word to her. Still, young men were flighty, their moods often puzzling.

Afterwards, Bartolomeo Capello had been uncharacteristically lenient. Since he did not know she had been with Pietro, he could not punish her for flirting. He had sneered at her '*very* close friendship' with Marco, but that was no more than she expected. He had, naturally, reprimanded her for leaving the palazzo against his wishes and for taking her mother's gown. Then, to her surprise, she had escaped with a single slap – and that half-hearted.

It would have been silly to force a quarrel by telling him that the gown was hers by right as the only daughter. Nor, though tempted, had she pointed out that her mother's jewellery was also hers by her mother's dying wish. She knew he kept the jewellery in a secret drawer in his writing-table, but saw no need to tell him she knew.

Bianca smiled again. Her image smiled back, distorted by the cracked looking-glass so that she had three nostrils and one eye. She laughed. There would be no more tears. God would help only if she fought for herself.

Father Sebastiano at the church of Sant' Aponal had urged her not to give up hope. He had promised that God would intervene in His own time. Although God was the old priest's stock in trade, Bianca had drawn courage from that promise.

Father Sebastiano had also advised her to appear to fall in with Bartolomeo Capello's wishes while awaiting divine intervention. That she could no longer do, not wholly.

Bianca looked round her small bedroom – and was comforted by the relics of childhood: the green bed painted with red poppies and the old black doll with yellow-glass eyes. Aunt Sophia always remarked on the rough furniture when she came to see that her brother-in-law was not mistreating her niece beyond endurance. The daughter of the wealthy Morosinis and, now, the wife of a successful lawyer, Aunt Sophia was used to luxury. Still, the green dresser on which the crazed looking-glass stood was undeniably crude, as was the stool before it.

The red-crayon sketch of praying hands was, however, far from crude. Aunt Sophia said it was a study for a larger work by Leonardo da Vinci, who had made his name designing fortifications. Her sister Pellegrina, Aunt Sophia said, had been given the sketch by a suitor from Milan. He was a count, but Pellegrina's father would not allow her to marry a foreigner. Pellegrina Morosini, a noblewoman of Venice, had, instead, married Bartolomeo Capello, a nobleman of Venice. Pellegrina had married dutifully – and, her daughter believed, regretted her obedience all her life.

Turning away from the looking-glass, Bianca dropped to her knees beside the bed, closed her eyes, and placed her palms together. She prayed to the Blessed Virgin Mary, who intercedes for women. When she rose, her spirit was refreshed. She was again hopeful – and she was even more determined to resist her father's tyranny.

Marco would have been proud of her; and he would have found a way to help her. But Marco was beyond reach. The *Galley of the Angels* had sailed four weeks ago, carrying an ambassador to Constantinople, the capital of the Empire of the Ottoman Turks, which stretched from the Indian Ocean across Arabia and the Middle East, through Egypt and Morocco to the Straits of Gibraltar. The mighty Ottoman Empire was the Serene Republic's chief enemy.

She had last seen Marco at the Mole of St Mark's when the *Angels* sailed, standing among his sisters, waving and promising to meet again in the New Year. That was late October, just before Bartolomeo Capello revealed his plans for her.

He had, Zia Rosa said, resisted the inevitable for half a year. But in mid-October, when the trading season was almost over, he had lost the last ship in which he had an interest – and thus forfeited his last hope of recouping his fortunes in trade. Lagging behind her convoy, the slow merchantman, laden with silks, dyestuffs and spices, had been snapped up by Dalmatian pirates only two days from port. Sea passage had been particularly perilous since the economising faction in the Senate sharply cut expenditure on the Great Arsenal and the Navy.

Bartolomeo had lost both his half-share of the ship and his half-share of her cargo. His profit on the luxury goods would have been seventy-five percent. Instead, he was crushed by the debts incurred to finance the voyage. He had imprudently guaranteed to his reluctant partners that he would assume all losses himself. So desperate was he.

Only one course was open then to Bartolomeo. He had summoned Bianca to his counting-room, where he had just dismissed his last remaining clerk. Gravely, with none of his normal bluster, he had then revealed his plan for her future. She remembered that scene with uncanny clarity, as she would all her life.

Bartolomeo Capello waved his daughter to the arm-chair beside his writing-table. Wary of his courtesy, Bianca stared at the drab-green wall behind him, her hands tensely gripping the chair's wooden arms. She relaxed with an effort and clasped her hands loosely in her lap.

The summer had passed pleasantly, for she had taken care not to provoke him. In return, he had neither made impossible demands nor hectored her. Almost believing he had shelved his unknown plans, she had allowed herself to be happy – and to look forward to the future.

Such confidence, Zia Rosa said, only proved the optimism and the resilience of youth. And Zia Rosa had been right.

'You'll be glad to know it's all settled,' Bartolomeo now said briskly.

'All the terms're agreed. You're to marry the Doge's Councillor and Guardian of St Mark's Basilica Missier Osvaldo Grimani before Lent . . .'

Bianca was shocked. Having no idea how to respond, she smoothed her scarlet skirt over her knees – and caught herself wondering inconsequentially whether she could ever bear to wear scarlet again. Surprised at her silence, Bartolomeo smiled.

'I knew you'd be sensible in the end,' he said. 'The honour alone . . .'

'Terms?' Bianca asked dully. 'What terms?'

'The usual: marriage settlement, residual rights, amounts allotted for children . . .'

'Children?' she echoed. 'I thought children were provided for *after* their birth, not before.'

'Oh, not your children, not yours and his.' Bartolomeo laughed. 'They're another matter. No, Osvaldo's children by his first wife. He's got . . . let me see . . . three sons and two daughters.'

'And all under sixteen?' she demanded. 'That *will* be nice.'

'How do you mean?'

'Only how nice to have a ready-made family. Every bride's dream. Naturally, they must all be under sixteen. Surely you wouldn't make me stepmother to children who're older than myself.'

'Well, to be perfectly honest, the oldest son is somewhere in his thirties.'

'You mean he's close to forty, don't you?' she riposted. 'What a lovely family we'll be, all living happily together in that great pile, Ca' Grimani. I won't even ask how old Missier Osvaldo is, certainly well past sixty.'

Bartolomeo did not speak. Although he had not expected telling Bianca to be easy, he had allowed himself to hope that she had truly come to her senses. He had braced himself for tears and pleas, not this biting sarcasm.

'So that takes care of me,' she resumed. 'And what about you?'

'What about me?'

'How are you profiting from this wonderful marriage? Surely the father of the bride isn't forgotten.'

'Now listen to me, young lady!'

Bartolomeo's temper was rising, despite his resolve not to let her see how much she annoyed him.

'Yes, Father?'

He controlled his temper and smiled. Holding the upper hand, he could indulge her childish spite.

'Well, no reason you shouldn't know,' he said genially. 'Though a true gentlewoman doesn't interest herself in business affairs . . .'

'How much,' she broke in, 'are you selling me for?'

Her language was unconscionable, but, at least, she had not flatly rejected the match. If she did, he would put her into a convent, the stricter, the better. But not as long as she did not openly defy him.

If he were forced to immure her with the Carmelites, it might put Osvaldo Grimani off. No matter how eager he was to enjoy his young bride, the Doge's Councillor would be upset at the public demonstration that he was taking to the marriage-bed an unwilling virgin a quarter his age. She had to appear willing. No man liked it said that he must buy a wife, especially if he were doing just that.

'I get a loan to pull me out of my temporary difficulties,' Bartolomeo responded. 'Honestly, Bianca, I expected you'd be happy. The Grimanis are among the richest and most respected families in the *Golden Book*.'

'An end to poverty,' she mused. 'That's the *only* attractive . . .'

Heartened, he broke in: 'A glorious match for you and a new start for the family. You should be very happy. We'll announce the betrothal on St Sylvester's Day, start your new life on the first day of the New Year. The wedding'll be just before Lent. Osvaldo's in a hurry, very ardent.'

Stunned by such haste, Bianca sat silent. Screaming defiance would do no good at all.

'We'll have a grand reception, throw the whole palazzo open: dancing, fireworks, acrobats, two orchestras, a troupe of players. And more besides! Three days of rejoicing'll make Damiano's reception for Ca' Capello look like a little jollification for fishermen and washerwomen.'

'How grand!' She smiled wanly. 'But I must think about all this. Please let me think.'

With a great effort, she smiled again. Closing the heavy wooden door behind her, she took great care not to slam it.

Bartolomeo congratulated himself. It had been easier than he had expected. No tears, no screaming, and she had been reasonable. True, she had not agreed wholly. But he could give her time to get used to the idea, for all she would go more smoothly if she were agreeable. He would allow her to pretend to consider before she gave in, as she must inevitably.

Bianca trembled with fury as she climbed the narrow staircase. She had smiled as warmly as she could to put him off guard. A bold face would not help her escape this trap, but what would? Closing her bedroom door, she only knew that she would never marry Osvaldo Grimani, an adroit politician who had a reputation among noble-women as a tireless lecher.

She would never marry Ducal Councillor Osvaldo Grimani! But she had no idea how she was to evade that marriage without ruining her life.

NOVEMBER 25, 1564
VENICE: CA' MOROSINI ON THE GRAND CANAL

Andrea Morosini was the younger brother of the Ladies Pellegrina and Sophia, Bianca's mother and aunt. The scion of a conservative old family, he was a leader of the progressive faction among the nobles who ruled Venice. The Youth, men had called his group since it sprang up at the University of Padua twenty years earlier. The Youth now met, frequently and informally, at Ca' Morosini on the Grand Canal to discuss sculpture and painting, literature and publishing, manufacturing and science, as well as government and foreign policy.

Bianca had begun attending their meetings in order to escape the grim Palazzo Capello, but had then found herself fascinated by the discussions. This was not the mere rhetoric of young men spinning ideal schemes they could never test in practice. Each of these men sat in the Great Council, which was made up of all noblemen over twenty-five. Many were officials or members of the Senate, which passed the laws and shaped the policies of the Serene Republic.

Being progressive, the Youth welcomed women, who, they felt, could make a unique contribution from their unique viewpoint. The Youth even believed a woman's mentality could be as powerful as a man's, although working differently. They, therefore, advocated equal education for their sisters. When she was still small, Bianca's Uncle Andrea had seen that she studied Latin, Greek, and mathematics, as well as rhetoric and logic.

Her father had not objected. He did not care what she did, as long as it did not decrease her value in the marriage-market. Uncle Andrea now boasted that her suppleness of mind and her breadth of knowl-edge were most impressive for a sixteen-year-old, male or female.

The easy manners of the Youth, so different from the starchy formality of traditional Venice, permitted outsiders to join their sessions, not only non-patricians, but foreigners. Even non-Venetian ideas, they believed, were valuable.

Ca' Morosini was the only house in Venice where a young patrician lady could speak with a Florentine commoner without raising eyebrows and setting tongues wagging. Biance had met Pietro Buonaventura at her uncle's house, not loitering on the street near the Salviati Bank, as her father believed. She did not enlighten him, since she did not want him to forbid her from visiting Ca' Morosini.

Two days after Bartolomeo Capello told her that she was to marry an old man with a long purse and a large family, Bianca sought refuge from her perplexities at Andrea Morosini's palazzo. Intellectual conversation might divert her thoughts from her predicament.

The Youth were discussing critical questions: *Were the Turks and aggressive Islam an unremitting threat to the Republic? If the threat had declined, could expenditure on the Navy not be reduced further?*

The issue went to the heart of the Republic's existence, but Bianca's thoughts wandered. The heart of her own existence was under even more immediate threat.

When Pietro arrived, she drew him aside, saying: 'I must speak with you.'

She did not know why she said that. An instant later, she realised she had to speak with a friend who was not mired in the morass of Venetian society, someone who could see beyond the walls of tradition and privilege that surrounded the nobility. She could expect no assistance, but could, at least, clarify her own thoughts by speaking to Pietro.

At the reception for the reopening of Ca' Capello half a year earlier, he had proposed with flowery compliments that they elope to Florence. His talk of their marrying had, quite clearly, been only talk. Knowing she could never marry a non-Venetian, much less a commoner, he had rhapsodised only to make her feel better. Marriage was doubly impossible. Venice was her home, and she would not leave. Besides, he still had his way to make in the world, although his prospects at the Salviati Bank were bright.

He had not renewed his proposal during the following six months, not even mentioned it playfully. An amusing fancy the first time, it would not be amusing on repetition.

Impulsively, Bianca now blurted out: 'I finally know what my father wants. I'm to marry a disgusting old man.'

Pietro frowned in sympathy and asked: 'Who is it, Bianca?'

When she told him, he frowned again.

'Grimani's quite a catch,' he observed. 'So the ladies say.'

'But not for me, not at my age. Pietro, what can I possibly do?'

Bianca had not known what she wanted of Pietro. She had, at least, expected sympathy, some balm for her hurt. She had, therefore, revealed her anguish – and drawn from him only prudent platitudes. Certainly no repetition of his proposal, playful or not.

'You must be brave and trust in God,' he advised. 'Providence will look after you, if that is what is meant to be.'

Such meagre consolation she had already received from Father Sebastiano, who had promised that God would come to her rescue. Pietro had not even gone that far. Arid counsel was more acceptable from the brown lips of an old priest than from a young gallant who had boldly flirted with her now for half a year.

DECEMBER 1–6, 1564
VENICE: PALAZZO CAPELLO IN SANT' APONAL

Summoning Bianca to his counting-room, Bartolomeo Capello told her curtly that her marriage would be celebrated by the Patriarch in the Cathedral of Saint Mark on March 6 of the coming year, 1565. The bridegroom was eager to claim his bride. Since the bridegroom was sixty-three, ten years older than his future father-in-law, his haste was understandable.

'If he doesn't hurry, he mayn't have much time to enjoy his delectable young bride,' Zia Rosa commented earthily. '*If*, that is, he can still rise to such enjoyment.'

Stroking Bianca's hair, the governess added glumly: 'Anyway, whatever pleasure *he* can still get, there's no question of anything else.'

'What do you mean, Zia?' Bianca asked. 'I know what happens in the marriage-bed. But I don't understand you.'

The older woman smiled in wry sympathy. Her precocious charge was learning that she did not know quite as much as she thought – or would like to know.

'Simply that, whatever pleasure he gets, he won't give you much – if any!'

'Why, Zia Rosa?' Bianca demanded. 'Don't make a mystery of it. Tell me what you mean.'

'Well, if you're old enough for marriage, you're old enough to hear . . . You know, I sometimes chat with the courtesans in the square. Fascinating tales they have to tell. Some're pathetic, but some're very cultivated and happy in their lives of sin. Better a mistress to many men than a slave to one, they say.'

'Very interesting, Zia. But do get on with it and tell me.'

'Well, my dear, Missier Osvaldo Grimani is well known among the courtesans. He's famous for his stinginess – and his . . . his . . . incapability.'

'That's a big word for you, Zia,' Bianca teased. 'What does it really mean?'

'There're other words for it,' the governess replied. 'But I won't use them to you. I'll just say he likes . . . *has* to do strange things, unnatural things. Or nothing happens for him.'

Bianca by now knew a great deal about Osvaldo Grimani, none of it, except his wealth, even remotely pleasing. She was even more convinced that she could not marry him. She had thought hard and long. She had talked for hours with Zia Rosa, encouraged by her governess's intelligence and compassion. But she had thought of no way out.

She had also talked with her Aunt Sophia, who indignantly advised her to reject the betrothal. Aunt Sophia had promised that her husband, Agosto Tron, now Attorney General, would intervene through the law or would try to buy off Bartolomeo Capello. For three days, Bianca had lived in hope that her aunt would rescue her.

Aunt Sophia returned empty-handed on the morning of the fourth day. Her husband, she reported, would do nothing to help her niece. She was, this once, unable to sway him.

The lawyer had declared emphatically that he could not come between father and daughter. To intervene would be not only unseemly, but illegal. A father's absolute right to dispose of his daughter as he pleased was too well defined to challenge. Either the state and its chief legal officer strictly maintained the letter of Venetian law or all would crumble.

'As for collecting a purse to bail out Bartolomeo Capello, don't be foolish!' he had added to that lawyerlike statement. 'He's a notoriously leaky ship, your charming brother-in-law. I couldn't raise a ducat if I tried. And, Sophia, my love, don't think you can help her on the sly. I'll put *you* in a convent if you dare.'

In desperation, Zia Rosa told Bartolomeo of Osvaldo Grimani's physical deficiencies – and his unnatural practices. She further implied what she suspected, but she did not know with certainty: Osvaldo Grimani was suffering from the Spanish sickness, the disease brought back from the New World.

'I happen to know Osvaldo has a weak chest from a fever when he was governor of Crete,' Bartolomeo retorted. 'If you'll lie about that, old woman, you'll lie about anything. You're disgusting! Filling an impressionable girl . . . a marriageable young woman . . . with salacious gossip and dirty lies. Get out of my sight!'

For daring to oppose him, Bartolomeo Capello exiled the governess to his dilapidated villa on Murano. He was responsible for his distant relation in the eyes of his fellow noblemen, whom he dared not offend further. But he would, he declared, no longer have that woman in his house filling his daughter's mind with filth and encouraging her to defy his just wishes.

Before leaving, Zia Rosa tearfully told Bianca: 'There's no hope for you, I'm afraid. There's no one in Venice who'll help you.'

LATE AFTERNOON: DECEMBER 10, 1564
VENICE: PALAZZO CAPELLO IN SANT' APONAL

Bartolomeo Capello did not speak to his daughter for days after banishing Zia Rosa. Yet he was ingratiating enough when he met her on the staircase in the late afternoon of December 10.

'How would you like to be Dogaressa?' he asked expansively. 'Osvaldo's very likely to be the next Doge.'

'If,' she retorted, 'he lives that long.'

'Those rumours of his illness?' Bartolomeo asked dismissively. 'Not true. Even if they are, you'll be a rich widow that much sooner.'

'Father, why can't you see? I don't want to be a widow, rich or poor. I *can't* marry anyone . . . not yet. Certainly not Missier Osvaldo Grimani!'

'You do owe me something, you know.' He strove to be reasonable. 'I am your father – and you owe me obedience. Not to speak of gratitude for the care I've lavished.'

There were worse fathers in Venice, Bianca knew, though not many. She kept silent, since she might otherwise laugh derisively.

'I tried, you know,' he continued. 'I tried other families, younger men. But they all declined. Think you're too much of a handful. And, to be honest, they know you *must* marry soon, marry a rich man or I'll be ruined. That didn't make them eager.'

Bartolomeo was candid, yet inflexible, his mind fixed on his own needs. Bianca's wishes, her needs, did not count. Her future was in pawn to keep him from bankruptcy – and give him the chance to throw away another fortune.

'As you know, Osvaldo's children and grandchildren will come in for a healthy share,' he added. 'But he's prepared to make you a very generous settlement, even after pulling me out of my temporary difficulties. Why don't you think of it as a temporary arrangement? Ill or not, Osvaldo can't live forever. And you're so young. Think of it as temporary when you stand before the altar and . . .'

'Stand before the altar!' Bianca erupted. 'I'll *never* stand before the altar with Osvaldo Grimani. I'd rather beg on the streets . . . or worse. His habits, they're disgusting. I'd do anything, anything at all, rather than marry an old man with stinking breath and trembling hands covered with liver spots.'

'Shall I send you to the Carmelites for life . . . your entire life?'

'You can't pay the dowry the convent demands,' she replied. 'They won't take me for life.'

'In Christian charity, they will take you for a year, maybe two. I could use the money your mother's father left entailed for your dowry.'

'Only if the court agrees,' she objected. 'And it won't. That money is *only* for when I marry, not for anything else, not for a nun's dowry. Those're the terms.'

'Maybe! Anyway later, when I'm once more on an even keel, the convent's dowry'll be a bagatelle . . . Wearing a coarse habit, living in a mean cell, up at all hours praying. Never gaiety or laughter. Is that what you want?'

'Rather than Missier Osvaldo? Almost!'

'Or else, the cherished wife of a very rich man, most likely the next Dogaressa. Then a wealthy widow, free to do whatever you please. Think about it again, Bianca!'

LATE AFTERNOON: DECEMBER 16, 1564
VENICE: CA' MOROSINI ON THE GRAND CANAL

Mist draped the alleys and passages with grey veils, as if Venice were mourning the premature death of the day. Less than a week ahead lay the shortest day of the year, and darkness was almost upon the city at four in the afternoon. But Bianca did not depend solely on the lantern carried by the black slave trotting before her. The pale half-moon and the candle-light glimmering through shutters closed against the cold cast an unearthly glow on the snow that mantled the unpaved lane leading to Ca' Morosini.

She blessed the four-inch pattens, like miniature stilts, that kept her feet out of the puddles glazed with thin ice. She would change into silk slippers at her uncle's palazzo, for she disliked the high pattens worn by true ladies of fashion. Bianca had no wish to be a lady of fashion, although she loved beautiful clothes. She was more an old-fashioned girl, she told herself, smiling, in her mother's old-fashioned winter dress and black fur cape. Even four-inch pattens would make her tower over everyone. Most women and many men were shorter than her five feet four inches.

High pattens, Bianca knew, had been contrived to keep ladies from venturing out alone, for they needed a man's support to keep from falling. The Turks simply locked their women up and set eunuchs to guard them, while the subtle Cathayans, as Ser Marco Polo, a noble-man of Venice, had reported centuries earlier, bound the feet of well-born female infants with tight bandages to make them tiny and unstable all their lives.

How could she, closely confined as she was by law and tradition, escape from Bartolomeo Capello's tyranny? Bianca swore that she would never again be totally dependent on any man – once she escaped the prison without bars that now confined her.

If she could escape!

Having spent a week assessing herself and her prospects, she believed she could. The sacrifice would be painful. But it was neces-sary, indeed unavoidable.

Bereft of advice and assistance, she had calculated her assets and her debits as coolly as any Venetian accountant. She had also defined her goals.

Her chief asset, she had concluded, was her well-stocked mind, which worked quickly and well. But, for the rest of the world, it was her striking appearance. Her flaming hair and her slender figure with pert breasts and rounded hips drew appraising stares from women as well as from men. She knew that her mouth was soft, yet firm, and she had learned that her candid expression and her wide green eyes were highly attractive.

Also deceptive! Others saw an innocent, indeed naïve, young

woman who knew little of the world. Her apparent vulnerability aroused protectiveness in men and maternal feeling in older women. It also cloaked her native intelligence and the hard lessons she had learned from experience.

She really should be grateful to Bartolomeo Capello. His brutal treatment had made her think hard about the direction her life was taking.

Bianca knew she could accomplish great things in the world. She could already outmanoeuvre most men, as she would her father. She could also inspire loyalty and devotion. If she had been a man, her talents and her name would have won her the command of fleets and the governorship of colonies, as well as independent wealth and opportunities to improve the life of the people under more just laws.

She could accomplish great things, but not in the Serene Republic of Venice. As a woman in Venice, she could only become the plaything of a lecherous old man. At best, she could win the lottery and become Dogaressa. But a Doge's consort was only a ceremonial figure, a gorgeously dressed doll whose freedom was even more limited than her own.

Not in Venice. That terse phrase summed up her predicament, her hopes . . . and her pain at the thought of leaving.

Yet only by leaving Venice could she escape the revolting marriage her father had arranged. Only by leaving Venice could she fulfil her destiny, whatever that was to be.

Leaving Venice would be like tearing off a limb. *Campanilismo*, they called it, that rooted attachment to one's native place, these islands in the lagoon hallowed by the lives of her ancestors for twenty generations. Venetians travelled far, but always returned to hear the music of the *campanile* in the Piazza of St Mark's. She now had to leave Venice, perhaps to return in triumph some day, perhaps never to return.

Bianca knew when she would leave and how. She would be gone within the next two weeks, before the detestable betrothal could be announced. Since she could not flee alone, Pietro Buonaventura must be her companion in flight.

Preparing for what might be the most critical encounter of her life, Bianca slipped on her yellow silk shoes in the tiny retiring-room on the lower-ground floor.

Bianca was grateful for the warmth of the small parlour. She was wearing the most demure dress she could find in her mother's chest, which covered her bosom and her shoulders, even her arms. She wanted to look forlorn, not wanton. But the total effect would have been spoiled if she had worn more than a shift and a single petticoat beneath the fine wool dress of a modest plum colour. She wanted the thin fabric to cling to her legs and hips when she moved. She wanted Pietro to see her breasts pressing against the bodice when she leaned forward. She wanted him to feel protective, tender – and ardent.

Finding Pietro sipping mulled wine, she drew him into the inglenook of the farther fireplace. Gazing intently at the flames, her shyness only partly assumed, she spoke of her predicament as if it had nothing to do with him. The door to his affections could only be opened by subtlety, not by force.

Bianca was a little surprised to find that her own feelings were by no means sisterly. She felt a certain affection for the tall blond Florentine with the brown eyes – and a certain desire, as well.

She was greatly surprised to find herself pushing against an open door. Obviously, his feelings, as well as his intentions, had altered sharply in the space of a few days. The door to his affections swung open at her first touch – and she was welcomed warmly within.

'I've been thinking, Bianca.' He took her hand. 'I think we ought to run away, elope. I'm serious, totally serious, now.'

'You've changed your mind?' she asked. 'Only last week . . .'

'I've finally come to my senses . . . realised I love you,' he declared. 'I've got to help you get away from that horrible old man.'

'But it's so hard,' she protested, leading him to take the initiative. 'How could we?'

'I'll think of a way.' He released her hand to swing his arm expansively. 'And my Uncle Giambattista . . .'

'Your uncle? He knows?'

'I couldn't do a thing without his help. He *is* the senior clerk at the Bank.'

'And he approves?'

'The first time I mentioned you, he was horrified. A nobleman's daughter, he said. Stay away from her. You'll make life impossible for both of us. But now he's all for our eloping. He'll cover up, so no one knows I'm gone for days.'

'You *are* talking about marriage, Pietro? I care for you, too. Very deeply, but I must . . .'

'Of course marriage. What else?'

'You know there'll be no dowry? Not for a long time, at least.'

'Dowry! Who cares? We won't need it, not with my connections in Florence. The Buonaventuras are important. Noble, too. Only the title's temporarily . . .'

'Noble blood is always important, but it's not the most important thing at the moment.'

'It's important for you to know you're not marrying a nobody. And there's wealth, too. Just as soon as we bring some law suits to their inevitable conclusion.'

'Pietro, you know about my dowry? Do you know we'll probably never see a penny?'

'I know twenty thousand ducats're put away for your dowry, put away where your father can't touch them. Giambattista checked the court archives.'

'Bartolomeo . . . my father . . . will *never* let me have it. It's his last hope. Twenty thousand ducats could buy him four new merchantmen.'

'He must! He'll have to let you have it in time. But it's not important.'

'What is important?' Bianca did not admire herself for leading him on, but he had to commit himself wholly. 'What is, Pietro?'

'*We* are important, *you* above all.'

'And?'

'Florence needs you almost as much as I do. Florence loves beauty, and you're the most beautiful creature I've ever seen. You're not appreciated in Venice. Come to Florence, the city of sunshine and flowers.'

Encouraged by her parted lips and shining eyes, he went on: 'You must leave dour old Venice: the fog and sleet, the stupid laws against beautiful clothes and delicious food, against natural enjoyment. You're much too beautiful to waste your life on a wrinkled, half-senile old man in a sour old city.'

Pietro had evidently been hearing the same tales about Osvaldo Grimani as had Zia Rosa. Bianca was, perhaps perversely, flattered that he had obviously taken care to learn more about her and to rehearse his declaration. She felt herself softening, although she reminded herself that she was moved as much by his profile as by his promises.

'You'll never, never in a hundred years, be adored here as you deserve,' he declared. 'Venetians have only their double-entry book-keeping. And the most beautiful daughter of Venice is ignored . . . or thrown to an ancient lecher.'

She smiled despite a twinge of irritation at his persistent denigration of her city. She let herself relax since there was no more need to manoeuvre him.

'I shall live only for you,' Pietro swore. 'Come with me to Florence, Bianca. Come to Florence with a son of Florence who adores you!'

NIGHT: DECEMBER 22, 1564
CHIOGGIA AT THE SOUTHERN END OF THE LAGOON OF VENICE

Progress was slow in the small sailing wherry, for the night was black, the moon was obscured, and the wind hurled snow into the helmsman's face. Zia Rosa's last gift to Bianca had been the name of a fishing family that was under obligation to her. Although himself uneasy, the father had overruled his sons' fears and agreed to take them the twenty miles to Chioggia, southernmost of the islands girding the lagoon. Half a ducat from Bartolomeo Capello's small hoard had finally persuaded him, but he insisted that they remain in the hold, which stank of fish.

In Chioggia they could not find a boat to take them up the Brenta to Padua. Even the offer of a ducat, a sixth of a good year's earnings, could not persuade the boatmen drinking in the dark little wine-shop to which the fishermen sent them. Bianca had taken only three ducats from her father's meagre savings. That, she told herself, was her due, her infinitesimal dowry. She had without a qualm removed her mother's jewellery from its hiding place in Bartolomeo's writing-table. But she was loath to tempt the boatmen, smugglers one and all, with a display of jewels.

Impatiently, Pietro interrupted her pleas to promise two ducats after he had cashed his letter of credit in Padua. He had not dared take a single coin from the Salviati Bank, not even from his own account, for fear of arousing suspicion.

His Tuscan accent, barely intelligible to the boatmen, confirmed the suspicions raised by their youth and their obvious desperation. The boatmen distrusted even Bianca. True, she spoke Venetian, but her accent was too refined.

Finding their slang much like the talk of the fishermen of Murano, Bianca listened in silence. Most of the boatmen believed Pietro and she were *agents provocateurs* sent by the State Inquisition to trap them into criminal acts. Some came too close to the truth, contending that the mysterious couple were fugitives who had committed some terrible crime in the city. Regardless, all agreed that it would be wise to steer clear of them. The smugglers wanted no involvement with their natural enemies, the Night Watch.

Yet Bianca sensed that the oldest boatman was weakening, and she tried again to win them all over. Whether their suspicions were right or wrong, she said, the boatmen would do well to see them on their way. If she and her friend were gone, they could not be arrested. No arrest would mean no case at law to ensnare the boatmen as unwilling witnesses, perhaps as unjustly accused.

The squat candle was guttering, and the fire was dying in the crude fireplace. Darkness draped them like a cloak. When the fire flickered, weathered faces shone ruddy and menacing for an instant.

Reaching out for Pietro's hand, Bianca found his hand simultaneously reaching for hers. In unspoken agreement, they rose to flee.

In an unfamiliar village on this black night, their chances of escaping were, however, minuscule. If they were caught by the Night Watch, it would no longer be a cruel father Bianca would face, but the merciless courts of Venice. Pietro and she had made themselves criminals. In law, it was a crime for her to defy her father's wishes and elope. In law, she had stolen the jewellery that was her mother's legacy to her.

The state prided itself on its normally severe treatment of all citizens under the law. But patricians were often punished more severely, as an example of even-handed justice. Yet Pietro's fate could be worse than her own: certainly torture for corrupting a Venetian noblewoman, perhaps execution.

Just visible in the dying firelight, a scarred hand twitched aside the old sail hung over the doorway to keep out the wind, and a hoarse voice advised: 'Get out, Y'r Ladyship. Night Watch'll be rolling up any minute! I'll snarl their nets much's I can . . . send 'em chasing moonbeams. Remember, keep to th' right, always th' right.'

A momentary rift in the clouds revealed a sliver of moon, which gave just light enough to pick out the three rocky paths leading away from the wine shop. The snow had turned to sleet, and the wind was blowing into their faces. They pulled up their scarves against the stinging pellets of ice, leaving only their eyes uncovered.

Bianca blessed the instinct that had told her to wear her oldest, sturdiest shoes with no nonsense about unsteady pattens. Shifting the bundle that held her few good clothes and valuables to her left shoulder, she followed Pietro into the night. The right-hand path led straight into the rising wind, but his body sheltered her from the worst blasts.

The wind dropped as if gathering for a new assault. In the momentary silence she heard dogs barking and the scuffing of leather soles. No boatman could afford the leather shoes the Watch wore. Stealing a glance over her shoulder, she saw a faint glow. An instant later, she heard voices raised in argument. The wind wailed again, drowning all other sound, and the glow shrank to a pinpoint in the white curtain of sleet.

Bianca clung to Pietro's belt, following him blindly and stumbling on the rocks that studded the slippery path. Her courage and her feeling for the common people had brought them this far. Now she had to put all her trust in Pietro. Only male strength could bring them to safety. She was almost seventeen, almost a grown woman. But she could not save herself without a man. She could only follow Pietro and trust in him completely.

Despite Zia Rosa's warning, there had been *one* person in Venice to help her. Marco was far away, but Pietro was there to rescue her from her father's smothering attentions. Whether Bartolomeo Capello loved her perversely or hated her perversely, she did not know – and she no longer cared. She only knew she had to be free of him, which meant being free of Venice.

She had delayed the inevitable pursuit by telling him she was visiting her Aunt Sophia for a few days – and telling Aunt Sophia she was staying with Marco's sisters. An intelligent woman could make schemes and plans, but she needed a man to carry them out.

She would never again allow herself to be at the mercy of any man, not even Pietro. Although he swore his funds would be more than sufficient for their needs, she had taken her mother's jewellery. Pietro believed she had removed only three or four trumpery rings and a gimcrack brooch or two. The jewellery her father had kept as his last resort would give his daughter some security and some independence in a world that was suddenly cold and hostile.

The wind snatched at her scarf, almost tearing it off. The wild gusts made it hard to breathe. Even Pietro paused for a moment under the hammer blows. But, through the wind's wailing, she heard a sailor's call: 'Ahoy!'

'Faster!' she gasped into Pietro's ear. 'Faster! Someone's following! Too close!'

The Night Watch, which knew the ground, had the advantage. Pietro and she had to keep to the path they could hardly see. Feeling their way, stumbling into the undergrowth on either side, they fled the pursuing voice.

Bianca stubbed her toe on a rock and slipped. She fell full length, instinctively thrusting out her hands. Pietro pushed onward for a few seconds before missing her hand in his belt. He turned and groped for her in the blackness. Her scarf had come away, and the pale oval of her face shone faintly.

'Up!' he commanded. 'You've got to get up! They're too close!'

His voice was tight with strain. If she had not known better, Bianca might have suspected a touch of panic. She tried to rise and slipped back. He shook her impatiently and hauled her to her feet.

'Come on!' he directed. 'I'm not getting caught.'

Rallying to his rough tone, she matched him pace for pace for several minutes. They bent forward to breast the wind, neither speaking. They needed all their breath for the struggle.

When Pietro slipped, they both went down. They lay in the mud for half a minute, until breath returned to their lungs. Then they rose, helping each other.

Again they heard the faint sailor's cry: 'Ahoy!'

This time it sounded ahead of them. Yet, unless their pursuers flew, how could they have passed ahead? Regardless, all they could do was keep to the path.

Pietro stopped abruptly. When she stumbled against him, he leaned down and said into her ear: 'It's hopeless! They're all around us!'

'Go ahead!' she gasped. 'Keep going! Until we're caught, there's always hope.'

'As you say.'

It was even worse for him than for her. He was surrounded by Venetians, who were alien to him, and he faced torment in the secret torture chamber of the Doge's Palace.

'Ahoy!'

The hoarse voice was so close they started. A lantern flashed for an instant. The faint light showed a hand with a broad scar and a face Bianca recognised as that of the oldest of the boatmen.

'Slow down,' the hoarse voice advised. 'Ye've led me a merry chase. Cuttin' cross country to catch you. But all's right now, Lady Bianca.'

She did not speak, afraid he was trying to entrap her.

'No fear, Mi'Lady.' The dialect was less extreme. 'I fought under your grandad, the Admiral, at Crete. D'ye think I'd betray a Capello?'

'The Watch?' she asked. 'They'll be on us in a minute.'

'I've sent 'em off on a fool's chase.'

'What now, old man?' Pietro demanded. 'Where do we go from here?'

'Can't understand 'is jabber,' the boatman said. 'But tell 'im he needn't worry, not while 'e's with you. Follow me. Only another mile or so down th' path's th' river. A little skiff's moored there. Do 'im good to row 'imself up the Brenta. A fair way to Padua, but 'twill do 'im good.'

CHAPTER IV

'I'M sorry, Marco. We can't block it any longer. I've been putting it off for months, but I *must* now let the process go forward.'

The nobleman's broad face, ruddy with hearty living, rose incongruously from the sombre black robe of his office. The Inquisitor's obvious delight in the pleasures of the flesh was not in keeping with this dark-panelled chamber where men hunted down conspiracies and span plots. The State Inquisition was housed in the 'secret ways' of the Doge's Palace, forbidden to the public. His tone was brisk, indicating that this minor matter merited no further attention. But his manner was indulgent towards the young nobleman he had himself recruited into the Secret Service.

'Your cousin Bartolomeo is bringing *great* pressure to bear.' The Inquisitor oddly stressed certain words. 'The Council of Ten *must* grant his petition within a month.'

'Or,' Marco Capello interjected, 'show cause why not!'

'*Precisely!* And in this case *no* cause can be shown. It's a straightforward question of *law*, since no one can dispute the facts. The Lady Bianca Capello and the clerk Pietro Buonaventura will be declared outlaws – to be *imprisoned* should they ever return to the Republic.'

'With no opportunity to answer the charges? Is this the celebrated justice of Venice? What of the words whispered to the prosecuting lawyer before every trial: "Remember the little baker!"?'

The Inquisitor laughed raucously, rocking back and forth in his red velvet chair, then lifted a goblet from the table before him.

'*In extremis, every* amateur lawyer introduces the little baker,' he said. 'That was a matter of *fact*. The baker was seen clutching a dagger beside a murdered patrician. "Open and shut case," they said, tried him, and hanged him. Later, the true *murderer* confessed. The baker had only drawn the dagger *out* of the wound, thinking to help the victim. The error was in fact, not law.'

'Precisely, my Lord Inquisitor,' Marco rejoined. 'And the facts in this case are not as stated.'

'How's that? The charges against her are: *absconding* in defiance of parental command. Against him: *corrupting* a noblewoman of Venice. Against them jointly: *stealing* jewels and monies, and, lastly, *fornication*. All proven!'

'Not so, my Lord! Firstly, they married. Secondly, the jewels were, are, Bianca's by her mother's express testament. She also took three ducats, a bagatelle. Thirdly, she fled her father's unnatural desires and the Florentine assisted her, as any gentleman would assist a lady in great distress. A different picture, my Lord, wholly different!'

'In your eyes, Marco. Not the law's. Firstly, subsequent marriage does *not* wash away the stain of fornication. Secondly, Bianca could have, *should* have, appealed to the courts for protection. Thirdly, three copper coins or three thousand ducats, theft is theft. Finally, the jewels are Bartolomeo Capello's *solely*, regardless of any dying wish of Pellegrina Morosini Capello.'

'But, my Lord Inquisitor, Bianca could not have appealed for protection without raising a scandal. She fled to save the family name from stain. From that necessary, nay, *noble* . . . deed, all else followed. My Lord, I shall raise such a protest at this miscarriage of justice that . . .'

'You will *not*, Marco! You will say no more to me . . . or to *anyone*!' The Inquisitor smiled thinly. 'You're getting a bad name as an *agitator*, my boy, a *malcontent*. That will *not* do. It will reduce your usefulness to the Secret Service.'

'But, my Lord . . .'

'Enough, Marco, enough!' The Inquisitor's hand slammed down on the table. 'I admire your *persistence* and your *ingenuity*. But you'll do better to use them in the service of the Republic. I have a critical, a *difficult* assignment for you.'

'My Lord Inquisitor, I shall obey!'

With that formal submission to authority, Captain Marco Capello of the *Galley of the Angels* gave up his fight to save his cousin Bianca from condemnation by the Council of Ten. Since there was no hope of winning, he submitted. It would be foolish, criminal, to sacrifice his usefulness to the Republic, as well as his career, to no purpose. He swore, nonetheless, to champion Bianca in the court of public opinion, which meant among his fellow nobles. But he would, for the time being, no longer strive to raise a general protest.

'Now where did that damned clerk put the file?'

The Inquisitor shuffled the documents that heaped his table, untidy sheaves threatening to burst the pink ribbons that bound them. Exasperated at not finding the right file, he gulped his wine. Before rummaging through the documents again, he refilled his own goblet and his subordinate's.

Marco sipped, suppressing a smile at the antics of the man he called Uncle Vincenzo outside this grim office. Nonetheless, the state's blind injustice towards Bianca had made him angry – and thoughtful. Uncharacteristically, he questioned the very basis of the Venetian state.

All Venetian nobles were equal, not, as elsewhere, divided into ranks like baron, count, and marquess, all addressed as Ser. In their eyes, no higher title existed than *Nobiluomo di Venezia*, Nobleman of Venice, except, of course, for the Doge, their Reigning Duke, whom they themselves elected.

Equality did not, however, mean insubordination. If all noblemen did not bow to authority, no nobleman would be secure in his position or his property. Despite occasional injustice to her children, the little baker and now Bianca, the Serene Republic was justly ruled. The structure had for good reason endured more than seven hundred years.

Inherent checks and balances restricted even the enormous power of the Council of Ten. Scores of rival courts, sections, commissions and departments constantly watched each other. Although not wholly independent, the Council acted quickly and decisively, having been created to avoid the interminable delays and the awkward compromises inherent in larger bodies, whether legislative, judicial, or administrative.

The State Inquisition answered to the Doge and the Council of Ten, two Inquisitors appointed by the Council wearing black robes and a third appointed by the Doge wearing red. The Inquisition in particular ensured the virtuous behaviour of all citizens, yet it did not suppress religious heresy. The Republic was not especially concerned with theological orthodoxy, but was greatly concerned with political orthodoxy.

To ensure virtuous behaviour the Inquisition mounted widespread surveillance. That vigilance had spontaneously developed into full-scale counter-espionage, which guarded against outsiders' penetrating Venetian secrets or subverting Venetian institutions. From the passive defence of counter-espionage at home it was a natural step to the active defence of espionage abroad.

Unlike Venice's ambassadors, the Secret Service was not bound by protocol. Its agents, who ranged from patricians to manure-collectors, had penetrated every layer of every foreign state. The Venetian intelligence service was acknowledged by her allies and her foes alike to be not only the pioneer of the art, but the best in the world.

Marco's reverie was broken by the Inquisitor's voice: 'I have them now . . . the damned *papers*. You understand, there's no *great* rush to sail. Take your time. Take a week, even two. I shall, however, *instruct* you on the mission today to give you *ample* time to plan. You'll see from this chart . . .'

Behind his goblet Marco smiled wryly. The State Inquisitor clearly wanted him out of the way as soon as possible. Once he had put to sea he could be gone for months. That would give the patricianate ample time to clean up the mess made by its unruly daughter Bianca Capello – with no danger of his interfering.

Bianca would almost certainly emerge as a monster of ingratitude, lust, and vice. Bartolomeo Capello would assuredly emerge as a martyr, a loving father betrayed by a daughter sunk in sin. Bartolomeo would undoubtedly also emerge with Bianca's most substantial dowry of twenty thousand ducats.

EARLY EVENING: JULY 16, 1565
FLORENCE: THE BUONAVENTURA APARTMENT

Bianca Capello Buonaventura told herself severely that she simply did not care. She was so cut off that her native city might have vanished, sunk without trace into the lagoon. But that did not matter in her new life, for she was now a Florentine like Pietro, her husband.

It was mid-July, and she had had no word, no news of Venice since fleeing last December. To be exact, she had had no word except a brief note from her cousin Marco, which was slipped into her hand by a ragged urchin while she was shopping for fruit and eggs in the street-market behind the church of San Lorenzo.

That was five months ago. Marco's note, written in haste, reported that her elopement was avidly discussed, 'making ripples on every canal'. That was no more than she had expected, the price she had to pay to escape. Although he could not wholly redeem her reputation,

Marco had promised to do everything he could to help her. That generosity she had also expected.

Since then, not a word from anyone, no inkling of events in Venice, public or private. She would know nothing more until she heard from Marco again. Clearly, no one else would write to her, not even her Aunt Sophia or her Uncle Andrea. Their silence hurt most.

Bianca missed the easy access to political and personal confidences enjoyed by the ruling circle of the Most Serene Republic. Her husband had no such entrée to the inner workings of Florence. Though fallen on hard times, the Buonaventuras were unquestionably gentry, perhaps minor nobility. But they were well outside the ruling circle.

That would surely change – and very soon. Even if the Buonaventura family fortunes were not restored, Pietro would undoubtedly be a spectacular success, not only in Tuscany, but out in the great world. Having mastered the art of finance at the Salviati Bank, he had also acquired a profound knowledge of international commerce in Venice, the world's chief seaport. When he struck out on his own, he would cut a great figure.

Hardly half a year had passed since their arrival in Florence. Great enterprises needed time to develop. Pietro was now making essential connections, impressing his worth upon men of substance and influence. His prospects were excellent, indeed brilliant.

Nonetheless, Bianca was strangely edgy today. Yet she saw no reason except the bake-oven heat of July so far inland, where no sea breeze could reach.

The Buonaventuras' apartment in a narrow tenement overlooking the cathedral of Holy Mary of the Flowers was pokey and airless. The whiff of decay from the open sewers five stories below mingled with the stench of chamberpots infrequently emptied when their contents were flung out of the window – and rarely scoured with sand. Also, their bedroom, Pietro's and hers, was no more than a storage space his parents had cleared for the newly-weds. It was actually smaller than the vestibule of her bedroom in Palazzo Capello. But such inconveniences were superficial – and, of course, temporary.

Giving up hope of the afternoon sleep beloved of Florentines, Bianca rose from the prickly straw mattress on the narrow board bed and slipped off the amethyst silk wrapper that was one of her few good garments. Wearing only a gauzy shift, which left her shoulders, arms, and legs bare, she sidled as close to the open window as she dared. Her breasts, almost entirely exposed, thrust against the transparent fabric. Unless the good fathers in the striped baptistery of the cathedral were spying on her, there was no one to shock.

What she really wanted was a cool bath. But there was little hope of getting the Buonaventuras' wall-eyed maidservant to carry the water up to the fifth floor from the cistern in the courtyard. And where put the hipbath if she did?

Bianca smiled at her own annoyance. These passing irritants Pietro and she would recall with nostalgic smiles when they had an entire palazzo to themselves, as well as a villa in the country. After laughing at the inconvenience, they would fondly remember the happiness of their first year together.

Really, Bianca chided herself, she had much reason to be happy – and little reason to be discontented.

Above all, she loved Pietro. Of course she did, though she had not expected that blessing when they fled Venice together. She had believed then she felt only fondness for the blond Florentine, though his masculine beauty stirred her: those burning brown eyes and that sensual mouth. She had believed she was only using his infatuation with her to gain his help in fleeing from her father. She now knew better.

On their journey to Florence she had begun to realise that her feeling for Pietro, who scrupulously respected her chastity, was more than fondness. He was not only kind and handsome, but intelligent and loving. He was also a true cavalier, dashing even beside Captain Marco Capello.

Bianca perched on the wicker stool before the unpainted chest that served as both dresser and dressing-table in the improvised bedroom. She stared at her indistinct image in the dim mirror with the chipped gilt frame, which had been the wedding present of her mother-in-law, who called it a 'precious family heirloom'. Dusk was falling, but her father-in-law's sharp nose would tell him the instant she dared light a candle – and he would again reproach her for being a spendthrift. She preferred to do without light.

The submerged thought floated to the surface of her mind: *Quite simply, she missed Venice. Here in the shadow of the bell-tower, the campanile of Florence, she was suffering from* campanilismo, *longing for her native city.*

Above all, she missed the waters and the waterways that were the unique glory of Venice; the intense clarity of the air, the palaces glowing like jewels in the brilliant light thrown up by the immense mirror of the surrounding waters. The myriad canals were not only smooth thoroughfares, but every tide flushed the city of wastes. And, beyond the lagoon, lay the Adriatic Sea, the high road to the oceans that linked the Republic to the farthest corners of the world – and shielded Venice from her enemies.

The door creaked open on its rusty hinges. Bianca instinctively reached for her wrapper.

'You're very shy, my dear,' Pietro laughed.

'A little mystery adds spice,' she riposted, leaving the sash untied.

'Let me see you!' His voice was suddenly husky. 'Against the light!'

Bianca laughed. Her back to the window, she posed for a few moments, lit by the scarlet glow of the dying sun, which kindled her red-gold hair. Grasping the skirts of her wrapper, she stretched out her arms and became an immense amethyst butterfly with a woman's white body.

Pietro stepped forward to embrace her, and she lay content for an instant in his arms. When he began to caress her back, running his fingers up her spine, she slipped away and tied her sash.

'Not now,' she whispered. 'Later. I do want you, but . . .'

Pietro smiled, surrendering himself to her mood with his usual grace. He never bullied; he was never harsh or demanding.

'Not feeling well?' he asked. 'Or is something wrong?'

'Pietro, just because I don't want to this instant doesn't mean something's wrong.' She smiled. 'You're insatiable . . .'

'Admit it. You love it, too.'

'Of course I do. It's . . . you're . . . wonderful. But not *every* moment of the day and night. Besides, the walls're so thin. Your parents . . .'

'Well, later then, when they're asleep.'

He stretched, yawned, and sank down on the bed, which was the only place to sit, aside from her wicker stool. Pulling off his pointed blue shoes, he stretched out his long legs in their new orange tights. He had to look prosperous, indeed opulent, to win backers for his great enterprise.

'You look tired,' she said. 'What've you been doing?'

'Just seeing some people. Things are beginning to come together but all this chasing around exhausts me. Tell me, are you sure you're all right?'

'To tell the truth, Pietro, it's not terrible exciting, my life, is it? Cooped up here most of the day. The only time I get out is to go to church or do some shopping. But I mustn't complain when you've so much more to . . .'

'No, tell me. I want to know.'

'Well, I'm idle. I'm not bad in the kitchen, thanks to Zia Rosa. But your mother won't let me near it. Says she couldn't eat my Venetian messes and she's happy with the maid's cooking.'

'Elvira with the funny eye?'

'We mustn't make fun of the poor thing. Thank God we can go out to the cookshops once in a while. The only one worse in the kitchen is that awful nurse of your mother's, Ariadna. She can turn an egg rotten just looking at it!' Bianca paused contritely and then blurted out: 'Oh, Pietro, I *am* sorry when you're trying so hard! I'm sorry to be a burden, a nag. It's just that . . .'

'Soon, very soon, everything'll . . .'

'I know that, Pietro. When we have our own house, of course everything will be different. We'll invite our own guests. But, now, it's an odd sort of life. No friends at all – and no family to visit.'

'My sisters . . .'

'. . . live in the country and are tied up with their husbands and children. If only I could see the Venetian community here . . .'

'You must become a Florentine, Bianca. I'm sorry, though, that the Venetians here are so hostile.'

'No more than I expected. They'll come round. Venetians're always practical, specially when money's involved. They'll flock to us once your enterprise begins to bear fruit.'

'You'll see,' he said. 'It's just a matter of time now . . . a few months at most.'

Bianca's heart sank, but she smiled brightly. She knew she lacked patience. She was used to the fast pace of Venice, not the provincial, almost rustic, languor of Florence. But she had made her choice, and she would abide by it. Besides, Pietro made up for everything – almost.

She had naturally been shocked by the difference between reality and the splendours he had promised. The Buonaventura apartment lacked even the solid comfort of the Palazzo Capello. The Palazzo Buonaventura in the Via Tornabuoni, Pietro explained, was still tied up by the drawn-out lawsuit that had also involved the Buonaventuras' country properties.

The magnificent wedding Pietro had promised in Venice became a meagre reality in Florence. Instead of the archbishop, they were married by a Franciscan friar in a dirty brown habit. Instead of the great domed cathedral, they were married in a minuscule chapel distinguished only because the poet Dante had there first glimpsed the Lady

Beatrice. Instead of a great organ and massed choirs, there had been a street musician with a viola da gamba, who tied his little white dog outside. The entire congregation had consisted of Pietro's father and his two sisters with their husbands. His mother was bedridden with rheumatism, the curse of the damp Florentine climate.

And, afterwards, no reception, only a cask of rough red wine and some leathery sausages shared with three of her father-in-law's cronies and two of her husband's classmates. Pietro had not asked the prosperous merchants and bankers with whom he hobnobbed, since he would have had to entertain them lavishly. Such display, he had explained, would influence the court that was pondering the verdict that must restore the Buonaventura fortunes.

She had never quite grasped that reasoning, but, as Pietro pointed out, Florentine ways were different from Venetian ways. She had been unhappy, and she was barely mollified when he assured her: 'We'll have a splendid reception at the Palazzo Buonaventura just as soon as things are settled. And that won't be long now.'

Seeing how hard he strove to make their fortune, Bianca was now happier. Above all, she knew she was in love.

But her eyes were not dazzled. She had not told Pietro how much of her mother's jewellery she had brought with her. Instead, she had taken a locked wooden casket to the Florentine branch of the Lombard Bank of Milan for safe deposit. A Florentine bank, susceptible to local pressure, would not keep her secret, while the Florentine branch of the Rialto Bank of Venice ultimately came under the authority of the Doge, the Senate, and the Council of Ten. Despite her occasional homesickness, her *campanilismo*, she did not trust the Serene Republic.

Having resolved that she would never place her fate entirely in any man's hands, not even Pietro's, Bianca kept to herself the value of the jewels. A thousand ducats or so was a tidy sum, though, of course, no fortune.

But, she told herself, she was not really keeping it from Pietro. She was only keeping it for him, saving it until they really needed it. Meanwhile, she would not expose him to temptation.

He had asked for a garnet ring to sell when they reached Padua on the second day of their flight, for it would clearly have been unwise to use his letter of credit. Why, he had asked, leave a trail for the Venetian bloodhounds to follow?

She had happily given him the ring. Only twice since then had he asked her to 'lend' him a piece of the jewellery she had kept out of the bank to wear. He would pawn, not sell, them, so that they could later be redeemed for their sentimental value.

He had told her three months before that he could no longer borrow from his father or his brothers-in-law, who had so little themselves. His letter of credit had been suspended by the Venice branch of the Salviati Bank, obviously under pressure from the Council of Ten. Yet they must have some funds.

Just two weeks ago, he had asked her to 'lend' him her aquamarine earrings to pawn. He had to maintain a *bella figura*, a prosperous appearance, to inspire faith in himself and his enterprise. His orange tights, as well as the red velvet cap carelessly flung aside and the padded doublet of green satin, had been bought with the proceeds of the earrings.

'Bianca, my dear, I hate to ask you again,' he said. 'But I'd like that pearl brooch with the little rubies I've seen you wear.'

'To pawn?' She stalled. 'Do we really need . . .'

'No, not to pawn. To give away.'

'Give away!' she protested. 'My mother's brooch! I don't see . . .'

'I've got it backwards, as usual.' He grinned beguilingly. 'You have that effect on me, always make my head whirl. I should have said first that just as soon as it all works out – and it will, very soon – I'll get you a brooch with twice as many gems. But I need yours badly right now. It's vital, absolutely vital – or I wouldn't ask.'

Bianca reflected. He had never pointed out that all her jewellery was rightfully – or, at least, legally – his. They had signed no marriage contract reserving certain property for herself, as great heiresses did. In the absence of a contract, a wife's property was her husband's in its entirety. Yet he never commanded, only asked.

'I need a showy gift for Gianni Giannini's mistress, Donna Laura,' he explained candidly. 'If she helps . . . really pushes . . . our project, the old man'll throw in enough to . . .'

Bianca had seen astonishing things since their elopement. Nonetheless, she almost gasped at his effrontery – and his candour. Who else would confidently ask his wife, hardly six months after her wedding, to give him her cherished brooch, her mother's bequest, as a present for a notorious courtesan?

She liked Pietro's directness, his refusal to lie to her. Another man would have invented an elaborate story to wheedle the brooch from her. But Pietro disdained falsehood. Since his confidence in her was perfect, her confidence in him must be equally so.

His project itself was brilliant in its simplicity. He would buy oriental spices through his Venetian connections, among them her cousin Marco. He would sell the spices in Florence, where they were always in demand. A few strands of saffron, less than a quarter of an ounce, brought four ducats, a groom's wages for an entire year. Having thus breached the Republic's monopoly, he would sell Florentine worked leather, Luccan silk, and Tuscan olive oil and wool in the Orient, again through his Venetian contacts. Venetian hostility would, she had told him, evaporate once her countrymen saw the money to be made in the new triangular trade.

The plan was sound, as well as audacious, but he needed capital to start the trade rolling. He had told her about Gianni Giannini, a rich miller in his late sixties who was looking for other places to put his surplus capital than the perfumed hands of his greedy mistress.

'I'm not quite sure.' She stood over him. 'It's such a beautiful brooch. I hate to think of anyone else . . .'

'My dear, I promise.' His voice was again husky with desire. 'I promise I'll find you a brooch such as never . . .'

She leaned down and kissed him gently, letting her hair trail across his face. He touched her breasts with his fingertips and reached for her sash. She leaned away from him. But she knew she would give in.

DAWN: SEPTEMBER 30, 1565
AEGEAN SEA: GALLEY OF THE ANGELS

The cockerel crowed twice in rapid succession. Red wattles quivering, it saluted the scarlet dawn. In the coops, a dozen hens obediently joined their lord in greeting the new day. In the pen, a single sheep baaed disconsolately, and two sows grunted their displeasure. They were all that remained of the livestock Captain Marco Capello had bought when the *Angels* touched Famagusta in Cyprus three weeks earlier. But meat and eggs were luxuries, and they could always trawl for the small tuna so plentiful in the eastern Mediterranean.

A greater threat hung over the galley. The fretful storms of the past ten days had not only depleted her livestock with waves that washed across the midships deck, but had contaminated her casks of fresh water. The water remaining would not last four days, no matter how stingily doled out.

Thirst disabled – and could kill in ten days. By that morning's count, the *Angels* was crammed with four hundred and forty-six men, well over her normal complement. Most of the excess were men-at-arms: swordsmen, pikemen, crossbowmen, musketeers and can-noneers.

Without water, hunger, too, would torment the *Angels*. Men-at-arms, seamen, and slaves would be deprived of their staple food, the hardtack invented centuries earlier by the stewards of the Great Arsenal. Marco had replenished his supply in Cyprus, where, as in every province of the Venetian Empire of the Sea, naval bakeries produced the iron-hard, long-lasting bread that was the staff of con-quest. Venetian seafarers were accustomed to a thick soup made by boiling hardtack with olive oil, spices, and whatever meat or fish came to hand. Without water, the cooks could not make that soup.

The cockerel, delighted that the violent gusts, the driven rain, and the waves like moving cliffs had finally subsided, crowed again.

'Four times,' the chief officer of the *Galley of the Angels* observed to his captain, who was peering anxiously at the horizon to the north.

'What of it?' Marco responded absently.

'The Turks think it's good luck when the cock crows four times,' the chief officer said. 'But when've you lacked luck?'

'I need some luck right now. I need the island of Santorini with fresh water, fresh meat, and fresh fruit, not a musical rooster.'

'It's in the skies, our luck: scarlet and gold, the colours of Venice.'

'I hope you're right,' Marco clapped his chief officer on the shoulder with rough affection. 'You're the devils for superstition, though, you mainlanders.'

Paolo Crespelle was an oddity in the Venetian naval service, an outsider, a native of Tuscany, where his father held the barony of Pistoia. Foreign mercenaries formed and commanded many of the Republic's land armies, but the premier service, the wooden ships that guarded her commerce and her Empire of the Sea, were normally officered by her own patricians. Paolo was an exception largely because of Capello influence.

He was, quite simply, indispensable to his captain. Although he was twenty-seven, six years older than Marco, they had been roistering through the ports of the Mediterranean together for five years now. A boon companion, Paolo Crespelle was also a superb seaman and a raging lion in battle. Feeling neither envy nor vanity, he was happy to serve his young captain. Aside from the mutual affection forged in common danger and common triumph, his captain was making him rich.

Paolo's share of the prize money for the ships they had captured was piling up in his account at the Bank of the Rialto. When Captain Marco Capello came aboard, the sailors said, they could already hear the clink of coins in their purses. He had never made a passage without taking at least one Turkish or Arabian vessel, corsair or merchantman, and usually more. Nor did he disdain a Genoese or a Pisan prize when politics permitted.

Marco Capello's skill also gave them all a far better chance of living to enjoy their riches. Although daring in action, Marco husbanded the lives of his crew. He had lost fewer men than any other captain in the Venetian service.

As Chief Officer, Paolo Crespelle valued the pleasures of wealth only a shade less than the joy of battle. He came of the impoverished hill nobility of Tuscany whose acres were largely vertical, fit only to graze a few sheep, grow a few inferior grapes for thin wine, and support a few twisted olive trees. Unlike most naval officers, he did not spend his gold on women, neither on respectable women nor on courtesans. After a wrenching affair with a lady of Padua a few years earlier, he had sworn never again to unlock his heart.

A few of Paolo's coppers might go to an honest whore from time to time, but there was usually no need. Making no particular effort, he for some reason attracted women of all classes. Perhaps it was his be-damned-to-you swagger, the manner of a warrior who has seen everything the world offers. Perhaps his refusal to pursue any woman attracted so many women. It was certainly not his looks, Marco joked – and Paolo gravely agreed.

His features, he had years earlier concluded, were wholly undistinguished: snub nose; long, bony face; olive skin burnt brown by the Mediterranean sun; light-hazel eyes. He was wiry, not obviously powerful, and he was three inches shorter than Marco. Today, even his clothes were workaday: a plain blue-woollen shirt and grey breeches that left bare his muscular calves.

Paolo Crespelle prided himself neither on his appearance, which, he said, was not merely ordinary but shop-worn, nor on his bloodline, which he said was running a little thin, since it went directly back to Father Adam himself.

He prided himself, rather, on his skill in running that complex organism, the *Galley of the Angels*, for a captain who was a splendid seaman but impatient of housekeeping details. He prided himself also on his lethal skill with the broadsword, acquired at the *sala delle armi* in the Medicis' Pitti Palace; and on his command of Turkish and

Arabic, acquired during three years of captivity among the Moslems, half the time as a galley-slave and half as sailing master of a Turkish warship.

'Land ahoy!' The lookout shouted from the wicker-work crow's nest. 'Land bearing four points off the starboard bow!'

Marco swarmed up the shrouds supporting the mainmast. Perched on the long yard of the lateen sail, he gazed at the low blue shape veiled by the morning haze. After measuring the angle with his thumb and forefinger, he shook his head. A minute later, he slid down a stay to the deck and studied the compass in its housing beside the helmsman's heavy tiller.

'Come to port,' he directed. 'Steer two seven zero degrees.'

Paolo commanded: 'Helmsman, tiller to windward. Sweeps out. Bring her round now.'

The warship changed course in an instant. When the helmsman swung the big rudder to the left, she was turned by the wind. She swivelled within her own length because thirty long oars pulled forward on her right side and thirty more backed water on her left.

Paolo Crespelle fussed with the set of her big faded red sails, one on the foremast, the other on the main. Finally satisfied, he turned to Marco with an inquiring lift of his eyebrows.

'It's not Santorini,' Marco explained. 'It's only Anafi. Far too small. They'd be on us in an hour or two. Santorini's big enough for us – with luck. I know a little cove among the cliffs, where no Turk ever sets foot. Anyway, the garrison's very small, not first-class troops. Albanians, not Turks. With luck, we can water there undisturbed. Maybe kill a few wild goats, trade with the peasants for cheese, grapes, some wheat. They're friendly Christians, most of them.'

'Let's put her on the beach and scrape off some seaweed. She's losing at least two knots, maybe more, trailing all that growth.'

'If we can, Paolo. But Santorini is hostile territory, even if we're not at war with the Turks this year, at least not formally.'

Shading his eyes, Marco peered around the horizon as the islet of Anafi dwindled in their wake. He saw no more than the endless indigo plains of the sea rippling with row upon row of white waves. The ancient philosopher Pythagoras was reputed to have made a device for seeing across long distances. Experimenters at the University of Padua had been trying to reproduce that device when Marco was a student four years earlier. They were still trying.

'Steer two ninety?' Paolo asked. 'We'll pass Santorini without even seeing it on this course.'

'Not yet!' Marco replied. 'Keep her as she is. I want the north wind in my sails as long as I can. We'll have to beat up to Santorini, use the oars, I'm afraid. But not yet.'

Marco drew his blue-and-orange captain's cloak against the chill, and the morning sun sparkled on the silver buttons that clasped its shoulders. His eyes were wary, and his mouth was set hard in suspicion.

The State Inquisitor had been eager to get him out of Venice. Afterwards it had been the usual bureaucratic muddle. The *Angels* had gone to sea in great haste – and then cruised aimlessly for a month waiting for authorisation to carry out her mission. The courier galley that finally appeared at the rendezvous off Corfu had carried not only the official despatch ordering him to sail to Cyprus, but a private note from the Inquisitor he called Uncle Vincenzo telling him that the proceedings of outlawry against Bianca and her husband were still pending. There had been no further word, official or personal, for him at Famagusta when he returned to Cyprus a month later.

'You may alter course now,' he told Paolo. 'But nurse the wind. We won't go to oars till we must.'

The *Galley of the Angels* inched north-west for an hour and a half, her triangular sails sheeted tight to catch the wind. Too close to it and the narrow craft could capsize, blown over despite the stability lent by her depth below the water. Too far off the wind and she would draw away from Santorini, which was still invisible. Its position was, however, marked by a parasol of cloud in the clear sky.

After two hours and ten minutes, Paolo Crespelle looked hard at Marco Capello, who nodded. The chief officer then gave a series of commands: 'Up helm. Sweeps out. Down sails. Row on my command: twelve strokes to the minute. Row!'

'Land ahoy!' the lookout called. 'Bearing fine on the starboard bow.'

Confident of their navigation, neither captain nor chief officer bothered to climb to a better vantage point. After twenty minutes, the peak of the volcanic island appeared on the horizon, a grey bowl floating in the flawless blue sky. During the next half-hour Santorini slowly revealed itself as a long crescent shape opening to the west.

Marco pointed to an indentation in the cliffs a few hundred yards from the south-western tip and said: 'We found the cove two years ago, Paolo, when you were on leave. A tranquil spot. We'll run up a Turkish flag, just in case we're observed. Also cover the cannon, then get my coat of arms and the commissioning pennant down. Now put on all speed.'

The chief officer gave another series of orders. A bass drum beat out the quickened pace for the oars, sixteen strokes to the minute, and a green flag bearing the silver crescent of the Ottoman Empire opened above the crow's nest on the mainmast. The galley was some three miles from her refuge in hostile waters.

A long black snakelike shape appeared from behind the tip of Santorini. A distant kettledrum demanded twenty-two strokes a minute from the slaves at her oars. Four minutes later, when she had cleared the point, the sweeps were drawn inboard. The three lateen sails on her three short masts billowed, catching the following wind. The snake-ship turned towards the *Galley of the Angels*, her flag, a white scimitar on a green field, streaming forward.

'No honour among thieves,' Paolo grinned, jerking his head at the green flag flying from their own mast.

'Not if they think we're a fat merchantman. A blessing we have that flag up. Nothing to mark us for what we are . . .' He pondered for a moment. 'The usual drill, I think. Turn her clumsily, very clumsily. Perhaps you could lose a sail.'

'I don't see why not.'

Within three minutes the tautly disciplined Venetian warship that had been ploughing steadfastly into the wind was transformed into an awkward merchantman whose captain and crew had panicked at the appearance of the Arab pirate. Her sweeps locked as they were drawn inboard, and two snapped like dry twigs. The big mainsail climbed halfway up the mast and then stuck, the halyard jammed. The foresail escaped its handlers and streamed out from its yard, flapping and ripping.

'Out of Algiers, I think.' Marco was unperturbed by the chaos on his ship. 'She's hunting a long way from home.'

'Probably very hungry!' Paolo observed, then barked at the helmsman: 'Steer wider, man – and wilder. Don't forget, you're pissing yourself with fear.'

'Men-at-arms, helmets off and armour covered!' Marco commanded. 'Down on deck, behind the bulwarks. I'll flog every second man if there's a single glint of armour or a shot fired.'

The black pirate bore down on the awkward galley like fate itself. And the panic on the galley's decks grew wilder. When the pirate was half a mile off, Marco nodded to Paolo.

'Let go your tiller, helmsman,' the chief officer said softly. 'Let her fly up into the wind. Now wait . . . a few seconds more. Good! Now edge her around. Let her get taken aback.'

Her sails flapping, the *Angels* was still moving forward under her own momentum. She stopped abruptly when the wind got in front of the mainsail, driving the red canvas against the mast. Apparently so paralysed by terror she could not even hoist a white flag of surrender, the galley wallowed in the swell, passively awaiting her gory fate.

By a feat of seamanship that made Paolo draw his breath in admiration, the Arab helmsman came within three feet of the Venetian vessel's side. Sharp-pointed grapnels trailing long ropes hurtled onto the *Angels'* bulwarks and rigging.

The ships grated together, bound along their entire length. White teeth in dark faces under coloured turbans gleamed as the pirates poured over the bulwarks. They met no resistance.

After twenty seconds, when more than fifty assailants had landed on the *Angels'* deck, Marco Capello shouted: 'Now!'

A hundred and twenty-six men-at-arms rose from the deck as one, and sailors swinging cutlasses dropped from the rigging. The silver crescent came down with a rattle, and the great battle ensign of Venice rose in its place: blood-red, twenty feet long and ten wide, the golden lion of St Mark roaring and flourishing its sword.

Astonished at the eruption of fighting men from a helpless merchant ship, the Arabs drew away. Their backs to the bulwarks, they rallied, their scimitars and pikes rattling on the soldiers' armour. Fresh assailants swarming onto the *Angels* were cut down by crossbow bolts and musket balls before they touched the deck. But not all.

'God, they fight well,' Marco gasped.

The heavy broadsword in Paolo's hand swung so fast it was a blur of silver. He parried and slashed, stabbed and cut, thrusting the scimitars aside. His lips drawn back in a savage grimace, Paolo led a boarding party sixty strong onto the enemy ship. A few pirates defended themselves as fiercely as they had attacked, but most were stunned by the ferocious counter-attack. Cutting down the last resistance, Paolo shouted in triumph.

The end came four minutes after the boarders had poured onto the *Angels*. Throwing down swords and pikes, the Arabs extended their open hands to plead for mercy. But Christian swords still fell, and blood puddled on the deck.

'Enough!' Marco cried. 'Enough! Take their surrender!'

Reluctantly, the Venetians disengaged. But a surreptitious thrust pierced the lungs of the Arab captain, and a halberd's axe-head sheared through the helmsman's neck before Paolo shook off the rage of battle and commanded: 'Sheathe your swords. No more killing! We'll need the prisoners.'

Marco Capello stood on the poop of the captured ship, his feet set wide apart to counter its unfamiliar motion. She was called *Akbar*, which meant Omnipotent, as his chief officer had just told him. With great satisfaction, he gazed at the rows of benches along either side of the ship, each seating three. The *Angels'* blacksmiths were knocking out the pins that secured the manacles of the slaves who had rowed under the Arab whiplash.

More than two hundred captured Christian seamen had worn those benches smooth with their toil. Living on a piece of bread and two cups of water a day, they had been burnt by the harsh summer sun and battered by the gales of winter. Only the toughest had survived.

'I like this best, setting them free,' Marco told his second officer, young Arnaldo Pesaro.

While the emaciated galley slaves rubbed their backs and grinned in delight, their former masters were chained in their place to the rowing benches. Not, however, the burly overseer, whose whip had left scars on every man's back. The big Nubian had surrendered when the counter-attack spilled onto the *Akbar*, but the first prisoners released fell on him.

Sickened at seeing a man ripped apart, Paolo nonetheless did not halt the carnage. Once a galley slave himself, he had not been sure he could – and would give no order he could not enforce. Anyway, it was finished in two minutes. The released slaves in their fury were more merciful than the overseer who had inflicted months, even years, of suffering on them. They killed him quickly.

'You'll have no trouble, youngster, on your first command,' Marco Capello advised Arnaldo Pesaro from the eminence of his twenty-one years. 'There're bound to be good seamen among the slaves we've freed. They'll work the ship – and keep an unsleeping guard on the new slaves. I'll give you six men-at-arms, as well as a bosun and half a dozen seamen. Can't spare more and you won't need them.'

He clapped the young nobleman on the back and added: 'I'll leave you food and water enough to make Crete. Re-supply there and take her home to Venice. Take her home! When she's sold our families will ensure we're not cheated of our share. I don't want a provincial prize court cutting into our claims.'

Seamen were already trundling casks of water, sacks of rice, baskets of dried fruit, and haunches of salt mutton aboard the *Angels*. The sailmaker helped himself to sailcloth and ropes, the carpenter to boards, oars, and spars. The armourers gutted her powder and weapons, leaving the prize only enough to defend herself on the short voyage through reasonably safe waters to Crete.

Within the hour, the *Akbar* had cast off and set sail for Heraklion, a hundred miles to the south. On her poop, her new captain stood self-consciously erect beside the helmsman. The voyage home to Venice would qualify nineteen-year-old Arnaldo Pesaro for appointment as a captain in his own right.

'Paolo, set a course to take us north clear of Santorini, so we're not seen from the island,' Marco directed. 'I'm sorry to stop the men going ashore, sorrier still you can't scrape her down. But we've made too much noise. Now I want to vanish.'

When the chief officer had given the orders, Marco resumed: 'We won't try that trick again for a while. I wouldn't without overwhelming numbers. Letting them board!'

'Not something I'd recommend every day,' the chief officer replied. 'But, by God, it went well!'

'Paolo, I think you'd better know about this mission. Sealed orders be damned.' Marco decided. 'Let's go to my cabin.'

Once under the poopdeck, he added: 'You recall we cruised off Anatolia for more than a month. We were clearly *not* looking for easy prey, as the crew was supposed to think.'

'But didn't. They never believed it.' Paolo stooped to enter the stern cabin. 'They're convinced you can sniff out a prize a hundred leagues away any time you want.'

'We were waiting for a courier, who finally turned up three weeks late. You've been very patient, not asking where young Arnaldo Pesaro and I went in the skiff those two nights.'

'I knew you'd tell me in time – *if* I didn't ask.'

'I was carrying a letter from Salomo Sagredo. You know who he is?'

'That Jewish banker who dabbles in chemistry. A great friend of your father, if I remember right. He seems open and honest. No slimy tricks. A good man . . . for a Jew.'

'I wouldn't say *no* tricks at all. Naturally, Sagredo wrote in Hebrew using a code I'm told is unbreakable. Both times, I landed alone north of Latakia. Pesaro has no idea what I was up to. The second time, I got the confirmation I needed. Our new rendezvous is the sixteenth of October on the island of Paros, the smaller twin of Naxos across that narrow strait. Joseph Nasi, the prince of the Jews, is our contact. What he tells the Turks in Constantinople, I've no idea. But Nasi himself is to meet me.'

Marco spread a chart on a folding table and stabbed his forefinger at a big island surrounded by a maze of smaller islands.

'Naxos, that's the real prize. Naxos and its isles, the Cyclades. The Republic ceded them to the Turks in 1540, when you were two years old, before I was born. There was no choice. We stood alone, deserted by our allies. The Council of Ten now believes we've a good chance of getting them back.'

CHAPTER V

MORNING: OCTOBER 12, 1565
FLORENCE: PONTE VECCHIO

BIANCA Capello Buonaventura was meandering through the Piazza della Signoria an hour or so before noon on a bright morning in the autumn of the year 1565. A lady might with propriety walk by herself in the centre of Florence, as she did when she went shopping. In Venice few ladies would wish – or be permitted – to go about unaccompanied by a male relation or a male servant. Any lady who did would wear a mask to conceal her features and safeguard her reputation. Since a mask would have been wildly conspicuous in Florence, Bianca wore a black veil, which at least obscured her features.

She was not yet at ease with the freedom she enjoyed in the capital of Tuscany, which in her thoughts she persistently and unfavourably contrasted with her native city. Even she would not contend that the mists of mid-October in Venice, though she loved their eerie isolation, were more pleasant than this sunlit day in Florence. Yet her freedom, was it not largely because her standing was so much lower here than at home?

Aside from Pietro, who was constantly busy with his enterprise, who really cared how she behaved? After the brief notoriety kindled by a Venetian noblewoman's eloping with a Florentine far below her in rank, she had become a nonentity. As she should have expected, the nobility of Florence had not welcomed her, but had taken her at their valuation of her husband, which was not high. Most of those who did take notice of her existence castigated her for seducing an innocent youth. Every Florentine from street-sweepers to counts knew with certainty that all Venetian ladies were love-crazed, using witches' potions and spells to lure the men they wanted.

Bianca knew exactly where she was going, but she took a circuitous route. She dawdled in the Piazza della Signoria, the Square of the Magistrates, beneath the tower of the stone castle that was the seat of the government of Tuscany. The Palazzo Vecchio, the Old Palace, they called it, but it was not very old. The cornerstone had been laid less than three hundred years ago. The cornerstone of the Doge's Palace was more than *seven* hundred years old.

Walking between the wings of the Uffizi, the offices of Duke Cosimo I, she saw one parallel with Venice. At home, too, they built slowly. Although the Uffizi was incomplete five years after the ground breaking, another structure was growing from it, a bridge over dry land. The universally talented Giorgio Vasari, poet, architect, and painter laureate to the House of Medici, was building an enclosed corridor over the roofs of the city. That aerial boulevard would cross the Arno over the houses and shops that lined the Ponte Vecchio, the Old Bridge, which was even newer than the Old Palace.

Bianca chided herself. She must stop carping at the deficiencies of Florence beside Venice. She must adapt and become a Florentine, as Pietro urged. There had been no word from home since Marco's letter last January. The silence was deeply depressing. She could, realistically, allow herself no hope of visiting Venice for years.

She picked her way through the builders' debris strewn on the cobblestones of the Old Bridge. It was no longer dangerous to cross to the south side of the city, as it had been a few months earlier, when bricks, stones, timber and bolts were falling from the hands of workmen hard-pressed to complete before December the project begun only in March. Duke Cosimo demanded haste. He wanted the road in the sky completed before his eldest son, Francesco, returned from Vienna with his bride Joanna of Austria, daughter of the Holy Roman Emperor.

A great conqueror who had made himself a duke and the most powerful prince in continental Italy, Cosimo was almost exhausted at the age of forty-five. He had already withdrawn into partial retirement with his latest mistress, having appointed his son Francesco Prince Regent of Tuscany. Cosimo now chose to live in the Pitti Palace on the south side of the Arno, while Francesco and Joanna were to take over the ducal apartments in the Old Palace on the north side. The Duke wished to go back and forth between the two palaces unimpeded by the mass of people in the streets. Giorgio Vasari had therefore conceived the extraordinary road in the sky.

Such arrogant extravagance, Bianca reflected as she paused before a greengrocer's shop on the Old Bridge, delineated the difference between her adopted home and her true home. Infinitely richer than this upstart city, the Serene Republic abhorred personal ostentation and enforced rough equality upon her patricians, as well as her ordinary citizens.

In Venice, the law curbed all excess; even the Doge used the common waterways. In Florence, princes and aristocrats in extravagant costumes were to fly over the heads of commoners, as if they were gods, not men. The Doge served the nobles and the people of Venice, but the nobles and the people of Florence served the Medici Duke.

She had learned to think for herself with the Youth, the intellectuals who met at Ca' Morosini. Her father had hated her 'spouting airy nonsense', as he called any mental activity that was concerned with neither money nor pleasure. Marco, convinced that two years at the University of Padua had made him a philosopher, enjoyed bandying ideas with her. Pietro was now disinclined to such conversation, although he had listened with fascination to the Ca' Morosini debates. Pietro was too busy fighting to make his way, *their* way.

The greengrocer's display gave off the scent of fennel, sage and rosemary. The elderly shopkeeper was one of her few friends in Florence. Having come from Mestre on the lagoon when he married a Tuscan woman, he loved to talk broad Venetian with Bianca. He had promised to get her some squid with inksacks intact, so that she could make a *risotto con seppie*.

'I told you, Lady Bianca, there wasn't no need for you to get up early in the morning.' His ruddy face beamed. 'Here you are. No, nothing to pay. My pleasure doing a small favour for a Capello.'

After conscientiously buying vegetables and fruit, Bianca drifted in a haze of well-being towards the southern end of the Old Bridge. It was ridiculous that so small an encounter attended by so small a kindness could make her glow with pleasure. She was normally alone, except for her ailing mother-in-law, her penny-pinching father-in-law, and their two cross servants. A touch of human warmth could make her happy for a day.

The thunder of hammers on anvils reverberated, and lightning seemed to flash from the forges where heavy-muscled blacksmiths toiled half-naked. Bianca wrinkled her nose at the urine-and-sulphur stench of the tanneries, which drew clear water from the Arno and poured back their stinking wastes.

The Old Bridge was a city in miniature. She was jostled by a juggler who kept a wheel of ninepins in the air as he strolled across the bridge. She was importuned by men leading donkeys laden with earthenware pottery. A tinker nursing his firepot chatted with a knife-grinder shouldering his grindstone. Butchers in bloodstained jerkins man-handling beef carcasses were avoided by fastidious ladies.

At the southern end of the Old Bridge, just before a granite arch, Bianca saw the black signboard that read in dignified gold-leaf letters: PALMIERI BROTHERS, GOLDSMITHS.

The Palmieris had been recommended by the Lombard Bank, where the casket with her mother's jewels was safely lodged. A lady who possessed a substantial amount of jewellery, the manager had said, must from time to time have need of a reputable craftsman who was a genius with gems and gold. Having little else to do, Bianca had visited the goldsmiths a number of times to admire their handiwork. The Palmieri brothers were happy to stop work to chat with a wealthy lady who must eventually give them a fat order. Working precious metals was only part of their craft, the easier part, Eduardo, the elder, often said. Patiently cultivating clients and catering to their whims was the harder side.

The Palmieris' shelves displayed intricate jewellery, as well as gold and silver salt-cellars, cosmetic-jars, hair-brushes, and the newly fashionable table knives and forks. Bianca loved the glamour of the goldsmiths' shop, just as she loved perfumes, beautiful clothes, and graceful furniture. But the frivolous side of her nature was muted nowadays. Like her father, her father-in-law sneered at her as 'a book-ish madam' because of her pleasure in learning.

She was not shopping for jewellery today. How could she?

Pietro was still looking for what he called 'the big, fat, beautiful chunk of capital to get my enterprise launched'. Though he was a persuasive salesman, the small sums he raised were consumed by their modest living expenses. Pietro desperately needed to be cheered up.

Bianca had flirted with the idea of buying him a handsome ring, saying, perhaps, that she had found it among her mother's jewels. Yet, no matter where she said she had got it, that gesture would make her look extravagant when they were struggling to survive. It could even make her look a bit stupid. Besides, she did not want him wondering how much more she had hidden away.

She had finally found a simple answer: the universal cure-all, money. If they had enough to live on for a few months, he could save the money he raised and build up the capital he needed.

She had decided to sacrifice the one good piece she had kept out of the Lombard Bank: heavy gold earrings shaped like buttercups with a handsome pearl in the centre. She would tell Pietro she had taken the money from her father's secret hoard before leaving the Palazzo

Capello – and kept it for an emergency. She would not tell him that she hid her jewellery under a loose board in their bedroom.

When he heard the tinkling of the bell on the door, Eduardo Palmieri welcomed Bianca as if she were already the lavish spender he hoped to make her. When she spoke of a short loan, backed by a piece of jewellery, he nodded sympathetically. His grey face assumed a knowing look, and his small, soft hands gestured deprecatingly.

He might as well have said: 'I know you ladies of fashion, always getting into scrapes you don't want your husbands to know about.'

Instead, he said: 'Of course, my Lady. If you'll come this way? We have a quiet little cubbyhole at the back for transactions that might embarrass our clients.'

Then he scuttled away like a conspiratorial mouse. The cubbyhole was separated only by a thin curtain from the shop itself. Eduardo Palmieri naturally liked to keep an eye on his precious merchandise.

'Mnn . . .' he murmured, studying the earrings through a lens. 'Yes indeed. Now I would say I could . . . Naturally a very good sum for your Ladyship, not what I'd give any Maria or Angela who drops in. I'd say they're worth about . . .'

The visitor's bell tinkled, and Palmieri broke off. He twitched aside a corner of the curtain and said: 'A gentleman. If you'll excuse me.'

Bianca was startled when she heard the familiar voice. Was Pietro following her?

Then she smiled. It was like a farce with the guilty wife caught by her husband selling her jewellery. She thought of popping out of the cubbyhole and surprising Pietro. They could laugh about this encounter, and there had not been much to laugh for for several months. But that would be childish. Besides, she did not want him to suspect she still had some jewellery left.

'Temporarily embarrassed,' Pietro's words echoed the words she had uttered a few minutes earlier. 'What can you give?'

'I'm deeply sorry I can't take you to the back, sir,' the jeweller apologised. 'I'm afraid I have another client . . .'

'No matter. Just give me a figure on this ring. In a hurry.'

'Well, it's not half as good as that other piece the other week, the pearl brooch with the fine rubies. I could let you have, say, two ducats.'

'No more?'

'I'm afraid not. Of course, if you want to sell this little bauble instead of just pledging it, I could see my way to, say, four ducats.'

'Done,' Pietro said. 'Give me the gold.'

Bianca sat stunned behind the curtain. Why, she wondered, had he not given her cherished brooch to Gianni Giannini's mistress Donna Laura? And how would he explain the disappearance of this ring?

But, of course, she could not ask him. She could not admit she still possessed even the pieces she had kept out of the bank, lest he suspect she had still more hidden elsewhere.

'Thanks, Edo,' she heard Pietro say. 'I need the cash, want to buy a present for my wife.'

Bianca smiled at her suspicions. How like her improvident, loving husband to buy her a valuable present when he had no money. She decided, nonetheless, that she would change her hiding place.

LATE AFTERNOON: OCTOBER 12, 1565
FLORENCE: THE BUONAVENTURA APARTMENT

Bianca disliked eating alone even more than she disliked the heavy midday meal the hearty Tuscans loved. Besides, strolling aimlessly through the streets emptied by the rush to luncheon tables, she simply did not feel hungry.

One moment she was warmed by Pietro's gallant gesture: buying her a present when his funds were so low. What, she wondered, was her present to be?

The next moment she was pierced by suspicion. What had he done with the money he'd received for the brooch that was supposed to win the goodwill of Gianni Giannini's mistress, Donna Laura, so that she would persuade the rich miller to invest in Pietro's enterprise? What, for that matter, did he do with the sums he raised beyond their modest living expenses?

The pendulum of her emotions finally slowed in perplexity. Could he really be as foolhardy as he appeared in recklessly taking her last piece of jewellery? Presumably, he counted on her not daring to question him about it. If so, he was contemptuous of not only her intelligence, but, even worse, her feelings. Perhaps she had woefully misjudged this man to whom she was bound for life.

Bianca saw suddenly that the streets were deserted and the shops shuttered for the Florentines' sacred afternoon repose, the long siesta. In her distress she had been wandering around the city for more than two hours. Her feet hurt, and her throat was parched by thirst. Seeing from the tall, narrow façades that she was in the Via Maggio, she crossed the Arno by the lovely Bridge of the Holy Trinity and walked down the Via Tornabuoni towards the Buonaventura apartment overlooking the cathedral.

When she struggled past the grey stone building with the carved oak doors and the grilled windows Pietro had pointed out as the former Palazzo Buonaventura, Bianca's full mouth curved in a smile devoid of either warmth or mirth. Was this truly the ancestral palace of the noble Buonaventuras? Or was that another of Pietro's fantasies?

Her hand went to her throat in dismay. She had never before that moment thought that her husband was a fantasist. Imaginative, a romantic, even a visionary, but a visionary whose achievements would match his heroic goals. She had never before acknowledged that he might be a fantasist who made up tales, perhaps to deceive himself, certainly to deceive others, above all herself.

If he did not change, they would be ruined. If he could not distinguish fact from fancy, if he could not chart a course based on reality, she would have to do so. Yet he was entitled to a hearing. He might well have an explanation for his inconsistencies and apparent falsehoods, an explanation that was not only plausible, but true. She desperately hoped he would.

Tired, thirsty, and, suddenly, hungry, Bianca climbed the five steep flights of stairs to the apartment. Her nose wrinkled at the fetid smells in the cramped corridors. The stench grew stronger, almost nauseating, when she opened the peeling wooden door.

Her father-in-law looked up nearsightedly when she entered the space that served as entrance hall, sitting-room, dining-room, and writing-room. He was, as usual, crouched over the scarred walnut table, which was, also as usual, heaped with legal documents. Peering through his thick-lensed spectacles held in place by tapes tied around his ears, he offered her his habitual scowl.

Bianca had realised months earlier that the scowl was not directed at her as an individual, but only as a member of the human race. His chalk-white face was heavily lined, the record of millions of scowls during his fifty-four years on earth. Pietro's father did not discriminate; he disliked everyone impartially. Sitting in the dark room from which he rarely ventured, he was a cave-dweller beleaguered by enemies he could not see, his only defence the volleys of legal documents he constantly shot out.

'Where've you been?' His scowl turned into a grimace, the nearest expression to a smile he could manage. 'We've missed you.'

'I'm sorry!' She was startled by his warmth. 'I've just been wandering around thinking.'

'Soon enough, you'll have your own carriage, no need to walk.' He tapped the parchment scroll held flat before him by two glass inkwells. 'This is it, the last stone in the arch, the keystone. When they get this final brief, the justices *must* decide in my favour. Another month, two at most – and it'll be all over.'

Bianca was to remember that assertion in the months ahead. At the time, she took it as no more than the latest flash of bravado behind the frenetic optimism that inspired his ceaseless litigation. With such a father, it was no wonder Pietro sometimes had difficulty distinguishing between fact and fancy.

'My son, he's in there waiting for you,' her father-in-law added. 'A herald came from the Venetian Embassy. All done up in scarlet and gold, even wearing a tabard. You know, a sort of tunic hanging down front and back.'

At the edge of her mind, Bianca felt the familiar annoyance at his belief that he had to explain the simplest words to his ignorant daughter-in-law. But her heart beating erratically, she was already opening the bedroom door.

It was most unlikely to be good news delivered in that formal manner. She would, nonetheless, allow herself to hope. Perhaps her father, who presumably loved her in his own way, had decided to forgive his only daughter, granting her both his blessing and her rightful dowry. Improbable, certainly, but not impossible. Regardless, she would not despair, either now or after she had read the formal communication, whatever it might say.

Pietro was lying on the narrow bed with his hands locked behind his head, staring at the rough-plastered ceiling. When he heard the door open, he looked hard at her – and she knew immediately that the news was bad.

His brown eyes, normally so warm, were filmed like those of an ancient lizard. Only that morning, a few hours ago at the goldsmiths', his male beauty had still moved her. But the vitality that lit his features had been snuffed out.

'Oh, it's you, is it?' he said perfunctorily. 'Well, it's all over . . . *finished.*'

'What, Pietro?' She forgot the doubts over which she had been anguishing. 'What do you mean, finished?'

'There!' He jerked his chin at the improvised dresser, where a crumpled parchment scroll lay beside a second scroll tied with pink ribbon. 'It's all there. I'll tell you what it said, what mine said. I daren't open your Ladyship's.'

He looked at her in silence for a long moment, and Bianca almost believed that she saw antagonism, even hatred, in those narrowed brown eyes. Then he spoke, his tone flat: 'My enterprise is all finished, Bianca, dead. I'm outlawed by Venice, so I can never trade through Venice. Well, it was a good idea . . . while it lasted.'

'Tell me now, Pietro!' Bianca refused to look at the scroll addressed to her before she had heard him out. 'Please stop moping and tell me.'

'Very simple. Addressed to Pietro Buonaventura, Clerk, by the Council of Ten. *Clerk!* I am commanded to present myself within a month before the Council to answer charges of fornication, theft, and corrupting a noblewoman of Venice. Failing, I am to be declared an outlaw, subject to arrest and imprisonment should I ever touch Venetian territory anywhere, either in Italy or the Empire of the Sea. I am informed that my uncle Giambattista has already been found guilty of encouraging and abetting my crimes. He's been taken across the Bridge of Sighs and committed for ten years to the *pozzi*, the cells under the Doge's Palace. The Salviati Bank has been fined a thousand ducats for harbouring such criminals. Not exactly an inducement to return to face the impartial justice of Venice.'

'Pietro! Pietro, my love, I'm sorry . . . so very sorry.'

'You should be,' he said flatly. 'But let's have the whole picture before you start weeping and wailing. Let's see what charming message the Council of Ten has for you.'

She slipped the pink ribbon off the heavy parchment cylinder, noting wryly that it was addressed to Nobildonna Bianca Capello, not Signora Buonaventura. The Council would not recognise a marriage contracted by a noblewoman of Venice without parental permission, whatever Holy Church might say. Ironically, in the eyes of the most powerful body in the Republic she therefore retained the noble rank she would have lost by a valid marriage to a commoner.

The charges against her were: defying paternal authority, absconding, fornication, and theft. She, too, had a month to appear before the Council – or be outlawed, exiled forever from her native land. No matter what she did, the dowry of twenty thousand ducats the court held in trust for her was forfeit to the state. To compensate Nobiluomo Bartolomeo Capello for the humiliation he had suffered, and, also, for the alienation of his daughter's affections and the loss of her services, the entire sum was to be paid into his hands.

Bianca laughed, and Pietro looked up in amazement.

'The aforesaid Nobleman Bartolomeo Capello,' she read aloud, 'desirous of demonstrating his continuing love for his sinful daughter, as well as his disregard for the monies placed in his hands by the justice of the state, hereby offers a reward of ducats two thousand for the return of his daughter or her paramour to Venice, either individually or severally.'

'A good profit for your loving parent,' Pietro said sourly. 'Eighteen thousand ducats *after* the reward. Enough to hire three and a half thousand men-at-arms for a full year, enough to change the map of Italy. Besides, the reward'll never be paid. They won't catch me. Venice isn't the only port in the world. Venice be damned!'

Stunned by the even-handed brutality of the verdict, Bianca was, nonetheless, heartened by the revival of Pietro's spirit. Only a moment earlier, he had appeared crushed, all fight knocked out of him. But he was now breathing defiance, resolved to batter down every obstacle fate put in his way.

Her husband, Bianca acknowledged, was weak in certain ways and sometimes unreliable. That was, however, only natural, no fault of his. He had been as unfortunate in his parents as she in hers. But his spirit was indomitable – and what else really mattered?

From this moment on, Bianca swore to herself, she would assist Pietro with all her strength and ability in all his endeavours. She would make up for what he lacked, just as he did for her. Together, they would conquer a hostile world.

She turned to Pietro with a confident smile to give him that pledge. He stared back at her coldly, shaking his head in puzzlement.

'You're a useless bitch, aren't you?' he said evenly. 'No cash, not a copper after all you led me to expect. And now you're grinning at disaster like a she-ape.'

Bianca gaped at her husband in astonishment, her entire being hollowed by such an assault. She could not breathe and her heart seemed to stop beating. Her body, as well as her mind, was stunned by the shock.

Only an instant earlier, she had believed that she finally saw Pietro clearly, his weakness and his strength, and that she could still be true to her vow to live with him all her life in mutual sympathy and support. Now, an instant later, she realised in anguish that there might be no future for them.

Her heart beat wildly, like a dove trapped in a chimney frantically flapping its wings. She sank onto the three-legged stool before the dresser. She still could not speak, even if there were anything to say.

'My Uncle Giambattista swore we'd get it: the dowry. A fortune!' Pietro Buonaventura's tone was low and vicious. 'What do you think I married you for? Your bookish talk and your clumsy love-making, perhaps? Why do you think I never fucked you till the priest said his mumbo-jumbo over us? I held off to make sure not to frighten you away. I had too much to lose! Everything to lose! Now it's all turned to shit!'

Bianca Capello, noblewoman of Venice, rose and looked down at her husband. She was as pallid as a marble nymph. But hers was the pallor of anger, and the tears that trembled unshed in her green eyes sprang from rage.

'The dowry would come to us anyway, Giambattista said!' Pietro went on in the same deathly calm tone. 'We'd get it all in time, even if it meant a lawsuit. After all, your mother'd bound it for your dowry, Giambattista said, and Venetian justice was fair, though slow.'

He paused and looked at her appraisingly, but did not move. As sensation and, with sensation, pain slowly returned to her, Bianca again heard his lifeless voice still abusing her.

'Well, my cunning uncle didn't reckon on your lunatic father getting us outlawed – and grabbing the loot for himself. My clever uncle had your damned family all mixed up, always talking about "the fabulously wealthy Capellos". He got poor Bartolomeo confused with rich Damiano. A fine mistake for a bank clerk!'

For the first time, fear or, perhaps, desperation invaded Pietro Buonaventura's despair.

'Well, Giambattista's now paying for those little errors of judgement: sitting in a cell that's half under water half the day. That's Venetian justice! And, as for me, I'll be paying for years. I'm landed with a highfalutin', prissy, penniless wife – unless I can get rid of you somehow. Why *don't* you go back to Venice? Who needs a cold, useless bitch like you?'

CHAPTER VI

THE Venetian warship was again masquerading as a merchantman under the crescent of the Ottoman Empire. The silvered six-foot tripod with the three lanterns of a captain in independent command had been removed from her stern, as had the shields bearing her officers' coats of arms. Ragged ends hung from her rigging, and ropes trailed across her patch-painted sides. No naval captain would allow washing to dry on his galley's shrouds, but the captains of the ragged coasters that plodded around the growing Turkish domain in the eastern Mediterranean had neither authority nor inclination to enforce man-of-war smartness on their under-manned vessels. Beyond her run-down air, the *Angels'* best disguise was her position: no Venetian ship, merchant or naval, would dare venture alone into the inner ring of the Cyclades, the islands scattered across the Aegean Sea, where the Ottoman navy was dominant.

'Paros harbour bears forty-five degrees off our starboard bow, distance six miles,' the Chief Officer, Paolo Crespelle, reported to Captain Marco Capello. 'Darkness falls two hours and thirty-six minutes from now.'

'Keep her steady on thirty degrees, Paolo. I want to pass the town openly, as if we had every right. I don't want anyone getting suspicious of an unknown ship skulking north . . . Slow her down. She's bowling along like a galley carrying despatches, not a dilapidated old coaster with a weed-fouled bottom.'

'Later, Marco, you'll be glad we scraped her. I'd rather have an extra two knots than four more cannon.'

'But for now rein her in. I want to dwindle into the dark, let them think we missed the tide and couldn't bring her into harbour.'

The Tuscan chief officer was even more proud of the galley than was his Venetian captain. He chafed at hiding her gunports under slovenly tarpaulins. He disliked bringing all but ten of her sixty sweeps inboard so that she would resemble a down-at-the-heels coaster that could afford no more than thirty oar-slaves, not the two hundred a crack galley carried. He was irritated by the men-at-arms' being told to exchange their uniforms for nondescript sailors' gear. Above all, he hated to compromise the perfection of the *Angels'* canvas.

Patched and faded cotton sails now flew from her tapering spars, each twice the length of its stubby mast. The lower corners thrust forward so that the galley, aided by her sweeps, could beat almost directly into the eye of the wind. The upper corners, high above and behind the masthead, captured the slightest breeze.

Paolo loved the voluptuous curves of a lateen sail filled by a following wind. But not today.

He resignedly gave the orders. The crewmen loosened the sheets, and slackened the halyards. The foresail hung limp. The mainsail bellied and flapped.

'Don't overdo it,' Marco directed. 'We want her to look sloppy, not like a scow manned by farmers. *Too* sloppy'll arouse suspicion.'

'Don't worry, Marco,' Paolo answered. 'I do know how a clumsy, leaky Arab merchantman is handled. Though, thank God, I only did three months on one.'

Normally happy to let his officers see to details, Marco was on edge. They had now been at sea for six weeks, more than four hundred and fifty men crammed into a vessel meant for at most three hundred and fifty for a two to three week stretch. The strain of living so close for so long bred cliques and quarrels, straining discipline. Marco was also nervous about the rendezvous, which was the crux of his first major independent operation.

The Council of Ten, he had already told Paolo, believed there was an excellent chance of reclaiming the Cyclades, which Venice had lost to the Turks a quarter of a century earlier.

Why, Paolo wondered, give that enormous responsibility to Marco Capello? Although he was already a seasoned captain at twenty-one, a major operation would normally be commanded by an older officer with much greater experience. Nor was he the only captain who was also attached to the Secret Service. Why, then, Marco Capello?

'I'll be going ashore on the northern point of the island.' Marco unnecessarily repeated his instructions. 'You will remain aboard in command. I am . . .'

'Marco,' Paolo touched his captain's arm. 'Isn't it time you let me in on the secret?'

Marco left his post beside the helmsman and leaned over the stern-rail, staring into the wake.

'I was about to say I am forbidden to share the details, except under stringent need. I now propose to exercise that discretion.' He grinned, no longer pompous. 'How these asses in the Admiralty could think I'd leave you sitting aboard the *Angels* with no inkling of what's going on! Anyway, the Inquisitor left it to me.'

Reaching under his black doublet, he pulled out a much folded sheet of heavy paper sealed with red wax. Tapping the stern-rail, he added: 'You're *not* to approach the shore, no matter what. Keep her two miles off. If I'm not back by dawn, leave me. Sail directly for Venice. Drive her as fast as she'll go. You'll like that!'

As he turned to face Paolo, Marco said emphatically: 'You *must* report my disappearance to the Inquisitor without delay. It's vital that the operation does not go ahead if there's any doubt. Arrangements will have to be cancelled immediately or . . .'

'Let me get this clear, Marco. You're ordering me to *desert* you?'

'Precisely.'

'And the letter in your hand?'

'If you do sail without me, please deliver this to Angela Tron. By your own hand, Paolo. Her family mustn't know.'

'I see!'

The chief officer's face was blank. Marco grasped his arm and declared earnestly: 'This is the great test: Can we restore the glory of the Empire of the Sea? Can we win back our territories without a major campaign depending on undependable allies? But, first, the background.

'There'll be four more galleys and a thousand men-at-arms waiting for us when we return to Crete. All to use at my discretion, no non-sense about waiting for clearance from Venice. But I promised you the whole picture. So bear with me if I tell you what you already know.'

The scores of isles known as the Cyclades, of which Naxos was the largest, Marco recalled, had become Venetian in the thirteenth century and remained Venetian for more than three hundred years. The archipelago had been a vital link in the Empire of the Sea, which extended two thousand miles from Trieste to Cyprus, its outposts the Venetian enclave in Turkish Constantinople and Venetian settlements on the Black Sea. The Ottoman Turks were the most recent and the most powerful of the Moslem hordes that had for eight centuries been hammering on the gates of Europe from Spain in the west to Bulgaria in the east. The Duchy of Naxos and the Cyclades had also been attacked by Greeks, Slavs, and, latterly, by Algerian pirates led by the merciless Khair-ed-Din, called Barbarossa for his red beard. The Serene Republic had, however, continued to rule through great colonial families of Venetian origin.

In the year 1538, Venice had girded herself to repel another assault. A Christian fleet had met the Imperial Ottoman fleet south of Corfu. Inspired by Venetian gallantry, the allies had been on the point of victory when the ships of the Holy Roman Emperor Charles V abruptly quit the battle.

The Emperor had no wish to bolster a rival whose splendour outshone his own. He was, rather, determined to dominate Venice and, in time, to conquer her. He had therefore instructed his docile admiral, Andrea Doria, a man born to cowardice and treachery, to withdraw if a great Venetian victory were in the making.

After the Emperor's flotilla fled, Christians were for the first time defeated by Moslems in a mass fleet action. By the peace treaty of 1540, the Serene Republic, having no choice, had ceded Naxos and the Cyclades to the Ottoman Empire.

'As you know, the Crispo family remained,' Marco went on. 'Our former vassals still rule – as vassals of the Turks.'

'Far too complicated and subtle for a straightforward Tuscan like me.'

'A certain Mehmet Ali, a loyal servant of the Ottoman Sultan, is governor of this island of Paros. He nominally comes under the Crispos, who rule the entire Duchy of Naxos and the Cyclades. But he is, as a Moslem, directly subordinate to the Sultan.'

'Loyal, you said?'

'Not quite! Mehmet Ali is really an Albanian, born to a petty noble family in Dalmatia who've served the Republic for two centuries. He was captured by the Turks as a youth, forcibly converted, and given high rank to attract other converts.'

'The threat of the scimitar is usually quite enough,' Paolo interjected. 'Immediate conversion by the sword.'

'Anyway, Mehmet Ali has now realised he is a dutiful son of Holy Church,' Marco laughed. 'Having discovered himself to be a Christian, he wishes to revolt against his overlords, the Christian Crispos, because they serve the Moslem Sultan.'

'No more confused than everything else out here. Logic doesn't operate east of Greece.'

'Now Mehmet Ali wants to rule independently. That means he

wants to cut himself a bigger slice of the spoils. He knows the Sultan won't tolerate a lapsed Moslem as a governor. He also knows he's too small to rule the Duchy of Naxos. He aspires to be no more than Count of Paros.'

'Then all it needs is Venetian ships and Venetian troops to put this charming two-times turncoat into power?'

'Not quite. Now enters our old friend and antagonist, Joseph Nasi, prince of the Jews, who once lived happily in the Ghetto of Venice. Nasi's to get the title Duke of Naxos once the Crispos have been pushed out of the islands. Nasi will then give Mehmet Ali the title Count of Paros – and everyone will live happily ever after.'

'An ecumenical plot,' Paolo commented. 'A false Moslem and a Jew who was once a false Christian both stand high in the favour of the Sultan. And both are determined to betray the Sultan. Where do the real Christians come in? If one can call Venetians Christians.'

'We only say: *We're Venetians first, then Christians a long way after!*' Marco laughed aloud. 'Since the Sultan won't give Nasi the title he craves, Nasi would have it of us. Besides, he has extensive business interests through the Hebrew communities in Europe. He's constantly dealing with Venice, France, and Spain, even the Vatican. He wants to come home to Europe, he says.'

'So Venice is to support the revolt, but *not* be seen to sponsor it,' Paolo summed up. 'When it succeeds, Venice will again be overlord of the Cyclades. And you command this simple little operation? Why you? Not the greatest master of intrigue in the Secret Service, are you?'

'Is that an insult or a compliment?' Marco laughed again. 'I'm in command because Joseph Nasi knows my family well. He knows that Damiano Capello fights to protect the Jews, as being valuable to Venice. I'm the only one who's both my father's son *and* an agent of the State Inquisition. Only I can give Nasi the assurance he demands: my word and my father's pledge.'

'The squadron of galleys, the battalion of soldiers to back the revolt? Who's to command them?'

'I am. Mehmet Ali will work only with the officer validated by his sponsor, Joseph Nasi. I am to command, but not as a commodore. Only as a captain.'

*   *   *

The wind off the sea had fallen as the dusk deepened. The night, already two hours old, was soot-black, the stars and the half-moon veiled by heavy clouds. The breeze now rising on the island, which lay south of the *Angels*, could not shift those clouds. But it filled the galley's new sails, which were so deep a crimson they were invisible on a ship already invisible in total darkness.

Tarpaulins hung over the prows muffled the sharp cutwater so that it would not fling up a luminous bow-wave and signal the warship's presence. Her running lights were not lit nor, of course, her great battle lanterns. The cookfires had been dowsed, as had the slow matches normally glowing to set off muskets or cannon. Paolo Crespelle had promised ten lashes to any man who raised his voice or let a weapon clang, however accidentally. To any man who struck a spark to light a twist of tobacco he had threatened a hundred lashes, which meant death. No man, however strong, could survive more than eighty strokes of the ten-tailed scourge.

Soundless as well as invisible, the ghost ship cruised slowly back and forth two miles off the cove at the northern end of Paros. To keep it from squeaking the rudderpost had been slathered with lard where it passed through the deck. Blocks and pulleys had been greased and wrapped with rope-yarn to make them noiseless. No word was spoken, not even helm orders. The helmsman came about when he felt a tap on his shoulder. The sails were not allowed to fly over the bow, slatting and flapping, but were drawn across by hand.

Marco Capello had gone ashore an hour earlier in a launch whose oarlocks were muffled with canvas. Before embarking, he had reiterated his instructions to abandon him if he did not return before dawn. He had also rejected his chief officer's plea that his boat-crew and personal guard of twenty-eight should be reinforced by the same number in a second launch.

He would depend on secrecy, rather than force, he had said, taking only five seamen to the rendezvous in the goatherds' shack on the hillside above the cove. The clatter of men-at-arms would alarm any patrol, though he expected none on sleepy Paros. Since discovery could imperil the rendezvous and, thus, the entire operation, he would rely on stealth.

Paolo stared at the black bulk of the hills silhouetted by the faint glow of the town in the distance. Unaccustomed to waiting while others went into danger, he stared even harder at the cove, where the necklace of white surf around the pale beach was just visible in the blackness.

Marco, the *Angels* boatswain, and five seamen were slipping through the coarse brush at the foot of the hill. With the sure instinct developed in a hundred landings, the boatswain had immediately found the goat-track leading to the shack. The ghost-scent of dead fires and the tang of wild garlic mingled with the brine of the sea; and the mewing of gulls rose above the twitter of small birds.

A vixen barked, and the Venetians froze. The boatswain tapped his captain on the shoulder, urging him forward. His unspoken message was clear: *The slightest sound will startle birds and beasts, but no man's hearing is so acute.*

Faces and arms burnt dark by the sun did not reflect the faint glow off the white-sand beach, and their clothes were black. When the glow of the beach faded into the darkness behind them, they felt their way inch-by-inch along the goat-track. The rasp of thorns on duck trousers was alarmingly loud, but the seamen's horny feet, bare except for rock-hard callouses, were silent on the stony path. The chorus of locusts in the trees sounded as loud as cannonading.

A man coughed no more than ten feet away. Marco's pulse raced, and he peered around wildly. But he saw only blackness and the boughs of olive trees silhouetted against the distant glow of the town of Paros.

The old boatswain again tapped him on the shoulder, urging him on. Automatically, Marco complied. Inching along the path again, he realised that he had heard a wild cat cough.

All his senses were alert, *too* alert. He had been landing by night on hostile shores for years, usually leading a large party. He was, nonetheless, nervy. The responsibility on his shoulders, no less than the future of the Empire of the Sea, made him start at the noises of the night.

Marco's heart thumped again. He thought he had seen a quick flash of red, but they still had half a mile to go to the rendezvous point. Red flashed again, followed by yellow. Scarlet and gold, the colours of Venice, were the recognition signal.

The boatswain replied with the harsh cry of a Mediterranean crow. In reply, a crow cawed twice in the darkness, then twice again.

Marco felt the presence of the men he was to meet, though he could not see them. He smelled scented pomade, sweat, and the stale breath of a heavy smoker of tobacco.

'Welcome to Paros, Ser Marco!' a man whispered in broad Venetian. 'God has brought you here.'

A hand on his arm guided him past the goat's hide hanging across the entrance to the goatherds' windowless shack. When the hide rustled back into place, a lantern was unshaded for twelve seconds. By that brief light, Marco glimpsed the original of the portrait his father had shown him: a long, narrow face dominated by a lean, straight nose beneath a black skullcap.

'Welcome, Ser Marco,' Nasi said again. 'I trust the Noble Lord Damiano, your father, is well.'

'Very well indeed, sir,' Marco replied. 'He sends you this gift. Only a book, but nicely bound: the scandalous *Dialogues of Aretino*.'

'What better gift! I have too little news of the arts of Europe.' Joseph Nasi was formal. 'Now, Ser Marco, please attend once more.'

The lantern flashed again, and Marco saw a second face lit from beneath: dark, round, and fleshy, crowned with oiled black hair beneath a dark-green turban.

'Our ally, Governor Mehmet Ali,' Nasi said. 'Soon to be Count of Paros.'

Marco regretted bringing the boatswain, rather than Paolo, who spoke good Turkish. Yet he could not leave his ship without knowing that the chief officer was in command. But the Governor of Paros greeted him in the simple port Italian larded with Arabic and Turkish words that was the common tongue of sailors of the Inland Sea.

Joseph Nasi spoke in the same tongue: 'Sit on this bench. Now, my plan is . . .'

The conspirators conferred for more than an hour in pitch blackness broken occasionally by lantern flashes to light a chart or a note. Sweat dripping from Marco's chin sizzled on the lantern. The homely smell of hot oil was swallowed by the rank stench of goats and herdsmen. The doorway, sealed against light, admitted no air, and the atmosphere grew heavy.

Joseph Nasi's strategy was meticulous. It was also straightforward, avoiding the temptation to be too clever that ruined so many plans. Sceptical when he entered, Marco was convinced when he left the shack that the coup could succeed. It would need luck, as well as coordination, but so did every worthwhile operation.

They had agreed that the rising would take place in a month. Earlier and there would be too little time to bring the Venetian task force into these waters undetected. Any later and the secret was bound to leak out.

'Cap'n, look there!' the boatswain said urgently. 'Dead south!'

Marco saw a rocket arch red over the distant town of Paros. A half-minute later, another rocket trailed green fire over the nearby hills. Distances were deceptive at night, but the second rocket looked no more than a mile away.

'Smugglers!' Mehmet Ali exclaimed in surprise. 'What a time for a smugglers' alert! I told all we'd have a quiet night, that I'd had an all clear from intelligence. I even gave the garrison leave. And now this.'

'*My* ship is the smuggler, my friend,' Marco said softly. 'The one thing I didn't reckon on: getting taken for a smuggler.'

'They won't, can't, turn out much force,' Mehmet Ali assured him. 'Except for the coast guard, which isn't under my direct command.'

'How many would turn to hunt a suspected smuggler?' Marco asked calmly.

'Three or four sailing launches, each carrying, say, twenty-five men. And on land . . .'

'You must leave right now!' Joseph Nasi intervened. 'Ser Marco, you must get back to your boat. If they find us, it's no matter. Who'll argue with the governor? But, if you're caught, we'll *all* be in the snare. Move now!'

Too hurried for silence, the sailors tumbled down the path they had crept up a few hours earlier. Breaking bushes, snapping twigs, and tumbling stones heralded their progress towards the pale glow of the beach below.

Nonetheless, Marco clearly heard Joseph Nasi revert to broad Venetian unintelligible to an outsider to shout: 'This is no betrayal, Captain. Only an accident. But I'll send you confirmation. Don't move without my confirmation.'

Coming down far faster than they had gone up, the Venetians reached the bottom of the hill after ten minutes. They still had a while to go across rocky fields and, finally, yielding white sand to reach the launch. Alerted by the rockets, the crew would be standing knee-deep in the surf ready to push off.

'Something's going on out there, Cap'n,' the boatswain said as they started across the sand. 'Can't see damn all. But it's surely more'n one vessel.'

The first officer had not expected to hear from his captain until the muffled splash of oars announced the launch's return. He was, however, uneasy, burdened by conflicting duties: responsibility for the galley to the Admiralty and responsibility for Marco's safety to Damiano Capello, as well as to the State Inquisition.

Paolo started at the rockets, but could do nothing. Then, almost five hours after the launch's departure, he heard stealthy splashing near the shore. He smiled in relief.

The smile froze on his lips. The splashing of oars was markedly louder than Marco would tolerate returning from a hazardous mission. Paolo heard a second series of splashes and, shortly, a third.

Forgetting his instructions, he ordered: 'Sweeps out! Sails down! Stroke for the shore! Attack speed!'

Within thirty seconds, the hundred and ninety foot long galley was knifing through the calm water. Within two minutes, seven hundred and thirty tons of warship, bow-wave glowing white, was hurtling towards the northern tip of Paros.

The galley overtook the first coast guard launch after six minutes and crushed it under her prow.

'By God, it's black tonight! Never saw him.' As always joyful in action, Paolo commanded: 'All cannon, load grapeshot.'

A rocket rose from the hills, casting a blue-white light over the cove. Momentarily reassured by that signal from their allies on shore, the coast guards were horrified when they turned their light-dazzled eyes towards the sea. A terrible apparition was emerging from the darkness into the cone of light: the most powerful machine of war ever made, her oars at full stroke, her cannon gaping, and her men-at-arms massed.

Paolo Crespelle did not pause when the *Angels'* ram splintered the launch. He heard the crackle of small arms' fire from the shore, though the Venetians carried only swords and daggers. His crossbowmen shot as they passed the third coast guard launch, but he did not pause.

The *Angels'* launch was floundering in the surf. He could just see by the dying flare that three men hung unmoving across the thwarts, while others tried to push her off. A file of men standing thigh-deep in the water faced the challenge from the shore. The flare expired, leaving a bright afterglow on his retina and the cove in blackness.

'Hard port!' he shouted. 'Now!'

The rudder hard over, thirty oars backing water and thirty pulling forward, she turned her side to the beach.

'All oars back water!' Paolo commanded. 'Guns two, three, and five, maximum elevation. On my command: *Fire!*'

Glowing slow matches touched the priming powder, and three cannon crashed as one. Aimed above the heads of the men standing with their captain in the surf, two stern guns and one prow gun flung a salvo of lead slugs, rusty bolts, and chain-links at the soldiers on the beach.

The Venetians scrambled aboard their launch and rowed for the galley, which was placidly backing water some ninety yards off the beach. Five minutes later, they had clambered aboard, their shipmates had pulled up the wounded, and the launch was under tow with the dead.

Paolo ordered: 'Take her out to sea. Oars full stroke. Set all sail.'

The night was still soot-black, and visibility virtually nil. The first officer found his captain on the midships deck. Clutching his shoulder, blood seeping between his fingers, Marco was taking the roll of the twenty-eight men who had accompanied him.

'Eleven wounded and four dead.' His tone was flat. 'Chief Officer, see to the wounded first. And keep her as she goes. I want to be out of sight of land by dawn.'

'Aye aye, sir!' Paolo gestured the boatswain to look after the men and said formally: 'Now, if the captain will come to his cabin, I'll have a look at his shoulder. *Twelve* wounded I make it.'

Marco did not reply, but led the way aft. He winced as he climbed the ladder to the poop, but said nothing. Checking the compass, he only grunted. Nor did he speak when seated in his cabin, with the portholes sealed against the light from the big lantern.

Paolo cut doublet and shirt from Marco's shoulder, flicking fragments of cloth away with the tip of his knife. Before applying a bandage, he poured grappa into the wound – and a grunt of pain escaped from Marco's clenched lips.

'A good clean wound,' Paolo said. 'The ball cut across the muscle, nowhere near the bone. It should heal clean in a week or two.'

'Thank you, Chief Officer.' Marco Capello spoke for the first time. 'Now if you'd be good enough to tell me why you disobeyed my clear orders and brought the ship in.'

Paolo shrugged, his meaning clear: *What else could I do?* The melodramatic Tuscan gesture fanned Marco's Venetian wrath, and he shouted: 'Good God, man, you could've grounded her. As it is, you've given away the rendezvous.'

'Captain, I spent a long time with the chart after you left. It's roughly accurate, but very roughly. That's why I didn't bring her closer. But I *knew* there was depth enough a hundred yards off the beach. I submit that I have given *nothing* away. No lights! No flag! No battle cry! A pirate galley, a smuggling galley, in the Turks' eyes. No more!'

Marco nodded, partially mollified. He lifted the bottle of grappa and drank deep before looking at Paolo again.

'The gravest charge remains,' he said. 'You disobeyed a direct order. I should have you court martialled.'

'If you will, Captain. But you have no case. I would have merited a court martial if I had *not* acted.' Paolo continued in the same flat tone. 'The captain, even acting-captain, of a warship of the Serene Republic is *finally* responsible himself for the safety of his crew and his ship. He cannot be bound by the orders of his predecessor. No more can he shift his responsibility to his predecessor. For all I knew you were dead, Marco, and it was my responsibility to bring the ship and the crew out of danger. *All* the crewmen I could save, including you. Acting on my own judgement, I did so!'

Marco shrugged, wincing at the pain in his shoulder, but smiled thinly.

'Next time,' he said, 'I'll put it in writing.'

CHAPTER VII

'YOU can hardly claim the marriage wasn't consummated, can you?' the Abbess asked Bianca Capello Buonaventura with a small smile. 'You are irrevocably married to Pietro and may marry no other as long as he lives. Mother Church requires you to be a dutiful wife, *unless* Pietro's behaviour imperils your life or your child.'

Bianca looked down at herself, almost expecting to see a gentle swelling to show she was fulfilling a wife's first duty: to be fruitful. But it was too soon for it to show. She had only been sure she was pregnant since her suspicion was confirmed three weeks ago by Sister Barbara, the midwife of the hospital for mothers and children administered by the Convent of the Oblate Sisters.

Bianca was now glad she was fruitful. She had raged for two days when the midwife told her she was pregnant; she had detested her body's being given over for the next seven months to nurturing the seed of a husband she now despised. After the nuns' selfless joy and the Abbess's tart counsel, she was happy that she was fruitful.

The Abbess had told her: 'Yes, it will be his child, but, above all, *yours*. After the . . . ah . . . initial act, a father can be important to his child. He can also be negligible. Knowing Pietro since he was four, I suspect he'll be little or nothing to your child, even, in time, to yourself. He's not a stayer. But a mother is *always* at the centre of her child's life.'

Chiara, Countess of Metrisanti in her own right and Abbess of the Convent of the Oblate Sisters by election, had not hesitated when Lady Bianca Capello Buonaventura came to her for refuge a month earlier after fleeing from her husband in the night. One noblewoman succouring another, she had taken the desperate Venetian into her convent and, after careful appraisal, into her well-guarded affections.

A simple act of charity had then become a friendship. Too long had the Lady Chiara been without an equal to whom she could talk unreservedly, as she could to the Lady Bianca. They came of different states, but the nobility of Italy, indeed of all Europe, were a single realm.

She was now casting Bianca out. Regardless of her own feelings, no conscientious abbess could harbour a fugitive wife who had fled an assault that was no more than verbal. Too many wives, ladies as well as commoners, came to the Hospital of the Oblate Sisters with wounds to bind up after being savaged by their husbands.

Being practical as well as dedicated, the Abbess had misled her friend. In fact, a marriage contracted under false pretences was not a marriage in the eyes of Holy Church, and Pietro Buonaventura had undoubtedly lied about his motives, as he always lied. The union should be declared null, as never having occurred, since mutual good faith, which was essential to the Holy Sacrament of Matrimony, had been absent. Yet the Abbess could not encourage her friend to take the long and weary road that led to an annulment.

There was as much chance of Bianca's winning an annulment as of her becoming Duchess of Tuscany. No decent woman should be tied for life to a shameless rascal like Pietro Buonaventura. But Bianca had neither friends nor funds to push her case through the Roman Curia. And how would she live even if she could rid herself of Pietro? He was a poor thing, but better than nothing at all.

'You're tied to him, but you needn't be his slave,' the Abbess resumed. 'You must stand up to him. He's weak . . . will give way.'

'I've been considering,' Bianca said. 'I couldn't bear being locked up with the Carmelites, but your house is completely different. You work in the world, even to help the world.'

'I'd never consider admitting you,' the Abbess replied. 'For some women, this is the right life. But not for you, Bianca. Not even if you could offer the dowry required of every high-born sister. Besides, a nun with an infant at her breast is an absurdity. Above all, you are too worldly, as I was until . . .'

The Abbess paused, and Bianca knew she was remembering the ambush that had deprived her at one stroke of her husband and her three half-grown sons. The starched white wimple that cast a faint shadow on her face in the pale sunlight of November made her unshed tears obvious. Her fine brown eyes were liquid, and she drew in her lower lip, which was still full and tender at the age of forty-two.

Bianca knew the Abbess was again reproaching herself for allowing all her sons to go with their father on the foray against a defiant smallholder who refused to pay his tithe to his overlord. But who would have thought that the fellow, who was hardly more than a peasant, would have the initiative, not to speak of the temerity, to lay a trap for his liege lord?

Until recently, as she had confessed to Bianca, it had done her good to remember the fate she had inflicted on the rebellious swine: hanging him up by his wrists for two days, then disembowelling him while he still lived. But the Abbess was now revolted by her own cruelty.

'I fear I may be becoming holy despite myself,' she had told Bianca. 'I, a daughter of the Metrisantis, the most vicious family in Italy.'

The Lady Abbess was not what one might expect. She was not a self-effacing motherly soul to whom one turned instinctively in time of trouble. Still worldly wise in spite of herself, the Lady Chiara was also still a great beauty with luminous eyes, a high smooth forehead beneath the white band of her wimple, and tautly moulded cheeks beneath high cheekbones. She was highly strung and slender, almost too slender. Her beauty was lit by her intelligence, rather than by her spirituality.

The Countess had come to the Convent of the Oblate Sisters only eleven years earlier, bestowing upon the community her large personal fortune. The community had chosen her as its head nine years ago, perhaps in gratitude for her largesse, but above all in appreciation of her wisdom. She still waged a daily battle against her own worldliness. Yet, having disciplined herself against bitterness, she exuded spiritual force.

The Abbess saw her convent as a tranquil haven for the unfortunate. Not merely to give refuge to women, but to make them independent. She would allow through the gates no prelate sent by the Archbishop of Florence, and every three months found a new priest to say mass for her nuns. She discarded confessors like old shoes, so that no man could become influential in the life of the convent.

Abbess Chiara had taken Bianca in against the counsel of her advisors. She was now driving Bianca out despite their pleas. The senior nuns wanted Bianca to remain a month or two longer. Even better, until her child was born.

That, the Abbess said, would be good neither for the Lady Bianca nor for the Oblate Sisters. They would corrupt one another. Bianca would become too soft for the world in which she must live, and the nuns would become frivolous, treating the Venetian and her child as if they were beautiful animated dolls.

'I'd prefer to keep you by me,' the Abbess confessed to Bianca, who was sipping strong coffee from a thimble cup. 'But it would only be using you. I do you no good, but harm, by putting off the inevitable. Besides, I'm already too self-indulgent.'

The walls of the Abbess's room were the pale stone the Florentines called sacred. They were hung with tapestries celebrating the glories of the Metrisanti family: the heroism of its men, the beauty of its women, and the magnitude of its wealth. The bright carpets from the Levant that lay on the flagstone floor were splashed with light by the sun-rays trickling through the leaded window-panes. Apart from the oak crucifix on which a life-size Christ twisted in agony, it could have been any room where a great noblewoman received her guests and plotted to further her husband's interests.

'I know I must go,' Bianca replied. 'But that doesn't mean I must go joyfully. Of course, you're right. After a year or two, I'd go mad cooped up here. But it looks so wonderful now, serene and secure.'

'Bianca, you're not made for peace and safety.' Feeling herself weakening, the Abbess Chiara, Countess of Metrisanti, spoke to herself as much as to her guest: 'You can now deal with Pietro. You're strong enough. I only wish I could send you back with enough gold to keep you and bring him to heel. But to what end? To make Pietro rich?'

'I don't want . . . need . . . the money.'

'Naturally. Once in your hands, it would all be his as the property of his wife. His to dispose of. You'd have no say, no rights. My dear, even when there appears to be no property, it is always a mistake for people of our class to wed without making a marriage contract. It's not sensible.'

Bianca smiled at the Abbess's relentless practicality, which had made the Convent of the Oblate Sisters the richest, as well as the best-administered, in Tuscany. But the habit of secrecy was now so ingrained that she would not tell even the Abbess about her mother's jewellery. Even that small wealth gave her a certain independence.

'Since I can't stay with you, Chiara, I must go back to him,' she said instead. 'What else can I do? Return penitent to Venice to be locked up by the Carmelites? Or take to the streets of Florence?'

'You'd never be on the streets.' The Abbess assessed Bianca coolly. 'You'd be a grand courtesan, beautiful, much wooed. But I can't see you in that role. You're too independent. Besides, why trade the tyranny of one man for the tyranny of many men?'

Bianca laughed at the pious woman's weighing the practical advantages and disadvantages of harlotry. Hearing that laugh, the Abbess added hurriedly: 'Even if it weren't a grievous sin, a daily insult to God.'

'Don't worry, Chiara. I shan't go on the streets or set myself up as a courtesan. I'll go back to Pietro – *not* to make him suffer, but to make use of him. Just as he planned to use me and the fortune he thought I'd bring him.'

'How will you manage with him?'

'I don't know, though I'm almost past resenting him. But I can't forgive myself for being such a fool, being taken in so easily. Not seeing through his lies!'

'You were very young. You still are.'

'But, now, I can see how tawdry he is. I still need him, though. To give me a roof over my head and to give the baby a name. Afterwards, I'll see.'

AFTERNOON: NOVEMBER 14, 1565
FLORENCE: THE BUONAVENTURA APARTMENT

The stench in the stairwell of the tenement overlooking the cathedral was unchanged: a miasma of excrement, urine, and vinegar only a gale could disperse. The atmosphere in the small apartment on the fifth floor was, however, quite different this mid-November afternoon.

Old Buonaventura's embrace and kisses went beyond the ritual welcome required of a father-in-law. Somehow, his greeting was warm, almost hearty. His habitual scowl was replaced by a beaming smile, and he wore a clean shirt. Even the normally greasy lenses of his spectacles were newly polished. He might have been welcoming a beloved daughter who had married a wealthy banker, rather than a foreign daughter-in-law who had not brought a single copper into the family.

The walnut table in the entrance-hall that served so many purposes was laden with a ham, roast beef, and a braised capon, as well as clams, oysters, fire-red lobsters with cloud-white flesh, and giant prawns in blush-pink shells. Such abundance was almost unimaginable in the mean apartment. Bianca saw, too, half a dozen bottles of sparkling Venetian prosecco and half a dozen bottles of the robust red wine of Montalcino Pietro knew she liked. There were even signs of attempts to wash the rough-plastered walls and scrub the scarred pine floors.

Bianca had tied her hair in a simple chignon and put on a workaday rust dress with a green overskirt when Pietro arrived at the convent to fetch her. Flaunting a new doublet of crimson velvet, he had kissed her lovingly after greeting the Abbess as an old friend. Pietro was exactly the same, but, somehow, he looked different. His brown eyes were no longer tender, but guarded. His blond hair was no longer youthful, but looked slightly bleached. His full mouth now appeared neither sensitive nor sensual, but self-indulgent.

While the hired cart clicked over the cobblestones, he told her repeatedly how much he had missed her. When he began to tell her how much he loved her, becoming erotic and urgent, she had nodded meaningfully at the driver's back.

Pietro had, nonetheless, whispered throatily: 'I can hardly wait for tonight . . . I looked everywhere for you. I nearly went mad with worry before Chiara told us you were with her. You know, I never meant what . . . what I said that night! Not a word of it. Only I was so unhappy, thinking how hard it would be for you, the deprivation, the little hardships. I felt I'd failed you. But I'll think of a way. I've got a new plan. We'll be rich yet. And, my dearest love, tonight we'll . . .'

Bianca had patted his hand to silence him.

No need to answer the torrent of sweet lies. But she would no longer fight him, for he was not worth the expenditure of energy and emotion. She would keep him sweet and pliable while she made the best possible use of him. He was not a promising instrument, but she had no other.

He was in for a surprise. Tonight would be not at all what he expected. There was a limit to her tolerance, as well as to her ability to dissemble. As Chiara Mentrisanti had pointed out, she would never thrive as a harlot because she could not pretend convincingly.

Yet, this heroine's welcome must go far beyond Pietro's fleshly desires, which he must have satisfied with willing partners in her absence. The penurious Buonaventuras had spent lavishly on food and drink, presumably using funds Pietro's 'new plan' had brought in.

Her mother-in-law's cracked voice called from the elder Buonaventuras' small bedroom: 'Bianca, my dear, is that you? At last! Come and give me a kiss.'

Her mother-in-law had never called her 'dear' before that moment, and the only kiss they had ever exchanged was a ritual peck on her wedding day, lips in the air not touching either cheek.

The bedroom smelled of herbs and blood. Evidently the leech had just called to dose Signora Buonaventura and to draw off a pint from her veins to relieve the pressure on her heart. Enormously fat, pale as a locust grub, perpetually perspiring, Pietro's mother lay heavily against the painted headboard whose gilt had flaked away.

She smiled with an effort and lifted her dimpled doll's hand. With a greater effort, she drew Bianca down to kiss her cheek, which quivered at the touch.

'My dear daughter, it is a great joy to have you back with us,' she declared tremulously. 'You must never leave us again. Never!'

Startled by the demand for a kiss, Bianca was surprised at being called 'daughter' by a woman who had hardly spoken to her in the past. She was astonished at being pressed to remain indefinitely in the cramped apartment. Her mother-in-law's strongest desire had been to get her out. Yet genuine tears seeped from the blue eyes past the rolls of flesh.

Bianca escaped to find Pietro opening the prosecco. Wondering if she were seeing visions, she took a tall glass with sincere thanks. Tears stood in her father-in-law's brown eyes, enormous behind his lenses, which were now greasy again.

'We've not treated you properly. We've treated you very badly,' he confessed. 'I must apologise. From now on you'll get the kindness and love you deserve. I'll see that this scamp of a son of mine behaves himself now that the Blessed Virgin has brought you back to us. Will you drink a toast with me? *To your return. May you never leave us again.*'

Bianca smiled, but her green eyes held no warmth. This flood of southern sentimentality would have offended her Venetian reserve even if she believed it genuine. Feeling it false, her flesh crawled.

But she smiled and drank and ate and said little. If either had known her better, if her husband had known her at all, her silence and her forced smile would have revealed how their play-acting disgusted her. Hardly knowing her and clearly not caring, the Buonaventura men evidently took her reserve as the modesty of a well-bred female.

Her father-in-law confided: 'My law suit, it's not working out well, not at all well.'

Although his son glared, he went on: 'To tell the truth, it's lost. We can try again once more, but it doesn't look good.'

'Never despair, Father,' Pietro interjected with forced jollity. 'I'll never give up the fight.'

'Of course not, my boy. We'll win in the end, no doubt. Meanwhile we've got to face facts. We can't count on another windfall like your last one.'

Bianca suddenly remembered that, leaving the apartment in a rage of disillusion, she had left a ruby ring on her dresser. She would look, but she was certain she would not find it. She took another half-lobster, determined to enjoy the feast she now suspected she had paid for.

'Another glass of prosecco, my dear?' Her father-in-law was attentive. 'Or, perhaps, the Montalcino? No, better wait for the beef.'

'Who cooked this meal?' Bianca asked, seeking something to say. 'It's splendid.'

'Wonderful, isn't it? I had it sent in from Antonini's cookshop,' Pietro replied. 'You didn't think Elvira . . .'

'Where is Elvira? I haven't seen her or Ariadna today.'

'I was just coming to that, my dear,' her father-in-law replied. 'You see, they've left us. Actually, I had to let them go. Elvira's a slattern, as you know. And Ariadna refuses to do any real work. So they both had to go.'

'Actually, they left when they realised they'd have to work a little harder, and . . .' Pietro began, but his father was already saying: 'So I let them go. But we'll manage very well without . . .'

Bianca asked quietly: 'How will we manage?'

'They were both getting on your mother-in-law's nerves,' the elder Buonaventura said. 'She's sometimes fretful nowadays, even a little demanding. But she's very fond of you, as you've seen. She's soothed by your lovely manners . . . by your beauty . . .'

Bianca did not hear all of that extraordinary praise, for she could already see which direction her father-in-law was taking. She could also see that, for the moment, she could do nothing but agree.

'. . . for you to look after my wife,' he was saying. 'I know it'll be no trouble at all for you. It would be an insult to you, to the daughter of the house, to get someone else in. And the few household tasks, they'll be nothing for a strong, healthy young lady like you.'

'Just for the time being,' Pietro interjected nervously. 'Till things're looking up again.'

Knowing her temper, if little else, he was obviously surprised when she remained silent. A moment later, when she murmured agreement, his eyebrows rose in astonishment.

Their demand was preposterous, but Bianca had no choice. She would have to play the household drudge, doing the work of two women with apparent good grace. She would, however, also play the helpless female – and insist that Pietro must support her entirely. Now, that would be interesting.

What would they say when she gave up the drudgery? Chiara Mentrisanti wanted her to return to the Convent in May, although the child was not due until mid-June. Once she was free to do so, she would seek her *own* fortune, as need demanded, as opportunity offered.

'To our new life together!' Her father-in-law poured red wine. 'To our new life of harmony and happiness!'

Pietro, who was hacking slices off the joint of beef, looked up in annoyance at his father. His glance swung to his wife. Finding no sign of the irritation he expected, he returned to his butchery.

Bianca raised her glass. She hardly had to pretend for these two. Her husband's insensitivity was only a shade less monumental than his father's. Neither would worry that her surrender had been too easy.

She welcomed the flush of wine that was rising to her head, for it alleviated her disgust at their stupidity. Even so, theirs was far less than her own stupidity in falling into this trap. In truth, rushing in! She laughed at her own stupidity, and her father-in-law grinned at her through a mouthful of beef.

Bianca knew she was getting drunk. But what did it matter? Although she could not match the Buonaventuras' gluttony, she would not stint herself tonight. She had obviously paid for this banquet, and she would enjoy it.

The feeble light from the candle on the makeshift dressing-table barely lit the gloom of the improvised bedroom. But Bianca undressed in the farthest corner before drawing on her amethyst silk wrapper, now more than a little worn.

Pietro smiled to himself complacently. She had obviously missed him and their love-making. Why this coyness, except to titillate him?

'Come over here!' He was lying on the bed, only a towel across his loins. 'Come and kiss me!'

Bianca knew she should have drunk a great deal more wine or a great deal less. If she had drunk more, she might have been able to overcome her repugnance and go into his arms. If she had drunk less, she might have found a graceful way to avoid his embrace. Although it was necessary to be agreeable to Pietro until she could make her own way, she could not force herself to make love to him. And she was no good at pretending.

Her smile, she feared, was not only forced, but tremulous. She did not want him to know she not only loathed him, but felt a certain fear of him. He could be violent, especially if he sensed weakness. And she was now vulnerable physically.

'I'm sorry, but not tonight, Pietro.' She could only be straightforward. 'I'm too tired . . . I drank and ate too much. Besides . . .'

'Besides!' His grasp on her shoulders, presumably meant to be passionate, was actually painful. 'Now's the time . . . *our* time. I've waited *so* long!'

'I'm afraid we'll have to wait a little longer,' she improvised. 'The Sister-Midwife said not during the first two months.'

Wondering what she would do when that time of grace was over, Bianca almost missed his question: 'What? What did you say? Who said what?'

'Why, Sister Barbara, the midwife. She's very experienced, and she said we mustn't . . .'

'Never damned . . . Never heard such damned nonsense!' His voice was a little thick. 'Why I just happen to know . . . happen to know damned well that . . .'

Pietro raised his dark eyebrows in incredulity. He shook his head and demanded: 'What did you say? Are you saying you're . . .'

'Yes, Pietro, it's definite. Some time in June, Sister Barbara says.'

The flickering light was deceptive, but Bianca saw neither pleasure nor anger on his face. Instead he looked annoyed, as if he had just heard that a small matter of business had to be postponed.

'Bianca, how wonderful!' Did he sound as false to himself as he did to her? 'I'm so happy for you, for us.'

It was very strange. She had been certain he would be delighted. Whatever his faults, Pietro genuinely wanted a son to carry on the name of Buonaventura. Why, she wondered with patrician disdain, bother carrying that name on? But a greater puzzle now faced her: *Why did he look disappointed when he should have been delighted?*

Pietro's normal devious charm deserted him, and he said outright: 'This is a nuisance, a damned nuisance!'

'What an extraordinary thing to say!' Bianca responded. 'What do you mean by nuisance?'

'Well, my dear, it's this way.' He spoke with exaggerated care. 'Things're not in good shape with the Buonaventuras. I don't want to deceive you.'

'No, Pietro.'

'You see, we, my father and me, we thought of a way. Nothin' else to do. There's nothin' for it but find you a rich patron. With your looks and your la-di-da manners, it'll be easy. We thought maybe Ferdinando de' Medici, the old Duke's younger son.'

'Ferdinando? But he's . . .' Bianca could not quite believe this extraordinary proposal. 'Why he's only, let me see, sixteen. Besides, he's a Cardinal.'

'What's that got to do with it? Sixteen, closer to seventeen, that's more than old enough. Anyway, there's lots of time now. Damned nuisance! We can't do a thing till after you . . . after the baby.'

Bianca's husband drew a blanket over himself, turned on his side in the narrow bed, presenting his back to her, and, two minutes later, was breathing regularly. Since there was nothing else for him tonight, he quite logically went to sleep.

She had liked the way he fell asleep so quickly and never snored. She was, however, now too angry to find any virtue in him.

But was she truly angry?

She should have been horrified. She should, at the very least, have been righteously indignant at this bland proposal to prostitute – there was no other word! – her for the Buonaventuras' convenience. She was, she realised, indignant and disgusted.

But she was not horrified. The whole matter was so extraordinary it was almost unbelievable – and, somehow, ludicrous.

Arranging her own blanket on the floor, Bianca smiled to herself. She was more indignant at his hogging the small bed, though she never wanted to be so close to him again. But his nonsense was really rather funny. How they could imagine that she would ever – and for *their* sake!

CHAPTER VIII

AS usual, the message had come late.

The endurance of a stone statue was essential when dealing with a bureaucracy, even if it were only the fledgling logistics of a conspiracy to overthrow Turkish misrule in the Greek Isles. Joseph Nasi's parting cry had warned Marco Capello not to move until he received the Jew's personal confirmation that the conspiracy was undiscovered. Two weeks late, the message had finally appeared on Marco's table in his quarters in the Cretan port of Candia.

Since none of the servants would admit slipping that folded sheet of paper under his plate, he had not questioned them. Although he would never have held a confidential conversation in such a public place, he hated feeling that he was surrounded by unknown agents. Yet it was unavoidable in the spy-ridden Orient. The counter-espionage service of the State Inquisition was virtually omniscient in Venice proper. But it could not penetrate the diverse secrets of the many peoples of the Empire of the Sea.

All in all, it was good to be at sea again. Watching the white wake the *Galley of the Angels* was raking across the dark waters of the Aegean at eight on a windy evening at the end of November, Marco smiled at his own indignation. He was now sailing to support rebels against the Ottoman Empire, and he was often a spy himself. But this spy hated being spied on.

The message had used a simple book cipher: a series of numbers referring to the order of words on specified pages of a single volume. Marco had the same edition of Aretino's bawdy *Dialogues* he had given Nasi, only less sumptuously bound.

I can now confirm beyond doubt that our plans are secure. You should, therefore, proceed as planned, the deciphered message read. *The incident actually strengthened our hand. It was put down to a pirate, since smugglers are normally loath to enter into combat. The people are enraged at the ineffectual authorities, who cannot prevent pirates harrying and slaughtering at will. All is in readiness. For last-minute coordination, as agreed, proceed to rendezvous point at eleven, evening of November 29th. /s/ Abraham*

No question about the origin: Abraham was the ancient forefather of the Jews, and Joseph Nasi was now the prince of Jews everywhere.

Marco had agreed to provide Nasi and his protégé Mehmet Ali, Governor of Paros, with a thousand men-at-arms and five galleys to back their revolt. The Venetians would, however, go into action only after the rebels had proclaimed a provisional regime, raised the flag of St Mark, and appealed to the mother city for assistance.

The Serene Republic could not to be seen to incite revolt. Venice was, at the moment, not formally at war with the Turks. It could not really be called peace, but it was not open warfare either.

The rendezvous point had been fixed six weeks earlier as a group of islets seven miles north of the sister islands of Paros and Naxos. If either side failed to appear, the other would try again the next two nights. Marco would not risk a longer stay in enemy waters. In command of a task force for the first time, he was acutely aware that his primary responsibility was the safety of his men and his ships.

They had left Candia, which the natives called Heraklion for the Greek hero Herakles, ten days earlier. But six galleys could not steal together into the Ottoman-held Cyclades, as had the *Angels* alone. To mislead ever-present spies, the squadron had sailed north-west towards the island of Cerigo off the southern tip of Greece. The ships had then separated to make the passage individually, disguised as merchantmen under a variety of flags from the Ottoman crescent to the green stripes of Genoa. The *Angels* herself sailed under the Lion of St Mark as a Venetian warship bound for a courtesy call on Constantinople. Late on the afternoon of November 29, the task force joined again precisely as planned – to Marco's delight and no little surprise.

The *Angels* now flew his personal pennant of command below the Wingéd Lion, and five galleys in formation followed her shaded sternlight. The big tripod of lanterns that marked the *Angels* as a flagship was unlit. The squadron could no longer pretend to be anything other than it was, but why attract attention?

Leaning over the stern-rail, isolated by the respect, almost awe, that surrounds a captain at sea, Marco mused on his mission. All had gone well so far. Fate was smiling warmly, and he was determined that no mistake of his would imperil success. Still, it had not been easy impressing his authority on captains older than himself.

Five galleys, rather than the four he expected, had been awaiting his orders when the *Angels* returned to Candia after his meeting with Joseph Nasi in the goatherds' shack on Paros. The fifth was the former Algerian pirate *Akbar*, which the *Angels* had taken in battle.

He had earlier instructed that she be sold as a prize in Venice. But the admiral commanding in Crete had pressed her into the Venetian navy and assigned her to the task force. Although irritated at being cheated of his spoils, Marco could hardly weaken his task force by sending her home for sale.

The admiral had also summarily removed nineteen-year-old Arnoldo Pesaro from command of the *Akbar*. That decision Marco could not let stand. If he did not back his man, his authority would be impaired severely, perhaps fatally. An hour after his arrival in Crete, he had relieved the senior captain appointed by the admiral and restored Pesaro to the quarter deck of the *Akbar*.

Marco knew he had angered the admiral, while the displaced captain, Paolo Crespelle warned, would defame him in Venice. But he could not lead into action captains who doubted his will.

His decision had been proved correct that afternoon, when, following tradition, he summoned a conference of his captains aboard the *Angels*. A *consulta* always preceded major naval action: one man might command, but the captains were all equal patricians, all entitled to an equal say. After Marco outlined the operative, the five captains, among them young Arnoldo Pesaro, almost overcome by his new status, had voted unanimously to endorse the plan. Since *consulte* had been known to rebuff their commander, Marco was pleased – and relieved.

Knowing he had to do nothing more before the rendezvous, Marco allowed his thoughts to drift to personal concerns. A pity he'd lost the prize-money for the *Akbar*, though he was glad to have an additional warship. If all went well, the *Akbar* could still be sold to the navy. Because the Board of Admiralty was notoriously mean, he would have preferred a civil sale in Venice. But there you were.

Jingling in his purse money of his own, not family money, he could think seriously about little Angela Tron. As yet, her father would not even consider him as a potential husband. But there was time, for she was just approaching the sixteenth birthday that would make her just marriageable. Angela had for years been an agreeable little thing who cast adoring looks at him. He had never thought of her as a woman until he had, somehow, felt compelled to write the letter he had given to Paolo to deliver if he did not return from the meeting with Joseph Nasi on Paros. He had, of course, reclaimed it.

The face that now rose before him in the moonlight did not burn with Bianca's fiery beauty. Angela's gentle charms, rather, glowed: a heart-shaped face between curtains of burnished gold hair; large oval eyes of the darkest blue; a delightful little straight nose; and a perfect small mouth whose smile revealed pearly teeth. Quieter, more restful than the ardent Bianca, Angela still had a spirit of her own.

He now knew that he wanted her, and he hoped she wanted him. They would have to fight the opposition of both families. For many reasons, some sunk in history, the Capellos and the Trons were bitterly at odds.

Gazing across the moon-silvered waves, Marco Capello could see the five ships of his task force following in a diamond formation, the *Akbar* in the rear. The west wind filled their lateen sails, driving them along at seven knots. Since they carried no running-lights, only foaming bow-waves marked their positions. The moon played hide-and-seek in the autumnal clouds, and the warships were dark silhouettes against the still-darker shapes of the scattered islands of the Aegean Sea.

His dream since boyhood had been to command a squadron of galleys in action. Once so distant, that ambition was now all but attained. What, he asked himself, half-mocking, could he possibly do afterwards that was half as glorious?

'Boat ahoy!'

It was not the lookout's normal loud hail he heard, but a whisper from the boatswain, the last link in a chain of men that began in the crow's nest, ran down the shrouds to the midships deck, and ended on the quarterdeck. Marco wanted the ship as silent as possible. No need to proclaim their presence in enemy waters.

Glancing over his shoulder, he saw a local craft, a caique with upturned bow and stern, that showed three bright lights. That signal would not draw others' attention, for caiques normally fished at night with lanterns blazing to attract their prey.

He turned to check the squadron again unhurriedly. His galley would not meet the caique for at least ten minutes. The dark warships merged confusingly with the black shapes of a clump of islets some two miles astern of the *Angels*. But their bow-waves assured him that all were following in good order.

The rhythmic pitching of the war-galleys against the unmoving backdrop of the islets lulled Marco – and distorted his vision. For an instant, he thought the islets, too, were moving. Strange fancies for the commander of a task force of the navy of the Serene Republic. Shaking his head, he turned to check the caique's position – and abruptly swung back again.

The islets *were* moving! A huge black shape was gliding out from among them. That immensity could only be a galleon, and there were no Venetian galleons in the Cyclades.

Damnable luck, this chance encounter! Must he signal his squadron to turn and fight? Must he reveal their presence and, perhaps, abort the operation?

Marco could not ponder his response. His first responsibility was the safety of his men and his ships. This operation was, however, vital to the Empire of the Sea, which was far more important than his task force. But there would be no operation if he lost his ships.

Five seconds after sighting the galleon, Captain Marco Capello was giving his orders. As the signal-lanterns rose on the *Angels'* mast, the *Akbar* vanished. The rearmost galley was eclipsed like the moon when the sun passes across its face. The huge black shape of the galleon, capped by black pyramids of sails, simply engulfed the *Akbar*.

Marco bellowed: 'Fire signal flares: *Turn and engage!*'

The *Angels'* bows were already swinging across the wind onto the opposing course. Paolo Crespelle had ordered the helmsman to put the tiller over.

'Out sweeps!' Paolo roared. 'Attack speed.'

Five Venetian galleys turned together towards the unidentified enemy, their stern-lanterns, now unshaded, flaring on the battle ensigns they loosed to the wind's embrace. Sweeps creaking and splashing in time to the overseers' throbbing drums sang the battle anthem of the galleys. Her crack oarsmen straining on smooth-worn benches, the *Angels* was overtaking the squadron.

'Flares to light the scene?' Paolo suggested.

'No,' Marco replied. 'Let's not make it too easy for them to see us. The operation's not aborted, not yet. If we can catch the galleon and kill her . . .'

'And her escort?' Paolo asked. 'I counted three galleys.'

A spark glowed on the dark horizon, a flare of yellow immediately extinguished. Seconds later, towers of flame revealed a blazing galley. Fire climbed her rigging and her masts, outlining the ship as if she were hung with lanterns for a festival. The Wingéd Lion of St Mark shone bright amid the flames.

Once a galley caught fire, she burned like a pyrotechnics display:

all that dry timber and cloth and cordage, all that inflammable oil and pitch. A fountain of flame rose, then a black cloud. The fountain fell, but the flames rose higher, casting their brightness across the sea. The *Akbar*'s gunpowder barrels were exploding.

In that macabre light Marco Capello saw that the galleon and her three attendant galleys had turned from the Venetian counter-assault to run for shelter in the tangle of islets. Retreat was only prudent, since the galleys were outnumbered and the clumsy galleon was vulnerable. But Venetians would have stayed and fought.

Marco ordered: 'Signal flares: *Attack! Utmost speed!*'

The red flare of the first signal was followed immediately by the gold-and-green of the second. The galleys lunged forward, their oarsmen, reinforced by men-at-arms, heaving together on the long sweeps. The overseers' drums demanded twenty-two strokes a minute.

A cannon barked on the prow of the leading Venetian galley, then another. The two foremost galleys fired a salvo from eight bow-chasers, trading the delay caused by the recoil for the chance of a hit. But the enemy ships were disappearing among the black crags of the islands.

The rage of battle subsided in Marco Capello's veins. His next command was the most painful he had ever given: 'Fire signal flare: *Break off and reform.*'

'No use!' Paolo beside him agreed bitterly. 'If we follow them into that uncharted maze, rocks'll rip out our galleys' bottoms. If only . . .'

Three of the four Venetian galleys were still sweeping forward, and Marco directed wearily: 'Fire again signal flares: *Break off action and reform on flagship! Immediate!*'

The *Akbar* still blazed, but the flames were guttering out when they reached the waterline. She was almost gone, overwhelmed and sunk in less than five minutes. Poor Arnoldo Pesaro had been so proud of his first command, which was likely to be his last.

The caique showing the three brilliant lanterns had prudently vanished.

Marco Capello had to risk a *consulta* to ratify his decision. He could not have it said that he had imposed his will without conferring with his captains, even if they should disagree. A very young task force commander could not risk the charge of arrogance. This melancholy dawn could, thus, be followed by a quarrelsome morning.

While three galleys rowed guard, the *Angels* and the *Lion* searched around the clump of islets, methodically tracing a series of squares on the roiled sea. Regardless of the danger of ambush, they could not leave the combat area without looking for survivors. Venetian war-galleys did not abandon their cohorts.

Bitter, like his officers and men, at having lost a ship with no chance to strike back, Marco prayed the Turks would come out and fight. But the sea was empty of other ships as the *Angels* and the *Lion* plodded back and forth.

Debris they found in plenty: spars, planks, oars, and sea-chests, as well as chicken coops with the long necks of drowned hens lolling through the slats. The pigs and goats, being heavier, had borne their pens to the bottom alongside men-at-arms dragged under by their armour. Sailors' bodies they also saw, scorched and blistered by flames. Of course, no oarsmen. The few free oarsmen had, as usual, been trapped below among the slaves, who were chained to their benches.

Marco hated using slaves almost as much as did Paolo, who had been a galley-slave himself. But few Venetians would now contract to serve as oarsmen, and the Senate found that conscripting free men raised too much turmoil. *La Decadenza*, the Decadence, writers were beginning to call this era in the millennium-old existence of Venice, when her people were enjoying the most abundant life they had ever known. *Il Periodo d'Oro*, the Golden Age, a diminishing few also called the era.

After an hour and a half, the galleys abandoned the search. They had not found the body of the *Akbar*'s young captain. Nor had they hoped to. Arnoldo Pesaro had undoubtedly been dragged under by his steel breast-plate; like men-at-arms, officers were invariably drowned by their armour if thrown into the water in battle. The attack on the *Akbar* had been sudden and overwhelming.

Clearly, the galleys would find no survivors. Nor, equally clearly, would the Turks venture out of their refuge in the tangle of islets, whose uncharted channels Marco Capello dared not enter for fear of ambush or grounding. Balked of revenge, thwarted in his life-saving mission, he signalled the squadron to sail south-west.

That course, which would take them back to Crete the roundabout way they had come, initially ran along the western coast of the island of Paros. The last pink trails of the dawn still streaked the sky as the Venetian formation sailed on, their triangular sails swollen by the morning wind. Marco could not summon his captains to a *consulta* while so close to hostile territory.

'Sail ho!' the lookout shouted from the masthead.

Every man's head swivelled. Every man prayed the Turks had belatedly decided to challenge them, the squadron commander most fervently. The dish he hungered for was revenge seasoned by spoils.

'Sail broad on the port beam!' the lookout shouted. 'Local craft.'

A shiver of disappointment swept from the quarterdeck to the fore-peak, leaving sailors and men-at-arms thwarted and angry. But the oarsmen on their narrow benches thanked God they were not to row blind into action this morning.

Marco ordered a small change of course. Only a messenger bearing urgent tidings would venture out the morning after the engagement that must by now be known to every islander. The *Angels* made a brave show of pursuing the caique, and, coming alongside, sent boarders onto her decks. Just far enough from shore to confuse any observer, Marco wanted it to make it appear the caique had been caught unwillingly.

The boatswain returned with a roll of paper. With some difficulty, Marco read the message set down in port Italian by Mehmet Ali, Governor of Paros. He handed the roll to Paolo with the comment: 'This confirms my decision. Damnably! I wish I'd never seen it. It'll make things even harder later on.'

'You know what I think,' Paolo said cryptically. 'But I'm not the task force commander.'

Obeying the flagship's signal, the squadron altered course to sail due west. The war galleys were out of sight of land after two hours. Leaving the *Angels* to Paolo, Marco transferred his pennant to the *Lion* and at last summoned his captains to a *consulta*. He chose the *Lion* because she had the weakest chief officer in the squadron. With Paolo, who was a better officer than any of the captains, commanding the *Angels*, only two galleys would be deprived of their captains during the conference. Both had sterling chief officers. An attack was unlikely, almost impossible, but a commander had to see first to the safety of the squadron.

Casually holding his ebony-and-gold baton of command in his left hand, Marco Capello welcomed the captains to the stern cabin of the *Lion* with elaborate courtesy. No one would be able to say that he had behaved arrogantly while holding temporary authority over his seniors. He welcomed them with wine, too, and chatted until the last captain was seated on a sea chest. All wore their best clothes for the conference, but only Marco wore the flat hat and the embroidered cloak with the shining shoulder-buttons of a task force commander.

'My lords,' he said, 'like our forefathers for centuries, we are meeting to agree on a course of action. I am eager to hear your views before proposing . . .'

'Trail our coats . . . draw 'em out . . . and kill 'em,' broke in the captain of the *Lion*, who at thirty-five was ten years older than any other man in the cabin. 'No point in shilly-shallying. I counted only three galleys with that monstrous clumsy galleon last night. No question we can . . .'

'Send a decoy ship,' the last captain to arrive offered. 'And draw the Turks out. They could have a few more galleys up their sleeve, but we're Venetians. Even two to one in their favour, we still outnumber them.'

Marco was not surprised, having expected just that vehement advice. Perhaps, when emotion was spent, the *consulta* would consider the issue coolly. But he wondered.

A third captain, one of the intellectual Morosini clan, asked: 'That caique you boarded, I imagine she passed you a message. From the rebels?'

'She did.'

'And it said?'

Marco replied: 'Mehmet Ali, our ally, wrote very briefly: *The revolt is still alive, needing only your support for success. Send me your men-at-arms – and I shall proclaim the provisional government. Then we shall win.*'

'That settles it, my lords,' the *Lion*'s captain observed complacently. 'A forgone conclusion. We can't turn down an opportunity like this. Let's take it. You'll issue the orders, Capello?'

Murmuring agreement, the four captains shifted restlessly on their improvised chairs. All were eager to get back to their ships and go into action.

'A moment, gentlemen,' Marco said. 'Respecting your wisdom, I do not find it a forgone conclusion. Admiral Ulluch Ali – damn all these Alis – who commands for the Turks here in the Cyclades has twenty galleys at his disposal. Any extended action would bring them down on us and . . .'

'You knew that when you drew up the plan,' the captain of the *Lion* intervened. 'What's different now?'

'The plan counted on a revolt, on the support of the populace, on merchant and fishing vessels converted into warships. Ulluch Ali was to be forced to guard his rear . . . to fear losing his base. None of that has happened.'

'And you propose?'

'To follow my orders, which are explicit: *Engage only after a provisional government is proclaimed and the Wingēd Lion flies again over Naxos and the Cyclades.* My lords, we shall return to Crete.'

Amid the babble of indignation Marco heard: 'Damned nonsense. From anybody but a Capello, I'd call it cowardice . . . It's mad to waste the opportunity to get the Empire of the Sea back intact.'

When the babble subsided, the captain of the *Lion* spoke for all: 'Captain Capello, we recommend immediate action, noting that we can withdraw later if necessary. But it won't be necessary. You command an independent task force. With the support of this *consulta*, you have full authority to take advantage of this unique opportunity for the glory of the Republic. I beg you. I am virtually a generation older, but I implore you. Do *not* let this opportunity pass.'

Tugging at his earlobe, Marco waited until the renewed babble of agreement had died away and the four captains were looking at him expectantly. He then said softly: 'My lords, my fellow seamen, I can*not* accept your advice.'

The babble again: 'Not for a century and a half, a *consulta*'s decision refused . . . They'll hang him in the Piazzetta.'

'My lords, hear me out!' Marco commanded their attention. 'This decision is agony for me! All my instincts are with you: to hoist our battle ensigns and dare the Turks to come out. But I can*not*. The intent, as well as the letter, of my orders is too clear. Besides, who knows whether we have been betrayed to the Turks? And what would follow then? But, above all, this is a political, as well as a military, decision. We want no war, not bereft of allies as we are.'

'What's different, I ask again, from your original plan?' the captain of the *Lion* demanded.

'If they had risen as promised and the Turks had been unprepared, we would have taken the Cyclades. We would then have put in additional forces, a strong garrison. The Turks would then have faced the Herculean task of reconquering a hostile population. As it is, *we* would face that task if I followed your advice. How conquer a myriad of islands with five galleys?'

'Nonetheless . . .'

'My lords, captains of the navy of the Serene Republic, this decision has cost me much. It is likely to cost me much more. But it is unavoidable . . . inevitable.'

'Why not just fight?' taunted the Morosini captain. 'Put it to the test of arms?'

'My lords,' Marco replied, 'it would be easy, very easy, to light my tripod of command and break out the battle ensigns. It would be very easy to die gallantly. No worrying about strategy or politics, only the courage for which Venice is renowned, a clear cut decision in the best traditions of the navy. Or would it?'

He paused, knowing he held their attention, and then declared: 'No, it would not! I am convinced it would be folly. I can see no likely gain, but great potential loss – not least, a war for which we are not prepared. Gentlemen, Venice needs a victory, not another glorious defeat. I do not propose to lead you to defeat and failure.'

'Do you want the *consulta* to vote formally?' the captain of the *Lion* challenged. 'Put it on the record officially?'

'No need, gentlemen. I note the sense of the *consulta*. Nonetheless, I must countermand the *consulta*. We sail for Crete.'

CHAPTER IX

SPRING came to Florence like a troupe of strolling players at Carnival, parading its beauties and its horrors. From outside the walls wafted the primeval smell of fresh-turned earth and the sweetness of unfolding blossoms. The mustiness of long habitation seeped from the palazzos on the squares and the tenements in the alleys. The bleating of terrified lambs and the gobbling of incredulous turkeys protested their sacrifice for Easter, lamenting the eternal mystery of death and rebirth.

Excitement seethed in the veins of men and women, birds and beasts, even, it seemed, trees and shrubs. It was a time of great joy. It was also a time when age-old sorrows ached in the bones.

Stepping through the open doorway of the frowsty tenement near the cathedral of Mary of the Flowers, Bianca Capello Buonaventura breathed the fragrance of the spring air. She caught, too, a whiff of blood and offal from the nearby slaughterhouse. The earth was moving once again towards the fruitfulness of summer, the season of fullness and birth. Yet all birth, human or animal, came amid blood, as her own child would not long after this mid-April morning.

The Easter just past had, as always, been the true miracle: blood and death, then sunlight and rebirth. The wonder of Easter was enhanced, not diminished, because it was also the Passover of the Jews, the fertility rites of Scandinavian tribes, and the Moslems' Ramadan. For all she knew, Chinese mandarins in skullcaps with jewelled buttons and Cannibal Islanders with human thighbones thrust through their woolly topknots also celebrated the season of resurrection in their own way. Bianca did not know, but she promised herself she would find out.

She found great pleasure in learning, but that taste was also a burden. Her cousin Marco had often teased her about her scholarly bent. Her father-in-law, like her father earlier, condemned her delight in books as unladylike.

Pietro Buonaventura now chided her for that taste – when they were speaking to each other. She had too much useless knowledge, he said. She took too much pleasure in abstract knowledge for anyone who was not a savant, far too much for a lady of noble birth. She should, Pietro said, be concentrating on her womb, not wasting precious energy on her brain. But Bianca knew she had too little learning.

She would, at least, have a few precious books when she was, quite soon, confined like a prisoner by her own body. This was not the last time she would trudge down five steep flights of stairs from the Buonaventuras' cramped apartment. But it was, thank God, one of the last times. She hated climbing those interminable stairs, burdened as if a twenty-pound sack of meal were strapped to her middle, always afraid of overbalancing and falling.

When she was confined, she would become bovine. She would lie all day on the narrow board bed, which Pietro had finally ceded to her. She would lie and eat and read and let the infant grow inside her and do nothing more.

She would be very calm, placid as a well-fed cow. She would not let herself be infuriated by her husband's vapidity. Nor would she fret at the cobwebs on the crudely limed plaster walls or the filth ingrained in the soft pine floorboards.

She had laboured for five months to bring cleanliness and order to the cluttered apartment, doing all the cleaning and cooking herself. She had performed distasteful services without complaint, carrying her mother-in-law's bedpans and washing that inert white hulk. She ached with sympathy for women of the people, who spent their lives in such drudgery. Until climbing the stairs became torture, she had almost every day bought fresh flowers from the street vendors to bring a little colour and light into the dark rooms, as few women of the people would think of doing. No point in expecting Pietro to remember to buy flowers, though he had carried up the heavier sacks of food.

But that was all over now – not because she had rebelled, but because she could no longer do the heavy work. She forced herself to ignore the slovenly ways of the slattern old Buonaventura had finally hired when it was clear his ballooning daughter-in-law could no longer cope with the domestic tasks and with his ever-complaining wife.

Money to pay the slattern, even money for food, came largely from Bianca's jewels. Knowing she had some source of income, the Buonaventuras watched her closely. But they had not discovered the source.

She hinted that she was borrowing from the Abbess of the Convent of the Oblate Sisters.

'Of course, Lady Chiara would let me have money if I asked,' Pietro had remarked complacently, 'but why should I, when you've struck up such a nice little friendship.'

The Abbess did not lend Bianca money, though she would have been glad to do so. The Abbess did lend her books and had promised to send a lay sister with a few volumes every week when Bianca was house-bound. But, the Lady Abbess reiterated, Bianca would come to the Convent for the final month of her pregnancy. There would be no nonsense about her enduring the fetid apartment in the steamy heat of June.

Sister Barbara, the midwife, was also adamant. When Bianca came to the convent, she would spend two hours every day walking in the grounds. Meanwhile, she was to go out as often as she could, no matter how gruelling the stairs. If she let her muscles get soft as butter, birth would be difficult and the child, perhaps, damaged.

How was it, Sister Barbara asked, that the women of the countryside stepped into the shade of a tree to deliver their infants amd were back at work in a few hours? Why did noble ladies struggle in great pain for hours, sometimes days, to push their infants into the world? Since all women were made the same, it could only be that the farm wives worked their bodies all the year round, while the pampered daughters of the rich moved about hardly more than houris in a Turkish harem.

Well, she was walking now, Bianca told herself, and that would please the imperious midwife. She was walking, although the weight she carried made her fear she would fall on her nose. She could have hired a sedan-chair once she was out of the sight of her mother-in-law, who stared into the street for hours like a great white cat at a mouse-hole. Then she would have avoided the earthy compliments and the nudges she seemed, curiously, to attract even more since her pregnancy began to show.

Men were very strange. She felt like a fat sow with a drooping belly waddling through the streets. But they saw something in her that had, evidently, not been visible earlier. For every bold invitation or, less saucily, every pair of fingertips now kissed in enchantment at her loveliness, ten other men turned to watch her.

Although acute, Bianca was young and inexperienced. She could hardly know that her splendid ripeness embodied all the beauty of all women to those men: mother, sister, and daughter, mistress and wife, wanton and saint, even the purity of the Blessed Mary who had borne the Son of God.

Unaware of her power to move men's hearts, Bianca strode through the cobble-stone streets in her voluminous emerald-green skirt and cerise overtunic. Those bold shades were quintessentially Florentine, beloved of popular painters. Her proud stride, her gold-toned skin, her delicately arched nose, and the side-glances of her wonderful green eyes enthralled male Florentines. Bianca coloured and looked down when a young gallant in an orange doublet called out: 'You're Botticelli's *Spring* in the flesh!'

Yet Bianca felt she waddled. She could, of course, not risk the unstable wooden pattens her countrywomen loved. Her flat shoes, their heels only an inch high, gave her a curious gait. Toes slightly pointed out, she swung down the promenade along the Arno, her bright auburn hair swaying at every step.

Disturbed by the attention she attracted, Bianca wished again that she had hired a sedan-chair. Never mind Sister Barbara! She would ask old Palmieri, the goldsmith, to call a chair for her return journey. She would then be carrying a small bag of gold coins. The Florentines could restrain their amorous instincts, but their greed they could never restrain. She would be happier – and safer – behind the screens of a sedan-chair.

Still, it was only three steps from the Lombard Bank of Milan to Palmieri's. The bank had offered to lend her money against her jewels, naturally after assessing their value. But she preferred to deal with Palmieri, piece by piece. She wished no one to know the exact size of her hidden treasure, which, having been modest to start, was dwindling all too rapidly. Now she was carrying a valuable piece, but the brief walk to Palmieri's was hardly dangerous in bright daylight.

She had taken from her casket in the strongroom a ring of white-gold worked with intricate arabesques around a star sapphire encircled by small rubies. It was most unusual. Admiral Rogerio Morosini, nicknamed *Malabranca*, the Evil Claw, had taken the ring by cutting off the finger of a defeated Genoese captain at Constantinople in 1296. The Genoese having taken it from a Moslem corpse, the ring was undoubtedly ill-omened. Almost glad to rid herself of it, even temporarily, Rogerio Morosini's great-great-great-granddaughter resolved that this would be the last piece she put in pawn to feed her idle husband and his parasitic family.

Bianca stood in the angle between the Lombard Bank and the Old Bridge where the Vasari Corridor, now completed, bent towards the

(114)

Pitti Palace, in which Duke Cosimo I lived in partial retirement. She paused to look down at the Arno. The river that divided Florence was flowing briskly, swollen with the torrents of spring caused by the snow melting in the mountains. Bianca stayed quite still for a minute or two, while the tide of passers-by flowed around her. She lifted her eyes towards the perfect symmetry of the arches of the Bridge of the Holy Trinity downstream, and the morning sunlight glowed in her red-gold hair.

Where would she be, she wondered, this time next year? Wherever, she would have her child beside her. It was very wearing, this uncertainty, the instability of her life with Pietro. Perhaps she should have married Osvaldo Grimani and waited for him to die, as her father wished.

She was a fool to have been taken in by Pietro's fantasies. Yet, whatever became of her, she could boast that once in her life she had acted entirely on her own, even if disastrously. Few noblewomen even once in a lifetime took a wholly independent decision. All were manoeuvred by their fathers, brothers, or husbands, especially queens and princesses.

Joanna of Austria, whose arrival after her marriage in Vienna to the Regent Francesco de' Medici had been celebrated with five days of festivity last December, was no more than a pawn in the hand of her father, the Emperor. Sadly, Florentine gossip, as accurate as it was biting, was already reporting that her husband, the Regent, found her graceless and boring. She was certainly no beauty with her long nose, sallow complexion, and lank hair. But few state marriages turned out well.

Bianca shivered. She felt as if someone were watching her. Of course someone was watching her, not just one, but several men. She should be used to the stares she had drawn since her pregnancy became so visible. Men would stare. She shivered again and turned towards the goldsmith's shop.

Before stepping onto the covered bridge, she glanced upwards at the Vasari Corridor. Through a window she saw a bearded face and a pair of large brown eyes that were indeed staring at her. The high forehead and the slightly melancholy mouth were unmistakable. Francesco de' Medici, Prince Regent of the Duchy of Tuscany, was watching her intently.

Warmth welled through Bianca, rising in her chest and radiating outwards. She had never felt quite the same before, at once weak and exalted. She stood very still – and smiled radiantly at that too serious face.

The Regent's grave look deepened. But he lifted a gloved hand in salute.

Bianca curtsied low, turned abruptly, and darted towards the gold-smith's shop. Out of his sight under the roofed bridge, she stopped to breathe deeply and slow her racing heart. Her hands went to her cheeks and found them burning. She was deeply agitated – and filled with inexpressible delight.

She knew that her eyes would never again meet the eyes of that man in perfect communion. The wife of Pietro Buonaventura would never encounter the ruling prince on remotely the same plane. Lady Bianca Capello, noblewoman of Venice, would have been received by the Medicis, but not the wife of a ne'er-do-well like Pietro, who at best was an impoverished petty nobleman.

Francesco de' Medici turned to Pandolpho Bardi, Count of Verino, who was riding beside him as they returned from a duty call on the half-mad Duke Cosimo in the Pitti Palace. The Regent's dark eyes were full for a moment, almost sightless, and they seemed to look inwards. An instant later, they glowed with wonder, and his full lips smiled eagerly.

'By God, Pandolpho,' he said, 'I've never seen anything like that in all my life. She's big with child, but, nonetheless, that face, that walk, those eyes.'

'Florence and the world are full of pregnant women every spring, Highness,' the count observed.

'So I see. My own wife, too, already. But none like that one, Pandolpho. Who is she? A lady or . . .'

The Count of Verino, who knew every attractive female in Florence between fifteen and thirty-five, replied: 'It's an interesting story, Highness. While you were away . . .'

CHAPTER X

'THEY wanted to try you for *cowardice*, Marco. They wanted you court martialled, degraded, and dismissed. The blockheaded admirals believe you ran away when you should have fought. I had to go the *Doge* himself to protect you.'

The manner of the State Inquisitor matched his sombre panelled work-room in the secret corridors of the Doge's Palace. The face of the man Marco Capello privately called Uncle Vincenzo was made to express pleasure and good fellowship. He now wore a grave look, grave, but not disapproving.

'I kept you from being relieved of command of the *Angels*,' he went on. 'But only just. I can't wholly protect you from the spite of the Admiralty . . . the ponderous displeasure of the Senate of the Sea.'

'I know, my lord,' Marco answered. 'I knew at the time. But it was the right decision. I'd do it again – and face the consequences.'

'If I were you, I'd let it rest.' The Inquisitor looked down at his fleshy hands, which were splayed on his writing-table. 'It'll be better if you're away from the eyes of the admirals for a while. Why not take a long leave, say six months? Travel by land, get to know Italy. Let your chief officer command the *Angels*.'

'Uncle, you forget. He's a foreigner, a Tuscan.'

'*No* impediment!' The Inquisitor, as usual, heavily stressed key words. 'Crespelle can keep the place *warm* for you. Your father's given enough cash for the fighting galleys! He and I can certainly dispose of the captaincy of *one* galley.'

'I'll think about it, Uncle Vincenzo. Not that I haven't had plenty of time to think . . . brood . . . lately. You know, it's May Day, just six months since the fiasco in the Cyclades. We should be drinking young wine and tumbling young wenches. But here we sit.'

Marco Capello, lately captain commanding a squadron of galleys on detached service, had just passed his twenty-second birthday. He was no longer the youngest captain in the Venetian navy, not even the second or third youngest; the bright aura of success he had worn for years was tarnished. Although heavily sunburnt, he looked strained and unhealthy. The ruddy darkness of his complexion only made more obvious the opaque sheen of his sunken grey eyes. His face was drawn so thin every bone stood out, the skull visible beneath the melting flesh.

'Do you feel like celebrating?'

'By Our Lady, I do not!' Marco swore bitterly. 'Celebrate what? Surviving? You know, Uncle, the Admiralty kept me patrolling for five months, useless patrols right up to Turkish shores. As if they *wanted* to lose the *Angels* – and me with her. The rules of engagement were ridiculously strict. In effect, they forbade me to take prizes. It was a long, hard, useless cruise.'

Marco lifted his goblet and squinted through the ruby wine at the flames burning low in the candelabra.

'They kept taking my galleys away,' he continued dully. 'Logically enough: no work to do. They peeled my ships off one by one, like a Turkish executioner skinning a man inch by inch. It hurt more that way. That smug bastard Fabrizio Grimani, who commands the *Lion*, they left him till last. How he gloated!'

'Marco, it's done. There's *other* work for you. Just forget for the time . . .'

The Inquisitor pushed the decanter across the table, and Marco refilled his goblet. But he was not mollified.

'They even stole the *Akbar* from me,' he railed. 'My only prize.'

'*Akbar?*'

'An Algerian pirate galley we took. I sent her back to Venice to be sold at the Mole of St Mark's. But the admiral in Crete drafted her into my task force.'

'Well, that was satisfactory, wasn't it?'

'We, I, lost her to the Turks. But she was already in naval service. The prize money's rightly mine.'

'I wouldn't press the Admiralty, Marco. Not *now*.'

'No, Uncle, I won't. But it's not just my loss. My officers and men, they've all lost their shares.'

'Perhaps an *ex gratia* payment from the Inquisition's funds. Yes, I believe it can be *arranged*. Including your own share. The *Angels* is the best *naval* asset the Service has had for years.'

(118)

'Thanks, Uncle Vincenzo, many thanks. No reason my crew should suffer for me. And I need a little money of my own.'

'The Tron girl?'

Marco nodded, and the Inquisitor advised: 'Don't let your father hear a word about that. Not till your name shines *brighter*.'

Marco smiled thinly and said: 'I've just got to remember one thing: I *will* take the *Angels* to sea again. There will be other days . . . other chances and other prizes. And Angela's very young, barely sixteen.'

'Your name is *without* stain in the eyes of the State Inquisition, on the rolls of the Secret Service. Naturally, we'd have preferred a *success*, but . . .'

'Naturally!' Marco echoed, smiling wryly. 'Who wouldn't?'

'But it was *never* on the cards. You did well, *better* than was expected. When I forced this operation through, the pessimists predicted *doom*. Swore you'd get us into war before we were ready.'

'You say I did well. I think it was a catastrophe.'

'Marco, we thought it was worth the *attempt*, also a chance for you to win your spurs. But *no* one expected success. So we gave you only a small force we could *afford* to lose. Yet you lost no Venetian warship, only a prize. And you showed us that much stronger measures will be necessary for Naxos and the Cyclades. *When* the time comes.'

'But the Admiralty's dead set against me.'

'I've spoken to them, will again. By the way, your enemies have not helped your cause. Was it *absolutely* necessary to make such powerful enemies? A senior captain *and* the admiral in Crete?'

'Not only necessary, but unavoidable.'

'Perhaps! Anyway, the simple sailors believe you failed to *grasp* an opportunity to destroy a Turkish squadron. The Turks were the aggressor, they say, so retaliating would not have provoked war. We know that's nonsense. It could have been war without a *single* ally at the Republic's side if you'd acted rashly. You did well, very well, but the simple sailors don't understand. So there you are.'

'Where am I?'

'*Praised* by the Doge privately and *esteemed* by the Secret Service. But in the Admiralty's bad books for the time being. By the way, have you heard about *Nasi*?'

'I came to you directly from my duty call on the Admiralty. I haven't even seen my parents. No, I've heard nothing. What about Nasi?'

The Inquisitor had been matter of fact, if grave, throughout the half-hour discussion. But he now looked troubled. His blue eyes no longer sparkled, and the natural ebullience faded from his blunt features. His expression, Marco realised, was pitying.

'We don't *really* know about Joseph Nasi,' the Inquisitor temporised. 'We're not absolutely sure.'

'What *are* you sure of, Uncle?'

'Last month, the Sultan gave Nasi the title he's been after so long: Duke of Naxos and the Cyclades.'

Marco winced and his hand went to the hilt of his sword.

'I see!' he said after half a minute of silence. 'So it was all a deception!'

'I do *not* know. If you were *betrayed*, which is not unlikely, but is not proved, if you were betrayed, it could have come as well from *Crete*.'

Marco mused: 'Crete is totally insecure. I know that. But are you sure Nasi didn't . . .'

'How can I be sure? Tell me, what do *you* think? You've met the man, spoken with him.'

'For an hour, I spoke with him. In a shack so dark I couldn't see his face. I'm no judge, but I'd say he did not betray us. It wasn't necessarily in his interest to betray us. My father, he knows Joseph Nasi well. My father looks on him as a prince among men, as well as prince of the Jews.'

'That was a *long* while ago.'

'So it was. Of course, he could've been working with the Turks. And the Turks may've wanted to lure us, wanted an excuse to destroy a Venetian task force, even to provoke war now. But their ships vanished, let us go without a fight. And no pursuit, either.'

'Therefore, I, too, think it was a chance encounter. But we do *not* know. We only know Joseph Nasi's been made Duke of Naxos and the Cyclades by the Ottomans.'

'The more reason to stay in touch with him, Uncle. To use him, as he may've used us.'

'A professional judgement, Marco. *Perhaps* he did betray us. But we shall keep contact with him, draw closer if we can. That is your assignment, your *long-term* assignment. You must purge yourself of resentment. If you *hate* him, you cannot work him. Healthy suspicion is another matter, essential to our trade.'

'And I get the *Angels* back, after my penance of six months ashore?'

'Assuredly! We need you with the *Angels*.'

Marco tossed back his wine and, unprompted, refilled his goblet.

The Inquisitor, normally so bland, professionally passionless, smiled approvingly.

'That's it. Let yourself *go*.'

'Thank you. But, sir, if there's nothing more to tell me, I'll go.'

'No, nothing more,' the Inquisitor said. 'Except, you haven't asked about your cousin Bianca.'

'I know, sir, she was outlawed. I heard while at sea. What else is there to ask, except, I suppose, is she well?'

'Bianca's very well, Marco. She's also very pregnant.'

Marco winced and asked pointlessly: 'Still with that bastard of a husband?'

'Afraid so, my boy. Very pregnant, and on very bad terms with Buonaventura. But the Countess Mentrisanti's keeping an eye on her. You know, Lady Chiara, Abbess of the Oblate Sisters. Also, there are the Morosini jewels.'

'Not worth that much, Uncle Vincenzo. Bartolomeo had already sold off the best pieces. It's infuriating to know there's nothing I can do for Bianca.'

'You might write to her, keep in contact. I'll see to delivery, as before.'

MORNING: MAY 3, 1566
VENICE: THE SQUERO ON ST VIO'S CANAL

The squero had been building gondolas on the bank of the Canal of St Vio in the Dorsosduro district for centuries.

As he stood in the May sunlight that splashed the boatyard, Marco Capello was far less gloomy than he had been in the work-room of the State Inquisitor. For the first time, he felt he had truly come home. The squero was so unmistakably Venetian: the tang of new-sawn wood, the swearing boatwrights, the black craft on trestles, the canal's aroma of salt and decay, even the gaudy flowers outside the Dantini family's wooden cottage.

Dantinis had owned the squero for centuries. Armando, the present Dantini, was a former boatswain of war-galleys. The senior boatswain aboard the first galley on which Marco served, he had looked after the novice officer, teaching him the ways of the sea and the foibles of the navy.

Genially paternal, Armando Dantini was happy to lend his cottage for an assignation. He, frankly, could not see why the Captain didn't take the lady to the White Lion or another hostelry whose proprietor was always delighted to oblige the nobility with discretion. Having said that, Armando Dantini had sent his wife to visit her sister and dispatched his younger son on a contrived errand to Murano. His two elder sons, who were learning the boat-builder's trade before going to sea, would be as silent as himself.

Nonetheless, Marco Capello hid his features behind a leering red mask with devil's horns and a pointed black goatee. He could not confess that this was no assignation, certainly not what the old boatswain thought. The lady and he would only talk, their hands hardly brushing. But he was more excited at the prospect of merely seeing Angela Tron that he would have been if Katarina Delfino, the city's most celebrated courtesan, had opened her arms to him without asking a single coin. Such anticipation, he supposed, was love.

A year ago, he would have laughed in astonishment if anyone had predicted that he would fall in love with a mere girl. But his recent misadventures had forced maturity upon him – and he knew now that he wanted Angela for a lifetime. He realised it would not be easy, but he also knew beyond doubt that he would win her in the end. For the moment, he was delighted just to look at her.

Angela surprised him. She came by land, not by gondola as he had expected, and her features were not obscured by a veil, as he had expected, but hidden behind a pale-blue coquette's mask with a tiny crimson bow of a mouth and rhinestone eyelashes. Watching her gracefully descend the wooden stairs from the alley to the squero, he saw why. She could hardly use a family gondola for a secret rendezvous, and no lady not escorted by a gentleman would trust herself to a hired gondola. But she was quite safe walking across the Rialto Bridge and through the tangled lanes at this time in the morning.

He ceremonially kissed her hand before they entered the painfully neat little parlour. Then Angela surprised him again. She slipped off her mask and then the shawl that covered her pale-blue dress. Saying not a word, she stood on tip-toe to kiss him on the lips. When he instinctively put his arms around her, she skipped out of his embrace.

'Welcome home, Marco,' she said. 'It's been so long. I had to give you a sisterly kiss.'

'Sisterly? It felt like more than that. I missed you desperately, but only a sisterly kiss?'

'Well, maybe a *little* more than sisterly.' She sat on the hard wooden bench beside the miniature fireplace. 'Oh, Marco, I missed you too.'

She had grown, he saw, become more womanly. They had, after all, been parted for nearly a year. Yet, only a little more than sixteen, she was still changing fast. She was *almost* a grown woman, but he would have to move slowly. Well, they had plenty of time.

Angela was very different from Bianca, with whom he had thought himself in love for one entire summer. Neither precocious nor fiery, she was instead serene and affectionate. If Bianca were a fierce, beautiful falcon, a female hawk, then Angela was a gentle, lovely dove. A falcon was exciting, but who would not rather live with a dove day in and day out?

The pains taken with Angela's hair were evident even to an inexpert male eye: strands of pearls were knotted in her looped-up plaits, and minute bouquets of enamelled daisies twinkled over her ears. Beneath those ornaments, her blonde hair, once platinum white, was mellowing to a rich gold. Her eyes, in girlhood an intense turquoise against her milk-fair skin, were now darker, almost royal blue. Several shades of blue repeated themselves in the snug bodice and the wide skirt of her dress, which ended just above her ankles.

Yet she had not changed much. Nor was she quite as mature as she apparently thought, either in appearance or manner. Her cheeks had not yet shed the roundness of adolescence; her hands were still dimpled by youth; and her small mouth, which now smiled enchantingly, could pout like a small girl's. One moment self-assured, the next she looked down at the fan she was nervously opening and closing.

With a surge of tenderness, Marco saw that she was at once woman and child. After another year, she would be much changed. But she was entrancing just as she was, fresh and innocent as this day in early May.

'You look very dashing, Marco,' she said. 'All the girls think . . . thought . . . so.'

'Thought so?' He smiled. 'In the past tense? Am I so old and crabbed now?'

'Of course not, Marco. I'm teasing. They're all hoping to see you at the Loredans' ball next week. Everyone'll be there. The hurrying and bustling and crying and shrieking, all the new ballgowns. It's very exciting.'

'I'm yours for as many dances as you can give me.'

'They'll all be jealous. But I must be careful. Not too many. My father . . .'

'Still detests the name Capello, does he?'

'He didn't mind you so much before. But now! That's why I said *thought* a minute ago. Marco, he says you ran away from the Turks. Is that true?'

'Angela, he could say that and be right – technically. He could also say I saved a squadron of galleys from certain destruction. You see . . .'

'You must tell me all about it when we have more time. But, today, I must get back very soon. So let's talk about important, urgent, things now. I want to be sure I'll see you at the Loredans'.'

'At the Loredans' or anywhere. Whenever you wish, wherever you wish, I'll be there.'

'Marco, that's very gallant. Speaking of gallant noblemen, did I tell you that my sister Alicia was going to marry . . .'

Her light talk was refreshing, a draught of sparkling wine to the spirit, so utterly different from the hoarse shouts of sailors and the self-important rumbles of admirals. Marco listened with delight to Angela's chatter.

CHAPTER XI

'ARE *you* in a position to disapprove, Marco?' Bianca's smile almost drew the sting from her words. 'I suppose you've never touched a woman, except to kiss her hand. Are you pure and unloved, waiting for your wedding day? In that case, don't lecture me.'

'I only said it would've been better,' her cousin responded feebly. 'You wouldn't face this degrading choice if . . .'

'If I'd consulted you before throwing my hat over the windmill? You weren't there when I had to choose. My Aunt Sophia failed me, everyone did. What could you have done?'

'A war-galley goes where she's sent, her captain with her. But we could have found a way. If only you'd waited.'

'I couldn't. After the betrothal, the shame would've been much worse – for the family as well as me. So now I suffer the consequences. But even now I'm not thrilled by the idea of being the consort of Osvaldo Grimani. *That* was the alternative.'

'Bianca, I didn't come to Florence to quarrel with you.'

'I'm sorry, Marco. It's good to know I'm not deserted by all the family. But, then, why not show it? Do this little thing for me.'

'Ordinarily, I'd be proud, honoured. But the consequences . . . It could be disastrous, even if it works. And what if it doesn't?'

'Then there'll be time enough to weep. Just tell me what else I can do. What possible alternative is there now?'

'As to money, I've told you . . .'

'After admitting you threw your prize money away. You're as poor as a Neapolitan tinker.'

'My father would be happy to make you an allowance.'

'Legally, the money would be Pietro's. Do you really want to endow the wretch I married? And I'd still be where I am now: with him.

Anyway, isn't it a crime to help an outlaw like me? You could both end up in the clutches of the State Inquisition.'

Marco could not tell her that there was no danger, since he was already in the clutches, as she put it, of the State Inquisition. Nor could he confide that he was happy in that position, as would be any Venetian nobleman privileged to serve in the Secret Service. Travelling as the Inquisitor advised, he had rapidly recovered his health and his spirits, the resilience of youth and the diversion of new sights proving better healers than any physician.

He had come to Florence with no particular purpose, except to see his headstrong cousin. Having initially been delighted that she was well and happy just four months after the difficult birth of her daughter, he was now worried. Desperation was so clearly visible behind her bravado.

Bianca had refused to let him call on her at the apartment she and her husband shared with the elder Buonaventuras. Instead, she had brought her daughter to the Convent of the Oblate Sisters, where they now sat in the Abbess's opulent parlour. Chiara, Countess of Mentrisanti, had told Marco before leaving them that she was a distant cousin on his mother's side. She had grimaced expressively when he mentioned Pietro Buonaventura.

Was Lady Chiara, Marco wondered, party to the plot Bianca was trying to draw him into? Quite likely, though it ill-became an abbess.

'Also, Marco,' Bianca pressed, 'think how it could serve the interests of Venice.'

'You've come a long way: from a desperate plan, a wild shot, to a triumph for Venice.'

'I know my own powers,' she responded earnestly. 'I *know* I can do it – given the chance.'

'Bianca, my dearest cousin, I'm no puritan, God knows. But to help you sin! How an abbess can possibly . . .'

'She doesn't let herself know,' Bianca laughed. 'We pretend it's only to introduce me to polite society.'

'Not such a bad idea.'

'How? Penniless and with *my* husband? Marco, this is the *only* way.'

Marco shrugged his shoulders, expressing neither assent nor refusal. The gesture merely acknowledged that Bianca determined to have her way was too much for him to withstand, perhaps too much for any man. She was counting on that.

Marriage to a wastrel who survived by minor fraud had not dimmed her attraction. The shadow that hovered in her wide-set eyes gave them depth and a touch of mystery. Her ordeal was reflected in her eyes, but her round Capello chin was even more resolute.

Bianca exuded confidence in herself and her destiny when she leaned down to draw aside the mosquito net covering her daughter's cradle. But she awaited her cousin's reply with candid eagerness.

'Beautiful! I've never seen a more beautiful baby.'

'How many babies have you seen?' Bianca laughed. 'Hundreds, no doubt.'

'Well, really, two or three. But she . . .'

'Marco, you're a liar. You know as much about babies as I do about galleys, less indeed. Now, tell me. I heard you won a great victory, but were out of favour.'

'No victory, great or otherwise. I did avoid a defeat, perhaps a disaster. No, I'm not in high favour in some quarters. But in others . . .'

'I'm delighted. I was worried for you. Then there's no reason you shouldn't do me this small service. You won't get into trouble by . . .'

'No, not really. It won't make things easier with the Council of Ten, of course. But that's not the reason.'

'Oh, Marco, I know that. I know you're worried about me, not yourself. I've never been one to calculate, too impetuous. But this time, this time *only*, I need your help. I've staked everything on one roll of the dice.'

She hesitated, drawing in her full lower lip, and her eyes widened in thought. Abruptly, she smiled, touched his forearm, and said impulsively: 'Marco, I think I love him. I can't be sure yet, of course. But, prince or ragpicker, Francesco de' Medici seems to me everything I've ever wanted. All my hopes . . .'

'Nonsense, Bianca!' He cut in brutally. 'You've only seen the man once, except for a few glimpses at a distance. How could you possibly . . .'

'I'm a silly woman, you mean? It happens to men, too. How could Dante Alighieri, after only one glimpse of Beatrice Portinari in this same city, love her all his life?'

Embarrassed by her ardour, Marco rumbled defensively in his throat, so that she heard only: '. . . Florence, maybe. Never happen in Venice.'

He distrusted her passionate folly, yet feared he would give in. He could feel it yielding, the prudence that normally curbed his own impetuousness.

Sensing that she was winning, Bianca attacked dramatically.

'It's too late to turn back,' she declared piteously. 'I've already done it. I've sold all my mother's jewels – and they weren't worth all that much to start with. I've taken a little house in the gardens of the Palazzo Ruccelai. After the six months' lease, furnishings, servants, clothes for myself and Pietro, there's not much left. Just enough gold for one grand reception. If that doesn't work, we'll all be on the street.'

'I'll see that you're not left in the gutter, Bianca!' he riposted dryly. 'All right, I'll do it.'

'Oh, Marco, I'm so pleased.' She flung her arms around him and kissed him. 'I know it'll work out perfectly. Chiara's already agreed to be godmother. Chiara alone Francesco de' Medici might ignore. With you as godfather, he *can't* spurn the reception after the christening. If you were only a nobleman of Venice and a galley captain, he might. Though he's curious about Venice, I'm told, thinks Spanish influence is too great in Italy.'

Intrigued, Marco began to ask a question, but Bianca pelted on: 'To make sure, I shall put your family title on the invitation. How grand it sounds: Count of the Lateran Palace and the Imperial Halls, conferred by the Emperor and affirmed by the Holy Father. He can*not* fail to come.'

'How do you know the Regent is curious about Venice and distrusts Spain?'

'Pandolpho Bardi, the Count of Verino, told me. He has come to me a number of times . . . told me Francesco's already fed up with his wife. A dry stick of a German, she is, always on her knees, whether in church or in her boudoir. She fills their apartments in the Old Palace with priests, German-speaking priests. She talks only of the next world, never this world. The Regent has a dreary life, Marco. He *needs* me.'

'How did this Count of Verino convince you that Francesco de' Medici needs you? Sounds far-fetched to me.'

'I may be romantic, Marco, but I'm not a fool. Yes, I am a little overwhelmed by Francesco. But I wouldn't strip myself bare, spend every last copper, if I did not *know* it was most definitely *not* in vain.'

'You *know* it's not?'

'Anything but. Francesco de' Medici talks to Bardi about me all the time. He's stolen more than a few glances at me. But he can't make the first move. He doesn't want me to feel it's *droit de seigneur*, like a marauding count taking a peasant girl. Also, he needs reassurance. He must *know* I want him before he can let himself want me totally.'

'Then why all this fuss? Your elaborate plot, the grand reception?'

'I can't have him feel he's lifting me out of the gutter. That's no way to start. Besides, he's shy. Hard to believe, but the Regent is shy. He's also suspicious. Who wouldn't be in his place? Also a practical problem: without such illustrious godparents, how could he honour the christening with his presence? The father is Pietro Buonaventura, not quite a gentleman, even if the mother is a noblewoman of Venice.'

'I see that. But, aside from Verino's chatter, what has Francesco de' Medici *done* to make you so certain?'

'You haven't heard? He's already warned the Venetian Embassy that Venice will be held responsible if anything happens to Pietro or me. We're outlaws to the Council of Ten, but not to Florence.'

'Then you've all but won,' Marco observed. 'So why this conspiracy, the subterfuge?'

'Don't be dense, Marco! His father the Duke, his ministers, his courtiers – all must see that he has *no* choice but to attend or affront the eminent godparents.'

'And when he does?'

'Everything else will follow. It's ordained. I know it.'

LATE EVENING: NOVEMBER 23, 1566
FLORENCE: PALAZZETTO IN THE RUCCELAI GARDENS

Bianca cast a nervous glance around the reception hall of her rented palazzetto, which was already half-filled by her guests. Most faces she did not recognise, although she knew the names her new major-domo announced in ringing tones. She knew the names from the guest-lists drawn up by Chiara, Countess of Mentrisanti and Pandolpho Bardi, Count of Verino, as well as by Marco Capello, Count of the Lateran Palace, before his departure to Naples. Even the Venetian Embassy had suggested influential guests for the reception celebrating the baptism of a child whose parents were wanted for trial in Venice.

That was Marco's doing. Now a powerful man, he had persuaded the Ambassador, who could, of course, not attend the reception, that Bianca Capello remained a loyal daughter of the Serene Republic, who could advance Venetian interests in Tuscany.

Bianca saw with a tolerant smile that her husband was playing the host grandly. Pietro swaggered among nobles and ministers he would normally never have met, showing off his new cloth-of-gold doublet,

(129)

which was almost the same colour as his blond hair. Although his only contribution to the festivities was the initial act of procreation, he strutted like a cockerel that was undisputed lord of its own barnyard. He all but crowed.

A woman had to look at her appearance, since her beauty and her charm were her only weapons. Not so a man. Yet Pietro Buonaventura was as vain as any woman; few women were more lost in self-love than he.

In the baptistery of the cathedral of Mary of the Flowers, Chiara Mentrisanti had once again warned Bianca about Pietro. Chiara sometimes appeared obsessed with his potential for doing his wife harm.

'You do realise all this grandeur will puff him up even more,' the Abbess had whispered. 'And it will draw you closer to him. You're making a great show of marital devotion.'

'Publicly, Chiara, publicly. I, we both, know the reality. But, publicly, I need Pietro.'

'Bianca, I'm almost sorry I helped you make this day. I'm glad of the joy it's giving you. And the sin you seek? There'll be time to repent. You're young enough. But be careful, *very* careful, how you handle Francesco and Pietro. The mixture's explosive.'

'Have I ever been less than careful? I even made sure his mother came. He would've forgotten, and the old man would happily have left her in her sickbed.'

Draped in violet silk, Pietro's mother overflowed the sedan-chair that had brought her the few steps from the tenement. Four chair-bearers had carried her down the five flights from the apartment, taking turns, two at a time, to make a sling of their clasped hands.

Bianca's father-in-law stood beside his wife. Washed, combed, and clothed for the christening, he would, as Pietro had said, 'not frighten any children today'.

Bianca's literal-minded husband had not suddenly struck a vein of humour. Children had truly run, screaming in fear, when Pietro's father made one of his rare sallies into the streets, grumbling loudly to himself and scowling. Today he had nodded graciously to the eminent guests seated among the thousands of blossoms that made the baptistery glow. Taking their presence as a tribute to the name of Buonaventura, he had said smugly: 'This will certainly do it! About time too! After this proof of my standing, the court *must* reverse its verdict.'

At least Bianca did not have to worry about the elder Buonaventuras now. Fearing that his mother's grossness and his father's obsession would mar the grand impression he wished to make, Pietro had persuaded his parents that the reception would be noisy and wearing. He was very good at persuading others to do as he wished, always for their own good.

Of Bianca's own family only Marco was present. Neither her Aunt Sophia nor her Uncle Andrea had made the journey from Venice. Too little notice, they had explained. Bianca assumed that her Aunt Sophia had been forbidden to come by her staid husband. And Uncle Andrea? Already suspect for his liberal views, he was only prudent.

Sophia and Andrea had sensibly avoided a public affirmation of their kinship with that notorious outlaw, herself. Nonetheless, both had sent loving letters and rich presents: Aunt Sophia a christening robe of silk and lace, Uncle Andrea a beautifully illuminated missal. From her father, Bartolomeo Capello, there was nothing, no word at all. Bianca had expected no more, but was, to her own surprise, nonetheless hurt.

The baptistery, itself a work of art, had been made even more glorious by the golden altar vessels and the gold-embroidered vestments of the Archbishop and his train. Following a great golden cross, the procession came through Ghiberti's golden doors and passed under arches of golden chrysanthemums entwined with hothouse lilies and roses. Above them on the vault of the dome a magnificent mosaic depicted on a gold background: the Creation, the torments of Hell, and the journey of the Magi to the cradle of the Christ Child. Over all, the benediction of Christ Himself and of John the Baptist, patron saint of Florence.

The Archbishop's consenting to preside Bianca owed to the influence of the Abbess Chiara and, she suspected, to a few words from Count Verino on behalf of his master, the Regent. She had herself given fifty ducats to the Archdiocese, and Marco had invoked the Patriarch of Venice, a kinsman of the Capellos. The gold-drenched late afternoon had crowned their efforts.

When the Archbishop sprinkled the infant's head with holy water and sketched a cross on her forehead, the godparents had stood beside the marble baptismal font: Chiara, commanding in her white habit, and Marco, elegant in the moss-green doublet and orange hose bought in Naples. Also, of course, the parents, herself in blue, Pietro preening himself in his new doublet of cloth of gold.

Her cousin had regarded her husband with distaste. More than distaste, Marco's eyes glinted with disdain, even detestation. He hated Pietro for the humiliation inflicted on his cousin.

Bianca's daughter had slept tranquilly until awakened by the cold water. The Little Pilgrim, named after her maternal grandmother, Pellegrina Morosini Capello, was now sleeping in her new nursery. Her mother had decided not to bring her down, for it would not, Bianca felt, be in the best of taste to flaunt her daughter before the guest she awaited most anxiously: Francesco de' Medici, Prince Regent of Tuscany, whom she hoped to win this evening.

She had known instinctively that her own costume should be in harmony with the palazzetto, opulent yet restrained. The brilliance of gold, which had dazzled the congregation in the baptistery, was now seen chiefly in the fine lines that outlined the door-panels and in the narrow fluting on the white-marble pillars that framed the blazing fireplaces. Bianca's pale blue satin skirt, six-feet around on its wooden farthingale, was subtly shot with gold. Her bodice was cut modestly, and her only jewellery was a single gold chain around her slender neck. Since understatement was not the manner of Florence, the hostess stood out among the over-elaborate costumes of her guests, male and female.

The repast, laid on tables with gold-fluted legs, was also opulent, but not ostentatious by the rarity of its ingredients, the complexity of its preparation, or the intricacy of its presentation. It was simply superb food, meticulously prepared and tastefully presented: salmon, oysters, prawns, and eels; a half-dozen varieties of pasta, that new passion of gourmets, kept hot in chafing-dishes: venison, hare, quail, and pheasant; beef, lamb, and pork; also a dozen sweet confections – all accompanied by the appropriate wines of Venice and Tuscany. But nothing too fanciful.

Francesco de' Medici, ruler of the most abundant region of Italy and heir to the greatest fortune in Europe, could command splendours of food and wine beyond the reach of the Emperor in Vienna, almost beyond the reach of the Pope in Rome. Since Bianca could compete with neither the ingenuity of his kitchen nor the resources of his wine-cellar, she had chosen refined simplicity. For a palate jaded by richness she offered tasteful relief.

Her knowledge and her wit could, however, easily compete with the Regent's untutored wife. One of Francesco de' Medici's chief pleasures was intellectual conversation. Quite remarkably among princes, he was deeply versed in the sciences, the classics, and the arts. He was, of course, a son of the cultivated Medicis. At his disposal lay all the luxuries of Italy, the richest and most advanced land of Europe. At his disposal, as well, lay virtually all the ladies of Italy and Europe. But Francesco was neither sybarite nor libertine.

Pandolpho Bardi, Count of Verino, had told Bianca with mock despair of his repeated failure to interest his master in the willing beauties he collected. An unhappy home life with a sour princess had not driven the Regent to philandering. Unlike his father, Duke Cosimo, and his younger brother, Cardinal Ferdinando, who paused in their womanising only to gorge themselves, Francesco de' Medici was no rake.

Ferdinando! Bianca smiled bitterly. Her husband had, almost unbelievably, urged her to seduce Ferdinando, to become the young prince's whore. That would have been not only ridiculous, but pointless. How long could a liaison with that restless youth have lasted?

When Ferdinando left her, she would have been pressed to lure another patron. Pietro now appeared happy to live on the wealth she had suddenly revealed, but he sensed that it was almost exhausted. He quite obviously considered the palazzetto a showcase to display her charms for other potential bidders. Yet, being neither light-minded nor lascivious, she was hardly suited to be a gilded courtesan.

Besides, it was wrong. Bianca would return to Venice, even to the grim cells of the Carmelites, rather than live a shameless life passed from one wealthy man to another, as her own husband proposed.

Francesco was different. She was greatly attracted to him, as he was to her. And not only physically, but for himself. She knew in her bones that he needed her as much as she needed him. Were he a hawker or a charcoal-seller, she told herself, she would probably be drawn to him just as strongly.

He had asked to meet her. He had told his confidant, the Count of Verino, that he was already half in love with her, this great prince who was virtually a puritan. He, who could have any woman in Florence, seemed to want her. She could not be certain that it was truly more than a passing attraction until they met. But she believed it was inevitable, their union, believed it strongly enough to hazard her last copper.

Impediments there were of course: his marriage of state and her marriage of folly. But impediments were made to be overcome. Neither fear of torment in the next world nor public scorn in this world would keep her from winning Francesco de' Medici.

Bianca mechanically acknowledged several farewells. Much of the food, she saw, had been consumed, and the candles were burning low. A reception so late was unusual, but the Count of Verino had said the hour was convenient for his master.

Bianca told her major-domo to put out fresh food and light new candles. She smiled at the musicians and asked them to play a new dance, Caroso's 'The Power of Love'. The ormolu clock over the fireplace showed almost eleven, very late for a society that rose at first light.

Would he never come? Had Pandolpho misled her? Had she spun a fantasy on a foundation of clouds? Perhaps Francesco was not really interested in her. And what would she do then?'

Doubts pierced Bianca like a volley of arrows, each wound a new fear. As she had told Marco, she knew she would win Francesco de' Medici, given the chance. Was she now to be denied that chance?

Bianca did not see the Prince Regent enter the hall. She only heard the general conversation diminish to a hush and then rise again. The musicians broke off the dance and swung into the song 'A La Battaglia, Into Battle', a favourite of the Medicis.

When she turned, he was smiling at her. She saw nothing else. She did not even notice his clothes. She saw only that smile, at once eager and shy, and his large brown eyes, which were sad and yearning.

'Your Highness, may I present Lady Bianca Capello Buonaventura?' Pandolpho Bardi's voice was far away. 'As you have observed, Highness, she is Venice's beautiful gift to Florence.'

Bianca, her eyes lowered, sank into a deep curtsy. She did not see the harsh look the Regent threw at the Count of Verino to reprove such familiarity. When she rose, she saw only the same smile, at once pleading and commanding, and his extended hand.

'My Lady Bianca, will you dance with me?'

His voice was soft and warm and deep, every syllable rounded with wonderful Tuscan clarity. She felt his hand tremble in response to the tremor in her own. When they touched, her body shivered. She saw now that he was dressed all in black, except for the white-lace collar around his throat. She saw also that the high forehead above his heavy black eyebrows was now without a single line of strain.

'My wife asked me to express her regrets.' His voice was now louder, speaking as much to the other guests as to Bianca. 'She is not well.'

They took the floor alone, and the musicians glided again into 'The Power of Love'. The regular, recurrent measures were emphasised by pronounced chords, the flute rising high, the bass viol responding low, while violin and zither sang the melody.

He was not a strong performer. Many noblemen prided themselves on the leaps and turns with which they embellished this popular dance, the *canario*. Francesco looked happy, he almost glowed. But he led her through the intricate movements gently.

Her temples throbbed, and her head seemed to reel. She felt weak, yet elated and triumphant. Such complex sensations so intricately intermingled she had never before known. It was true, then. One could be struck by love, as by an arrow or a bolt of lightning.

'I'll never forget that moment,' he said softly when the dance drew them close. 'A spear went through me when I looked down and first saw you.'

Bianca smiled enigmatically, then confessed: 'I, too, Highness!'

The dance separated them for interminable seconds, and she yearned for his next words. When they came together again, he said: 'I have seen you several times since. I made the opportunities, though it is hard for me to be inconspicuous. I cannot go through Florence disguised as a porter like Haroun al Rashid in Baghdad.'

'I never saw you, my Lord.' She was surprised by his knowing the *Arabian Nights* tales, which had only recently been translated in Venice. 'Not like Scheherazade.'

The dance kept them together, as she twirled around his outstretched hand. His deep voice caressing, he spoke just loud enough for her to hear.

'That meeting, that glimpse of you, was hardly believable,' he declared. 'Too much like a myth, a fairy tale.'

'Why did you wait so long to tell me?' she whispered.

'My Lady, I could not make the first move. How could I overwhelm you with my . . . ah . . . position? I wanted to know that you, too . . . Also, I hated to interfere in a marriage. But now I know yours is as unhappy as mine. Above all, I did not want to force you to . . .'

'How could you, Highness? How could you take by force that which is already given?'

The musicians were now once more playing the 'The Power of Love'. No longer tentative, but committed, Bianca swayed closer to hear his low, impassioned words.

'I want to be with you again . . . very soon . . . alone.'

'As you command, Your Highness,' she answered. 'When you command!'

CHAPTER XII

'*ENOUGH!*' The cavalier in the cloth-of-silver doublet smiled wolfishly as he came through the door of the boudoir. 'Enough! Make yourself any more beautiful, and the moon'll hide herself in envy. You don't want to be guilty of that, do you? Enough on your conscience already, isn't there?'

Bianca Capello Buonaventura looked up from the gold-backed mirror her hairdresser held. The remark was in her husband's usual style: florid, insincere, and barbed. But the barbs were a little sharper today.

She was struck still by his physical attraction. Yet, how differently she had felt six years ago, when she first saw the intense dark eyes framed by the sleek blond curls. He was still beautiful himself, this worthless husband of hers, quite beautiful for a man. But she could no longer enjoy that masculine beauty. Whatever had been between them he had systematically destroyed, not just during the poverty-pinched first period of their marriage, but over the years.

She motioned to the hairdresser to continue dusting her breasts with the rose-scented powder, imported from Constantinople. The gold brocade gown she had chosen for the ball tonight would, in the manner of Venice, bare her breasts almost to their nipples. Why should she not display her beauty as did noblewomen of the city of her birth? Not only her lover Francesco de' Medici, but even her husband, rhapsodised over her splendid bosom.

'Angelino,' she said to the hairdresser, 'the beauty patch? Perhaps a bit to the left . . . not quite so near my mouth?'

When he had made the minute adjustment, Bianca nodded approval. The tiny black silk heart was meant for just one man. Too close to her lips, it would appear to invite the attentions of others.

Too far away, and it would appear she had no interest in other men – or, worse, could not attract them.

An intelligent woman did not fan the devotion of a capricious prince by showing herself utterly abandoned to him, beyond the possibility of any love but his.

In truth, she was only his and would always be. But, a sprinkling of doubt would season Francesco's devotion to her. It must never appear that she was wholly blind to other men or incapable of exciting their passion.

'Pietro, you know it would be foolish to skimp,' Bianca at length answered her husband. 'We must live up to our . . . to *my* . . . means.'

She did not like giving him that cool reply, for she wanted none of his tantrums today. This was a night for frivolity, for sheer pleasure. But it was necessary to remind him that she alone kept them from ruin. He often appeared to seek trouble, as if bent on destroying himself and her, too.

Pietro had killed her love by his lies, his womanising, and his feck-lessness. Her enemies said she was as calculating as a grizzled merchant of fifty. But she *had* to be.

Yet she had set out to charm Francesco de' Medici – and had ended by falling in love with him.

Bianca smiled at her husband to heal the hurt she had to inflict. She nodded dismissal to Angelino. The hairdresser would wait in the *souterranea*, the servants' domain in the basement of the mansion on the Via Maggio near the Medicis' Pitti Palace.

Bianca glanced around her boudoir, delighted and reassured by its muted splendour. The hairdresser's unguents, paints, and implements were laid out on a side-table of Carrara marble. On the flower-sprigged silk wallpaper opposite the windows to the balcony hung a portrait of Francesco playing with her spaniel Don Juan. He could never marry her. But, in the absence of marriage lines, the charming domestic portrait testified to her rights: for Bianca almost as good as a title deed to Francesco de Medici.

Seeking favour, the Florentine artist Bronzino had given her the painting. But Francesco had paid eight ducats for the view of the Church of Sant' Aponal that hung where she would see it when she awoke. The master Tintoretto saw no need to flatter the Prince Regent of Tuscany or his mistress with gifts. He was an independent Venetian, not a fawning Florentine.

'I'm sorry Angelino took so long,' Bianca placated her husband.

'Now we have time. And, Pietro, please don't sulk in front of the servants, I understand, but Angelino . . .'

'He understands, too. All Florence understands.' Seeing her frown, Pietro changed his tone. 'Anyway, I don't mind waiting. I could stand silent watching you for hours.'

'Silent?' She laughed. 'I can't imagine you silent for hours.'

'True. I couldn't be silent so long, not looking at you. I'd have to praise your beauty and your . . .'

Bianca was no longer listening, though she nodded from time to time. Loving the cadences of his own voice, as he loved the contours of his own features, Pietro span endless compliments.

Coolly inspecting her image in the mirror, Bianca saw that her red-gold hair was drawn back into precisely the regal chignon she wanted. Like a merchant taking stock, she saw, too, that she was even more striking after Angelo's subtle cosmetics. No need for the bold carmine and apricot paints many Florentine ladies favoured. Behind the thick fringe of her lashes, which she now darkened a shade, her eyes were limpid green. Their candour required no enhancement from blue or silver shadows on their lids.

Bianca did not hear the patter of compliments falling from her husband's lips. In her inner ear, she remembered the bewitching voice she had heard in the autumn and winter of the year 1564. 'You are the most beautiful creature I have ever seen,' Pietro had rhapsodised. 'But you are not appreciated here. Come with me to Florence, the city of art and sunshine and flowers. You'll never be adored here as you deserve!'

Almost seventeen, ripe for marriage, she had been swept up by the tide of words. She knew that he loved her and valued her above all else. She also knew that his family was old and noble. Florence would truly appreciate her.

Six years later, she was celebrated in Florence, but not as he had predicted. The city of flowers had proved far less welcoming than Pietro promised; except for its ruler.

All foreigners were suspect to Florentines, especially Venetians with their close ties to the menacing Orient. The Venetian lady who had become their uncrowned queen was, therefore, mortally resented. Naturally, the female populace, great ladies and whores, hated Bianca. She had stolen their prince, who, they devoutly believed, should have sought solace from his sour foreign wife in the arms of a fellow-countrywoman. She had snatched their rightful prey.

Bianca's Florentine maid Lucia, whose father was Venetian, kept her mistress apprised of what they were saying in the streets. Between laugher and indignation, she had yesterday reported overhearing a conversation between a market-girl and a lady.

'Poor man!' said the market-girl. 'With that awful German wife he deserves any consolation he can get.'

'*Not* from *another* foreigner, a Venetian,' the lady rejoined sharply. 'Anyway, she only got him by trickery . . . magic. She's always dabbling with herbs, making up potions and unguents. It's as plain as the nose on your face she's a witch . . . trapped Francesco by witchcraft.'

Naturally, the women turned the men against her, Bianca reflected, gazing through the painting of the church of Sant' Aponal into the past. Down a street from the church the tiny Crooked Bridge spanned the threadlike canal of Sant' Aponal. Beside the bridge stood the five-storey Palazzo Capello, its round-arched windows covered with lichen-green shutters. Gaps in the Venetian red stucco revealed the weathered bricks beneath. Her father's villa on Murano was equally dilapidated and badly placed. The villas of the great families stood on the *terraferma*, the mainland, along the Brenta.

She had lived in a palazzo. But names were deceptive, as she had explained to the Ambassador of the English Queen, who often called upon her '*unofficially*, but gladly', he declared with true English warmth. The Ambassador said candidly that he wished to please the mistress of the ruler of Tuscany. He had also called *officially* upon Joanna, the sour, priest-ridden Austrian princess who was Francesco's consort.

'Officially,' he twinkled, 'but not so gladly!'

A villa, she had told him, could mean any country house with more than three rooms, although it overlooked a midden. A palazzo was not a 'palace', as he called it in his language. A palazzo was simply a tall building with many rooms, whether occupied by one family or by many.

In her rebellious seventeenth year the only charm of the Palazzo Capello had been its closeness to the graceful ochre building of the Salviati bank. Twenty-one-year-old Pietro Buonaventura, she now knew, had been a very junior clerk, hardly more than an apprentice. Her eyes dazzled as much by her own yearnings as by his braggadocio, he had appeared a gallant cavalier with vast knowledge of the world. Breathless with excitement, she had finally yielded to his pleas and eloped to the wonderland of Florence.

She had fallen in love twice in her twenty-three years, or had, at least, thought herself deeply in love. Both times, Bianca reflected wryly, she had been wildly impetuous. Her heart had driven her, though she told herself she was cool and rational.

She had thrown over her entire way of life, given up her homeland, to elope with Pietro. In fairness, Pietro had been an escape from her father and the horrifying husband chosen for her. Then she had put every last copper she owned into the setting in which she won Francesco. In fairness, again, Francesco was an escape from Pietro – though, of course, far more. But what would she have done if he had not wanted her as much as she wanted him or had afterwards proved unfaithful?

She could not deny the contradiction. She had sworn to herself that she would, after her father's tyranny, never again be dependent on any man. Yet she had twice put her life into the hands of a man.

But it was *not* contradictory. She was *not* dependent on Francesco, not as the world saw it. They were equals, for he was just as dependent upon her as she was on him. Only, he took more managing.

Forced by Pietro, she had learned self-reliance quickly, but she had not learned to hate Pietro. She detested his posturing and the fecklessness that led him into foolish scrapes. Now emotionally independent, she felt neither particular hatred nor particular affection for her husband.

Their present arrangement was a fair trade. She needed his presence to make her a respectable married woman, and he needed her patronage. Pietro Buonaventura lived happily with his wife and their daughter in the mansion her lover Francesco de' Medici had given her near the Pitti Palace, where he lived unhappily with his dry and pious wife Joanna of Austria.

Her own wooing by Francesco, facilitated by his loyal courtier the Count of Verino, was another tale for another day. So was Pietro's glad collaboration in that wooing. All had now come about just as she had first dreamed – and then planned.

She had not planned to fall utterly in love with Francesco.

In her reverie, Bianca heard Pietro's voice from a distance: 'You know, we make a good team.'

His tone drew her back to the present. When he dropped florid compliments or span his fantasies aloud, his voice was butter-smooth. It was now a little gritty.

'How is that?' she asked warily.

'Look what we've done. Look what we've achieved working together. Better than your fondest dreams.'

'You know I appreciate all your help.'

'My help?' Refusing to be placated, he whipped himself into a state of indignation. 'Who planned it? Who keeps it all on an even keel, as your fishermen ancestors would say?'

Pietro had got it into his head that only a century ago her family were poor fishermen. He taunted her with that presumed disgrace when he was in a disagreeable mood.

'I'll never understand you Florentines,' she sighed. 'To think there's something *wrong* with hard work. Now, the Medicis . . .'

'Don't change the subject.' His tone now was abrasive. 'Though it always comes down to the Medicis . . .'

'So it does,' she agreed silkily. 'For you, as well as for me.'

'For you, yes. But for me? What do I get out of it?'

'It? What do you mean by *it*?'

'Bianca, I've said it before, and I'll say it again: *You've got no delicacy*. You lack the natural reserve of a true noblewoman.'

'Be that as it may, what do you mean by *it*?' She wanted to dispose quickly of the quarrel he was fomenting. She wanted it done with so that she would be serene, rather than agitated, when the ball began. Besides, she did not want him to become sullen and then drunk. Since he had a formal role to play at the ball, it was best to let him vent his anger now.

'*It*, woman, is letting that jumped-up coxcomb of a Medici use . . . I said *use* . . . my wife. In bed and now virtually in public. How do you think I feel when . . .'

'How *do* you feel?' she retorted, finally angry. 'Your scruples certainly don't keep you from enjoying . . .'

'That's the point.' His dark eyes were narrowed in anger. 'I have . . . have my own interests.'

'Mistresses, you mean? Those shop girls of yours? The seamstresses you dote on?'

'No, Bianca. Only one now: Mariarosa. A true lady who truly cares for me. *She* is proud of me. But I must have more money. Position, too.'

'And you want me to . . . ?'

'. . . to ask your lover. The post of chamberlain is now vacant in his household. I thought . . .'

'And if, this time, I refuse? Or can't persuade him? What then?'

'You think you're discreet. But you and your lover are a public scandal in Florence. In Venice, too. You had a bad name when you came here. But it's far worse now. If I cast you out, who'll protect you? Who'll cover you with his name . . . conceal your sins as I do?

(141)

If I denounce you, even Francesco will think twice about going on with you. You'd be penniless and alone. And your pretensions: your grand balls and your high position . . .'

Bianca sighed wearily. Why, she wondered, must he always work himself into self-righteous rage before making another demand upon her? Why did he not reflect upon *who* had seduced her and given her a bad name?

Yet his threats had never been as bald – or as frightening. In a rage he might well do as he now threatened, though it ruined himself as well.

'I'll consider it, Pietro,' she finally said. 'I'll consider it, perhaps see if it's possible.'

MIDNIGHT: SEPTEMBER 14, 1570
FLORENCE: THE PALAZZO ON THE VIA MAGGIO

Pietro Buonaventura had discreetly left his house on the Via Maggio, which was really his wife's house, shortly after eleven, when the ball ended. He had no fear of the footpads who preyed on lone pedestrians on moonless nights like this. He counted on his enveloping black cloak to make him inconspicuous and on his basket-hilted broadsword to protect him. Never deficient in physical courage, he was a superb swordsman.

Besides, it was only a ten-minute walk to the small apartment he kept for his new love, Mariarosa Santini, in the tenement where his parents lived. The second apartment was cheaper because he was already paying their rent – or Bianca was, which amounted to the same thing. Besides, visiting his parents accounted for his frequent comings and goings at odd hours.

Pietro prided himself on his discretion, which he had just displayed in leaving the palazzo on the Via Maggio unseen so that Bianca and Francesco would be undisturbed. Since he was now a public figure, discretion was essential.

In reality, all Florence knew that its leading cuckold, the husband of the Regent's mistress, kept his own current mistress in the ramshackle tenement near the cathedral. Nor did Pietro reflect that it was to the princely indiscretion of Francesco de' Medici that he owed his own prominence. Francesco disdained to attempt the concealment he knew he could not maintain. Pietro was neither cowardly nor stupid. Quite the contrary. But he never pursued any thought that might tarnish his own shining image of himself.

For that reason, he almost never thought of Bianca and Francesco together. Not because he loved her, being capable only of self-love. Not that he was jealous of her as a possession, being rewarded with more negotiable possessions for his forbearance. Yet he was really neither as complacent as he himself thought nor as complaisant as his wife thought. Although he would once happily have prostituted her for his own advantage, his vanity was hurt by her so clearly preferring Francesco to him as a man, let alone as a protector. Somehow, he felt, Bianca was not playing fair with him, though he could not say why, even to himself. He therefore preferred not to think of her alone with her lover in her boudoir.

Bianca traced the intertwined arabesques with her fingertips. The small rubies were sharp to the touch compared to the glossy smoothness of the star sapphire they encircled. She was wearing the ring looted by her ancestor Rogerio Morosini because Francesco could not bear to see on her finger the paltry gold-washed wedding-ring Pietro had given her. Her lover had redeemed every piece of jewellery she had pawned before they met and almost every piece she had sold outright. His agents were still searching for two or three minor pieces that had apparently passed through a number of hands.

This prince of hers, who was more at home with the logic of science and philosophy than the too human and too unpredictable hurly-burly of governing, was, quite illogically, jealous of inanimate objects. He could not bear to think that any ring or necklace once hers now adorned another woman. Nor was that distaste merely a pretext for restoring to Bianca every gem and every copper she had spent to support herself and, of course, the Buonaventuras, as well as to create a social setting in which he could take notice of her.

'If I let you,' she observed suddenly, 'you'd probably collect my fingernail parings to go with the lock of hair around my portrait.'

'No bad idea!' Francesco pulled out the gold chain that hung under his shirt and tapped the ivory case of the miniature. 'Bianca, you have no idea what it means to me to have one person with whom I can be entirely open.'

'Because she is entirely yours, dependent on your lightest wish?'

'Perhaps, but I don't really think so. No, it's not that. It's because I can trust you utterly.'

'You're absolutely sure?' she teased. 'I might surprise you some day.'

'Absolutely sure!' He laughed, but she knew he was deadly earnest. 'Not only because your interests and mine are identical, as are no one else's, not even, *particularly* not, my wife's. But because I know your mind and your heart. We don't think alike, far from it. But I almost always know how you'll react.'

'Isn't that rather dull? So predictable.'

'I said *almost* always. After four years you can still surprise me.'

'And you me, Franco. Pray it'll always be so.'

'What's wrong? You sound doubtful.'

'No, not doubtful. Only Pietro's been at me again and . . .'

'Not tonight, Bianca!'

His hand slashed the air imperiously, and she remembered that she was dealing with a prince, as well as a man who loved her. Extraordinary how infrequently she had to remind herself that he was the absolute ruler of hundreds of thousands. He never thought of his dignity when they were alone, and she was, whatever her enemies said, devoted to the man above the prince. She could have had a supremely comfortable and satisfying life in Venice if she were concerned primarily with wealth and power.

'I'll discuss that creature, that mosquito, you married another time. I'll do what I can for him, within reason and propriety. But *not* tonight.'

'I'm sorry I, when you're so tired . . .'

'He's a cross we both bear. Only later.'

A frown-line marred the smooth skin between Bianca's arched eyebrows. She was not concerned for herself; the ground on which they stood, Francesco and she, was firm enough to bear without shifting tremors a thousand times as strong as this one. She was concerned for him, his evident tiredness. She was sorry she had not cancelled the ball this evening, although it had been eagerly awaited for three months.

She should have cancelled it. Francesco had today returned from a two-week tour of his domain and had then, as she had known he must, sat through a series of irritating meetings with his ministers. But he had insisted that the ball not be postponed.

The Prince Regent of Tuscany was sitting in a ridiculously small boudoir chair on silk cushions with narrow pink, black, and silver stripes. Staring unseeing at the portrait of himself with Bianca's spaniel Don Juan, he was fumbling with the laces that held his trunk hose. His fingers were clumsy, and he was making hard work of a task he rarely performed for himself.

'Let me do it,' Bianca said, slipping to her knees beside him. 'Let me be your *valet de chambre* tonight.'

He gently touched her shoulder, bare under her wrapper. His fingertips moved up her neck and danced around her ear. Bianca shivered at his touch and grasped his arms. He kissed her lightly on the lips, then returned to the knotted laces.

'I can do it,' he said. 'How can I manage Tuscany if I can't manage my own laces?'

'It's not your role,' she replied, settling again on the stool before her dressing table. 'That's what others are for. A valet, myself, to make you more comfortable.'

The soothing words fell automatically from her lips while she studied him. He was very tired, drained by the cares of state he did not yet wish to discuss. They would undoubtedly talk about what was disturbing him when tomorrow they rode out to the unfinished villa at Pratolino. He loved playing the country squire, conferring with his architect on plans and discussing crops with his farm manager.

How smooth was her life beside his! Pietro's follies were all she had to worry about, except for the enmity of the Florentines. But she was hardened to both irritants.

Although they never discussed the subject, Francesco knew she did not sleep with Pietro. She had not, in fact, done so since the night, even before Pellegrina's birth, when Pietro proposed that she become a public courtesan for his benefit.

Francesco had to sleep with Joanna for dynastic reasons. He needed a male heir, not the three daughters she had given him. Besides, he did not wish to be chided by his brother-in-law the Emperor for failing in his marital duties. Imagining herself a man as best she could with her feminine mind in her female body, Bianca shuddered. If she were a man, she would hate to sleep with the bony, sour-breathed Joanna of Austria.

Francesco drew on the light woollen robe he kept in her wardrobe in the antechamber of her boudoir and threw another log on the fire. The evening was mild, but his exhaustion evidently chilled him.

Rising from the stool, Bianca stood over him. Meditatively, she traced the contours of his features with her fingertips. His face was surprisingly soft, but she felt new lines in his cheeks. His deep-brown eyes were lustrous, but melancholy, and the delicate skin beneath was stained by fatigue. Normally, he looked less than his thirty-one years because he was so vigorous, physically as well as mentally. Tonight, however, he looked older. His high sloping forehead was creased; his neat pointed beard was dishevelled; and he was stooped from his five foot eight inches of height.

'It's not Ferdinando again?' Bianca asked impulsively. 'I'm sorry. I shouldn't ask, not when you're so tired.'

'Not absolutely exhausted, as you'll find out in bed.' He grinned, then answered soberly. 'Yes, Ferdinando's plotting again, yapping at my heels, though the old Duke's still very much alive. His latest trick is . . . But I can deal with him.'

'And what else? Or would you rather wait?'

'Let's be brief tonight. It's the accursed Spanish. King Philip would eat us all up if he could. So I must stay on particularly good terms with my brother-in-law. Philip, my cousin, and he are always conspiring. My brother-in-law Maximilian wants his own piece of Italy, starting with the Venetian domains. Well, as long as my Aunt Catarina is Dowager Queen of France and rules her son, the King, we'll be safe.'

'Poor Francesco, such a complicated family. And I'm an embarrassment with all your royal relations!'

'God no! You don't come into it. Maximilian's no prude. He knows a man needs relaxation, companionship, excitement. And he's certainly not devoted to his sister. It's only . . . but don't worry. It's nothing to worry about.'

'*What* am I not to worry about?'

'Bianca, I'd let Joanna go, whatever the cost, rather than lose you. But that's not it. It's only, I know, that the Emperor, her family, wouldn't mind in the least if you were some feather-brained girl, the sillier the better. What bothers them is that you can think, not to speak of reading and writing.'

'I'm sorry,' she laughed. 'Shall I write to apologise? No, that obviously wouldn't do.'

'It's not important, Bianca. What can they expect with the miserable woman they married me to? How could I possibly talk to her? She's wholly ignorant. You know, that woman can't speak Italian. That's understandable, if not excusable, for a princess of the Holy Roman Empire. But she can't even speak Latin, only her barbaric German dialect. She's totally uneducated – and so narrow!'

'I do have other uses than conversation,' Bianca said innocently.

She held out her arms, and they rolled together onto the big bed.

After a short while, they came together gently, as if their bodies, too long apart, were again learning to know each other.

Seeing that he was already half-asleep, Bianca snuffed the candle on her bedside table. She stretched, feeling tired, yet not sleepy. It was not so much that she was aroused and unfulfilled, but that she had hoped for more emotionally, as well as physically.

Yet she knew they would awake sometime that night and fall on each other ravenously. That stormy coupling would undoubtedly occur, as it had so often in the past after separations shorter than two weeks.

Clutching that thought like a talisman, that meant so much more, she finally slept.

CHAPTER XIII

THE State Inquisitor had left Marco Capello to ponder the dispatch in the cubbyhole off his workroom. The stiff official handwriting on the stiff official form gave no hint of the identity of the agent who had sent the report. The despatch Marco held had been set down in plain language, by a cipher-clerk who knew the agent only as F109. F stood for Florence, though the true number of reporting agents in the Tuscan capital might be less than a hundred, might not even be nine. The Venetian Secret Service keep its secrets, even from its own men.

Still a captain, unpromoted since the action in the Cyclades five years earlier, Marco Capello was at the age of twenty-six a powerful officer in the Secret Service. He had learned to curb the Capello impulsiveness; and he had never been inclined to accept the most popular view as the only or, even, the correct view. That detachment made him invaluable as both a director of agents in the field and an analyst of their reports.

Marco had been at sea for half of each of the four years since he had seen Bianca in Florence. During the present year, the *Galley of the Angels* had played a distinguished role in a campaign that was barely creditable for the Venetian fleet. The performance of the Christian alliance against the Turks was wholly discreditable. The new Ottoman Sultan, called Selim the Sot from his fondness for wine, had brilliantly exploited the vacillation of both the Serene Republic's allies and the Venetian Senate itself.

Marco laid the dispatch on the rickety table and turned up the wick of the single small oil-lamp the Service provided with true Venetian frugality. He rubbed his eyes wearily.

He must not think of his personal disappointment: the enmity of the old admirals still denied him command of a squadron. Nor should he dwell on the Republic's vulnerable position: Cyprus, the keystone of the Empire of the Sea, was in danger of falling to the Sultan, who, it was said in bitter jest, coveted its strong wines.

He picked up the dispatch again. The author, whoever he was, was a true writer. His words painted individuals and scenes so vividly Marco pictured them before his eyes.

He had never seen the palazzo on the Via Maggio given to Bianca by Francesco de' Medici. But the dispatch evoked it in a few phrases: '. . . tall and narrow of pale-grey stone inscribed with white graffiti in the shape of nymphs, satyrs, and beasts, twinned always for symmetry; and, lately added in their centre, supported by an angel with outspread wings, the coat of arms of the Capellos of Venice.'

That same coat of arms rippled on the flag that flew from the mizzenmast of the *Angels*: a silver upper half and a royal-blue lower half with, superimposed, a tall hat, blue above and silver below, tied by red crossover ribbons and emblazoned with a golden fleur de lys. Bianca's boldness in displaying that shield, topped by the Wingēd Lion of Venice, was a little surprising. The agent F109, while acknowledging that he did not know her mind, speculated that she had been emboldened by the growing favour shown her by the Prince Regent.

'Also, perhaps, by her frustration,' the dispatch declared. 'Since she cannot be the recognised consort, she asserts her unique position by showing in place of the Medici arms, which she is denied, not the arms of her husband (fabricated as they are), but her own arms.'

Regardless of her motives, that display had provoked – or appeared to provoke – a stormy response from the Florentines, who resented her power over their Regent. The anonymous agent wrote:

'I was drawn to the Via Maggio at five on the afternoon of October 8 by wild shrieks and the beating of sticks against iron pots in derision. Before the white-scrolled face of the mansion we must now call the Palazzo Bianca Capello, I saw a mob of some two hundred, chiefly loafers and bravos for hire, stiffened by ten men who were visibly uncomfortable without breastplates and helmets. Two I recognised as officers of the household guard of Ferdinando Cardinal de' Medici. There were also a score or more of women of the town, the lowest kind of harlots.

'The mob was chanting: "Send the whore back to Venice!" And alternately: "Burn the witch!"

'The figures were indistinct in the deepening dusk. Nonetheless, I clearly saw cobblestones hurtle through the air. Most fell short or wide, but a few struck home, smashing one window, then another. A female figure appeared at a shattered window to hurl back a cobblestone. Other hands snatched her to safety. I later learned she was the Lady Bianca herself.

'All the while the chant continued, hoarse and menacing: "Expel the whore! Send her back to Venice!" Also shrill shrieks from the harlots: "Burn the witch! To the stake with her!"

'Torches flared, lighting the mob like demons in the fiery Pit. Two daring fellows, clearly men-at-arms, dashed forward to lay a billet of wood and straw soaked in oil against the barred door. They set it alight with their torches and dashed back into the mob's embrace. The flames leaped, taking hold on the door.

'The door opened, and a man with white-blond hair stepped out, followed by three manservants. Together they kicked away the blazing billet and stifled the flames on the door with their cloaks.

'The startled mob stood stock still. But shouts from the two guards officers urged them forward. Swords and daggers in their hands, the disguised men-at-arms attacked. The little party of defenders was overwhelmed, and the mob surged towards the open door.

'Suddenly the mob fell back. The blond man was revealed in their midst, wielding a broadsword with great skill. He beat off the men-at-arms, wounding three, one, it later proved, fatally. The door slammed shut, and the mob, disappointed of easy prey, fell back.

'For some ten minutes, the mob hurled cobblestones, bricks, and flaming torches at the palazzo. Some fell wide, but many hit the mark, hurtling through the shattered windows. The blond man, who was, I saw, Pietro Buonaventura, stepped out of a groundfloor window, challenging the men-at-arms again. Now wary, they formed a circle around him. Pressing inward together, rather than offering themselves individually to his deadly sword, they forced him back.

'There could be no hope of the few defenders holding the palazzo. I expected the mob to pour in, looting and killing.

'A rattle of drums and a blaring of bugles halted them. A company of the Prince Regent's household guard advanced from the Pitti Palace behind their blue-and-gold banner, which bears the Medici arms surmounted by a small coronet.

'The mob broke before the guard's spears. The officers of Ferdinando's guard stood irresolute for a few seconds. Then they, too, scurried away.

'I later learned that they were under orders not to fight the guard should it intervene. Nor were they to kill or maim the Lady Bianca, if it came to that.

'The purpose of the attack had already been attained. It was to blacken the name of Lady Bianca and her husband, as was demonstrated two nights later. Returning from his mistress's bed at four in the morning, Pietro Buonaventura was waylaid by six thugs. When his broadsword came out of its scabbard, they fled. But the assault was known to all Florence by eight that morning.

'Buonaventura, it was said, had been attacked by thugs hired by his mistress's mother. Some declared that the Council of Ten was carrying the feuds of Venice into the streets of Florence. Others swore the assault was to frighten him so that he would deal fairly with the creditors he creates faster than his wife can pay them off. In any event, the moral was clear to read: *Bianca and Pietro Buonaventura are provoking unrest and strife. The city would be better without them.*

'In reality, I have learned, Cardinal Ferdinando paid those thugs, as he had paid the mob that besieged the Palazzo Bianca Capello. His purpose is clear. He wishes to strike at the Prince Regent through his mistress. Ferdinando evidently hopes to displace Francesco and himself take the crown when Duke Cosimo I dies, as cannot be long averted.

'I speculate above, but I have confirmed the fact that Cosimo encourages his younger son's folly. The old, half-mad Duke in the Pitti Palace, where the Prince Regent Francesco and Princess Joanna now also reside, passionately hates his eldest son's mistress.'

Marco laid the dispatch down again and stretched wearily. He could not pace the cubbyhole as he did his quarterdeck. One stride would take him to its limits.

Yet he could not leave until he had digested the dispatch and set the intelligence in the context of Venetian interests at a time of crisis. Still standing, he considered the information, deliberately excluding his concern for Bianca from his mind.

The unknown agent had closed by citing reasons for Duke Cosimo's enmity towards Bianca, which led him to encourage his younger son to actions that could undermine the Medici dynasty. The indulgent Prince Regent, the agent added, would not discipline his unruly, treacherous brother. He did not consider the threat offered by Ferdinando to be serious.

'Cosimo disapproves of the Lady Bianca [the dispatch reported] because: 1) The relationship is making Francesco, and through him Medici rule, unpopular. 2) He believes she is plotting on behalf of Venice. 3) She is too intelligent and not sufficiently respectful to himself. 4) He, Cosimo, is very fond of the Princess Joanna, whose marriage to Francesco he considers a coup of his own statesmanship.

5) He fears that Lady Bianca's prominence will alienate the Emperior Maximilian, since she implicitly humiliates his sister, Princess Joanna. Finally, the old lecher and tosspot is becoming highly moralistic as his end approaches.'

Marco grinned at that expression of personal distaste. Such human touches, though officially discouraged, made a dispatch more valuable. He could visualise the bitter, ageing Duke who no longer ruled. He could also assess the dispatch better now, having a sense of the character of its unknown author.

And how did events in Florence bear on the Venetian Republic's predicament? How could these developments be utilised?

At the beginning of the year, Sultan Selim had told the Senate that Cyprus belonged to him. He had underlined his claim by the vigour of his threats, as well as by arresting scores of Venetians resident in Constantinople and seizing dozens of Venetian ships in its harbour. Venice then threw Selim the Sot's challenge back in his teeth and bundled his ambassador home.

By mid-year, more than a hundred Venetian galleys had sailed for the disputed waters. Neighbouring cities and towns launched new galleys, and funds were raised by all means, including the creation of eight new Guardians of St Mark's. Wealthy patricians paid well for the honour of bearing the highest title in the state beneath the Doge. But the resources of Venice were inadequate against the immense Ottoman Empire, whose population outnumbered her own a hundred times.

The Republic urgently needed support, but her Christian allies wavered. Emperor Maximilian had signed a treaty of peace with the Turks, which, he told the Venetian ambassador, still had five years to run. Catarina de' Medici, Dowager Queen and effectively Regent of France, was engrossed in a quarrel with King Philip II of Spain over the Netherlands and would not help. Philip, however, sent fifty warships under Admiral Gian Andrea Doria. That name was loathed in Venice, for this one's uncle, Admiral Andrea Doria, had twice betrayed the Republic's trust in the war that lost Naxos and the Cyclades a generation earlier.

True to form, Gian Andrea Doria advocated, first, caution and, then, retreat in the councils of the combined fleet. He was supported by the minor allies and opposed effectively only by Sebastiano Venier, second-in-command of the Venetian forces. Without ever sighting the enemy, the Christian fleet had, therefore, turned and run for home. King Philip, agents reported, was so pleased with Gian Andrea Doria that he was to reward him with Spain's highest military rank.

With such allies, Marco reflected, Venice might better depend on her nominal enemies. Joseph Nasi, Duke of Naxos and the Cyclades, was still in communication, but Marco was puzzled by his actions. He felt the need to test the intentions of his former ally.

A purpose was forming in Marco's mind. He let his thoughts focus again on Bianca Capello Buonaventura, her strong position and her misadventures.

Ironically, her father Bartolomeo was prospering at a time of troubles for his city and his daughter. He had invested Bianca's twenty-thousand-ducat dowry, never morally his, in trade with Northern Europe at the right moment. Of course, Bianca now had no need of the money. She was virtually mistress of the vast resources of the Medicis, the richest family in Europe, as the mistress of the effective head of the family.

Somehow, Marco reflected, all those tangled skeins could be woven into a coherent pattern pleasing to Venetian interests. He folded the dispatch, turned down the wick of the gimcrack oil lamp, and knocked on the door to the work-room of the State Inquisitor.

'I've read the dispatch,' he said. 'I would recommend much closer liaison with Florence. The Prince Regent stands aside from the conflict, but he is linked to every player.'

'And who's to undertake that liaison?'

'Myself, sir. I think it's time for me to pay another visit to Florence.'

CHAPTER XIV

'IT'S not like Venice here,' Bianca Capello Buonaventura chided her cousin Marco fondly. 'It's not all devious plots and puritanical rules and hiding behind masks to enjoy yourself. Not darkness, but light. Florence lives in the open.'

Marco smiled at that fulsome praise for her adopted city from a noblewoman whose scandalous life was truly an open book to critical Florentines. Two minutes earlier, she had been yearning for her native Venice, for the gaiety of feast days, the savour of the seafood, and the elegance of dress. Yet she was now reading him a lesson on the virtues of Florence. He listened idly, intrigued by the single dimple that appeared when she smiled.

They had just come to Florence, Captain Marco Capello of the *Galley of the Angels* and his chief officer, Paolo Crespelle. They were dressed as petty merchants and were staying at a second-rate inn. It would have aroused suspicion, even antagonism, if they had appeared in their true character: Marco as the cousin of the lady many Florentines cursed for her influence over their Prince Regent; Paolo as the estranged eldest son of the Baron Crespelle, who would not bow to the Grand Duke of Tuscany, but maintained his independence in a weather-beaten castle in the hills above Pistoia.

They had, as Bianca instructed in her letter, entered the mansion in the Via Maggio through the small rear-door opening on an alley. Her Venetian doorkeeper and her half-Venetian maid had made sure they were not seen by the other servants. The door to the antechamber of her boudoir was locked. Yet she was now saying their purposes would be better served by candour.

'Florentines love grandeur,' she explained. 'Not like your dour Tuscan hill folk, Paolo. Or your secretive Venetians, Marco. And they're endlessly curious. If you slink through alleys, they won't rest until they know your business down to the last copper. What they don't know, they'll invent, as they do with me.'

'Bianca, my dear,' Marco broke in. 'You're as charming as ever – and as illogical. One minute you're yearning for Venice, which has put a price on your head. The next minute you're rhapsodising about Florence, which curses you. First you want us to be discreet, nearly invisible. Then you tell us to swagger about like Spanish grandees.'

She laughed at the jibe, her green eyes shining, her head thrown back showing the long white curve of her throat. But an anxious pulse beat in the hollow above her collar-bone, and she twisted the great ruby that was her only ring. Marco was sad to see her so tense, although her insecurity was promising for his mission. The palazzo had been repaired after the mob's attack, but it would take longer to restore the confidence of its mistress.

'If you're open, even showy, Florentines will take you at your own valuation,' she insisted. 'They're not subtle.'

The Venetian officers nodded. Rather than skulking in disguise, they preferred to appear in their own persons and, they were confident, dazzle the ladies of Florence.

'Still, it would probably be better,' Bianca mused aloud, 'if Paolo, my new friend, the comrade of my best-loved cousin . . .'

Knowing that tone, Marco wondered suspiciously what she had in mind, but Paolo was unwontedly gallant.

'Yours to command, my Lady,' he said.

The Tuscan sailor-of-fortune was clearly in love with Bianca ten minutes after meeting her. His lean face, capped by short rust-red hair, inclined eagerly towards her. His hazel eyes glowed with devotion no other woman had evoked for years.

'. . . better for Paolo to pay a visit to his father, the old bandit of the crags,' she continued. 'Better not to fan old feuds by staying in the city.'

'Yours to command, my Lady,' Paolo repeated, and Marco marvelled at the docility of his often insubordinate lieutenant. 'This time of year only a forest fire could warm my father's stone castle . . . or his stony heart. Still, I wouldn't mind seeing the old tyrant.'

Paolo Crespelle bowed, pushed aside the brown felt curtain hung over the doorway against the cold December wind, turned the key, and was gone before his captain could say farewell. Bianca carefully locked the door again before turning to Marco with eyebrows raised.

'Well, my dear, no cousinly kiss for a long-lost relation?' she asked.

Bianca moved closer. When her red-gold hair brushed his cheek, he instinctively drew her to him. She flung her arms around his neck and pressed close for the space of a long breath. Feeling his body respond as it had always responded to her closeness, he released her. Beneath his automatic lust, he felt great tenderness for his wayward cousin who now lived on the heights – over an abyss.

During the six years they had been apart, Bianca had matured, as well she might. She had been unsure in her youth, despite the precocious perfection of her face and form. She now appeared to have outgrown the lack of self-esteem, verging upon self-distrust, that had made her so vulnerable to flattery – and to deception.

She appeared perfectly self-possessed, her own façade as impressive as her setting. Both bespoke the self-confidence engendered by great wealth and great power.

At five in the afternoon, the octagonal antechamber to her boudoir was lit by sixteen candles in a glass chandelier from Murano. Marco found it ugly, indeed vulgar, those intertwined blue-glass branches with green-glass leaves and, as candle-holders, flowers of red, orange, and yellow glass. But for Bianca the chandelier was evidently a comforting memento of her birthplace. The crimson silk that covered the walls was embroidered with cherubim in flight, only their bright faces and rudimentary wings visible. Her chair was placed so that she could look at a portrait of Francesco de' Medici in gold-inlaid ceremonial armour.

Beneath their heavy brows, the Prince Regent's dark eyes stared at Bianca with passion – and, perhaps, distrust. They would see a serene lady richly, but quietly, attired. Her dress of maroon cut-velvet was plain by the standards of Ducal Florence, fit for modest occasions, a dinner for thirty or a *musicale* for a hundred. The square shoulders were heavily padded, and the puffed sleeves were picked with lace, as was the demure décolletage. Her only touches of grandeur were a ruby ring and a necklace of enormous cabochon rubies. In the cleft of her bosom shone a plain gold crucifix.

Impulsively, Marco kissed her perfumed cheek. His dark curls contrasted with her fiery hair, his ruddy complexion with the golden undertone of hers. Above the Capello chin, rounded but strong, her lips were very red and very soft. Their fullness hinted at sensuality, their fragile cast at vulnerability.

'Taking stock, Marco?' she asked. 'Will the merchandise do?'

'Perfect!' he laughed. 'Far too good for export.'

'Sometimes I wonder: should I have eloped?' she said abruptly. 'But how could I let my father put me in the Convent of the Carmelites?'

Marco knew then that she was desperate. Behind her façade of casual self-assurance Bianca was tense with fear, on the verge of tears.

She wanted advice, but she clearly wanted comfort even more. He murmured sympathetically, but did not speak. She was on the brink of self-revelation, and he would not deflect her.

Bianca was barred from the confessional by her long liaison with Francesco de' Medici, but even flawed confession would be good for her soul. In whom else could she confide, certain she would not be betrayed?

'Marco, I must tell you . . .' She paused. 'But it's only foolish female fears. Anyway, you haven't told me about yourself. You are now, let me see, almost twenty-seven? And still not married?'

'Alas, no!'

'Why, Marco? Surely that little Angela Tron who was always at your heels. Angela must be nineteen, ripe for marriage.'

'Angela won't have me.'

'Why, Marco? The Trons are very grand, but a Capello of Ca' Capello on the Canalazzo isn't quite a peasant.'

'All sorts of reasons.'

'Then there's hope. So many reasons mean *no* reason. What does she say?'

'She loves me, she says, but she won't let me approach her father. That old feud between the Trons and the Polos, I seem to have inherited it with my Christian name.'

'You mean the nonsense about *il Milion*, our ancestor Marco Polo, cheating some long-dead Tron? A silly feud three hundred years old?'

'Silly or not, it's there. Besides, she says she's too young. She'd bore me. Also, her father has another bridegroom in mind. I'm becoming inpatient. But, Bianca, I do love her.'

'We Capellos, always romantics. Tell me, does she show affection?'

Marco flushed as he replied: 'A little, but not much. There are still *some* virgins in Venice. Angela's one of them.'

'Be a little distant, Marco. That's trite advice. But it usually works – if she's worth having. Otherwise, forget her.'

She smiled when he raised a hand in protest and said: 'Bianca, I'm afraid of losing her.'

'I know it's easy to solve someone else's problems, far easier than solving my own,' she acknowledged. 'I *do* have problems, Marco.'

'There was never a time when you didn't. If you must live like the heroine of a Greek tragedy.'

'I'm afraid,' she said. 'I know I look very secure. With Francesco,

I mean, despite his brother's attempts to drive me away. We do fit together, almost perfectly. Considering my past, it looks ideal, except for the marriage lines. But it's all threatened.'

'You're vulnerable,' he responded carefully. 'You're living on the slopes of a volcano. Still, I know how you love to flirt with danger. Fear makes your blood race, doesn't it? What exactly do you fear, Bianca?'

'There'll be no more direct attacks from Florentines. Francesco's seen to that. But my father's agents, his assassins. He's sworn it again: to seize me and take me back to Venice to face the courts. Then to wall me up in a nunnery. Marco, I'd die in a nunnery.'

'Your household, the power of Tuscany, surely there's protection . . .'

'My household isn't my own. In this house loyalty is divided between Pietro and Francesco. There's little left for a Venetian adventuress. The guards, the servants, they'd do anything for gold. Florentines don't like us, Marco. They fear and envy Venice. They say I was sent to enslave their prince.'

'So I've heard,' he acknowledged. 'And worse.'

'My father's hand in glove with the State Inquisition. And you know it's the world's best secret service. Most ruthless, too. They could kill Pietro.'

'After so long?' he encouraged her to talk on. 'And would that be a great loss?'

'I bear Pietro no ill-will. And I need him, the shield of a Florentine name. Without him, I'd be no more than an adventuress, a whore as some Florentines say. Then they *would* drive me out of their virtuous city.'

'Certainly the Regent can . . . will . . .'

'Not *certainly*. Francesco has fits of conscience. Every so often, he talks of sending me away, going back to Joanna. Also, his father, who's still Duke in name, is quite mad. The old Duke hates me.'

She grew more eloquent as she grew increasingly agitated. When, Marco wondered, had she last been able to speak to anyone so candidly? He was saddened by her distress, but it was not for him to dam the river of her words. Not for her own sake, as well as his. Let her vent her feelings – and reveal her needs.

'And Pietro,' she sighed. 'In Venice he lied to me like a rug merchant. He's never stopped lying, though now I can usually sort out the few kernels of truth.'

Bianca paused, assessed her cousin speculatively, evidently made up her mind, and continued: 'But I can't keep him from lying and strutting outside the house. He tells his new mistress he's not just First Gentleman of the Wardrobe to the Prince Regent, the post I had to enveigle for him to keep the peace. He tells her . . . and everyone else . . . he's Francesco's confidential Chamberlain, consulted in all decisions.'

'He fantasises. But what's the harm, except to himself?'

'Francesco's patience is wearing thin. And that new woman of Pietro's, his latest, it's such a *public* affair. He does it to avenge himself on me . . . humiliate me. She's a widow, thank God not a wife. But, if Francesco doesn't lose his patience, her brothers will. And God knows what they'll do.'

It was like a morality play. His beautiful cousin had sinned, and she was being punished by terror. Yet he could help her.

'Rarely do duty and inclination run so close together,' Marco declared pompously. 'A fortunate coincidence.'

Bianca looked at him in surprise. Her smile was amused, but her eyes were wary. The lady whose terror had so moved him a minute earlier now laughed heartily. She no longer appeared vulnerable, but formidable.

'You sound like an astrologer,' she said. 'What's this fortunate coincidence? Are Mars and Venus in the same house? Are they behaving scandalously?'

'You might say precisely that, Bianca. Regardless, I can help with your problems.'

'I wasn't asking you to . . .'

'I know that, my dear. But just listen to what I have to say.'

'Very well, proceed.'

'I can make you safe from your father and from the Secret Service. I can have the decree of outlawry rescinded. With luck, I can see that you *never* suffer from your husband's foolishness. I can make you invulnerable, I can even bolster you against the Prince Regent's moody conscience.'

'What must I do for all that?' She laughed nervously. 'Seduce the Pope?'

'Even *you* would have difficulty,' Marco responded in the same vein. 'The old man's close to death.'

Bianca crossed herself and demanded: 'You *are* serious, aren't you?'

'Never more so. Though I cannot help your immortal soul.'

'Leave my soul aside, Marco,' she directed icily. 'Just tell me what you're offering – and what you expect me to do.'

'Don't be haughty with me, Bianca.'

He had provoked her. But Marco reacted as if they were still boy and girl together, squabbling and making up.

Bianca directed imperiously: 'Tell me what you're offering . . . all those miracles . . . and how I have to earn them. Quickly, Marco. I expect Francesco within the hour.'

'I . . . ah . . . have connections with the State Inquisition, the Secret Service. I can make your father give up his vendetta and withdraw all charges against you. I can make the Inquisition designate you a protected personage. You're now classified: *potential danger to the state*. I can get that changed to: *great asset to the state, to be safeguarded*.'

'Your price will be high. No Capello, no Venetian trader, offers a tenth that much without demanding ten times as much in return. But, before you hand me the bill, Marco, tell me how you can possibly shield me from Pietro's recklessness and, even, Francesco's over-active conscience.'

'Simply by the Senate's declaring you a "True and loyal Daughter of the Venetian Republic".'

Bianca gasped: 'Marco, that's impossible. That title, it's like being royal anywhere else. The Senate's only given it once, to Queen Catarina of Cyprus – in exchange for Cyprus. How could you possibly?'

'I did say *with luck*, Bianca. If your work is superb, yes, it could be done. And then, almost royal, as you say, you'd be beyond Pietro's malice, safe even from Francesco's bouts of piety. An affront to you would be an affront to the Serene Republic herself.'

Marco knew the Senate would never give that ultimate accolade to Bianca while she was merely the mistress of the ruler of Tuscany. The Secret Service badly wanted her influence and her information. But Venice would not bestow the virtually royal title, Daughter of the Republic, on anyone but a reigning princess or the consort of a reigning prince.

Francesco de' Medici might well wish to marry the noblewoman on whom he lavished presents, the latest a splendid villa in the hills at Pratolino. But he could not marry Bianca while his lawful wife, Joanna of Austria, lived.

The State Inquisition would consider assassinating the unhappy princess a peccadillo if policy required it – as long as the crime could not be brought home to Venice. But Marco knew he would refuse to play any part. He would wade up to his knees in the sewers of espionage, but no deeper. He was, above all, a captain of galleys on secondment to the Secret Service, and he would not besmirch his conscience with murder.

'The . . . the work must be enormous,' Bianca said tentatively. 'For such a reward.'

'It is, but *your* part isn't. You only have to do a little better what you already do so well.'

'What must I do?'

To hear Bianca ask that question Marco had come to Florence. Yet he hesitated before speaking.

The cause was undeniably just, even noble. He was not only serving Venice and her unique ideals; he was also fighting for the survival of Christendom against the hordes of the East. Everything he promised Bianca, even the royal title, he could deliver – if she did her part and fate were kind.

Nonetheless, he loathed himself for an instant. Like a pimp, he was inducing her to use her body and her charm for *his* purposes. True, he was asking nothing of Bianca she had not gladly done of her own will. Moreover, he was offering her an opportunity to serve Christendom and thus, perhaps, redeem herself in the eyes of God. Yet he felt tainted.

'Christendom, the West, is now guarded by the alliance of Venice and Spain forged by the Pope,' Marco finally said. 'But the alliance is unravelling, and Pius is dying. Slowly, but dying nonetheless. I want you to knit up the alliance . . . make it stronger.'

'And on the seventh day may I rest?' Astonished, Bianca could only joke. 'Marco, you're ridiculous.'

'If I am, Venice is in desperate danger, and the leaders who are fighting to save her are fools,' he answered portentously. 'Worse, Christendom itself is threatened. Please, just hear me out.'

'Yes, Marco,' she said meekly, 'I'll listen.'

Any envoy of Venice, official or private, would have been received by the Venetian mistress of the Prince Regent of Tuscany. But she would truly listen only to him. He had always been able to compel her attention, even, sometimes, her obedience – for a time.

'You must get Francesco de' Medici out of his stinking laboratory, out of the artists' studios. I can't argue with his experiments in science or his supporting artists. Both are noble pursuits. But they're not enough. You must make a statesman of him.'

'God knows I'm always trying – for Venice and for Florence. But with no great success. How . . .'

'By giving him a great cause to champion, the greatest imaginable: the salvation of the West and the preservation of Christian civilisation. Since Tuscany is not immediately threatened by the Turks, he does nothing . . . only plays at statecraft. You must convince him with the intelligence reports I'll send you that Tuscany, too, is in grave peril. And that he *must* act.'

'How?'

'There are four doors, and your Francesco holds the key to three. He's close to King Philip of Spain, who must be won to wholehearted participation. He's cousin to the King of France, nephew to the Queen Dowager. And he's the brother-in-law of Emperor Maximilian. Venice needs their help . . . their men and their ships.'

'Joanna!' she exclaimed. 'You want *me* to persuade *him* to work through *Joanna*?'

'You *must*, Bianca!'

'Well, I suppose I'll do no harm, though how much good . . .' She smiled mirthlessly. 'And the fourth door?'

'Is the Papacy. Pope Pius is the great champion of the Christian Alliance against the Turks. But he's dying, almost gone. The Vatican *must* continue his policy whoever succeeds him. Francesco must mobilise the cardinals he controls, including his brother Ferdinando.'

'Now that is absurd. Ferdinando hates me and hates Venice. He even hates Joanna. He's afraid one of us'll produce an heir and do him out of Tuscany.'

'He's not a priest,' Marco recalled, 'but a lay cardinal.'

'. . . so that he can smoothly succeed Francesco.'

'Regardless, you must do all you can. We have other levers, of course. Our cousin, the Patriarch, obviously. The Vatican is crucial, but the least difficult of the four doors.'

'And that's all, my dear Marco? You're quite sure that's all? All I have to do is change the world? Then you'll make me safe and cover me with honours?'

Marco unconsciously pulled at his left earlobe. Bianca observed the telltale gesture, common to her father and his cousin, Marco's father. She smiled at the memory, but waited tensely for his explanation.

'Bianca, the last part is, so to say, a little fanciful. But, if it works . . .'

'I suppose it's the key to my title, Daughter of the Republic, *if* God carries Joanna away. Please tell me.'

'You know of Joseph Nasi, Duke of Naxos?'

'That horrible creature! An anti-Christ, a treacherous dog of a Jew in league with the Turks!'

'Who apparently persuaded the Turks to attack Cyprus . . . to conquer our colony. Well we're in touch with this Duke of Naxos. He could be useful.'

Bianca did not speak. Not merely sceptical, she was unbelieving.

'This Jew and his complicated family lived in Venice before fleeing to Constantinople,' Marco continued. 'Sentence of death was passed on him: to be hanged between the pillars in the Piazzetta of St Mark's. That sentence has now been repealed – for good reason. Nasi is in close touch with France, with the Emperor, and with the Vatican, chiefly through the network of Jewish bankers and merchants. His tentacles are everywhere.'

'And you plan?'

'To use Joseph Nasi, now the Sultan's strength, against the Turks. We are in touch with him, but too loosely. I want to send a secret envoy to Joseph, one who appears to be an ordinary trader. But not a Venetian and not too clever, so that he's not suspected. Now, there *is* one . . .'

'Pietro, you mean? Send Pietro to Constantinople?'

'Exactly!'

Bianca's surprise turned to thoughtful consideration: 'I wonder. He's always talking about the fortune to be made in the trade of the East. He'd go happily. And that could save him from the consequences of his own folly here. Also, I wouldn't have to worry about him or the damage he does me.'

'And . . .'

'Best of all, no one would suspect.' She had grasped his argument. 'Who would suspect a libertine, a fop who looks a fool? Who would think him an agent of Venice?'

Marco nodded his approval. She was an apt pupil in the dark arts of espionage.

As if to prove that judgement, Bianca added: 'Go now, Marco. I shall not present you to Francesco. You must leave Florence today. Go quietly, very quietly.'

CHAPTER XV

MARCH was the time-in-between in the city with one foot planted in Europe and the other in Asia. Constantinople, renamed Istanbul by its Turkish rulers, spanned the Bosphorus, the straits that separated the continents. The same duality coloured the seasons. Neither truly winter nor truly spring, early March was a battlefield on which the two seasons clashed. Ice no longer rimed the reeds blowing on the shores of the straits, but the night frost painted white arabesques on the trees among the close-packed houses on the banks.

At the end of the first week of March 1571, Pietro Buonaventura came ashore from the Genoese merchantman that had carried him from Livorno through the gales of late winter. Barely visible in the dusk, the single-plank gangway was slick with freezing sleet. His cloth-soled shoes slipped on the icy surface, and he drew his crimson cloak around him.

Pietro shivered. The night was dark, although a sliver of a crescent moon flirted through rifts in the clouds that hid the stars. Determined to make a brilliant first impression on the city he had come to conquer, he was wearing the exuberant court costume of the High Renaissance: thin violet-silk hose, puffed blue-satin trunks, and a gilt-pommelled rapier. Only his brocaded doublet, which was heavily padded to give him a heroic figure, tempered the icy wind.

His inborn authority had, Pietro knew, carried him unscathed through a searching interrogation by three port officials. His wax-sealed, scarlet-ribboned passport signed by Francesco de' Medici, Prince Regent of Tuscany, he conceded, had also smoothed his way. Giving no rank or title, it simply requested all to allow him safe passage. Yet how many travellers could boast of a passport at all?

It was the least his wife and her lover could contribute, when both were delighted to be rid of him. He also carried in the purse on his belt letters of introduction to Florentine and Genoese merchants. Since neither city was a friend of Venice, they were excellent cover for his mission.

Sewn into the right shoulder-pad of his doublet was a letter from Marco Capello's father Damiano to the bailo, the chief among the Venetian merchants who, though under house arrest, still traded in the Ottoman Empire. Although at war, neither state saw a need to forgo commerce entirely. That introduction, Marco had told him, was only for a crisis.

Sewn into his left shoulder-pad were three big rubies Bianca had given him 'for emergencies' and an unaddressed onionskin message meant for Joseph Nasi, Duke of Naxos and the Cyclades. Folded into a pellet no larger than a grain of wheat, it had been written in Hebrew in code by a Jewish banker, who was an associate of the Capellos. It read, he had been told, like a report of family events and business transactions. Should it be discovered, he could plead that it had been hidden without his knowledge by a Jewish tailor.

Pietro was irked at being thought a fool by his wife's cousin who had, he suspected, once been her lover. Hiding the messages, ostensibly for his safety, was really for Venetian security. If the secret messages were found, only a very dull Turkish security officer would believe him an innocent trader. However, he had just cleared the first obstacle, the suspicious port officials.

By the light of a bonfire on the pier he saw two muscular Nubian slaves armed with enormous scimitars waiting with three porters. The older Nubian, who wore an enormous green turban and a white robe, held up a slate reading: *Caravanserai of the Golden Horn*. When he nodded, the Nubian strode off, his torch blazing a golden trail. The second Nubian, who wore a blue turban, fell in behind the porters.

The escort was welcome. The adventurer Pietro Buonaventura, always laughing and optimistic, was uneasy. He was alarmed by his first sight of Constantinople, the richest city of the world except, perhaps, for the distant capital of Cathay. The metropolis appeared mean and menacing to him. He was accustomed to cities that flaunted their wealth, but Constantinople *hid* its riches.

The capital of the Ottoman Empire seemed not one city, but two cities superimposed on each other. The few wide streets and the innumerable narrow alleys were alike palisaded with blank walls topped with spikes. Behind those walls must lie the secret city of wealth and power as yet invisible to him. Beneath those walls, families lived miserably in hovels that were no more than upended packing cases.

He had not expected so many women on the streets of a Moslem metropolis. Some wore makeshift veils that barely concealed their grimy faces and sagging bodies. But most went unveiled in coarse rags grey with filth.

Looking away from the people, he felt himself pierced by their hostile stares. His clothing, which he had half an hour earlier believed dashing, now seemed garish. Vastly self-assured, he had always thought himself at home wherever he went. Tonight, for the first time, he felt an alien – and in danger.

Pietro saw with a shudder that half the people were blind – in one eye or both. Their milk-white irises seemed, nonetheless, to stare balefully. Their faces were sullen, almost unreadable. But he saw envy, malice – and naked hatred.

The Nubians cleared a path through the throng with the flats of their scimitars and the threat of their edges. Slaves though the big blacks were, the impoverished free men shrank from their master's power, which inspired their arrogance.

The life of the streets was frenzied. Pietro was jostled by hawkers of every known commodity – and some he did not know. Food vendors cried the virtues of their goods: hot chestnuts, kebabs on wooden skewers, thick soups served in battered mugs and crab apples on sticks. The fragrance of wood smoke and meat roasting mingled with the sour stench of poverty and the heavy sweetness of musk.

Although accustomed to the uninhibited throngs of Venice and Florence, who also lived largely in public, Pietro was shaken by the immense numbers and the ceaseless movement of Constantinople. He reminded himself that the Ottoman Turks abhorred that name, because it recalled Constantine, the first Christian Emperor of the East. He must learn to call the city Istanbul.

EARLY MORNING: MARCH 7, 1571
ISTANBUL

'Above all, be discreet,' Marco Capello had warned him. 'You'll be safe as long as you act like a merchant of Florence. You can be flamboyant, but don't give offence. The Turks are prickly. Above all, do nothing to arouse the suspicion that you are not exactly what you seem.'

Aside from confirming the mutual distaste Marco and he felt, those training sessions had been useful. Pietro, who already knew he had a flair for espionage, had decided to follow Marco's advice – subject, of course, to the realities he found on the ground.

After a convivial meal with two Florentine wool merchants also staying at the Caravanserai of the Golden Horn, Pietro returned to his opulent chamber and pulled aside the linen counterpane. The landlord's candle-clock showed an hour after midnight, past time for sleep in a city that rose early for a business day broken by a long siesta.

Tomorrow he would play the eager merchant in earnest. Yet, he wondered, could he miss an opportunity to further his mission? Would it not be foolish not to take advantage of the dark night to meet the fabled Duke of Naxos and the Cyclades?

Marco had told him that the Turkish security police never began their routine surveillance of newcomers on the night of arrival. Lazy and self-indulgent, they asked themselves the obvious question: *Where could a newcomer, friendless and alone, possibly go on his first night in an unfamiliar city?*

Much of Istanbul was, however, already as familiar to Pietro as the back alleys of Florence. Marco had made him memorise street plans, and he knew the route from the Caravanserai of the Golden Horn to the palace of the Duke of Naxos as if he had trodden it every day for years.

Throwing a dark cloak over his gaudy garments, Pietro exchanged his flimsy rapier for his broadsword. He congratulated himself on his foresight as he crept down the stairs, his soft-soled shoes silent as cat's feet.

He slid through the deserted dining room, which was lit only by the dying fire under the empty spit, and slipped out of the side door. With the habitual caution of a professional secret agent, he worked the latch onto its hook with a length of twine, which he then withdrew through the latch-hole. He would return through the same door. Long before this mission, he had been practised in opening latches from outside with twine tied to a pebble.

Delighted with his quick thinking, Pietro circled the block. He stayed in the shadows and avoided the sleepers on the pavement. In the fashionable district around the Caravanserai of the Golden Horn, street people were few. The police saw to that.

Circling the block a second time, Pietro knew he was not being followed. A dark, unobtrusive figure, except for the white osprey plume in his black velvet hat, he set out for the palace of the Duke of Naxos.

Despite the street-plan in his head, he took several wrong turns. Each time, he went back to a landmark he knew and set out again. It was almost three in the morning when he saw the white marble walls of the palace of Joseph Nasi, Duke of Naxos and the Cyclades, which was called Belvedere for its magnificent view across the Bosphorus to the European shore.

Beside the palace stood wooden houses painted green or blue, five stories high, but very narrow. Land on the straits was inordinately valuable. A measure of Joseph Nasi's wealth was the eighth-of-a-mile water frontage of his castle. Pietro could see one end of the walls, but the other end was invisible in the mist. Oddly, the street people were almost as thick here as in the rough dock area. Under his cloak Pietro slipped his wrist through the lanyard of his broadsword and grasped its basket-hilt.

He slipped between two lean-to stalls to study the gates of Belvedere. The gilded steel pickets topped with spearheads were backed by sheets of wood to keep passers-by from looking in. How, he wondered, would he enter without awakening the staff? Had he once again been too impulsive?

Feeling a plucking at his cloak, he looked down at the extended hand of a beggar, which shone sickly white in the faint moonlight. Not really a hand, but a misshapen stump seamed with scarlet scars. The creature was a leper. Pietro drew away in horror – and an arm encircled his throat.

Whirling, he shook off the arm, tossed his cloak back, and drew his broadsword. A stiletto darted out of the shadows. He felt the blade tear his left biceps before the shock numbed his entire body. All strength drained, his left arm fell nerveless to his side. He wanted only to lie down and rest.

But he knew he must fight back – or die. In desperation, he lunged into the shadows and felt his blade cut through a soft substance. His sword arm was jarred to the shoulder by the impact, and he knew he had struck bone.

Springing like imps from the shadows, a dozen ruffians surrounded the Florentine. Back against the wall, he whirled his sword round and round to fend off their daggers and clubs. He cursed his left arm, which hung limp, a useless encumbrance. But he blessed his foresight in taking the broadsword rather than the rapier.

His assailants' shrieks hardly seemed human speech, but the raving of devils out of Hell. Eyes glittering in the faint moonlight, they pressed upon him. He could not draw back, for he was hard against the wall. A spearhead sliced his sword hand, and dashed his sword out of his hand, leaving it dangling from his wrist by its lanyard.

Almost despairing, Pietro closed his fingers on the hilt, which was slippery with blood. Unthinking, he shrieked the war cry not of his native Florence, but of Venice.

'Saint Mark!' He appealed to the grey sky. 'Save me, Saint Mark!'

A club crashed on Pietro's left shoulder, and the lightning of pain seared his useless arm. Staggering, almost falling, he clutched his sword again. But he could raise it no higher than his waist. Spread-eagled against the wall, he waited like a sacrificial animal for the death stroke.

A ram's horn blared, so distant and so faint it was assuredly an illusion. Through his pain and fear, Pietro recognised the throaty roar. In the Ghetto of Venice on a Jewish holy day he had heard a ram's horn blare, the same blaring that once brought down the walls of Jericho. Why was his mind playing tricks on him?

He heard the gates of Belvedere crash open, and he heard the thud of running boots. A club struck him on the temple, and he fell to the muddy ground. He heard no more. Nor did he see his assailants scatter before the men-at-arms pouring from the open gates of the palace of the Duke of Naxos.

Dawn was flooding through blue-glass windows when Pietro Buona-ventura opened his eyes. Feebly, he pushed away the vial beneath his nose and closed his eyes against the pain that lanced his temples. Gasping at the pungent fumes, he turned his head away. A hand grasped his chin, forcing him to breathe in the ammoniac reek. Cough-ing and spluttering, he opened his eyes again.

'You've given me much trouble.' A man's voice, deep and sonorous, spoke in Italian marred only by the trace of a Venetian accent. 'I hope you're worth it.'

No pity here for the wounded, Pietro reflected with wry self-pity, no balm of sympathy for the afflicted.

He squinted. Amid the brilliant circles whirling before his eyes he saw a tall man with a short red beard streaked with grey. The man's features wavered, crumbled into bits, then resolved, only a little blurred.

He saw a long face with penetrating eyes of the darkest blue above high cheekbones. The forehead swelled as grandly as the great dome of the cathedral in Florence. The skullcap on the man's thick grey hair was the same colour as the blue stripes on his white robe.

'Now, what's it all about?' The tone, like the words, was stern, but not brutal. 'You were looking for me?'

'Joseph Nasi?' Pietro asked. 'The Duke of Naxos?'

'And the Cyclades, if you please.' The red lips within the thicket of beard smiled. 'What do you want of me?'

'I carry . . . carry a message . . . from Venice.'

The Duke's stern blue eyes commanded him to continue, but Pietro glanced around warily. A black slave with a wisp of a white beard was stirring a drink on a low table, and a man-at-arms guarded the door. No one else was visible, although the tapestries covering the walls could have hidden a battalion.

'Why the devil did you come at night?'

Surprised by the abrupt digression, Pietro said weakly: 'Why . . . for safety. At night, I thought, visitors are not so noticeable. My mission, it's secret.'

'Did they tell you to come by night, your masters?'

Pietro shook his head slowly, wincing at the pain. He said softly: 'No, but I thought . . .'

'You *thought*!' Joseph Nasi raised his eyes imploringly. '*Only* by coming at night could you arouse suspicion. The Turks, the Sultan and the Grand Vizier, *expect* me to have many callers, strange callers, every day. I'm very useful to them because of my connections and my informants throughout the world. Then you come stealing in by night – and call attention to yourself.'

The Jewish nobleman shook his head in disbelief and mused aloud: 'Maybe you're not a liar, though a fool. I'll have the security police around my ears. Well, knowing your purpose, I can deal with them.'

The old black servant offered the Duke a frothy drink in a silver cup on a silver salver. He sipped, sighed with satisfaction, and handed the cup to Pietro. Sighing again, the Duke sank into the cushion-heaped chair beside the pallet on which Pietro lay.

'Egg beaten into milk, my physician prescribed, with powdered opium for your pain. In a week you'll be fit to go back to your tavern. Meanwhile, you must endure my hospitality.'

Surprised at hearing the best hotel in Istanbul called a tavern, Pietro matched his host's new civility. He was, he said, honoured to be the guest of the famous Duke of Naxos and the Cyclades He profoundly regretted his error in coming by night and profusely apologised for the difficulties he had created.

'You're no Venetian.' The Duke was suspicious again. 'No matter-of-fact Venetian merchant ever made such a graceful speech. And your accent's Tuscan. Of Florence itself, I'd bet. But you come from Venice, you say?'

'A Venetian?' Pietro spoke through his pain. 'How could they send you a Venetian, Your Grace? Nonetheless, I come from Venice, from the Senate itself.'

'Then it's peace?' The blue eyes lit eagerly. 'You come to sue for peace – and to confirm my titles?'

'To confirm your title to the Cyclades, not yet, my Lord.' Pietro had been drilled in that answer. 'Under certain circumstances later, yes. But I know nothing of a suit for peace.'

'Then why the devil *have* you come?'

'To bring a message and convey your messages to Venice, my Lord.'

Pietro concluded that he would have to trust the Jew with the rubies. To a man who possessed incalculable riches himself and could draw on the illimitable wealth of world Jewry, the rubies should be a bagatelle.

'In the left shoulder pad of my doublet, you'll find a message,' he said. 'The few stones are my own.'

'Enough to get you killed three times over in Istanbul,' the Duke observed. 'They'll kill for far less than the thin purse at your belt.'

MARCH 19, 1571
ISTANBUL: THE BELVEDERE PALACE

Pietro stayed at the Belvedere not for a week, but almost two. When his anger cooled, Joseph Nasi grew fond of the Florentine. The Duke was, after all, a European, although a Jew and an exile. In Pietro Buonaventura he found a candid, if not entirely truthful, informant on the present condition of Europe and, also, an appreciative audience for his own tales.

Joseph Nasi needed an audience. His extensive family had already heard his tales too often or, like his wife, Brianda, had been actors in those dramas. Even his physician, the man called Hillel of Damascus, was too familiar with his patron's extraordinary life to react with satisfactory wonder.

The physician, who had come to Istanbul with Joseph Nasi in 1557, was himself a Venetian. As Hilario Damasceno, he had enjoyed a reputation as a comic playwright among Christians as well as Jews. He wrote in Italian with a Venetian intonation. Although Jews were required to reside in the first Ghetto in Europe, the city was tolerant intellectually, as well as commercially, and even socially. Jews used Venetian names, spoke Venetian Italian, and were received in enlightened patrician salons.

Hillel had met Joseph Nasi twenty years earlier. Then called John Miches, the future Duke had come to Venice with the two remarkable Mendes widows, both of whom were his distant cousins. The ladies were extremely wealthy, still controlling both the spice-and-pepper trade and the financial empire built by their deceased husbands, a pair of Jewish brothers who had traded from Lisbon.

The sisters-in-law had fled to Venice from persecution in Antwerp. Their legal status was confused. They were neither professed Jews nor practising Christians, but Marranos, 'swine', as born Catholics called those converted by force to Catholicism. The Holy Inquisition everywhere took a benevolent – and brutal – interest in their souls. But Venice, which was tolerant of Jews, especially wealthy Jews, as she was of other dissenters, did not permit the Holy Inquisition to pursue souls within her territories.

The ladies' young cousin, John Miches, started by managing their businesses. He later became even closer to them, marrying first Brianda Mendes's daughter, Beatrice, and later, confusingly, Beatrice Mendes's daughter, Brianda.

He had eloped with Beatrice to Ravenna, where he had good connections. His mother-in-law had wanted an independently wealthy banker or merchant for her daughter. At worst, a physician or a rabbi. But not her distant kinsman who, although brilliant, had no capital of his own.

Even Pietro Buonaventura's appetite for complicated and scandalous gossip grew jaded when the Duke described the convulated legal processes that followed. Pietro only remembered the upshot.

The enraged Brianda Mendes and her ducats had secured an extraordinary verdict from the Council of Ten. Her son-in-law John Miches, convicted of abduction and embezzlement, was exiled from Venice forever. Should he return, he was to be hanged between the twin columns in the Piazzetta of St Mark's. Neither remission nor pardon was to be granted except by the vote of two-thirds of both the Senate and the Council of Ten, which was virtually impossible.

The bond between the Duke and the courier of the Venetian Secret Service grew stronger when Pietro confided that he, too, had been outlawed by Venice for abduction. The Duke did not confide that he was already informed on the man whose wife was the mistress of the Prince Regent of Tuscany. Nor, beyond alluding to his influence at the French and Spanish Courts and his friends in the Vatican, did he explain how he had managed to have his own sentence revoked.

Yet the Duke was hardly tight-lipped. Delighted with his new audience, he ranged from the nature of the Ottoman Empire to the Jewish religion. But he did not reveal the contents of the message Pietro had brought him. He only observed cryptically: 'A holding action, no more!'

Pietro considered that casual remark a deliberate evasion. He was convinced that he had almost lost his life defending a vital link in the secret diplomacy between the belligerents, Venice and Istanbul. He further believed that the attack on himself had been instigated by enemies of Venice, almost certainly the Genoese.

Although the Duke would say no more regarding the message, he continued to be almost embarrassingly confidential regarding his private life. He had, he said, been separated from his wife Beatrice by the intrigues of her mother Donna Brianda. While mourning his loss, he had been engaged in espionage on behalf of the great powers – and on behalf of his own rapidly expanding ventures in trade and finance.

'That,' he observed complacently, 'was how I acquired informants and agents in every capital of Europe and Asia Minor. There are today more Christians and Moslems than Jews in my network.'

In 1556, Donna Beatrice Mendes and her daughter Brianda had left an increasingly anti-Semitic Venice for Istanbul, where the Moslems regarded the Jews as elder brothers and sisters. Forty cavalrymen escorted mother and daughter into the Ottoman capital. Their entourage rode in four gilded-and-begemmed carriages, followed by a retinue of five hundred servants. Astonished reports of Donna Beatrice's having been received like a reigning princess were sent to all European states by their ambassadors in Istanbul.

Donna Beatrice could now live openly as a Jew. She could also openly assist thousands of Marranos, those Jews who had, like herself, been forcibly converted to Catholicism, but were still persecuted. Her great influence at the Court of the Sultan was enhanced the following year by the arrival of John Miches, her cousin and business manager.

'I didn't want to outshine the lady,' the Duke told Pietro. 'So I kept my escort to twenty cavalrymen and my entourage to two carriages. But I couldn't stop the thousands of poor Marranos who streamed after me.'

Pietro Buonaventura was no more sympathetic to Jews, especially Jews who had recanted their baptism, than were most good sons of Holy Church. He was even more inclined against the troublesome Jews because Damiano Capello and Marco Capello, whom he detested, favoured them. Although disgusted, he listened with apparent sympathy to the Duke's tale.

'In Istanbul I could practise my own religion,' his host said. 'I was circumcised and readmitted to the community. But not as an ordinary member. That's where I received my new name: Nasi for chieftain of the Jews; Joseph for the Jew who became a great man in Egypt, as I have become a great man in the Ottoman Empire.'

Yet the Duke spoke with cold candour of his hosts. Always questioning all motives except his own, Pietro wondered at that dangerous frankness. But, he realised, the canny Jew was taking no risk at all.

He, Pietro Buonaventura, was now helpless in the Belvedere. Later, he would not dare betray the man who could so easily have him beheaded by the official executioner as a spy or stabbed by a street assassin for a few coins. Besides, the Turks *expected* Nasi to hold conversations with strange informants. Finally, whatever he said on returning to Italy would only enhance the mystery and the glamour that surrounded the Duke of Naxos and the Cyclades.

'The Ottomans are nomads, marauding nomads who have, *not* by chance, conquered an empire,' his host told him. 'To deal with them, my friend, you must understand their ideas.'

'Which are?' Pietro dutifully asked.

'Three chief ideas. *Jihad*, the first, is Islam's Holy War against unbelievers like you and me. That concept they acquired when they took on the Moslem faith.

'Even more fundamental is *ghaza*. The moving force of Ottoman life is periodic expeditions for plunder and conquest, constant expansion in other words.'

The Duke drew on his water-pipe before continuing: 'Last is the *kafes*, the cage-prison in which a new Sultan locks all males with any conceivable claim to the throne. By the "law of fratricide", he then executes *all* his brothers and *all* their sons, as well as his uncles and their sons. So he ensures that his rule is not challenged.'

'How can the Ottomans ever make peace with their neighbours or with Christians?' Pietro forgot for a moment his host's claims that he could reconcile Venice and Istanbul. 'How can you possibly hope for peace?'

'Not in the long run,' the Duke replied undisturbed. 'In the long run, the Ottomans must either conquer or be conquered. But, in the short run, we can arrange mutually advantageous truces between Istanbul and Venice that are also advantageous to you and me.'

'They must be incredibly difficult to deal with!' Pietro exclaimed. 'Always walking on eggs – or the scimitar's edge.'

'Not at all. The Sultan is the soul of courtesy and generosity. He knows that I serve him wholeheartedly and that I cannot become a threat to him. Therefore, he trusts me more than he trusts any nobleman of his own race. He lets me practise my own religion, even use a small building on my land as a synagogue. You'll find it interesting. It's not like a church. A synagogue isn't consecrated. Yet it's sacred, like the Torah, the Scroll of the Law. My Torah has a velvet case set with diamonds and rubies.'

And the Jews, Pietro reflected, called Christians idolators because they made images of God and His Saints. What hypocrisy!

'The Sultan has given me a city,' Joseph Nasi continued. 'Tiberias in the Holy Land of Palestine. There I am building a new Jewish nation, the new kingdom of Judea and Israel.'

Pietro crossed himself against such an abomination: a new kingdom of the Jews. Mindful of his vulnerable position, he made the sign under the thin blanket that covered him.

He regarded his mission to Istanbul primarily as a chance to enrich himself with profits from trade and his stipend from the Secret Service. For the first time, he now asked himself the vital questions: *Would Joseph Nasi use his great influence for peace, as he said he would? Or would he urge Sultan Selim II to increase Turkish pressure on those bastions of the Venetian Empire, Cyprus and Crete?*

MORNING: MARCH 31, 1571 – MORNING: JUNE 11, 1571
ISTANBUL

By the end of March, Pietro Buonaventura was well enough to leave the Belvedere. Having become close to the Duke of Naxos during his convalescence, he was frequently at the palace on the Bosphorus afterwards.

Pietro could not read the messages he forwarded in the cargoes of pepper and cinnamon to Ravenna. All were in the Hebrew code known only to Joseph Nasi and one Jewish banker of Venice. The Duke had excellent connections in Ravenna, as he knew from the Jew's account of his personal history. Why, Pietro's restless intelligence asked, was an intermediary like himself necessary?

He felt in the pit of his stomach that Joseph was playing not a double, but a triple, game – with Venice and himself as dupes. Pietro, who could barely puzzle out a bill of lading, could read the lightest expression on a human face. He had for years made his way in the world by playing on the half-revealed feelings of men and, above all, women. Underestimating Pietro's shrewdness, the Duke was sometimes marginally indiscreet.

Intuition now told Pietro that Joseph Nasi was talking peace in order to split Venice from her wavering allies. At the same time, he was probably urging the Sultan to attack the Venetian fleet, the only force that stood between the Ottoman Empire and domination of the Mediterranean from the Golden Horn to Gibraltar. Yet the Duke was clearly prepared to profit from peace if that plan went astray. Pietro admired his acumen and his agility, while ritually condemning his duplicity.

Pietro himself bet heavily on war. He had already sold Bianca's rubies. Seeking large loans from his Genoese and Florentine associates in Istanbul, he invoked the name of Francesco de' Medici. Why should he not use the influence he possessed because everyone knew of his wife's liaison with the Prince Regent? Thus financed, he doubled and redoubled his shipments of spices.

Any enlargement of the war would cut off all trade for at least a year. Any merchant holding large stocks of spices in Italy could make his fortune; and his partners in Florence would not dare cheat him grossly. When the Florentine-worked leather he had ordered failed to arrive in sufficient quantities to pay the interest of twelve percent a month on his debts, he borrowed further from Joseph Nasi himself.

The Duke cherished his reputation as a hard bargainer and a reluctant lender. He spread tales of his close-fistedness to counteract the impression of weakness created by his open-handedness towards the thousands of Marranos he resettled in Galilee near Tiberias. Yet Pietro found the Duke accommodating, perhaps because he valued good relations with Francesco of Tuscany, the richest banker in Europe.

While Orient and Occident teetered on the knife-edge of greater war in April and May of the year 1571, Pietro Buonaventura prospered through his ties with the Duke of Naxos and the Cyclades. Despite his inbred anti-Semitism, he grew fond of Joseph Nasi, who apparently returned his affection. He had finally found in the older man the father he could respect: Joseph Nasi aroused awe, which Pietro had never felt for any human being. His greed as robust as ever, the Florentine exploited the friendship, telling himself that Nasi was also exploiting him.

Yet Pietro Buonaventura suggested to Marco Capello in their private code that the State Inquisition should contribute five thousand ducats to the Duke's project aimed at creating a new homeland for his persecuted people. Pietro even donated a hundred ducats of his own. He also promised that Venetian fishermen would teach their skills to the settlers in the Holy Land when peace came. He further undertook to recruit Florentine masters of wool and Luccan masters of silk. He was manoeuvring not only to consolidate the Duke's favour, but to give the Duke reason to prefer peace.

In the warehouses of Florence and Ravenna, Pietro built up an enviable stock of spices, which had quadrupled in value as soon as they touched Italy. He also built up staggering debts in Istanbul when the trade goods he ordered with his profits were slow in arriving. Marco Capello, who did not want his agent imprisoned for debt, found a solution.

Ottoman nobles coveted Murano glass for their palaces: chandeliers, mirrors, dishes, goblets, and vases. But the remaining Venetian merchants in Istanbul, virtual prisoners in their own houses, could not meet that demand. Anyone who could slip quantities of Murano glass through the Venetian and Turkish embargoes would make himself very wealthy at a stroke.

Bypassing the Venetian embargo for the benefit of Venice, Marco shipped seven tons of glass, well packed in straw inside enormous baskets, on the Tuscan ship *San Moisé*. The manifest prepared by the master forgers of the Secret Service showed that the glass had been shipped two years earlier to a concern in Lucca that soon went bankrupt. Reclaimed by creditors, it was now offered for sale in Istanbul, clearly no longer Venetian, but Tuscan, glass.

On the evening of the 11th of June, 1571, the *San Moisé* put into Istanbul a week late, having been delayed by storms near Crete. Her rigging was tattered, and her sails were patchwork. But an anxious examination of eight baskets in the top tier of the hold proved that her cargo was intact.

Pietro was ecstatic. All his fantasies were coming true at once.

He could sell every piece in the morning – at prices inflated by scarcity. He had already collected deposits on most of the cargo.

He could now repay the money he had borrowed and the exorbitant interest. He could also give the Duke a princely present. And he could pay the customs officials the substantial bribes he had promised to have them endorse the legal fiction that the glass was Tuscan, not Venetian. He could, further, donate five hundred ducats to the settlement at Tiberias – to please himself, he realised with surprise, as well as the Duke.

Despite those outlays, he would by tomorrow's glorious close be liberally endowed for life. Moreover, the demonstration of his commercial prowess and his goodwill, as well as the show of Venetian amiability, should further incline the Duke towards peace.

EVENING: JULY 12, 1571
ISTANBUL: THE BELVEDERE PALACE

In the early evening of that day of enormous promise, Pietro Buonaventura entered the Belvedere sadly, his tread funereally slow. His world had collapsed between six in the morning and two in the afternoon, when all Istanbul retired for the siesta. Sure of his welcome at the Belvedere, he was sure of nothing else.

The first five baskets from the top tier of the hold had been eagerly received by their consignees, their contents displayed with pride on the dock.

'Ever seen such beautiful colours and shapes?' the happy customers asked. 'Even if they are infidels, the glassblowers of Murano are true artists.'

The purchasers of the next five baskets happily took them home, as instructed. They kept their wives locked up in harems, but obeyed their wives in household matters. The ladies wanted the pleasure of seeing the baskets of wonderful glass opened.

Four customers returned within an hour and a half. Their wives' keen eyes had found hairline cracks in articles ranging from perfume bottles to ring-holders. His stomach a cold pit, Pietro recognised the Xs he had scrawled on two of those baskets when he examined them in the poor light of the hold the night before. He felt the earth shift under his feet as basket after basket yielded cracked or broken glass. The storms that delayed the *San Moisé* had defeated the skill of the packers.

Pietro faced not only great debts, but angry customers demanding their deposits back and the murderous glares of customs officers deprived of their bribes. In desperation, fearing for his life, he turned to the only man in Istanbul who was truly his friend, the one man he respected, almost loved.

The Duke of Naxos and the Cyclades received Pietro in an ante-room. His stance was rigid, and his blue eyes were icy. For the first time in his twenty-seven years, Pietro Buonaventura despaired, his last hope crushed.

'You lied to me. From the beginning, you lied,' the Duke asserted. 'Didn't you?'

'Lied, Your Grace?' Pietro protested. 'How lied?'

'You lied about Venetian intentions. Venice has no intention of making peace, not on any terms.'

'How could I lie about Venetian intentions, Your Grace? I have no idea of Venice's intentions!'

'True enough! You're a dupe as well as a villain. But you led me to believe Venice wanted peace.'

'And does she not, Your Grace?' Pietro tried to evade the accusation.

'By God, no!'

'But how? What . . . what've you learned?'

The Duke ignored the question and charged: 'You also lied about your prospects. Francesco of Tuscany hates you, and you are penniless. My loans to you are water . . . pissed away like bad wine.'

'Your Grace, I . . .'

'Do not interrupt or I'll have you whipped till your back is raw, red meat. If you're lucky, I'll only have you whipped. Worst of all, you misled me about Galilee. None of you disgusting Christians has the slightest intention of helping Jews, Marranos, swine as you call us, to build again the kingdoms of Judea and Israel! I was a fool to believe even for an instant.'

'Your Grace, I swear . . .'

'You swear, *you*! Do not perjure yourself further. Just leave! Get out! If you're still here after two minutes, I *will* give you to the executioner.'

The older man clasped his hands together to keep from striking the younger.

'I loved you once,' he said. 'Loved you like a son. Get out now! Get out before I . . .'

Pietro Buonaventura crept out of the white marble palace in abject humiliation. He had often been scorned and had sometimes been beaten, but he had never felt himself broken, as he did now. He had, he realised, loved the stern Jewish nobleman as he had never loved his own father or any other human being.

Now he loved no one, not even himself. But he would save his life – for what it was worth.

The *San Moisé* was sailing at ten that evening. Determined to escape the storm brewing over his cargo, the captain had bribed the port officials liberally. As soon as they completed the laborious documentation, he was to be allowed to leave, providing he took his cargo with him. Pietro knew that he himself would, somehow, be aboard.

Love had turned to hatred before he saw the gilded spearhead atop the front gates of the Belvedere. The grounds were deserted, for the Duke had ordered that no one should bid farewell to the Christian he had trusted and loved. Pietro's dragging feet took him almost against his will towards the small synagogue beside the wall.

The cypress-wood door was open. The interior was dark except for the single candle that burned in a rose-red glass bowl before the gilt tabernacle that housed the Torah, the Sacred Scroll of the Law. Pietro now knew what he had come to do, and he was for an instant appalled.

Nonetheless, he moved remorselessly towards his goal. He had come to avenge himself on the man who had rejected him – and he would have his revenge. With caustic self-contempt, he told himself he would also profit from his revenge.

He would need a nest egg when he returned to Florence in disgrace, for both Francesco de' Medici and Marco Capello would turn against him, perhaps Bianca, too. But he would not be dependent on any of them. He might, in fact, never return to Florence.

He opened the fretwork doors of the tabernacle. He slipped the green-velvet case off the Torah, feeling the diamonds and rubies rough against his fingertips. He wiped his sweating face with his sleeve and rubbed his wet palms on his doublet. In the light of the single candle in the ruby bowl his face was scarlet, and his lips were drawn back from his teeth.

Hating his own actions, he slid his dagger from its sheath. The edge sliced the scroll, vertically first and then horizontally. He heard a horrified gasp behind him, and someone wrenched at his arm.

Instinctively, Pietro turned, his dagger thrust forward. Instinctively, he buried the blade in the belly of the lean man in the long kaftan and jerked it upward.

Beyond feeling, he wiped the blade on the man's kaftan and slid the dagger into its sheath. Since no one could survive that stroke without immediate medical attention, this man would die. He was Hillel of Damascus, the physician of the Duke of Naxos.

Pietro thrust the Torah case under his doublet and left the synagogue. He carefully drew the door shut behind him.

All his life Pietro was to remember in fearful detail every moment of the next hours. He wanted to forget, but his punishment was to be unable to forget.

He remembered slipping over the wall into an alley and creeping stealthily through the back alleys of the midnight city to the harbour, expecting every moment to be seized. Not only the police and the street thugs would be after him, but, also, the Duke's men-at-arms, his own creditors, the customers he had mulcted of deposits, and, finally, the infuriated customs officers balked of their promised bribes.

The irony was bitter. This once he had striven to be honest, reasonably if not perfectly honest. Yet he had, quite inadvertently, cheated on a grander scale than ever before – bringing the fury of an entire city upon his head.

He was always to remember the exact shape of the driftwood log he found on the beach, its every knot and hole. He was to remember as clearly his long wait for the *San Moisé* in the tepid water, which stank of urine and rotten fish. He was to remember, too, the barnacles on the trailing anchor line of the slow-moving ship, which cut his palms to shreds as he climbed. He was to remember, as if he saw a painting before him, the astonishment on the face of the captain when he clambered, soaked and bleeding, onto the lantern-lit deck. Finally, he was to remember the captain's resigned shrug.

That gesture said everything: *Yes, you can stay aboard, hidden at first. We're victims together, victims of fate and fugitives from the Turks.*

Pietro heard the clanking of broken glass in the hold each time the ship rolled. That funereal clanking was a dirge for all his hopes.

On the third day, the *San Moisé* passed close to Crete. The lookout spied a war-galley with the big white cross of the Knights of St John on its crimson sail. The knight who came aboard was grateful for all they could tell him of İstanbul, which he called Constantinople.

'Why such haste?' Pietro asked, again dressed like a gentleman from the captain's wardrobe. 'Stay and drink a bottle of wine with me.'

'Of course! You don't know!' the knight exclaimed. 'The Christian League was proclaimed in St Peter's by the Holy Father, Pope Pius, three weeks ago. Our galleys are joining the fleets of Venice and Spain to attack the Turks. I cannot tarry.'

Pietro Buonaventura then knew the treachery with which Joseph Nasi, Duke of Naxos and the Cyclades, had charged him. He had, he realised, been thoroughly duped by Marco Capello, ordered to seek peace when Venice was already bent on war.

CHAPTER XVI

GREY boulders stood sentinel on the Greek shore to the north. The shelving beaches of the Peloponnesus lay out of sight to the south. Before the war-galley's bow a bluff headland reared.

On the hillsides, gnarled trees stooped under the weight of the hard green olives the peasants had left unharvested to flee the fighting. When the morning breeze ruffled the boughs, the leaves flashed silver against the hard blue sky. Rippled by the breeze, the narrow gulf glinted in the dawn sunlight.

'Perfect fighting weather!' Marco Capello observed to the bald helmsman of the *Galley of the Angels*. 'Galley weather, thank God. But the oarsmen can enjoy their holiday a little longer.'

'Give 'em a lot o' rest!' The helmsman advised his captain as to an equal. 'They'll be gasping their hearts out . . . sweating blood tonight – them that live to see the sun go down.'

Marco was suddenly aware of the stench of sweat and urine rising from the half-naked men on the rowing benches. He did not normally allow himself to think of the two hundred rowers as men who could sweat and bleed and die, but only as the power that moved his lean galley. Detached in order to command, he no more smelled them than he did the smoke of the cookfire or the stagnant water in the bilges. As much as the salt tang in the wind, such stenches were part of life at sea, a way of life unchanged for tens of centuries. But all his senses were preternaturally keen this morning.

North to the hills and south as far as he could see, the morning glinted ruby, gold, and silver. The armadas' banners and sails shone crimson; the gold-leaf on the warships' figureheads and their giant stern lanterns gleamed yellow. As dawn moved slowly westward over more than three hundred ships of the Christian and Moslem fleets, the men-at-arms' breastplates and helmets flashed a brighter silver than the olive leaves.

Darius, Emperor of the Medes and the Persians, had sailed from the port now called Constantinople or Istanbul in the four hundred and eightieth year before the birth of Jesus Christ with the greatest fleet ever seen to meet the Athenian galleys at Salamis. More than two thousand years had passed, and now two such vast armadas again confronted each other in the Gulf of Patras hardly a hundred miles from Salamis.

The Turkish force was even larger than the hundred and sixty-two warships of the Christian League, which united Venice, the Papacy, Spain, and the Knights of St John. The multitudes of Asia were once again pitted against the elite of Europe this seventh day of October in the year of Our Lord 1571. After the most heartfelt mass of their lives, the champions of Christendom were challenging the unbelievers this Sunday morning.

The Christian League had given supreme command to Don John of Austria, the bastard son of the former Emperor Charles V. Since Don John was the half-brother of Philip II of Spain, the Pope hoped his appointment would help keep that mercurial monarch from leaving the alliance. The vital interests of the Spanish Empire lay in the western Mediterranean around the Balearic Islands, Tripoli, and Gibraltar. The vital interests of the Venetian Empire lay in the eastern Mediterranean around Greece and Asia Minor.

The reports of the best espionage service in the world had stressed, almost monotonously, the desperate position in which the Serene Republic found herself. Not only her Empire was threatened, but Venice herself. Even the Republic's control of her home waters, the Adriatic Sea, was disputed by Moslem warships and pirates. Turkish armies were attacking her colonies in Dalmatia on the eastern shore of the Adriatic, as well as her more distant colonies in the Greek Islands, which were the foundation of her commercial and military power.

The walled city of Famagusta, the last Venetian stronghold on the island of Cyprus, had fallen to the Turks a month earlier. Every fighting man of the fleet knew that the Venetian commander had been promised an honourable withdrawal if he surrendered the remnants of the starving garrison that had withstood the Turkish siege for ten months. Yet he had been paraded through the sacked city naked and confined in a cage. While the Turkish general licked his lips, the Venetian's skin had been slowly peeled from his living body until, at last, he died when he was from the waist down only raw and bloody flesh.

The Venetians also knew that, after a glorious life of nine centuries, the very existence of the Serene Republic lay in the balance. If the Turkish armada were victorious, Venice would be defenceless.

After the Christian armada put forth from Sicily at the end of September, the High Admiral Don John of Austria had moved with dispatch and courage. Almost as if he were a Venetian himself, he had pursued the Turks to their stronghold at Lepanto on the northern shore of the Gulf of Patras.

Then came a lull. Only glancing contact had been made with the enemy. Turkish scouting galleys had turned their sterns when challenged, though some inconclusive engagements had been fought between isolated galleys. But there had been no mass test of will and power.

The High Admiral now tensely awaited the Turkish response to his challenge. If he attempted to mount a protracted blockade, he knew, his mixed fleet would splinter of its own internal stresses. If he attacked the enemy armada where it lay under the protection of heavy cannon in stone fortresses, great losses were certain and a humiliating defeat was likely. If the Turks did not come out and fight, there would be no glory – and the mortal threat to Venice would remain,.

'A ducat the Moslem swine don't come out in the next hour,' Paolo Crespelle, chief officer of the *Galley of the Angels*, taunted his captain. 'Even money.'

'Make it two to one,' Marco Capello laughed. 'They're still inside. Inertia's in your favour.'

'Even money,' replied the chief officer. 'You won't catch me with your Venetian tricks. Inertia's not in it. Either they come out or they don't.'

'You know damned well odds are they *won't* come out,' Marco laughed again, fighting the tension that gripped him. 'Much better for them to wait for the Grand Fleet to break up of its own squabbling. Just like last year: Spain against the Papacy – and both against Venice. But I've got a feeling . . . All right, even money.'

'My mother taught me to beware of generous Venetians.'

Paolo thought again of the warship that flew the long red-and-gold pennant of Vice Admiral Sebastiano Venier, the Venetian second-in-command of the Grand Fleet of the Christian League. When the *Angels* parted from the main body to sail north with her flotilla, two sticklike figures had hung from the mast of Venier's ship, their feet brushing the great cross on the bellying sail. The Vice-Admiral had hanged two Spanish officers for forcing a duel that divided his mixed ship's company. In retaliation, Don John of Austria now refused to communicate directly with his deputy, who was his senior by almost half a century.

'Also beware of Tuscans laying bets,' the bald helmsman interjected. 'But, mostly, watch out for Spaniards picking a fight.'

Marco Capello was almost alone among Venetian captains in encouraging his crew to speak their minds. Not only Paolo Crespelle, his lieutenant for years and his closest friend, could speak his mind, but even the boatswain at the helm. Open give and take between officers and crew, he believed, made for a happier – and a more lethal – warship.

He believed in practising even at sea the rough equality among her citizens that allowed Venice to be ruled by elected Doges, rather than by hereditary princes. He believed as strongly in the checks and balances that kept any individual or group from becoming dictatorial. He also believed passionately that the hereditary rulers of the Republic, the nobility, were uniquely wise when sitting together in council, if not always individually.

Marco Capello stood on the platform in the prow above the bronze ram. Head thrown back, he sniffed the salt breeze. His face, reddened by sun and wind, was shadowed by his helmet's visor. He looked competent, Paolo Crespelle reflected, not heroic, despite his crest of three ostrich feathers, a silver between two blue, his gleaming breastplate, and the black tights that moulded his muscled legs. Just five foot eleven, tall for a seaman in an age of low 'tweendecks, he looked coolly businesslike.

He should, at the least, have been commanding a squadron of five galleys, for he was more than qualified by experience and seniority. But he still commanded only the *Angels*. The Admiralty had a long memory for his reputed cowardice in these waters five years ago. Marco was, therefore, determined to prove himself again today.

Paolo Crespelle gazed at the bleak headland before them, willing the Turks to come out and fight. He lifted his orange-crested helmet and wiped his face with a silk kerchief. His back to the red cross on the white sail that alternately bellied and sagged in the fitful breeze, he used the gleaming steel helmet as a mirror to observe the ship and her crew.

Paolo saw the drummer poised to give the beat to the oarsmen who now lounged on their rough benches. Aboard the *Angels* no overseer normally lashed the oarsmen with a bullwhip. And neither sailor nor oarsman had been flogged in punishment for three months, a record in the fleet.

Most vessels under sail alone, their long sweeps cocked high in the air, the armada bore eastward. The half-moon formation, all fighting ships, extended more than five miles across the placid sea. The High Admiral, Don John, had sent to the rear both the supply ships and the slab-sided floating fortresses called galleons. Although a galleon measured more than three hundred and fifty feet and mounted more than a hundred cannon, they were clumsy and slow, depending on sails alone to manoeuvre.

Since the Battle of Salamis, every captain sought to lay his ship alongside his enemy so that his men-at-arms could board her. Lacking oars, galleons could not catch the agile galleys, and only an idiot galley captain would be enticed within range of their heavy cannon.

Although he distrusted the untried galleons, Don John of Austria, just twenty-seven, was a young – and an innovative – admiral. He was enthusiastic about the equally untried galleasses lately produced by the Great Arsenal of Venice. Heavily built to carry seventy heavy cannon, galleasses were slower than galleys. But they used oars for manoeuvrability in battle. If the galleasses were effective today, naval warfare would be radically altered – for the first time since Salamis.

The destructive power of the galleasses' cannon would be pitted against the galleys' well-proved rams, as well as the muskets, crossbows, swords, and pikes of their men-at-arms. The lean galleys did carry cannon, normally five in the prow and, sometimes, five at the stern. But galleys, lightly built for speed, could carry only light cannon. Their true strength was their speed and their agility. They could turn in less than two of their own lengths and make twelve knots in bursts, water creaming white along their sleek sides.

Paolo saw that Marco was warily studying *Queen of the Seas*, the galleass the *Angels* had been ordered to escort. The *Queen*'s oarsmen were already stroking hard to keep pace with the galleys on either side, which ghosted under sail in the light airs. The *Queen*'s high poop and forecastle made her hard to steer, even in the calm sea that allowed her to open her gunboats. Paolo shuddered. The weight of metal those green-bronze cannon threw could crush a galley's hull – and sweep all her crewman off her deck.

Marco Capello grinned, his teeth white against his weathered face, and asked lightly: '*That* is the new queen of battle, the mistress of the seas? Without us to keep off enemy galleys, she's just a big, fat target. Our day's not over yet.'

'Sail ho!' The cry fell from the lookout's basket high on the mainmast. 'Enemy in sight!'

Rising behind the headland, a rocket soared into the implacable blue sky and erupted into orange fireballs that momentarily rivalled the molten red sun. Far to the south, a dozen rockets responded, and a cannon fired thrice. A distant bugle shrilled, and a hundred bugles answered. Their soprano shriek tore at the Christian seamen's nerves like talons.

High-pitched drums throbbed. Out of sight Paolo counted twenty-four a minute, an extraordinary demand on the oarsmen. Ten galleys raced from the shadow of the headland, their long sweeps flashing silver, their multicoloured pennants fluttering. At their mastheads green banners bearing silver crescents streamed in the wind of their passage.

Long black whips writhed like snakes in the limpid air, lashing the slaves and prisoners on the rowing benches. Turkish galleys carried twice as many oarsmen as they needed, not to rest the weary, but to replenish constant deaths. Remembering the whiplash burning like liquid fire across his bare shoulders, Paolo shuddered. A Moslem victory today would be catastrophic for Western civilisation. This armada was the vanguard of the Turkish tide that had already covered not only Asia Minor, but also North Africa and Eastern Europe from the Balkans to Vienna.

Ten more galleys appeared, banners streaming and bugles shrieking. Then ten more, twenty more. The drums pounded louder and louder, frantically insistent. Horns and trumpets screamed in crescendo, furious and threatening.

Above the din, rose the bass chant: '*La llaha illa llah! Wa Mohammed rasul ullah!* . . . There is no god but Allah! And Mohammad is His prophet!' Half-prayer and half-war cry, that chant Paolo knew well from his captivity, as he knew the shriek of hate that followed: 'Kill the Christian curs! Kill! Kill the unbelievers!'

One moment, the sea was empty except for a score or so of Turkish galleys pulling out from the headland in the north. The next moment, the horizon was blanketed by enemy galleys, stretching south in a great crescent to the limit of sight.

*　　*　　*

The jubilation of horns and the exulting of zithers were no longer as sweet as they had been half an hour earlier in the ears of Ali Pasha, Grand Admiral of All the Seas in the service of Sultan Selim II, Emperor of the Turks, King of Kings, the Shadow of Allah. The Grand Admiral was distracted by the rumbling of heavy guns and the blaring of Venetian trumpets across five miles of open water to the north.

His lookouts could see a great distance from the tall masts of his flagship, the *Sultana*, the largest vessel in the two armadas fighting for mastery of the Great Inland Sea. He awaited their reports with anxiety. He had promised his master the Sultan that he would by the year's end drive the infidels from the Inland Sea by capturing their bases and destroying their fleets. The lookouts' shouted reports to the deck a hundred and ten feet below were disturbing.

Ali Pasha nervously stroked the full grey beard that made him look like a kindly old uncle. His soft brown eyes and plump cheeks enhanced that likeness.

He was gentle towards his family and his officers, nothing like the Christians' image of a Turkish nobleman as a tyrant who beat his many wives and treated his subordinates cruelly. He adored and was a little afraid of his chief wife, who in turn loved his two junior wives, and he had to restrain his inclination to treat his junior officers like younger brothers.

The Grand Admiral was a kindly old gentleman. He was also a fierce warrior. He hated the Christians for their threat to the integrity of the Sultan's domains and the lives of the Sultan's subjects.

Today he could not allow his hand to tremble or his eyes to lose their confident lustre. He could not let his staff sense that he was shaken by the opening moves in the critical contest played with warships as pieces on the great chessboard of the Gulf of Patras. He could not allow himself even a fleeting frown. Nor could he peremptorily silence the musicians who squatted on silken cushions as if playing for the Sultan and his ladies in the harem on the Golden Horn overlooking the Bosphorus.

Those narrow straits were secure because both shores were held by the Great Ottoman Dynasty. The Gulf of Patras and its naval bases should have lain just as securely in Ottoman hands. But infidels now challenged the Imperial suzerainty. At twenty minutes to nine this warm October morning, the initial skirmishes were not reassuring.

Ali Pasha smoothed the embroidered robe that covered his body armour. His officers would put down the slight tremor of his hands to his age, rather than to his fears, for he was almost seventy. Too old to climb the mast and see the opening manoeuvres for himself, he awaited reports standing under the silk canopy that kept off the sun. He had sent aloft an intelligent staff captain of twenty-seven.

'Excellency, I beg to report.'

Telsouk Ahmed stood before the Grand Admiral flushed with excitement. His eyes glittered, but his voice was firm.

'Excellency,' he said when the Admiral nodded. 'The engagement to the north is still inconclusive. At the beginning it appeared we had won. The tide then turned. It may be turning again, but I cannot be certain.'

'Details, man?' the Admiral prompted. 'Speak out.'

'The enemy galleys broke before our first attack, and the galleasses could not hit our galleys. Our fear . . . ah . . . caution about their broadsides appeared excessive. Heavy-gunned they are, but clumsy. You'll recall, sir, signals from the northern flotilla reporting the enemy admiral Barbarigo slain. And, five minutes later, his second-in-command, as well. It seemed conclusive. But the heavy cannonading we've heard, the screeching of Venetian trumpets – and no further signals from our fleet . . .'

'You saw no more? What *were* you doing up the mast so long? Day-dreaming?'

'It *is* some distance, sir. And the powder smoke obscures the action. If only we had a device to see from far off . . .'

'As soon a magic carpet, Captain!' The Grand Admiral was testy despite the need to maintain a calm demeanour. 'What do you *think* is happening?'

'I hesitate to say, sir. But I fear that in the north . . .'

A rasping voice with an Egyptian accent shouted from the lookout's basket: 'Signal from the southern fleet coming in: *Rear-Admiral Uluch Ali reports to Grand Admiral Ali Pasha* . . .'

The Grand Admiral waited, his half-smile confident. His southern flotilla, which was commanded by his most experienced rear-admiral, had earlier reported that it outnumbered the enemy's southern flotilla by half again, more than ninety Moslem vessels to sixty Christians. Further, the flag of the Spanish King Philip's favourite admiral, Gian Andrea Doria, had been sighted. Ali Pasha had benefited from Doria's timidity in the past. Yet, his calm dissolved when forty-five seconds passed with no further report.

'Damn you, report!' he exploded. 'Report now!'

'Signals're hard to read, sir. Cannon fire's commenced and manoeuvring's rapid,' the Egyptian voice responded. 'Here it is, Admiral. Flags read: *Fatimah, Aleppo, Baghdad, Bosphorus, Medina, Jedda, India.*'

'Enemy in flight,' Telsouk Ahmed interpreted the message. 'I am in pursuit. Request permission to deviate from plan and break enemy line so as to take him in the rear.'

'Make *Hegira*,' the Grand Admiral ordered. 'Permission granted.'

He gestured to his personal slave, a stick-thin Nubian, to bring his water-pipe, and directed: 'Go aloft again, Ahmed. I want to see this action unfold north and south, particularly south, with your young eyes. It's now unfolding just as I planned.'

Ali Pasha seated himself with conscious dignity on the sofa under the silken sun-canopy. He sucked hungrily on the amber mouthpiece of his pipe, and the water in the clear bowl burbled. The sound mingled congenially with the cheerful old song the horns and zithers were playing to the martial beat of a muted drum: 'Saladin Conquers Jerusalem'. The music was again sweet in the ears of the Grand Admiral.

LATE MORNING: OCTOBER 7, 1571
THE GULF OF PATRAS OFF LEPANTO

Visibility was bad aboard the *Galley of the Angels*, which lay alongside the battered flagship of the Christians' northern flotilla. Blood streamed from the flagship's scuppers as her captain gave his orders. He had begun the battle as the senior flag captain of the flotilla. The death of Rear-Admiral Augustino Barbarigo, followed closely by the death of his deputy, had now given the flag captain overall command by default.

After the first onslaught by the galleys flying the silver crescent, Marco Capello had depended primarily on his hearing to follow the battle's course amid the billows of powder smoke. The Venetian galleasses had fired wildly, missing their targets. The *Angels* had charged into the cannons' smoke like a blind bull. Emerging from the smoke, the long bronze ram had struck a Turkish galley amidships, splitting her hull and sending her to the bottom. A great stroke, but a lucky one.

Whether by chance again or by Divine Providence, as Marco believed, the tide of battle had then turned. Somehow, he had known in his bones that the Christians were winning.

Squinting against the stinging black powder fumes, he had been struck again by the stench from the half-decked hold where the oarsmen sweated. Gasping and half-blinded by the smoke, he had conned his ship largely by instinct. Then, guided by reports from Paolo Crespelle, relayed by a string of ship's boys from the foredeck a hundred and ninety feet away, he had given his orders to the helmsman and the overseer of the oarsmen.

The *Galley of the Angels* had twice evaded death blows. Marco himself, warned either by the reek of the scent the Moslems used so freely or by a shift in the light wind, had sensed a hostile presence off the stern. Responding to his orders like a machine, helm and sweeps had spun the *Angels* around in her own length. Instead of her vulnerable stern, the Turkish galley had confronted a powerful ram – and a death rain of arrows, crossbow bolts, and musket slugs.

As the first assailant sheered off, Paolo had reported urgently from the half-visible prow. Glimpsed through a rift in the smoke, two Turkish galleys were aiming their rams at the *Angels*. For the first time, the Venetian overseers' whips curled in the air to lash the oarsmen's bare backs. Their stroke rose to a muscle-tearing twenty-six to the minute, which they maintained for more than thirty seconds. Amid the din of guns, bugles, drums, and screams, the stench of their sweat and their blood filled their captain's nostrils. But the *Angels* sprinted towards the gap between her assailants at thirteen knots.

The chief officer had aimed his prow cannon at the Turk on the left. Beyond question Providence directed the flight of the shot and brought down the Turk's mast. In falling, the heavy timber shattered the Turk's starboard bank of oars and left her fluttering in circles like a pheasant with a broken wing. At the same time, the *Angel's* archers, crossbowmen, and musketeers aimed at the Turk on the right. The rain of missiles checked that enemy galley for a few seconds, just time enough for the *Angels* to slip between her enemies.

Both captain and chief officer were eager to strike at the enemy – and to take the spoils from captured ships. But Marco dourly obeyed his instructions to protect the clumsy galleass, *Queen of the Seas*. Before the battle began, Rear-Admiral Agostino Barbarigo had told him sternly that he was to beat off attacks on the *Queen*, and *not* to go off and attack on his own.

When the rear-admiral's galley drew away, Marco had sworn at the injustice of fate. Why, he had demanded of the mute sky, was the *Angels* forced to nursemaid the galleass? The big, graceless vessel was useless in battle. She was not a weapon, but a burden.

The Turks had obviously shared his view. Although the freshening wind was clearing the powder smoke, they had ignored the line of three galleasses. Massed to strike the Christian galleys a single mortal blow, their war drums demanding twenty-four strokes a minute, the Turkish warships had passed contemptuously close to the galleasses. The guns of all three battleships had then spoken at the same moment, more than two hundred heavy cannon thundering.

When the wind whipped aside the pall of black-powder smoke emitted by those broadsides, the scene had altered magically. Thirty galleys had been rowing hard, their green battle-flags streaming behind them, water foaming white along their sides. Seconds later, the Turkish formation had disintegrated into a broken rabble. Some galleys were already sinking; others lay unmoving among the whitecaps while fire licked their wooden flanks.

Suddenly there was silence. No longer the war-drums, but shrieks of despair. No longer the war cry: 'No god but Allah, and Mohammed His prophet!' The bass chant had fallen, receded, and expired.

The acting rear-admiral had then ordered the *Galley of the Angels* south to report the Turkish rout to High Admiral Don John of Austria and Vice-Admiral Sebastiano Venier of Venice. The galleasses would follow at their own slow pace, escorted by other galleys. Marco's anger at being cut out of the spoils was allayed by being given command as acting commodore of the ten galleys detailed to reinforce the critical centre of the Christian armada. At last, he had a squadron again.

The northern flotilla could well spare those warships. Those Turks who could were beaching their battered ships and fleeing on foot towards their fortified base. Some Christians were pursuing them on foot; other Christians were looting the abandoned ships.

Trimming its cross-emblazoned sails to the rising wind, the squadron sailed southward. All hearts were buoyed by victory, but many brains were disconsolately calculating the loss of booty. The galleys sailed briskly towards the main fleets, where the battle would be won or lost – and the mastery of the Mediterranean would be decided.

* * *

Grand Admiral Ali Pasha was elated by the reports from the south. Rear-Admiral Uluch Ali had destroyed ten galleys manned by the Knights of St John and captured their flagship. Flying their tattered red battle-flag, with its bold white cross, beneath his own pennant, he was pursuing the remnants of the Christian southern fleet under Gian Andrea Doria, the timid admiral of King Philip of Spain.

Grand Admiral Ali Pasha was pained, but not dismayed, by the destruction of his northern flotilla. It was his smallest unit, and he had never hesitated to sacrifice a knight to take a queen. Besides, he had no time to mourn his losses.

He was fighting for his homeland and for his family – to keep them safe from pillage, arson, rape, and murder by the barbarians who worshipped the minor prophet Jesus Christ as a god. The decisive engagement in the centre had already begun, and the enemy flagship *Royal* was already under attack. Peremptorily waving the musicians to silence, he pondered his next move.

'Hoist signal-flag *Messiah*,' Ali Pasha directed.

Staff Captain Telsouk Ahmed hesitated perceptibly before relaying that order. The Grand Admiral was putting himself and the armada in grave danger. The bold manoeuvre called Messiah was intended to crown a victory – or, in desperation, to salvage a defeat. Hoisting that signal would command all Turkish ships, led by the flagship *Sultana*, to converge on the Christian flagship. While performing that complex manoeuvre, they would themselves be virtually defenceless. Impelled by the Grand Admiral's soft brown gaze, the staff captain finally repeated the order to the signalmen.

The sea was already paved with ships, enemies and friends inextricably, almost indistinguishably, interlocked. Hand-to-hand fighting spilled to and fro across that unstable platform.

Hostile galleys lashed together were deaf to the din of battle as their men-at-arms fought backwards and forwards. Broadswords, scimitars, and cutlasses rose and fell, throwing silver sparks into the sun. Red pinpoints glowed: fuses to touch off the guns' black-powder charges. The popping of muskets and the barking of the galleys' light cannon were underscored by the bass coughing of the galleasses' heavy cannon.

Some men died with their features frozen in astonishment at their fate. Some died in triumph, their pikes impaling an enemy as an enemy blade slipped between their ribs. Some slipped in the blood and sea water that greased the decks – and were trampled to death. Others fell screaming in terror between hulls that were scraping against each other so hard their timbers cracked. The mailed men-at-arms tried to maintain their tight formations, but were swept piecemeal into the mêlée.

Somehow, the Turkish flagship *Sultana* pierced the entangled mass of ships to smash her high forecastle into the sterncastle of the Christian flagship *Royal*, which flew the black two-headed eagle of Austria. Marco Capello's *Galley of the Angels* barely escaped being crushed when the two towering hulls grated together. Pushing at neighbouring hulls with poles, pivoting on a sinking galley's mast, and sculling with the rear oars where the others were blocked, the seamen had sprung her loose. The captain thereupon ordered his helmsman to steer as clear to the interlocked flagships as he could.

Marco had earlier been rewarded with a quick smile from the High Admiral for his report on the victory in the north. His feet planted well apart, light cascading from the lozenges incised on his stubby broadsword, Don John of Austria had praised his Venetian allies. He had then ordered Marco's ten galleys to guard the flagship.

Like the others of her squadron, the *Angels* was virtually untouched. Hardly a plank was marred, and only one man wounded, a seaman struck in the hand by a stray arrow. Yet Marco could not appeal to his fellow Venetian, Vice-Admiral Sebastiano Venier, to detach his fresh galleys to attack on their own. Not when the Christian flagship was for the second time boarded by Ali Pasha's janissaries.

The janissaries were the elite of elites, the most formidable of the millions of warriors of the vast Ottoman Empire. They invariably mounted their ferocious attacks to the booming of kettledrums that threw out overwhelming waves of sound to stun their enemies. Most janissaries were light-skinned Christians captured as small boys or conscripted as infants – to be forced either to toil as slaves or to fight. All now devout Moslem converts, they were the Sultan's personal slaves. But they were slaves rewarded for their victories with wealth, well-born brides, and high rank.

Eerily identical in their white uniforms, four hundred screaming janissaries poured over the bulwarks of the battleship *Royal*. They looked so like good Christians the men felt as if under attack by brothers-in-arms.

Christian galleys closed on the *Sultana*, determined to divert her fury from their flagship. Interpreting his orders liberally, Marco hurled the *Angels* into that assault. He was, he told himself, counter-attacking to save the flagship, not deserting his duty to guard her.

Marco clutched a rope dangling from the *Sultana* – and was pulled off his feet when the Turkish flagship rolled. Waving his men upward, he screamed the drawn-out war cry: 'Saint Mark! Saint Mark . . . and Venice!'

For the first time, the vigorous young galley captain felt the burden of the thirty pounds of steel that were his body armour and helmet. Panting and silent, soaked with sweat, he climbed the sheer side of the *Sultana*, which towered thirty-six feet above his galley's deck. Clinging to the rope with slippery hands, he laboured upward inch by inch. He could not dodge the balks of wood, the loose blocks, and the chunks of metal hurled from the *Sultana*'s decks. Thrice he blessed the burdensome helmet that turned those missiles, though his head rang with their impact. And he blessed the unseen hand that twice saved him when he was falling.

Marco Capello boarded the enemy flagship on all fours. He clambered over the bulwarks and was immediately entangled in the nets slung to keep off boarders. He tripped and sprawled on the deck.

Exhausted, he lay still, staring at a coil of pink and grey tubes. A fecal stench filled his nostrils, and he raised his eyes to a dark face smiling benevolently under a spotless white turban. With relief he saw that the Turk lay still in death. With horror unbecoming a seasoned veteran, he saw that the Turk had been ripped open from throat to groin by a Christian blade.

Rising gingerly, Marco felt the deck rough under the thin soles of his boots. The white planks, that morning holystoned glass-smooth, had been ripped by lead slugs and cannon balls. His feet were wet inside his sodden boots, for the splintered planks were awash with a slimy pink liquid. The seawater sloshing in the scuppers glinted iridescent in the sunshine, blood coiling in terrible yet beautiful spirals on its surface.

Through his soles Marco felt continual pounding, as if hundreds of demented carpenters had chosen this moment to overhaul the *Sultana*. Turkish and Christian gunners were firing a few yards apart, ripping great swathes through each other's ships. He marvelled that any gunner was left alive to fight the gargantuan duel of cannon muzzle to muzzle. Lashed firmly together, the flagships were destroying each other.

Marco felt the vibration, but he could not hear the cannons' reports above the enveloping din. Only bugles and horns rose shrill over groans and curses, over musket shots and explosions, over the thud of falling spars, the creaking of anguished timbers, and the grating of the hulls.

Yet the overwhelming roar of the janissaries' kettledrums had ceased. Once already, the Christians had driven the Turks off the *Royal*, and then, storming the *Sultana*, had themselves been hurled back. Their second counter-assault had now silenced the kettledrums, which the janissaries never yielded short of death.

Marco Capello, feeling he had used time assessing the battle, drew his cutlass from his belt. Yet the man who had followed his frantic scramble up the ship's side, the man who had kept him from falling, was just climbing over the bulwarks. Only a few seconds had passed, he realised, seeing with surprise that the man was his chief officer, Paolo Crespelle.

'What are you doing here?' The captain shouted over the din. 'You're station's aboard the *Angels* when I lead boarders away.'

'Not this time!' Paolo shouted back. 'The second officer can keep the guns firing. There's no other danger, and you need me here. Frankly, I don't trust you out of my sight.'

Marco Capello shrugged, grinned, and sketched a mocking bow of welcome.

Only after the *Angels*' forty men-at-arms formed in a wedge did they throw themselves into the ragged battle swirling around them. Earlier engagements had proved to them that ten men in close formation were as formidable as a hundred, each fighting on his own.

For an instant that became a prolonged moment and, finally, lasted almost a full minute, the wedge wavered. Grand Admiral Ali Pasha's janissaries had retreated to their flagship under relentless attack. They now turned in fury on their new enemies, and the Venetians gave way.

The two Venetian officers battled side by side. His cutlass flying like a shuttle, Marco slashed and parried. Without turning, he felt through his skin that the will of his soldiers was failing. Their mailed wedge was cracking.

Two tall, blond janissaries hammered at him with battle-axe and scimitar. But, beside him, Paolo's heavy broadsword swept aside the battle-axe, in the same stroke slicing through the chain-mail clothing the arm that wielded it. When the janissary looked down in horror, Marco's cutlass stabbed him in the throat, which was bare just above his breastplate.

Wrenching his cutlass free of the shattered cartilage, Marco joined Paolo to attack the second janissary, who was already waxen from loss of blood. Paolo's broadsword scythed the Moslem's legs, and the scimitar dropped. Held erect for an instant by the crush around him, the dying man then crumpled to be trampled under foot.

Paolo's triumphant cry pierced the din and Marco was again astonished by his friend's primitive joy in battle. He himself exulted in the turmoil in the blood and the preternaturally sharp vision when every terrifying instant seemed a joyous hour. But Paolo was battle-mad.

Intent on their own fight, the officers were cut off from the formation. They heard the men-at-arms shouting their rallying cry: '*Angels! Angels!*' But they could not cut their way back to the wedge.

While High Admiral Don John of Austria led the defence of his own flagship, Vice-Admiral Sebastiano Venier hurled the Christian fleet at the Turkish flagship. The explosion of shells and grenades reverberated through the beleaguered *Sultana*. Acrid powder fumes swirled in the heat waves rising from the flames that licked at her decks and masts. A curtain of smoke dimmed the sunlight.

Joined by six men-at-arms, Marco and Paolo cut their way towards the sterncastle, where they would find the Turkish commander-in-chief, if he still lived. Marco swarmed up a rickety ladder, his hands hardly touching the charring rails. He peered over the edge of the deck, then hurled himself forward. Behind a screen of six janissaries, an old Turk with a full grey beard was slashing with his scimitar at a swarm of enemies. A pike thrust his green turban from his head, but the Grand Admiral was untouched.

Instinctively, Marco and Paolo flung themselves down on the blood-greased deck just before a salvo of small cannon balls shattered the mêlée. Five janissaries fell, entwined in death with four Spanish soldiers and a pair of Venetian sailors.

A ball struck the Grand Admiral square on the forehead. The old Turk died before his broken head touched the deck.

A Spanish soldier wearing an enormous bloodstained ruff drew his sea-knife. Gritting his yellow teeth, he sawed off the Grand Admiral's head and impaled it on his pike. His mouth gaping in a scream of triumph, he flourished the pike joyously. Grinning in delight, the Spaniard waved the old man's head to and fro as a priest waves an olive branch dipped in holy water over his congregation.

*　　*　　*

'Sebastiano Venier of Venice won this battle!' Marco asserted in the relative quiet of the Grand Admiral's cabin. 'Not Don John of Austria.'

'Less Venetian braggadocio, if you please!' Paolo grinned. 'True, Venier took Ali Pasha's flagship. But Don John sent the galleasses forward. And their big guns won the battle. The galleys' day is over.'

'A fluke, perhaps? We'll see. But where's the hiding-place?'

The *Angels'* six men-at-arms were stationed outside to keep all others out of the big cabin, which stretched across the *Sultana's* stern. Paolo had led him to the great cabin, swearing they would find the Grand Admiral's personal treasure there. He knew the Turks' ways from his years as a galley slave and, later, though still a slave, as sailing master of an Ottoman galleon. Three minutes later, Paolo pointed triumphantly into the cavity he had found by twitching aside the Grand Admiral's silk prayer mat and lifting a loose plank.

Marco smashed the damascened lock with the hilt of his cutlass and reverently opened the lid of the cedar chest. Inside, a vellum Koran set with semi-precious stones lay beside a worn battle-flag. Marco impatiently tossed book and flag aside – then froze in astonishment. Neatly compartmented, the chest displayed an emperor's hoard: gold coins, unset gems, gold cups, and jewellery.

'For a rainy day, no doubt!' Paolo laughed in delight. 'Or shipwreck. The Doge *will* be pleased. More loot for the public coffers.'

He reached for a necklace of blue-white diamonds with matching brooch, earrings, and bracelet. Marco watched warily, but did not interfere when his chief officer also took a handful of unset stones. He poured half into Marco's hand.

'All is to be given over to the state,' Paolo said. 'We shall turn it all over, shall we not, my captain. Aside from, say, a hundred ducats to split among the *Angels'* crew. All the rest for the state, though.'

Marco pulled gently at his left earlobe, considering the matter.

'Must we then?' he finally asked. 'Every last stone?'

Marco was incapable of hypocrisy. That trait, Paolo had often told him, was a grave handicap in the race for riches and power. And, Paolo usually added, he was also regrettably respectful of other's property for a free-booting galley captain. If more inhibited by scruples than most patricians, Marco was, however, not incapable of intelligent self-interest.

He carefully selected a necklace with rubies set between pigeon's-egg pearls, a jewelled dagger, and a tiara of sapphires and diamonds. Paolo nodded approvingly, but Marco shook his head when the mate's hand reached again into the chest.

'A fair return for our trouble,' he said. 'But the rest belongs to the state.'

'. . . which will dole out our further shares,' Paolo said silkily. 'A captain's share and a mate's share. Riches enough!'

CHAPTER XVII

GIOVEDI GROSSO, Fat Thursday, the last before Lent. All Venice was still celebrating the great victory at Lepanto, relishing the few remaining days of Carnival, when not only Mother Church, but even the State Inquisitors, briefly relaxed their vigilance. The nobility and the middle classes went masked to avoid the scandal that might follow their being recognised amid the revels. Only the plebeians showed their own faces to the world.

Commodore Marco Capello was out of tune with the jubilation of his countrymen. He twitched aside one of the blue-and-red-checked curtains that framed the windows of his apartment in Ca' Capello and gazed pensively down at the rear courtyard into which the land gate opened. The cannon balls set into the balustrade of the outside stair-case leading to the portego on the second floor alternated with gilded iron tracery that had, only a few months earlier, framed the great stern lanterns of Turkish war galleys.

Smiling wryly at that private monument his father had built to the glory of Lepanto, Marco pondered the battle's effect on his life and the life of Venice. He had himself been triumphantly vindicated, his acting rank of commodore confirmed by Vice-Admiral Sebastiano Venier after the battle. He had also become rich from the state's division of the spoils of victory, as well as from the loot he had taken privately. And the Republic? Her people were still dancing in the streets, drunk with second-hand glory. The immediate threat of Turkish domination had been quashed, and Venetian prowess was celebrated throughout Christendom. But, he wondered, how much had really changed?

Mechanically, he picked up the letter he had written shortly after returning from the battle. He held the draft in plain language, not the ciphered version he had sent to his cousin Bianca Capello Buonaventura in Florence.

Bianca had already proved her worth, beyond the use made of her husband to deceive Joseph Nasi, Duke of Naxos, and Selim II, Sultan of the Ottomans, regarding the West's intention to fight, rather than make another humiliating peace. Above all, Bianca had successfully encouraged her lover to act the statesman.

Pressed by his brother-in-law, Francesco de' Medici, Prince Regent of Tuscany, the Emperor had smiled on the Christian League. Under the same influence, Philip of Spain had joined his fleet to the Christian armada. Unfortunately, Gian Andrea Doria had proved it was unnecessary to command him to desert his allies, as Philip had done the preceding year. He had shown himself to be not only a traitor and a coward, but a shockingly inept admiral. As for France? But who could do anything with the French, particularly when they were ruled by Catarina de' Medici, an Italian woman?

It had been vital to keep Bianca active in the service of Venice. Marco had, therefore, given her a full report of the battle to reinforce her patriotism. He had been wholly candid, even telling her of deeds he should in self-protection never have set down on paper. A little sheepish, he began to read his own words in order to recall the events they described. But he was soon reading with pride of authorship.

'Much thanks for your compliments, but it was not *my* victory. It was Venice's victory, Christendom's victory, and Admiral Sebastiano Venier's victory. The old man is justly hailed for carrying the battle to the enemy when Don John was on the defensive. He'll be the next Doge, if he lives long enough. He's taken a fancy to me for my part in the battle, and who knows what may come of that?

'When we came to count, we found we had sunk or captured a hundred and thirty-one enemy ships. And lost only thirteen of our own, almost all in Gian Andrea Doria's ill-fated southern flotilla.

'God knows how many Turks we killed and captured, at least forty thousand. Our own losses were heavy, inevitable in five and a half hours of hand-to-hand fighting. But we did not lose half that number, and we freed fifteen thousand Christian galley slaves.'

He flipped over a page devoted to details the serious-minded Bianca would relish and read: 'The *Angels* made port on the 18th of October, just eleven days after the battle. The Vice-Admiral sent us home with the news because of the *Angels'* speed and because he wished to give me the honour of announcing the victory to the Republic. Still, the fast passage knocked the stuffing out of my oarsmen.

'All Venice was still locked in fear when I arrived. It was eerie. Any moment the Senate and the people expected the Turkish armada to come over the horizon – and the city had been stripped of her defences to equip and man our fleet. Remembering the atrocities of Cyprus, the flaying and the torture, even the stoutest hearts skipped a beat.

'We sailed into the lagoon with all our banners flying, trailing the Turks' battle ensigns and their long turban-cloths in the water. Our decks were piled so high with spoils the sailors had to clamber around them to work the sails.

'Venice went mad with joy – and relief. When I stepped ashore on the Mole of St Mark, they mobbed me.

'The word ran through the city like lightning, and everyone turned out. Only paralytics and the dying remained inside. The agéd were carried on men's backs, and even newborn infants were brought out to join the revelry. Tens of thousands danced in the Piazza. They draped the Rialto Bridge, the entire Rialto quarter, with heaven-blue hangings set with golden stars.

'That night, the whole city flamed. It was brighter than day. Every building, every square, even the narrowest canals and alleys, all were lit by bonfires, torches, and candles. Hundreds of thousands of candles like starry constellations fallen to earth.

'It was the greatest victory celebration in two centuries! Wholly uninhibited. Some of the sights I saw that night filled me with amazement. Prudently, the Senate declared that all might wear masks. So everyone danced . . . and did more . . . on every corner to a hundred orchestras and ensembles.

'When I got a mask on, they finally left me alone . . . left off lionising me . . .

'Then I could see to my own affairs. After paying my respects to my mother and father, the first thing was the tiara. I had "found", may I say, a splendid sapphire-and-diamond tiara of Florentine workmanship among the effects of the Grand Admiral Ali Pasha. Naturally, I made it a present to Angela Tron. I tell you, Bianca, she is the most wonderful . . .'

Embarrassed by his impassioned praise of his lady, Marco skimmed through the next three paragraphs. He noted, nonetheless, that he had, a few months earlier when he wrote that letter, been more optimistic regarding his prospects with Angela than he was now. He also saw that he had not been as sanguine about the prospects for Venice as he might have been in the train of the great victory.

In reply, Bianca had discussed the dangers facing Venice with the acuity and foresight he now expected of her. But, womanlike, she had surprised him by devoting as much space to questions about Angela. He had, he recalled, replied in haste, but at length, shamelessly using the couriers of the Venetian Secret Service for his personal affairs. He valued Bianca's insight and her counsel greatly.

'I can't persuade Angela to set a date,' he had written aggrievedly. 'I can't even arrange to speak with her father. The time's not ripe, she says. Here I am, certified as a hero of Lepanto by the Vice-Admiral himself. And I have, thanks to the fortunes of war, now got enough put aside to ensure that we would live very well. Also great prospects in renewed trade with the East through Joseph Nasi, the old Duke of Naxos, with whom I have resumed relations. But Angela won't let me speak to her father. She's afraid the old Capello-Tron feud and the Marco Polo bitterness still . . .'

Bianca and he had exchanged a number of letters during the next few months, for there were affairs of state to discuss. Marco continued to use the Secret Service's couriers to carry letters that were in part personal. The personal note strengthened Bianca's loyalty to Venice by reinforcing her loyalty to himself, who embodied her native city for the exile. Somehow, their exchange was more like a discussion face-to-face than a correspondence, as if they could speak directly across two hundred miles.

'Marco, there is only one way to find out whether her father will have you as a son-in-law,' Bianca observed. 'Just ask old Tron to his face. As I recall, he loves money. Your new wealth should wash away old bitterness.'

'Angela won't let me,' Marco replied with resentment. 'She says it's all off if I do. She says I could spoil everything. Even that first night, my first night back, when we met in our usual place behind the church of San Fantin. Oh, she kissed me and held me, held me tight, all right.

'I was full of bonhomie and joy and relief at having survived, and, I suppose, full of wine. I just assumed it would be all right now. But she drew away and said we must still wait. When I asked why, she told me the old story. Then I asked if there were anyone else, and she laughed at me. Did I think that she would be with me on this night, above all nights, if there were anyone else?'

Anticipating the question Bianca was sure to ask, he explained: 'Paolo Crespelle, as you may know, will stop at nothing, nothing at all to get what he wants – or I want. He had Angela followed for two weeks by a small army of spies disguised as Benedictine friars, street-walkers, beggars, sweet-sellers, hooded penitents, water hawkers and a dozen other guises. No, there's no one else. There couldn't be. So why . . .'

'And she's still a virgin?' He resented Bianca's quick reply, though he knew she asked out of concern for his welfare. 'A virgin in Venice at twenty? She sounds too good, perhaps a little insipid. She's not turned towards her own sex? You're *absolutely* sure, Marco?'

He bristled at the implicit slur, then answered defensively: 'Virginity's *not* totally unknown among young patrician ladies. Yes, I'm *absolutely* sure. A man can tell . . . from experience. She'll do anything with me, anything except . . . I swear she's normal, also passionate. But a virgin, unquestionably!'

'In that case, there's only one answer.'

Despite himself, Marco resented Bianca's questions and, even more, her judgements. But she was the only woman to whom he could speak so candidly. She was also very shrewd about men and women, although her inborn impulsiveness had twisted her own life.

'Your Angela's afraid,' Bianca continued. 'She's afraid of growing up . . . of responsibility and marriage, not just afraid of making love. You *must* confront her. Do not let her wriggle out of it. Either she tells her father and lets you talk to him – or it's all over. Then you'll know.'

Marco had begun a letter of protest, but Bianca had anticipated him: 'Of course, you're afraid to lose her. And she knows it. So she plays you like a fish on a line.'

Marco Capello bundled up the correspondence and locked it in his safe. He was seeing Angela tonight, the climax of the Carnival. Would he confront her as Bianca advised? He was not sure.

Angela cocked her head quizzically, but Marco could not see her expression. He could only see her pink mask, which was strewn with gold sequins. His own voice sounded hollow inside his severe white mask with the jutting nose. Masked, they could wander unknown through a Venice that was after four months still celebrating the great victory that had restored her dominion over the seas. Yet the revellers' masks gave the city a sinister air, as if they were not human, but puppets or demons with fixed grimaces.

Angela had told her mother she was visiting a girlfriend, while her friend's mother believed her daughter was with Angela. Each could thus go where she wished – with whom she wished. Normally, young ladies were safe at home by ten in the evening. Normally, their mothers would not take such a tale on trust alone. But this was no normal night.

Jostled by the throng, Angela and Marco strolled hand in hand down the twisting streets. Twice they stopped in shadows to lift their masks and kiss fervently. But Angela refused to take a gondola. She said frankly that she feared the temptations of the dark little cabin. Instead, they came to the Piazza of St Mark's, where hundreds of stalls were lit by guttering torches.

Under enormous green-and-scarlet umbrellas were spread the goods of all the world: silk from China and caviar from the Caspian; coffee from the Indies and tobacco, that curious weed, from the Americas; pearls from Madagascar, salt herring from Holland, woollen stuffs from Flanders, and furs from Muscovy.

The plebeians were dancing across the Piazza, lapping at the café tables and then receding, like the tides of the mother sea. Waves of sound thundered like breakers as they roared the perenially popular 'The Lion of Venice': 'A hymn to St Mark and an anthem of war . . . As our warships sweep down to the sea . . . Hail Venice! Hail Saint Mark! Hail the glory of our magnificent lion!'

The spectacle of the torch-lit Piazza of St Mark's by night normally moved Marco deeply. The great square, dominated by the most beautiful cathedral in Christendom, was the heart and the symbol of the Venice he loved. But, again, this was no normal night. Irritated by Angela's coyness, he was further irritated by the need to contain his annoyance. If he questioned her, she might just walk away from him.

Instead, he said provocatively: 'Angela, it's theft, but theft on such a grand scale that it's made noble. *La Serenissima* is based on theft. Even Saint Mark was stolen from his sepulchre in Alexandria seven centuries ago,' he persisted. 'The four horses, they're spoils from the sack of Constantinople in 1203. Even the lion, our glorious lion guarding St Mark's, was taken . . .'

Angela tugged at his arm, and he stooped to hear her amid the tumult. Her voice was oddly remote through the mask: 'Marco, you can't make fun of *everything* that's made us great.'

He drew her into the quiet passage under the archway that led to the Doge's Palace, where they could talk without shouting.

'I'm just stating facts,' he replied. 'I was about to say it's *truly* a miracle. From evil deeds, criminal acts, has sprung the greatest city in the world. *La Serenissima* is unique . . . crowns human achievement. A government controlled by neither the mob nor degenerate royal dunces, but by the educated elite. What more could anyone ask?'

'Then why go on about loot and theft and evil?'

'Because, Angela, that *is* the miracle. The glory of Venice exalts the evil deeds. Venice is magic, an alchemist's stone. Not transforming base metals into gold, but base deeds into golden ends.'

'You're not going to start all that again, Marco, my dear, are you? Lecturing me on our wonderful system. I do know how Venice works.'

She was unusually testy. Still, her cutting remark proved she was not the smiling doll her mask made her look, but an intelligent and spirited woman. They laughed together and broke the tension. Then they pushed through the throngs in the Piazzetta towards St Mark's Basin, where merchantmen and galleys lay at anchor lit with coloured lanterns. In the Piazzetta, men and women of all classes were drinking wine and watching street entertainers perform by the light of torches and bonfires.

A Harlequin waving a cucumber club berated a red-lipped Columbine on the stage of a puppet theatre. A bear on a chain, eyeing his master's whip warily, capered to a tinny mandolin. A juggler kept eight yellow-and-red wine glasses whirling aloft so fast the colours melted into a fiery wheel.

As they approached the Mole, Angela shuddered and grasped Marco's arm. Its outspread hood displaying a white eyeglass pattern, a black cobra swayed in a woven-grass basket.

A dozen public gondolas normally awaited passengers at the Mole. But, this evening, only two still bobbed on ropes tied to silver-and-orange poles.

'Outsiders find Venice claustrophobic . . . locked in,' Marco observed. 'So small, and they have to choose between expensive sedan-chairs or walking everywhere.'

'Or taking an expensive gondola,' Angela laughed. 'You're trying to inveigle me into . . .'

'I am,' he admitted cheerfully. 'It'll be wonderful on the Canalazzo tonight, away from the crowd.'

'Marco, you agreed . . .' she began, but abruptly conceded: 'Very well then, but not in the cabin. We'll remain outside.'

'No one'll know us, Angela. If it gets cold, my cloak'll easily cover both of us.'

'Don't forget!' She stepped gingerly onto the strip of carpet that covered the foredeck. 'You promised . . .'

The late February night was damp, and puffs of fog drifted over the water. Open to the chill wind from the sea, St Mark's Basin was markedly cooler than the land. It was still cool when they entered the Grand Canal, which was brightly streaked by the lights of the palazzos on the banks. Although the little cabin would be warm, Angela and Marco perched on a narrow plank seat in the open.

She shivered and pressed against him. She had not objected when he drew his boat cloak around them both or when he put his arm round her shoulders. But she pulled away when he bent to kiss her.

'Gondoliers,' he reminded her, 'are blind to their passengers.'

'That's only a way of speaking, Marco,' she replied. 'Like two trees making a forest on stage. He can see as well as you or I.'

'Then come into the cabin,' he urged. 'It's warmer – and no one could see us there. Not that there'll be anything to see.'

'I hope not.'

Angela, sounding prissy even to herself, followed him inside, rather than sit alone in the prow looking foolish. But she shrank into the farthest corner, holding herself rigidly erect on the worn velvet of the little sofa.

To her surprise, Marco did not attempt to embrace her. Instead, he reached into a battered pewter bucket for a bottle of *prosecco*, and gave his attention to drawing the cork.

'It'll be on the bill, of course,' he remarked. 'But it's damned pleasant.'

'Of course,' she said meaninglessly and clinked her glass against his. 'I never knew they . . .'

Her first alarm was fading, but Angela was still on edge. She had never before been alone with a man in an enclosed room, and this doll's-house cabin was very much enclosed. She held herself aloof. But she swayed back and forth as the gondola rocked on the swells, each time almost falling into his arms.

Angela chided herself. She was on the verge of panic, and that was ridiculous. She knew Marco's reputation as a philanderer, even the three married noblewomen with whom he had been involved. But what did that have to do with her?

Those ladies had been willing, even eager, as she was not. He had sworn he was finished with casual affairs. He wanted to marry her, not merely dally with her. And he had never imposed on her, but had always awaited her signals. She would signal unmistakably that it was hands off tonight.

The dark cabin was lit only occasionally by flashes as the gondola passed through the beams of the lights on the banks. Even so, Angela relaxed, logic having dispelled panic. She sipped the wine, and enjoyed its fizzing on her tongue.

The little cabin provided a secure little world of their own. Unguarded for an instant, Angela mused aloud: 'The old wives say more girls have gone wrong in gondolas even than in bedrooms.'

'Not tonight,' he laughed. 'I'm not after your virtue, but your hand.'

Despite his casual reply, Angela was abashed at her own daring. She had not meant to be provocative, only amusing. She had merely wanted to show him that she was not the prim little girl he might think her. Just so long as he did not press her too far. The wine was making her pleasantly relaxed, and surely there was nothing to be afraid of.

The gondola struck another swell and threw her into Marco's arms. He laughed, but did not release her. She felt his lips on hers, first feather-light, then harder and more demanding.

Her arms tightened around his neck. She felt free, as if floating in the air, but wholly in control of herself. Marco shattered her mood with a few words. She wanted to feel his hands on her body, but his hands did not stray from her back. His voice was muffled, his lips pressed into her hair.

'Angela dearest, there has been more than enough time for you to speak to your father. How does it move? How much longer . . .'

'Hush, my dear,' she coaxed. 'First, kiss me again.'

He did, and she could feel his excitement. His breathing was quicker, and his arms were tense around her. She wondered how she could control him if he should now . . .

Instead, he persisted: 'I want to be able to kiss you at any time – all the time. This is no boy-and-girl flirtation, not a passing affair, only for a thrill of pleasure. It's for the rest of our lives . . . for the families also.'

His voice was urgent. Not the shallow insistence of a youth, but a mature man's deep urgency.

She felt a prickle of resentment. Why must he be so earnest? Why could he not just let them enjoy the pleasure of the moment? Within bounds, of course.

'It's not . . . not good, my darling,' she said hesitantly. 'Father wants me to marry, says I'm overdue for marriage. He's picked out his ideal son-in-law. When I mentioned your name in passing, only talking about your bravery in the victory, he ranted: "There's an example for you, a *bad* example. Any husband would be better than one of those scapegrace, radical Capellos. They want to turn the world upside down. Consorting with Jews and liberals, they're a bigger threat to the Republic than the Turks . . ."'

Her mimicry was so realistic, Marco could hear the pompous tones of Leonardo Tron himself. He sat up very straight. She felt him draw away from her in spirit, although his arm still rested lightly on her shoulders.

'So it's all pointless, is it?' he at length said. 'The battle and the booty. I've half a mind to give it all back . . . to say in the heat of battle I took more than I should. First, give back the tiara, then the rest.'

'Marco, don't . . .'

'Don't what? Don't despair or don't give back the loot?'

'Don't do either. It's not hopeless, you know. We only need to be patient.' Her soothing tone abruptly altered, and she mimicked a greedy courtesan: 'Above all, do *not* even *think* about giving back the jewellery. Especially *not* my tiara.'

In spite of his anger, Marco laughed at her raillery and asked as lightly as he could: 'Who's the lucky man?'

'The *un*lucky man is Alvise Pisani. This'll interest you. His father's that Pisani, the one who's always saying sea commerce is finished. Little Alvise parrots his father. He says land is the thing: the *terra-ferma* with farming, wine-making, and manufacturing.'

'A fool as well! Our forefathers had it right: *Forget the land and look to the sea!* But he still sounds lucky to me.'

'Marco, dearest,' she declared. 'I'll *never, never* marry little Alvise Pisani. Better the cabin of your galley, better a hut in Dalmatia, than all the Pisani villas on the mainland.'

'Of course you'd hate the ninety-room mansion the Pisanis are building on the Brenta at Stra!'

Ignoring his sarcasm, she answered: 'Not without you, my dear. Only be patient.'

Her eyes shining, Angela lifted his hand from her shoulder and placed it on her breast. Marco pulled her close, and his mouth bore down on hers. Her lips opened, and her tongue darted between his teeth, exploring and enticing.

Angela felt his hand slip between the buttons of her dress to caress the exposed upper slope of her breasts. She started, but steeled herself not to pull away. His fingers slipped under her bodice to touch her nipple with surprising delicacy.

Delicious warmth seeped through. Pulling him closer, her fears were smothered by sensations and feelings she had never before known. The strength of her responses astonished her, and she yielded to them. She abandoned herself to his embrace and the delight of his hands moving over her body.

Instinctively, she reached out to touch him. Abruptly, she snatched her hand back. She stiffened, her entire body going rigid. She shook her head as if awakening from sleep – and pushed him away.

Marco released her immediately and sat back on the sofa. Neither spoke, but the bottle clinked as he filled their glasses. Angela drew in her breath, letting the air fill her lungs till it seemed they would explode.

He did not seem greatly disturbed by her rejection. Or, at least, he was pretending not to be.

'Yes, Angela,' he finally said, 'I'll be patient.'

Embarrassed, she recalled that she had just implored him not to press her about speaking to her father. Flustered and eager to fill the pause, she said without realising that the subject could itself prove awkward: 'Marco, I've been thinking. You cannot deny things have changed from the palmy days of seafaring.'

'After the victory of Lepanto?' His voice was too level, too patient. 'Yes, things *have* changed. A new era of glory is beginning. It won't be easy, but . . .'

'That's not what they're saying in the banking houses.' She persisted in spite of herself, as if driven to force a quarrel. 'They're saying Lepanto's not being followed up . . . might just as well never have happened.'

'And what else are they saying in the counting houses, all these wise men?'

'Well, my father says we, Venice, have to get back to the old ways. The government is too liberal, too loose. The people need more discipline. Enough, he says, of dealing with foreigners, especially the pestilential Jews. Enough of mortgaging ourselves to the Jews to finance risky ventures abroad . . . to fight purposeless battles very expensively.'

'And what would he do with the Jews who're our guests?'

'Send them away, as other cities have. Let them all go to Constantinople to join their brother, the treacherous Duke of Naxos. That's what Father says.'

As usual, Marco reflected, Leonardo Tron was speaking for the worst segments of Venetian society: the decadent nobles who were afraid to fight for the Empire of the Sea, and the dregs of the common people, who wanted only to enjoy themselves in idleness while blaming others for their troubles. Both groups had turned on the inoffensive Jews in the Ghetto, charging that they were in league against Venice with their co-religionist, Joseph Nasi, and through him with the Turks.

Marco had joined his father to fight the rising tide of anti-Semitism – for the sake of Venice, not primarily for the Jews themselves. The truth was, as always, more complicated. One might even say the Duke of Naxos was in league with Venice against the Turks through Venetian Jews like the banker-chemist, Salomo Sagredo, who wrote to Nasi in their unique code on behalf of the Secret Service. Marco himself was a major player in that hidden drama.

Since he could not babble such secrets to Angela, he only asked: 'And where would he get money to defend Venice without our trade overseas, without the Jews to lend it in need?'

'Why from the land, from the *terraferma*.'

'At the price of ceaseless strife with our neighbours in Italy? War on the land, where we're always at a disadvantage?'

'He said you'd say something like that and . . .'

Horrified by her rash revelation, Angela waited in fear for Marco's response. It was a long time coming.

'So you *have* discussed me with him?' he finally said softly. 'You said you hadn't . . .'

'Not *specifically*, Marco. He was talking about the Capellos in general. The old Marco Polo feud, Capellos and Trons always at sword-point . . . Well, I may have let your name slip, just generally. Anyway, you've been pressing me to . . .'

'You *did* talk about me as a husband, then.'

She nodded sheepishly, and he pounced: 'What did he say, Angela?'

'I told you it was no use trying with him just yet. He said that I *would* marry Alvise Pisani. If I refused, I would *never* marry a Capello. Marco, it's not you personally, but . . .'

'That's a consolation! Anyway, here we are at the Rialto.'

They disembarked at the landing-stage beside the wooden bridge lined with shops. Marco tossed the gondolier a silver coin, and his generosity was rewarded with extravagant thanks.

Angela automatically turned towards the lane that twisted towards Ca' Tron on the Grand Canal. Marco would say his goodbyes now, rather than at her father's door, lest they be seen together. But he would walk a dozen steps behind her to ensure that she was not troubled by bravos or beggars on her way home.

'Angela, I *know* I can change his mind . . . force him to give consent.' He grasped her arm and offered her an ambiguous farewell. 'But you must think . . . think hard . . . about what you *really* want – me or some other nice, safe Alvise Pisani.'

CHAPTER XVIII

HER two lateen sails, cocked diagonally on the short masts of the *Galley of the Angels*, fluttered as they felt the onshore breeze. The golden image of the Archangel Michael flourishing his two-handed sword, which was her figurehead, plunged into the green Adriatic swell. The *Angels* was beating through the Porto di Lido, Venice's gateway to the world, where the Doge on Ascension Day solemnised the symbolic Marriage to the Sea.

When the galley turned south towards the Mediterranean her sails filled, and she heeled sharply. Captain (Designate) Paolo Crespelle, whom the crew called the Tuscan Wild Boar, ordered the oars brought inboard. Senior Commodore (Designate) Marco Capello jumped lightly from the poop rail, where he had been observing the squadron of eight galleys under his command. Wheeling one after another at precisely the same point like disciplined swans, the squadron sailed to join the Armada of the Christian League off Greece for the decisive battle with the Turks. It was less than a year since the great victory at Lepanto.

The crimson-and-gold banners bearing the Lion of Venice shone as bright as the gold leaf on the galleys' sterns. The morale of their crews shone as bright. The Venetian seamen *knew* that they would this time sweep Moslem naval power from the seas forever. Their commodore's confidence was shadowed by caution. He knew from the latest intelligence summaries that the Turks were stronger than they appeared and that the Christian Allies were, as usual, disunited.

Marco owed his appointment as senior commodore to his patron, Admiral Sebastiano Venier, the most powerful man in Venice. The Senate of the Sea would in its own good time confirm Marco's rank, and he would then confirm Paolo as captain of the *Angels*. Few outsiders had ever commanded Venetian galleys, though many had commanded Venetian regiments, which were considered less vital by

(214)

the seaward-looking city-empire. Since a senior commodore at sea during hostilities could appoint a captain, Paolo soon would have the permanent rank as well as the responsibility.

If only, Marco mused, his personal affairs were as promising as his career. But the signs were as mixed as the prospects for the coming battle. He still knew he would win Angela, but he also knew now how hard the fight would be.

Angela and he had not said goodbye in anger. They were too adult and too fond of each other to mar a parting that could be forever. They had felt not the heat of anger, but cold perplexity. She had been alternately warm and cool since that last Thursday of Carnival, sometimes aloof, but just as often affectionate. Perhaps he should not have been so hard after her rejection that night. Perhaps he should not have told her so sharply that she must make up her mind whether she really wanted to marry him or preferred to avoid the conflict with her family. Perhaps he had been unfair, although he was thinking chiefly of her own good.

She had told him only a week later that, after pondering deeply, she wanted him – and no other. But she did not act as if she believed it. Bianca had warned him that Angela would be cold physically until she matured and could take on the burdens of marriage. Angela had also cooled emotionally, even intellectually. Not only her body rejected him, but also her heart and her brain.

Somehow, she was no longer as ingenious at evading the vigilance of her parents. The constant feast days and civic celebrations had, as always, provided many opportunities, but she had not used them as eagerly as before. Suddenly, the young noblewoman who had blithely deceived her father said, 'I simply can't defy him any longer.'

Nonetheless, she swore she would withstand Leonardo Tron's pressure to marry Alvise Pisani, whom she despised. Better to be shut up in a convent, she said, than to be the Gentildonna Angela Tron Pisani. But she was afraid to tell her father that she would marry *only* Marco, son of the detested Capellos. Nor would she tell Marco clearly whether she had ever informed her father flatly that she wanted to marry him.

He made no attempt to force the truth from the increasingly reticent young woman. He wanted to marry her, not to quarrel with her.

There matters had stood for four months – and there they still stood until the hour before the *Galley of the Angels* sailed through the Porto di Lido to storm down the Adriatic towards Greece. Marco Capello could command nine war-galleys and their complements of more than two thousand men. He could *not* command a twenty-one-year-old Venetian maiden who said she loved him.

Last night Angela had come out, while her old nursemaid guarded the bedroom where her mother believed she lay with a headache. In the shadows of the Campo Rialto she had assured him again that she loved him dearly. But she had then thrust at him the velvet bag containing the diamond-and-sapphire tiara of Florentine work he had taken from the Turkish Grand Admiral's hoard.

'You say you love me,' he exclaimed. 'But you're giving back my gift. I don't understand.'

'It's not right,' she replied. 'I can't keep a gift like this unless I *know* I can marry you. I won't hold you to your word, not if you find someone else. So . . .'

'Find someone else in the middle of the Mediterranean? On a Turkish galley perhaps? Don't be foolish, Angela. I'm bound to you, regardless. Keep the bauble. Someday you'll wear it to a ball – proudly!'

'I hope so, Marco.' Her dark blue eyes were liquid in the torchlight, and she asked: 'What *is* to become of us, my darling?'

'If you'll let me, I can face your father,' Marco assured her. 'Suppose we eloped? He'd have to forgive us. You're no Bianca, and I'm no Buonaventura.'

'I should hope not,' she said stiffly. 'So we can't behave like them.'

'Angela, we'll work it out when I get back. It won't be long. And for God's sake keep the tiara.'

'Till then, at least.'

They had talked, going round and round, until she kissed him and said she must get back to Ca' Tron. But her casual dismissal lingered – and festered – in his mind: 'Till then, at least.'

Whatever that meant!

Angela was also sounding more and more like her reactionary father, who wanted to go back to the past. Not the recent past, but back nearly a thousand years. He wanted the Republic to turn her back on the sea, which had made her noble, wealthy, and glorious.

The clique led by Leonardo Tron refused to believe that the Turks menaced their way of life. The threat was vastly exaggerated, they said, in order to keep the Great Arsenal producing ships, guns – and profits. They also advocated spiritual and intellectual submission to the Papacy, while decrying the Christian League, which the Vatican continued to sponsor after the death of Pius V in May of this year. Yet Venice had won glory by standing against the Papacy's intolerance and dogmatism. For centuries men had said: '*Veneziani, poi Christiani!* . . . Venetians first, then Christians!' Leonardo Tron wanted to abandon the great tradition of intellectual independence, along with the Empire of the Sea.

'What good has Lepanto done us?' Angela had demanded, parroting her father. 'The Turks still hold Cyprus, our former island. That Jew dog Joseph Nasi still calls himself Duke of Naxos and the Cyclades, our former domain.'

Marco was again mute. He could not tell her that he was once more in touch with Joseph Nasi. The Duke sincerely desired reconciliation with Venice and the Papacy. He wanted to be free to pursue his business interests in Europe and to protect his fellow Jews in Europe from extortion and persecution.

Marco could not argue that the great victory at Lepanto was conclusive. Immediately after the battle, Don John of Austria had withdrawn to Sicily on the orders of King Philip of Spain, rather than follow up the victory by attacking the Turkish bases. Nor could Marco deny that only intense pressure by the Papacy had persuaded His Most Catholic Majesty to rejoin the Christian League.

Marco certainly could not tell Angela of the influence exerted on King Philip by Francesco de' Medici, inspired by his Venetian mistress, Bianca Capello Buonaventura. Yet, if the Secret Service had not reported that Philip was subject to that additional pressure, the Senate would not have taken the decision to sail against the Turks. Venice would be supported only by a single Papal squadron, if Spain remained outside the Christian League. But the Senate's bold decision had finally shamed Philip and forced his hand.

Now, however, victory was once again within reach, a conclusive victory that could regain Cyprus and restore Venetian domination of the eastern Mediterranean. The Sultan had cobbled together a new fleet of a hundred and fifty galleys supported by eight galleasses, the new battleships whose heavy cannon had proved decisive at Lepanto. But the Turkish fleet had been built by officers working in mad haste to fulfil the Sultan's impossible demands in insufficient time – and thus save their necks from the executioner's scimitar. The Ottoman shipyards had used green timber to put together jerry-built ships, armed them with faulty cannon, and manned them with inexperienced crews.

Nonetheless, the Turks would fight like demons. The Sultan had sworn to decimate the families of his officers if they again broke before the Christian fleet.

Eyes fixed on the whitecaps, Marco heard himself singing under his breath the great anthem, 'Our Lion of Venice'. The outburst of rejoicing for the victory at Lepanto had produced much new music and many new songs, like the sentimental ballad that went: 'There's silence on our canals when our gondoliers row the war-galleys . . . Venice my beloved homeland, all-powerful gem of the sea, thou are girt with glories, with hopes – and with love!'

The battle would be fierce, but he would return as a victorious senior commodore. Leonardo Tron's obduracy would then melt before his renown as a hero of Venice – and before his own forcefulness.

He had good reason for hope, even confidence: the vision he had seen and the words he had heard on the Mole of the Great Arsenal two minutes before the *Angels* cast off the hawsers that bound her to the land. He had not foreseen Angela's sudden appearance to wish the war squadron good hunting. He could still picture her among the throng of ladies in their bright summer dresses. That image he would carry in his heart through the campaign.

Her hair, the dark gold of a candle's outer flame, hung free, caught only by a clip of diamonds and sapphires. Her heart-shaped face was soft above her small white ruff, and her heavy-lidded blue eyes were so dark they looked black in the sunlight. Her hand fluttered beneath her orange scarf, and her full lips parted to show small white teeth. Her nose, which was small and straight, ended in the minute roundness the old wives said showed a passionate nature.

Curtseying to the commodore, Angela had whispered: 'I had to come, Marco! To tell you I'll do whatever you wish. I'll speak to my father . . . even elope . . . whatever you wish. Only come back to me!'

She had then risen abruptly and turned away. His blood tingling, he had swung over the bulwarks onto the galley's deck and ordered his squadron to sail.

Elated by the memory, Marco caught himself on the point of telling Paolo to shake out the reefs in the triangular sails and set all auxiliary sail. A commodore did not tell a captain how to handle his ship, but only directed him to make all possible haste. He had not spoken, but he heard Paolo giving those orders, which the crew obeyed enthusiastically.

All the men were eager to come to grips with the Turks. All believed that inevitably they must win the last great victory – and take the enormous booty that victory would bring.

CHAPTER XIX

THE sliver of moon that lit the pale Pitti Palace recalled to Pietro Buonaventura the crescent symbol of the Ottoman Empire. Although the night air was hot and damp, he shivered and wished for a warmer garment than his linen cloak.

Most Florentine gentlemen were happy to go about in their shirts, leaving off doublets in late August, when the summer heat lay like a stagnant weed-choked pool in the valley of the Arno. But Pietro wore the black cloak to make himself as nearly invisible as he could when he slipped through the shadows of the back alleys. Yet he was now chilled by the sight of the moon, that unwanted reminder of his time in Istanbul.

Pietro hated the memory of those three months in the Turkish capital. Ashamed of his craven flight, he was even more ashamed that he had fumbled the opportunity to enrich himself. He detested himself for the gold he had not amassed, as, he felt, others detested him for not possessing gold. Not only wealth, but the power and the independence gold brought had lain in his palm. But he had not grasped them.

Still, to his surprise, neither Francesco de' Medici nor Marco Capello had lifted a finger against him. Neither had reproached him for the theft of the Torah-case or the death of Hillel of Damascus, not even for the scandal of his defaulting on his debts and fleeing. To his astonishment, he had even been permitted to collect the profit from his first shipment of spices, after, of course, paying off the original loan and the interest due.

To Pietro's mind that forbearance demonstrated conclusively how badly both Florence and Venice needed him. He was beyond doubt indispensable to both the Prince Regent of Tuscany and the State Inquisition of Venice as the husband of record of the woman loved by the Regent. His wife, he believed, manipulated her lover for the benefit of Venice. Yet, without Pietro to sustain her and shield her, Bianca would be lost.

As the essential link between two of the richest states in Europe, Pietro felt himself extremely powerful. Having survived the débâcle of Istanbul, which was not, after all, of his making, he also felt virtually invincible. No need to stoop to threats. They knew he could bring their houses crashing about their ears by telling all he knew, but they dared not eliminate him because they needed him.

Cheered by his own logic, Pietro let the cloak fall back and took off his black hat. No further need for the broad brim to hide his features and the gleam of his golden hair, which his valet now regularly tinted. At twenty-nine, he was beginning to go grey. Still, a touch of white at the temples would give him an air of distinction. He was sometimes not rendered the respect he merited because he looked so young, not just because of his lack of money.

Aside from that irritation, Pietro Buonaventura was filled with a sense of well-being. The night with Alessandra had been delightful. He had proved his prowess three times, until she moaned that she could take no more of him. But her splayed white legs and her open, engorged sex contradicted her protestations, and he had mounted her again. Alessandra Bonciani was a noblewoman who had been widowed very young. Not even Bianca, his spiteful wife, could say his conquests were all shopgirls or artisans' wives, not when he lay with Alessandra in affection and pleasure. If only her brothers were less jealous of the family honour, the affair would be idyllic.

Whistling softly to himself, Pietro slung his cloak over his shoulder. He fanned himself with his hat as he entered the alley behind the mansion on the Via Maggio. Only a dozen yards from his own back-door, he need no longer worry about being recognised.

Not that he feared attack if he were recognised. His skill with the sword was too well known. Besides, he enjoyed the protection of both the State Inquisition of Venice and the Prince Regent of Tuscany. But Florence in August, brimming with idle visitors, was a paradise for cutpurses who did not scruple to cut throats as well.

Behind him, Pietro heard another whistler – and realised with quick anger that he was being mocked. He had, unaware, been whistling the Turkish ballad, "Saladin Takes Jerusalem". His unseen pursuer had taken up that tune, embellishing it with derisory trills and flourishes. He whirled round, his hand resting menacingly on the pommel of his sword. The gesture alone would frighten robbers away. They wanted easy loot, not a fight.

Two men were following a dozen paces behind. Muffled in cloaks, they were shapeless figures in that pre-dawn grey before the first rays of the sun. They came on steadily, undaunted by his threatening gesture.

Nor did they hesitate when he unsheathed his light sword. Throwing back their cloaks, they revealed the hilts of heavy cavalry sabres. Both wore white Venetian masks with jutting noses. One stepped back like a courteous second at a duel when the other drew his sword.

Pietro was chilled. They clearly meant to attack him, and they were two to his one. Yet if, as it appeared, only one at a time engaged him, his chances were far better than even. They had reckoned without his dazzling mastery of the light sword, whose speed and agility would in any fair match invariably defeat the clumsy heavy sabre.

One of his pursuers leaned casually against the wall of the alley like a passer-by stopping to enjoy the fight. The other threw off his cloak, revealing massive shoulders and legs like gnarled tree trunks. He wrapped his cloak around his left arm and lifted his sabre to high guard, eerily like a gentleman before a duel. Yet he said not a word, and his features were hidden behind the white mask.

Pietro Buonaventura had never lacked physical courage. He only felt a quickening of his blood now that he had to fight, whether one or two. He too wrapped his cloak around his left arm, regretting that the fabric was not heavier for better protection. He raised his sword to high guard, matching the duellist's politesse of his opponent – and leaped at the squat, muscular figure.

Surprised by the sudden attack, the duellist barely turned the lunge aside. His parry was awkward. Heartened by such clumsiness, Pietro feinted at the heart, but at the last moment turned his blade to slash at the sword-arm. Blood seeping from his arm, his opponent thrust wildly at Pietro's side.

Throwing up his left arm for protection, Pietro felt his enemy's blade slice through the thin fabric of the cloak. A whiplash of pain coiled around his forearm. Recovering from his parry, he thrust again at the man's sword-arm.

To his astonishment, his stroke was checked. His arm was jarred to the shoulder as the point of his opponent's blade slid under the guard of his hilt. He expected his sword to be wrenched from his grasp and sent flying through the air. But his opponent released the lock with a disdainful flick. His blade singed Pietro on his left side just above the waist. Somewhere birds were singing a morning chorus.

For the first time, Pietro felt cold fear. He knew he must fight defensively, wary of his opponent's proven skill. Neither man cried out, although both grunted with exertion. Aside from the clashing of steel and the distant birdsong, Florence was quiet as the grey dawn turned pink.

Mockingly, the second man whistled the chorus of 'Our Lion of Venice'.

Angry at that mockery, Pietro lunged into the attack again. He knew he could kill the man – but only by concentrating all his skill and strength, only by risking an all-out attack that would leave him vulnerable. His sword darted back and forth, over and under, so rapidly it was a blur of silver in the air.

His attack was turned aside. His attack was parried, clumsily and painfully. But it was turned aside.

Pietro Buonaventura gasped in surprise and fear. He had already known he was fighting for his life against a powerful and skilled opponent. He now knew he faced a fencing master, a professional swordsman as well as a professional killer. Only a professional could have turned back that whirlwind of steel. He fell back, exhausted by his efforts. He panted heavily, and his sword drooped.

The fencing master did not strike for his heart as Pietro expected. Instead, the heavy sabre slashed at his right side. He was, it seemed, to be sliced inch by inch, as in a Turkish torture.

Pietro ducked under that slash and let his sword-point drop. Screaming in triumph behind the white mask, the fencing master lunged at his right shoulder. Pietro's blade flickered under that high thrust to take the man beneath the ribs. The shriek of triumph ended abruptly, and the heavy body sagged on the blade that impaled it.

Pietro struggled to free his sword to meet the certain attack of the second man. Yet, unknowing, he allowed himself to relax, as much in exhaustion as in elation. He desperately needed an instant's respite before playing the charade of the formal start of a duel with his next assailant. His left arm and left side dripping blood, he was undoubtedly weakened. But victory was a splendid tonic, and he was ready to face the next assault when it came.

Lightning flashed before his eyes. For several seconds, he felt nothing and could see nothing at all. Then came the pain, giant claws that raked his side. His left arm, he saw with disbelief, was hanging useless, and blood was seeping from his shoulder.

There was no gentlemanly overture for the second murderer. His sabre had struck while Pietro, expecting a respite, was girding his nerves for battle. Still cloaked and masked, the new enemy raised the dagger in his left hand to slash Pietro's cheek. For the first time he spoke.

'You're not so pretty now!'

At least, Pietro knew who had sent the assailants. Only an assassin hired by Alessandra's jealous brothers would mock his good looks.

At least, then, he was dying for love, a notion he had always thought ridiculous. Short of a miracle, he was certainly dying. Weakened and exhausted, he could not turn aside this fresh assault by an enemy who had struck his first blow from behind.

Pietro's vision blurred, and his head drooped. Mechanically, he parried. The thrusts that struck home were meant to maim, rather than kill outright. He was being methodically carved up like a carcass hanging from a butcher's hook.

The dagger slashed his face again, and he heard a terrible grating as his nose broke. Frantically, he charged forward, his sword held before him like a spear. For an instant he felt resistance as the blade touched his opponent. Then nothing – and he fell, hurled to the ground by his own momentum.

A foot scornfully turned him over, and the hollow voice within the mask said: 'I am instructed to tell you why you are dying . . .' The murderer spoke a name, then a brief sentence like a judge summing up the crimes of a convicted criminal.

Pietro Buonaventura just heard those words. But he heard no more. When the sabre fell to cleave him from shoulder to hip, he jerked in automatic spasms. His soul had already fled.

Francesco de' Medici, Prince Regent of Tuscany, wore a sculptor's smock splotched with paint stains and acid burns when Bianca let herself through the secret door of his private laboratory in the cellar of the Pitti Palace. He was staring intently at the blue liquid in the glass beaker he held over an alcohol flame, and he did not look up until she said softly: 'Franco, I'm sorry to interrupt. But I must talk to you.'

A spasm of irritation crossed his high, sloping forehead, and he did not answer. When the liquid began to turn red, he set the beaker down on the marble laboratory table and sighed with satisfaction. A smile lighting his large brown eyes, he turned indulgently to his mistress. His heavy eyebrows, already lifted interrogatively, rose higher in surprise when he saw her costume.

Bianca always took pains to appear before him at her best. She even veiled the candles in her bedchamber with pink gauze, so that the soft light flattered her face and her body when they made love. At twenty-four, he had told her, such pains were not only unnecessary, but mildly comical. Nonetheless, she persisted, and he was grateful that she wished to give him the greatest possible pleasure whenever he looked at her.

Yet this morning, with the time already past ten, she was wearing a plain dress of green muslin with a straight, unhooped skirt and only a small collar. Such a dress a middle-class wife might wear to supervise her meagre two or three maids. Perhaps she had slept late as she sometimes did, scandalising the early-rising Florentines, who battened on the gossip from the servants' quarters of her mansion on the Via Maggio. The city loved to talk about its most notorious woman.

She had stinted her normal make-up, sparing though she was always with cosmetics in the morning. He saw no eyeshadow, no eyebrows emphasised with dark pencil, but only a dash of red on her lips. She was twisting a lace handkerchief around her long fingers, and her eyes were red. She made no move to wipe away the grey streaks left on her face and hands by the cobwebs that hung in the secret tunnel from her mansion to his laboratory.

Clearly, this was no simple matter of feminine vapours over a trivial upset. Anyway, Bianca hardly ever gave way to such frailty, except, perhaps, over the ailing cats, dogs, and, even, foxes she collected at their villa in Pratolino. Francesco had seen her as distraught as this only once before, when her daughter Pellegrina lay blotched with a scarlet rash and burning with fever. It had been several days before the physicians could tell Bianca and Pietro, who was apparently concerned, that the rosy rings were not the plague, but a virulent, yet not mortal, childhood disease.

'Franco,' she said again, 'I must talk to you.'

His smile broadened to show he was attentive, accentuating the fullness of his broad face over the cheekbones. Like his wide eyes with their heavy lids, that fullness made him look a little fragile, not weak, but, perhaps, too open, too trusting, and too tolerant.

'I'm sorry, my dear,' he said. 'I had my mind on other things. What has made you look so worried? You hardly ever cry . . .'

'It's Pietro! Franco, he's . . . he's dead. His body, we found him in the alley behind the house. Horribly cut up. The murderers even cut off his right hand.'

'Murderers? More than one? How do you know?'

Suspicion flashed through Bianca's mind. He was so calm, so unsurprised, that she wondered if he had already known of Pietro's death. Could Francesco have known before it occurred? Could he have ordered the murder?

Yet that would have been foolish. Worse, it would have been unnecessary, which was not Francesco's way. Pietro had been behaving well for him, not threatening, not trying to extort money or position. He had even made an effort to keep his latest affair discreet.

'My question, it troubles you?' Francesco asked gently, as always sensitive to her unspoken reactions.

'Yes,' she answered candidly. 'I wonder why you're not surprised. Did you know before I told you?'

'His way of life made it inevitable. He was bound to die by violence. The only question was when. And no, I didn't know before. You said *two* assassins?'

'Yes, Franco. A stranger's body was lying next to his. It's all . . . all so horrible. I didn't, couldn't, love him. Not for years, certainly not since you and I . . . But he was my husband and Pellegrina's father. I keep thinking what he might have been. The total waste!'

'I hate it, Bianca. I hate to see you suffer. And for what? All he brought you was misery. You know I never liked the wretch or his fawning charm.'

'Because he was so afraid of you, Franco. And he envied you so. You were everything he always wanted to be. You even had me, the woman he wanted.'

'Amazing! *How* he could dream! Now, tell me what you've done?' He was incisive, this prince whom his enemies charged with indecision. 'But, first, let us clear up one matter: *Do you still suspect me?*'

'No, Franco, no longer. It was a passing foolishness. You would never . . .'

'No more than you, my dear. Certainly not *this* way. You might've struck at him in anger, even said so that your friends could hear: "Oh to be rid of this rascal!" But you would never hire killers.'

'I didn't think . . . It didn't occur to me that . . . that anyone would suspect me.'

'Assuredly, they will. Just as they'll say I ordered it, that we conspired together. That's inevitable. But tell me: what have you done?'

'Very little. My old gatekeeper, my dear old Venetian gatekeeper, he reported the . . . the discovery. Only the gatekeeper and Lucia, my maid, only they know. They put the bodies in the cellar, behind the wine-casks.'

'Good,' he mused aloud. 'The less done the better. The murderer's body we'll leave on the Ponte Vecchio. Another unknown corpse won't raise an eyebrow there. Buonaventura must be found far from your house. But not too far from the widow Bonciani's palazzo. No great harm if people think her brothers . . .'

'Franco, it could have been anyone. He made enemies wherever he went. La Bonciani's brothers were swearing to avenge the family honour. Outsiders thought Pietro is . . . was . . . an obstacle to our love, yours and mine. Though it was really the other way, they'll blame us. And my father still cherishes his hatred of Pietro. He was always threatening to have him killed.'

She would not mention the other strong likelihood. Her cousin Marco had only mentioned Pietro's scandalous misbehaviour in Con-stantinople – and never complained. Yet Pietro had acted very badly. Perhaps Marco had ordered him killed in retribution.

But Marco's squadron was blockading the Turkish fleet, which had run for shelter into the port of Navarino. Still, his superiors in the Venetian Secret Service could have sent the killers. Pietro had been silent during the two years since his return, but he was not famous for his discretion.

'What will you do?' she asked.

'As little as possible. An autopsy will be necessary, and some attempt to identify the dead assassin. I'd be astonished if it succeeded. Otherwise, a modest funeral. And no protracted inquiry. Visitors die every day on the streets of Florence. I regret it, and I do everything I can to make the streets safe. But still . . .'

'Pietro is to be another unexplained death then?' she asked. 'It seems so cruel. It *is* cruel. You'll just write him off as another victim of the footpads?'

'Yes, I'm afraid so . . . Bianca, I understand your feelings. I feel with you and I grieve, grieve deeply – because it hurts you. But otherwise?'

CHAPTER XX

FRANCESCO DE' MEDICI had just given Bianca Capello Buonaventura public recognition – with almost indecent haste, she feared. Nonetheless, he had finally granted her the position and the power she craved and merited. Yet she had never felt more an outsider than she did this late afternoon in mid-May in San Lorenzo, the parish church of the Medicis.

Joanna of Austria, her sallow complexion turned to waxy pallor by her black head-dress and black gown, sat beside Francesco I, Grand Duke of Tuscany, as was her right and her duty as his lawful consort. But she, Bianca of Venice, was seated in a rear pew among the representatives of lesser Italian cities, having been strictly enjoined by the Court Chamberlain to keep her features hidden behind a heavy black veil.

This funeral was a family, as well as a state, occasion, and she was *not* a member of the Medici family. Although she was now publicly acknowledged as the true mistress of the new Grand Duke, she was not entitled to sit beside him in his family church, now when he needed her.

The privileges conferred by her new dignity were severely limited. With their usual bold logic, the French had coined the term *maîtresse en titre*, meaning official mistress. The hard-headed French knew that a reigning prince could need a more sympathetic, more intelligent woman than the princess he had married for reasons of state. As *maîtresse en titre* to Francesco I, she, Bianca Capello Buonaventura, could now counsel and sustain him in public.

She could also adorn some ceremonial occasions, although not a solemn dynastic ceremony like today's. When she appeared at court, she was seated in a chair, rather than on a throne, albeit a splendidly worked chair, a step below the dais where Francesco sat on his throne.

Joanna would have been enthroned beside him, if he had wanted her or she had insisted.

Someday, perhaps, she, Bianca, would sit beside Francesco as his Grand Duchess. Never strong, Joanna was worn out by bearing five daughters and one sickly son in nine years. Bianca could not wish for Joanna's death, although it would relieve Florence, above all Francesco, of a dreary and oppressive presence.

No, Bianca told herself, she would not think of Joanna's dying. Ambassadors, courtiers, artists, poets, and philosophers could now call upon her openly in her palazzo in the Via Maggio. All remarked on the wit and beauty with which it was furnished, so unlike the lugubrious piety and shoddy taste that surrounded Joanna of Austria. Her palazzo, Bianca resolved, would become a second court for the Duchy of Tuscany. At *her* brilliant court, Francesco would find amusement, rather than boredom, and love freely given, rather than constant complaints.

Nearly two years had passed since Pietro's death, for which the Florentines naturally blamed her. That death had freed Francesco's hand. But her lover had waited until another death freed both his hands to make her *maîtresse en titre*. Fear, as well as propriety, had delayed him. Although Prince Regent for nine years, Francesco had still feared the displeasure of his half-mad father.

The forceful Cosimo, first Grand Duke of Tuscany, who had greatly extended his domain and his power, had not liked his son's mistress. He had barely tolerated Bianca, of whom he was suspicious because she was Venetian. Above all, he had found her insufficiently pliable. Cosimo liked women who were decorative and pleasing, as Bianca assuredly was. He did not, however, like women who thought for themselves and fought for their principles.

Today Francesco de' Medici was bidding a formal farewell to his father. At the same time and by the same act, he was giving notice to the world that power over Tuscany had passed, unbroken and undiminished, into his hands. He was at once asserting the dynasty's continuity and casting off his subordination to his father.

Cosimo I had died on April 21 in this year of Our Lord 1574. The hawk's-beak nose that had once sniffed the air for conquests, now shrunken to the bone, rose gaunt from a face wasted by disease. The black widow's peak that had accentuated his bold features and inspired ladies' sighs was grey and as ragged as if gnawed by rats. The hands that had despoiled his neighbours' treasures and his neighbours' daughters, were barely-fleshed claws that could no longer either hurt or help any other being.

Those wounds of time the embalmed body bore, but not the waxen effigy Francesco had commissioned of Giambologna, his favourite sculptor. Hands and face, all that was visible in the robes of state, showed the features of Cosimo de' Medici in his matchless prime to the throngs that passed the bier in the Old Palace, the seat of government of the city that had recently been a republic and was now a monarchy.

Francesco and Bianca had decided upon that royal display to emphasise the message: *The Duke never died, only the mortal who for a time occupied his body.*

Bianca was a good daughter of Holy Church, although denied the Holy Sacraments because she could not give up the love of Francesco, which was the core of her life. But she shuddered at the immense mausoleum that the artists of Florence had made the Church of San Lorenzo. Holy Church was obsessed with mortality and the macabre.

The tall apse was draped with black hangings, some drawn aside to show backdrops painted to simulate the marble-and-granite interior of an immense tomb. More than life-size, yet grimly realistic, skulls and skeletons alternated along the sides with tableaux glorifying Cosimo I.

The penitent's robe with the pointed hood and the white cross on its breast in which the new Duke sweated was like that which King Philip of Spain had worn at the funeral of his father, the Emperor Charles V. Such a garment would please the Pope, who was always to be reckoned with. It further asserted Francesco's absolute inheritance of his father's power, as Philip had thus asserted his succession to Charles.

Francesco's detractors would undoubtedly sneer that he was atoning, among his other sins, for the murder of Pietro Buonaventura. They would have said so whatever he wore. The Florentines delighted in blaming Francesco and Bianca for the murder they had not done. Above all, they blamed her. It did not matter that Pietro alive had given her a gloss of respectability, while Pietro's death had benefited her not at all.

A mist of incense swirled through the crypt-like gloom, the sweet, heavy smoke stifling. By the feeble light of the candles on the altar, a host of cardinals and bishops, assisted by innumerable priests, dragged their way through the highest of high masses. The eulogies had already taken two hours – and would take at least two more.

Examining her conscience, as the nuns had taught her, Bianca Capello Buonaventura found it heavy enough. Her present way of life was wrong, but to alter it would be death for her. She might, in the past, have been more dutiful to her father, but he had wanted to lie with his own daughter, an abomination more heinous than anything she had ever done. Yet, even now, at the height of her power and glory, she would alter her life, abandon her constant sinning, if only God showed her the way.

A tear for the man who should have been her father-in-law touched the eye of the woman Florentines swore never wept. Also a tear for herself. Yet she knew that she was serving those Florentines well. She was doing far more good than evil in bolstering Francesco's confidence and encouraging him to rule for the benefit of all his people. Moreover, he and she together created beauty by supporting artists, and they fostered knowledge by employing scientists.

Despite all logic, Bianca blamed herself for Pietro's base death. She might have behaved otherwise. She might have resisted her love for Francesco. She might have settled down to be a middle-class housewife.

But Pietro had never given her the opportunity. From the very first day he had lied and stolen, wasting his talents in wild schemes to enrich himself without work. In truth, Pietro had contrived his own death. In truth, she had kept him alive longer than he would have survived on his own. Nonetheless, she would bear the burden of his death as long as she lived.

Wearied by her self-examination, the repetitious rites, and the fetid atmosphere, Bianca dozed off. Her maid Lucia, sitting beside her, smiled maternally and cradled her head on her shoulder.

Bianca awoke when the great catafalque, heavy with bas-relief scenes of Cosimo's triumphs, was borne down the aisle. Still drowsy, she rose with the congregation and found herself face to face with Joanna of Austria, who was walking, hunched and dull-eyed, behind Francesco.

Against their will, the women's eyes met. Biance knew that Joanna recognised her behind her heavy veil. The new Grand Duchess's mouth worked frenetically. Spittle trembled on the thin brown lips, and Bianca drew back.

With a visible effort, the Grand Duchess controlled herself, but the veins stood out on her temples. She crossed herself very deliberately, but her glare was malevolent. The Austrian princess endowed her pious gesture with the detestation of a Sicilian peasant woman making an obscene sign to avert the evil eye.

Francesco turned his head and looked for an instant at his two women. His face was pale and expressionless beneath his pointed black hood.

No more than a foot from her rival, moving at the solemn pace of the cortege, Joanna of Austria spat out a single word: 'Whore!'

Astonished, Bianca instinctively responded: 'Parasite!'

MAY 23, 1574
FLORENCE: THE MANSION IN THE VIA MAGGIO

Francesco de' Medici was not normally devious. He was, indeed, straightforward compared to most men who held power in the late sixteenth century. Yet Bianca Capello Buonaventura could not suppress the disloyal feeling that he was acting deviously when he came into her bedchamber as she was dressing on a sultry evening, a week after his father's funeral.

Still glowing from her bath, she wore only a light dressing-gown. While her maid Lucia brushed her hair, Francesco chatted about her latest cause. Accompanied by her daughter Pellegrina, now ten years old, Bianca had spent the day in the countryside to the north. The roads, really no more than hill paths, were hot and dusty, and the farm families were awed by her sudden appearance.

She felt her discomfort and their discomfiture were well worthwhile. Her surprise visits, followed by promises of assistance and threats of punishment, worked near-miracles in improving the peasants' care of their livestock. The patient white oxen and the hardy little donkeys were better treated and, therefore, happier and harder-working. So reported the agents she sent to follow up her efforts.

'Of course, the peasants think I'm mad,' she chattered happily to Francesco. 'Carlino, my youngest footman, came back the other day and said they called me the "mad Contessa". I like his honesty. He also said even the sheepdogs work better now they're fed decently and not tied up at night.'

Often reluctant to meet his own courtiers, the Duke marvelled at her ease with peasants who spoke only their own rough hill dialect. He looked on her concern for animals as a charming frailty, a mild disorder of the mind that could not harm anyone. But he knew better than to challenge that devotion.

Instead, he nodded dismissal to the maid and came to stand behind Bianca. He admired their joined image in her mirror: he dark and saturnine, she golden fair with fiery hair. She reached up to touch his hand, and he stroked the back of her neck.

She smiled and drew away in mock alarm when his hand slid down to caress her breast. In truth, she loved such moments, when she stirred him unaware and was herself stirred in return. She turned and gave him her lips.

Francesco kissed her tenderly, but without passion. Still amused and playful, she pouted and asked: 'Is My Lord Duke displeased with me? Such a chaste kiss!'

'As always, I'm tempted beyond endurance.' He matched her tone, then added earnestly: 'But not now. Bianca, you must do something for me.'

'Yes, Franco. Whatever you wish.'

'Listen first, then give me your word! I want you to meet Joanna. She will receive you in the Old Palace. She still likes the Old Palace best for the murals of Austria my father ordered for her.'

'Because she doesn't like Tuscany . . . never has.' Remembering the encounter in San Lorenzo, Bianca spoke with vehemence she rarely allowed herself.

'That is neither here nor there.'

'Unfortunately! If she were there, not here, she would be much happier.'

'Don't joke, Bianca. I'm very serious. You *must* meet Joanna.'

'Franco, My Lord Duke, I cannot. I *will* not. You don't know what you're asking. If you were a woman, you'd understand why . . .'

'You can! And you *shall*!'

'In the name of God, why? What possible use?'

'I will not have this squabbling, your slanging her in public. I will not have my people gossiping about your hatred for each other. You must show amity.'

'Then, tell her . . .' Bianca began hotly, but he broke in to say: 'Nor will I have you insulted in public. Never again. I've already spoken to her . . . as I'm now speaking to you.'

'My Lord Duke, if you love me, please do not force me . . .'

'You must meet amicably, so that everyone, everyone from Florence to Venice, knows that you two are no longer quarrelling. It is absolutely necessary. I won't have them saying I cannot control my women.'

'My Lord . . . Franco . . . please. I beg you!'

'You *shall!*'

Bianca bowed her head to hide her tears of rage. When he spoke in that tone, as he rarely did, she obeyed.

He was a strange man, even to her, this sensitive son of the aggressive Medicis. He had to have his secret places, not only the laboratory in the cellar of the Pitti Palace, but a room in the Old Palace, and of course, the Vasari Corridor over the Old Bridge so that he could cross from the Old Palace to the Pitti Palace unseen. Yet he was a good man, devoted not only to her, but to the arts and the sciences. Also to his people, though she sometimes had to remind him that he was dealing with creatures of flesh and blood, men and women, each an individual soul, not with abstract concepts.

But the people did not warm to him. He was too aloof, lacking the vulgar appeal they expected of their ruler. They therefore gossiped viciously about him and, naturally, about herself. Scurrilous verses attacked them and, sometimes, posters appeared on the Old Palace itself.

His father Cosimo had humiliated a loving, intelligent wife for a succession of mistresses. Francesco barely neglected a dull, whining wife for one mistress, to whom he was utterly faithful. By the standards of Florence, even the stricter standards of Venice, his fidelity was eccentric. Yet the Florentines attacked him for immorality, as they had not attacked his hail-fellow-well-met father.

Bianca nodded, and Francesco said with obvious relief: 'Well, that's settled. I'll tell you when. And, Bianca, you're not going as a penitent, far from it.'

She smiled and blinked back the tears she despised, disdaining to play on his sympathy by blotting them with her handkerchief.

'We must present a solid front.' It was as close to an apology as he could ever come. 'Everything is even more unsettled since that appalling treaty last year.'

'Franco, Venice had no choice,' Bianca interjected. 'The Serene Republic was deserted by everyone. What else could she do?'

'Venice abandoned her allies, betrayed her promises to everyone, all her pledges to me.'

'With Catarina and Charles of France, as well as the new Pope, all lukewarm against the Turks, Venice was herself deserted. Remember how Don John left the Venetian squadrons in the lurch? How he sailed away, abandoning the blockade of the Sultan's fleet at Navarino after only a few months? On the orders of his brother, King Philip, no doubt. With France intriguing in Constantinople, and raising the Spanish Lowlands against Philip, Spain had other worries.'

'Your Venice had sworn to carry the offensive to Constantinople itself. Only an all-out offensive, the Venetians had kept saying, could keep the Turks from dominating the world.'

'That's true.'

'Then to make peace . . . to sign away Cyprus . . . to pay an indemnity to the Sultan. Abominable! Lepanto might never have been fought.'

'You're quite right. Disastrous from *our* point of view. Remember, I was against our coming out publicly for Venice. We agreed we had to look after our own interests. With *everyone* looking out for his own interests, Venice had no choice. Either the treaty with the Turks . . . or lose everything.'

'Bianca, I must know what's going to happen next,' the Duke said. 'I want you to go to Venice. Incognita, of course. Call yourself the Countess of Prato. I want you to watch and see and use all your contacts. Venice still knows more of the true state of the world than anyone else. I want that knowledge – and your own assessment.'

First the rod, Bianca reflected, then the reward. First, the abhorrent meeting with Joanna, then the joyous return to her native city, protected from any possible harm, indeed assured of great honour, by the might of Tuscany.

'First, though, you must see Joanna.' The rod flicked her again. 'I depend on you.'

JUNE 2, 1574
FLORENCE: THE OLD PALACE

Bianca curtsied.

It was the hardest act of her life, far worse than nerving herself to escape from her father's perverted desires. It was the most galling act of her life, more galling than the jeers of the street crowds when Francesco and she were first known to be lovers. It was the most humiliating act of her life, more humiliating than anything she could imagine, except, perhaps, being paraded naked in chains through Venice.

(234)

But Bianca Capello Buonaventura, noblewoman of Venice, curtsied to Princess Joanna of Austria, Duchess of Tuscany. And she smiled as she curtsied to the one woman in Florence to whom she was obliged to pay formal respect.

Joanna of Austria did not smile. Nor did she nod to acknowledge the homage of her rival. She sat unmoving on her small green-and-silver throne, attended by none of her ladies-in-waiting. The thin brown lips under the long nose were turned down, and the long pale hands that were her only beauty were clasped on her stomach. But the dull grey eyes for once glowed – with the fire of hatred. In mourning for her father-in-law, whom she had loved, she wore a plain black gown, and a necklace of funereal garnets. Her skin sickly yellow, she looked much older than her twenty-seven years.

Joanna had loved Cosimo in good part because he had valued her so highly. She had, Bianca knew, insisted on this meeting in the Old Palace because it was virtually a monument to herself. Cockahoop at snaring the Emperor's daughter for his son, Cosimo had ordered the octagonal entrance hall to be covered with murals depicting her Germanic homeland. Veronese and Veneziano were among the masters who had painted the panoramas through which Bianca had just passed – so that she would know she was approaching an Imperial princess.

Bianca's Venetian eye for grandeur had found the view of Vienna imposing in a provincial way, and Passau charming in an elvish way. As for Grätz, it looked rather as it sounded.

She was now exposed to further Austrian quaintness in the canvases hanging on the walls of the cold minor salon where Joanna had chosen to receive her. Behind the throne, hearty Tyrolean peasant women with red cheeks and hyacinth-blue eyes laughed and flirted with men wearing leather knickerbockers. Skirts kilted around their hips, their sturdy brown legs trod out grapes in a wooden vat. On the opposite wall, jolly peasants, snug within their hut while snow lay deep outside, lifted their tankards.

Joanna still remained silent, and Bianca could not speak before the Duchess did. She wondered idly if she had chosen the proper dress. She concluded that her grey-and-purple gown with its high neckline and long, straight skirt was right, as were her earrings and bracelet of amethysts. She, who was not formally a member of the Medici family, could not compete with the Duchess in the depth of her mourning.

Still unspeaking, Joanna of Austria stared at Bianca as if she were an animal in a menagerie. Staring forthrightly back, Bianca marvelled that this parched, worn woman was only a year older than herself.

'His Highness, the Duke, desired that I receive thee.' Joanna finally broke her silence, her Italian halting and heavily accented. 'Accordingly, I am receiving thee.'

Not just once, but twice, used, the familiar *thee* galled. So Bianca would speak to her maid, who would reply with the respectful *you*, or so she would address an equal. Joanna was not addressing her as an equal.

'I am Your Highness's servant,' Bianca replied formally. 'Command me.'

'Then begone from my Duchy of Tuscany,' Joanna directed, in curiously stilted language as if she had rehearsed the words. 'Release my man from thy talons and leave me in peace. That is my command.'

'He has been my man for nearly a decade. He came to me freely after he was forced to marry *thee*.' Still standing because she had not been asked to sit, Bianca snapped at her unwilling hostess. 'He is my man by choice, not *thine*.'

'*Thy* man?' Joanna rose in anger, and they were on equal terms. 'Before God, in holy wedlock, *my* man alone . . . And thou dare say *thee* to me!'

'As long as *thou* speak so to me.'

Bianca wrestled down her anger. She was not helping Francesco by brawling with his wife. Yet there was no point to this demeaning encounter if it did not help Francesco.

'Your Highness, I have come at the command of the Duke,' she said carefully. 'I know that you love him and wish him well. And he wishes there to be peace between us. Can we not together . . .'

'Peace with a usurper, a courtesan like you! Peace between a creature who sins every day of her life and myself, the true wife of Francesco de' Medici and a princess of the Holy Roman Empire!'

'A princess barely equal in lineage to a noblewoman of Venice. Besides the Capellos, the Hapsburgs are newcomers. I have bent my knee to your position. Not to your blood, which is less noble than my own. I am glad you did not call me whore again . . . that you no longer call me *thee*. Perhaps we can now talk like sensible women.'

Joanna's thin lips remained stubbornly pressed together, and she angrily twitched the coral rosary in her hands. When the silence had lasted for almost a minute, Bianca saw that she would have to set the pace. Short of giving him up, she would do anything for Francesco – and he wished her to make peace with his wife.

'Your Highness, each of us can give the Duke something different,' Bianca said. 'You, your prayers and the support of your brother, the

Emperor. An heir as well. I, in my own way, give him gaiety and a little brightness to light his life. Also a certain adroitness in the politics of Italy. He needs us both. Can there not be peace between us? At least a truce, if not perfect peace?'

'Never! My soul would be damned if I condoned the Duke's immoral liaison. How could I condone your great sin, your sin and his? All the Duke needs I can give him.'

'You, Your Highness, can give him sickly children and snivelling prayers,' Bianca retorted angrily. 'You can give him boredom and tension and fear of the hereafter. You can give him dry kisses and sour breath. And you do!'

Joanna sat stunned by the onslaught, but Bianca's temper was unleashed after enduring so much humiliation.

'I give him love, ungrudging love, and joy in bed,' she went on unchecked. 'I give him judgement and knowledge almost equal to his own, free play between minds, as you cannot. I give him laughter and music and friends. You cannot – or you will not. He needs me to sustain himself as a man *and* as a prince.'

The rosary in Joanna's hands snapped, and the coral beads rolled on the marble floor. She said nothing.

'Can we not, at least, agree not to plague him with our quarrels, Your Highness?' Bianca pleaded, now repentant. 'A show of amity in public is all he requires of us – for Tuscany and for himself.'

'Whore!' Joanna of Austria spat out the word amid a spray of spittle. 'I, Joanna, Duchess of Tuscany, a Hapsburg princess, to make a show of amity with a common, scheming slut . . . a sinful, evil whore!'

Bianca curtsied even more deeply than she had when she entered. She curtsied and withdrew without speaking again.

She had tried. God knew she had tried for Francesco's sake! And his cold sour wife had called her whore again.

Joanna of Austria was right. From now on, there could only be war between them. And to the vanquished no mercy!

CHAPTER XXI

'FORGET the austerity laws,' Commodore Marco Capello whispered to the lady called the Countess of Prato. 'For royalty, we always forget them.'

'I'd almost forgotten.' Her tongue stumbled over the clipped Venetian dialect. 'It's been ten years . . . a long time.'

'My dear Bianca, you can't have forgotten. You screamed loudest in '62 when they prohibited almost everything. And they sent the police into kitchens to make sure no host served more than three kinds of meat at one banquet. Also never marzipan or sugar figures.'

'Bartolomeo Capello, my father, liked that,' she recalled. 'Less expense for him. Not like last night.'

'Nothing like last night,' Marco agreed. 'He poured out the ducats like water.'

'Who wouldn't?' she asked. 'Won't you tomorrow?'

He nodded, and she continued: 'You know, Marco, it always irked me. He put up two thousand ducats for anyone who'd kill my . . . my husband . . . or me.'

'Irked is putting it mildly.'

'What *really* irked was the small sum. Two thousand ducats, only forty times what he pays his cook now that he's wealthy – from my *dowry*. Only two thousand ducats for the head of his only daughter. Well, he got my . . . he got Pietro.'

'He didn't, Bianca. Bartolomeo had no more to do with Pietro's death than I did. Not that I might not have liked . . .'

'You're sure, Marco? I must know . . . get this burden off my shoulders. That leaves only his mistress's brothers, washing the family honour in blood. Six months later, Alessandra was dead, too. So . . .'

'Not them either, not as far as I know.'

'And you would, wouldn't you?' she said suspiciously. 'Who then?'

'I'll tell you later. It's a long story, and this is hardly the place.'

Bianca looked across the still Basin of Saint Mark's, which glinted a deep, almost unreal, blue in the July sunlight. Pietro and Florence, even Francesco, seemed very far away. On this the third day since she had returned, her heart, her mind, and her senses were wholly taken up by the unending miracle of *La Serenissima*, the most serene, the eternal Venice.

The Doge's Palace shone like a spun-sugar castle against a sky of blue a shade lighter than the bay, but equally unreal. The round Romanesque arches below and the pointed Gothic arches above airily balanced the tan-and-white brick tracery of the façade. Above the central balcony she could just make out the marble figure of the former Doge Andrea Gritti kneeling before the Wingēd Lion of St Mark – and, above all else, Justice with her terrible sword.

The bucentaur of Doge Alvise Mocenigo was moving towards the Great Arsenal, the engine of Venetian power. Seated beside the Doge on a golden throne, the new King of France eagerly took in every sight. He appeared to be greatly impressed. But, as Marco had observed, he had to be *overwhelmingly* impressed by the power and the wealth of Venice.

The Royal bucentaur that carried the new King of France did not only symbolise the majesty of the Doge and the maritime power of the Serene Republic. The vessel grandiosely displayed the commercial city's wealth, which was both the source and the fruit of her power.

On the gilded bowsprit, the gilded Lion of St Mark stood sentinel over a gilded angel, which hovered beneath a gilded Justice holding gilded scales and a gilded sword. All that was not crimson hangings or crimson lacquer was golden: the mermaids, mermen, and cherubs carved on her bluff sides, as well as the life-size satyrs and nymphs, gods and goddesses, saints and heroes that alternated, male and female, along her bulwarks. On the afterdeck, the immense Ducal throne, big enough for a Titan, was covered by a golden carapace studded with semi-precious gems.

Bianca glanced at the figure on the throne. The Doge's attire was more than regal. Venice might elect her ruler and jealously curtail his power, but she clothed him with truly imperial grandeur.

Over a crimson robe heavy with gold embroidery, he wore a mantle caped with three rows of ermine. On his head rested the *cornu*. Beside the Doge, Henry III of France, dressed all in white with gold lace trim, was a boyish figure, appealing but slight.

Providence had given the Serene Republic a second chance by the sudden death of Charles X of France, who had cunningly manoeuvred her into making a humiliating peace with the Turks. His younger brother, who was now Henry III, was reputedly less wily, though also the son of shrewd Catarina de' Medici. Henry, who was on his way to Paris to claim his throne, had to be convinced that the might of Venice made her an ideal ally, not, as his elder brother had believed, a pawn well sacrificed to increase the power of France.

But Bianca Capello Buonaventura, travelling as the Countess of Prato, was not thinking about the strategy of her native city. Looking at Henry, his hair fair and his expression open, she wondered what her son would be like, the son she was determined to bear Francesco. Would he be one of the dark, scheming Medicis or a Medici of light and laughter like this twenty-three-year-old who had just inherited the crown of France? Would hard Venetian commonsense dilute Medici ambition? Would her impulsiveness or Francesco's caution be dominant in their son?

She smiled at her fantasy, ruefully recalling that they had been trying hard for a year. Yet she had not yet been able to conceive. Well, trying was also its own reward.

So was this moment of pure glory. She was an honoured guest on the gold-and-crimson vessel that today bore not only a doge, but a king, a cardinal, and three dukes. The ten intervening years might almost have been wiped out. Then, her father had forbidden her to join the ladies attending the Doge for the Marriage to the Sea. Now, six patricians had been assigned to her as ladies-in-waiting – and they sighed over her romantic story.

The title Countess of Prato was deliberately transparent. All Venice knew that the wild daughter of Bartolomeo Capello had returned in triumph. The Senate and the Doge were eager to please the noblewoman who all but commanded Francesco of Tuscany, whose net of influence and wealth covered all Europe. Venice was paying her wayward daughter quasi-regal honours, second only to the honours protocol and policy rendered the young man who was going home to be crowned King of France.

Bianca marvelled at the extravagant spectacles already mounted for Henry and the even more lavish spectacles planned for his week in that city of Europe most esteemed for its splendour.

'This is the city that bans high living?' she asked. 'What's become of all the laws against waste and ostentation?'

'Suspended for the visit,' Marco answered, 'as I told you.'

'Suspended? More like turned on their head. Everything that *was* banned *now* encouraged. Everything that *was* encouraged practically banned: thrift, modesty, humility.'

'What else can we do without allies, even the Pope turning his back?' Marco confided. 'We can only parade our wealth. This is all a trick mirror . . . to make us look bigger and stronger than we are.'

Marco, she reflected inconsequentially, had talked little about Angela, who was now his wife. Welcoming his cousin to Ca' Capello on the Grand Canal, where Angela and he lived with his widowed mother, he had said only that his wife was visiting relations on the *terraferma*, but would return to act as hostess at Ca' Capello's reception for the King on the next day, July 19.

Anticipating Bianca's unspoken question, he had assured her that Angela and he were 'perfectly happy together'. That was an odd choice of words for a man who had courted his one love for five years and married her only six months ago. Heeding the implicit warning in that modest claim, Bianca had gossiped about politics and Florence and the family, having been joyfully reunited with her Aunt Sophia and her Uncle Andrea. She had not again mentioned Angela.

'Well, my parent seems at home with the new ways,' she said. 'To think of Bartolomeo pouring out gold like cheap wine.'

'And bowing his knee to his daughter,' Marco laughed. 'Saints aren't the only ones who work miracles. The Senate works miracles every day.'

'Lord, how he's prospered!' she marvelled.

'With a daughter who is one of the most powerful ladies in Europe, what else? Why do you think the Senate had the King spend his first night at Palazzo Capello on Murano? Not to see the glassblowers. And not to please the old man, but you, my dear.'

Marco spoke with the frank, almost naïve, cynicism that always delighted Bianca. He saw nothing odd in such forthrightness, although most men and women rarely spoke their minds. His candour was the outlet for his keen sense of the ridiculous. Except for a sprinkling of grey like the first faint frost on his black hair, Marco also looked much the same: dark, ruddy, hump-nosed, and vigorous.

'It used to be just a country villa,' she said. 'But we've all become so grand it's now a palazzo.'

Marco grinned, and Bianca realised again that he was the only one in the world to whom she could talk with unguarded frankness. She was straightforward with Francesco, for she could not dissemble successfully for any length of time. But she could not always speak to Francesco without reflection. Nor dared she too often show him her frivolous side – or reveal her occasional despair. With Marco she never had to hold back.'

'And the old man, Bartolomeo Capello.' She was still reluctant to call him father. 'He was in seventh heaven. What a show! Every wall hung with tapestries or cloth of gold. Forty young patricians dancing attendance on the King and sixty halberdiers in gold. Not to speak of eighteen trumpeters and a dozen drummers.'

'Just the prologue to this spectacle, as you'll see. How did your father strike you?'

'Not much changed. A little more grizzled and a little more domineering now that his fortunes've been miraculously restored. And that same old look in his eye.'

'What look?'

'Never mind, Marco. I'm not sure what I meant.'

He let that evasion pass. If he pressed, the lighthearted Bianca who revelled in her return could in a moment become the haughty tempestuous Bianca who led one of the great potentates of Europe on a silken rein.

On six anchored rafts bobbing just outside the pilings that marked the channel crouched a monster never seen on the sea since Noah rode the Flood. The beast's gaping mouth, which was studded with three rows of immense teeth, belched flame, and smoke poured from its cavernous nostrils. Its gigantic dragon's body of copper, steel, and glass glowed with the fires inside. Enormous flukes flailed the water in time with its unearthly roars.

Eighty oars backed water to halt the bucentaur and allow the chief of the Guild of Glassblowers followed by ten porters to clamber up her side. With flourishes worthy of a royal chamberlain, he presented King Henry with a service of five hundred crystal plates and goblets, all made inside the monster. While the King said his words of thanks, five more porters climbed to the deck bearing two hundred crystal platters and tureens.

The royal guest must not be allowed time to be bored – or to reflect. His mind must be fully occupied by the splendour and the might of the Serene Republic. New prodigies succeeded the glass-making sea monster when the bucentaur once more got underway.

All the guilds of Venice had helped fit out the fifty-odd vessels with bright sails and brighter banners that now traced intricate patterns around the royal vessel. A barge had been transformed into a huge dolphin with a gigantic Neptune riding on its back. Winged horses and winged lions drew several craft. Another displayed a giant panorama of the lagoon with all its islands, so detailed it showed the murals, the plaques, and the statuary on every façade.

Half a dozen craft sent up showers of brilliantly coloured fireworks into the afternoon sky, anticipating the displays that were to light up the night sky. Green, red, and yellow comets flared in the blue dome over the city.

When the bucentaur tied up at the mole of the Great Arsenal, the royal party prepared to disembark. The ladies were not expected to risk their fragile shoes or their delicate gowns amid the hurly-burly of the biggest manufactory in Europe. But Bianca insisted upon seeing the Arsenal, which produced not just cannon and small arms, but, above all, warships.

When he heard her request, Doge Alvise Mocenigo looked grave and shook his head decisively. His ruddy complexion, full black beard, and bulbous nose all made him appear simple and direct. But his wily dark eyes constantly measured the dignitaries surrounding him. A counsellor wearing the fur-trimmed crimson robe and yellow stole of the Attorney-General whispered in his ear, and the Doge smiled.

'Certainly, Contessa,' he said. 'Your wish commands me.'

Marco Capello said softly as he helped Bianca down the gangplank: 'No harm in impressing Florence, as well as Paris. Two Medicis with a single stroke, so to speak. For a moment, the old boy forgot who you now are. He saw only another pushy Capello.'

Horns and pipes played King Henry's entourage through the marble archway supported by double columns of Greek marble. The pediment bore an enormous winged lion, and, above all, stood a marble Justice. Inside the red-brick wall, the royal party saw a different realm.

The clanging of hammers, the whining of immense saws, the groans of drill-presses, and the roar of giant bellows almost overwhelmed the creaking of pulleys and the shouts of workman. Black smoke blew from innumerable fires, and soft coal soot covered every surface. The scent of the sawdust blowing everywhere recalled distant pine forests.

'Sixteen thousand men, Your Majesty, sixteen thousand!' The Admiral commanding the Great Arsenal bellowed over the din as he had over gales at sea. 'The staunchest sons of the Serene Republic. And they produce . . .'

The Admiral had little new to tell Bianca about his workmen – and nothing to tell Commodore Marco Capello. Both had been brought up on tales of the heroic corps of Arsenalotti who were as quick to quell a riot or dowse a conflagration as to cast a cannon or shape a mast, all for *La Serenissima*. On that human foundation rested the security of the state. In return, the state paid them highly, housed them comfortably, entertained them well, and ensured them an old age free of care or want.

Bianca had also heard much about the wonderful machinery of the Great Arsenal, which dwarfed every other manufacturing complex in the world, but she had never seen it. Speaking into her ear, Marco explained what the machines and men were doing. Nonetheless, her impressions melted together: Satanic fires, cavernous sheds, tall masts, long oars, slick slipways, daredevil riggers, muscled foundrymen wearing only brief trousers, and, over all, the musty odour of burning coal contending with the tang of new-sawn wood.

Unlike the King, Bianca did not have to chat with naval architects and master craftsmen. But she watched with interest when the Admiral offered Henry a sharp adze and asked him to mark the long, heavy balk of timber that lay at his feet. Spying a shape like an H in the grain, the King whimsically drew three strokes to make his royal monogram: *H III*.

Pressed to explain his request, the Admiral smiled enigmatically and implored the King to be patient. Piqued by the mystery, Bianca was, above all, fascinated by the galleys under construction. They were like fabulous beasts coming to birth.

First, long, heavy timbers were laid down as the keelson, the backbone. Then, thin, upward-curling ribs grew from that keel-spine. Next came the long horizontal stringers, as Marco called them, that held the ribs together. Finally, the planking of the hull and decks grew like skin over the skeleton. Each time, the embryo galley was trundled on rollers to a new team of workmen. Looking back from a slipway as a completed galley slid into the water, Bianca saw its successors in varying stages of construction moving forward into a gaunt procession.

EVENING: JULY 18, 1574
THE DOGE'S PALACE

The King had much time to cultivate the virtue of patience. Six hours were to pass before he saw the last act of the Admiral's little drama.

After washing and changing his clothes in his regal apartment at the Ca' Foscari on the Grand Canal, the King was fêted at a banquet in the Hall of the Great Council in the Doge's Palace. The guests sat beneath Tintoretto's immense mural showing myriad souls in Paradise striving towards an enthroned God and Veronese's great ceiling painting of the Apotheosis of Venice, which depicted the city as a majestic pagan goddess robed and crowned by angels.

Even Marco and Bianca, inured to Venetian magnificence, were impressed by the spectacle the Senate had mounted. The young King appeared awestruck, as his hosts intended.

Three thousand noblemen and noblewomen sat down to dinner at the long tables around the golden canopy beneath which King Henry III and Doge Alvise Mocenigo dined with their courts.

The bill of fare was printed in an intricate calligraphic style created for the occasion. The King's copy was hand-lettered; its pictures were illuminated with gold leaf; and they sparkled with pearl and diamond dust. Twelve hundred different dishes were eaten from silver platters chased with gold, an additional set of three thousand platters being displayed around the Hall. They ate with silver forks, a utensil unknown north of the Alps, except for those introduced to the French Court by Queen Catarina, born a Medici, who was teaching the French how to cook.

Oysters stuffed with caviar and whole lobsters served cold in cups hollowed from large oranges followed the first sprinkling of vinegared and spiced cold titbits: tiny squid, prawns, sea urchins, scallops, conch, and the like. Each group of four guests was then presented with a single egg: the size of a man's head, it was made by separating and boiling in a pig's bladder first the yolks of twenty-five ordinary eggs and then, around the yolk, the whites. The monster egg came to the table wrapped in gold leaf on which was embossed the winged lion and the fleur de lys of France.

Next came pasta, rice, and polenta, those new luxuries of the wealthy. The crown of rice was a true work of art. Stuffed with sausage from the Abruzzi and with chicken breasts from Asolo, the rice was flavoured with dried porcini, the great mushroom of Tuscany, and with white truffles from Alba. It needed fifteen distinct steps before the rice, moulded into the shape of a king's crown, was placed on the table.

The fish displayed Venetian ingenuity with the fruit of the Mother Sea: of course *sarde in saur*, the characteristic sardines in a sour sauce; tuna cutlets fried in breadcrumbs; swordfish marinated for two days in vinegar, wine, salt, fennel, coriander, and cinnamon, grilled lightly, and then covered with a mixture of crushed walnuts, hard-boiled eggs, raisins, honey, and mint. The same taste for mixing sweet with natural flavours was apparent in the meat dishes, which numbered two hundred and thirty-two. By the time the ingenious sweet desserts appeared, few were still eating.

Jewels, shimmering ballgowns, and brocade doublets dazzled the eye, and Venetian virtuosi bewitched the ear with their mustic. The Venetian musician, Zarlino of Chioggia, had created a new art form for the occasion. He called it an *opera*, a work. While the King, who had inherited his mother's passion for the theatre, watched entranced, singers and actors performed a musical drama. After two hours, Bianca, who was seated with the elect under the golden canopy, saw that Henry had fallen asleep.

Awakened by rolling applause, he cried: '*Bravi! Bravissimi!*' Then he praised the opera inordinately. Would he have been so full of praise, Bianca wondered, if he had seen the entire performance?

As was customary, the King and the Doge left first. Instead of the big gondola that had brought Henry from his lodging in the Ca' Foscari, an armed galley lay at the Mole of St Mark's. Her new banners fluttered, and her new sails flapped in the light breeze. Her oarsmen sat ready to push off, and the torchlight gleamed on the armour of her men-at-arms. Redolent of new paint and fresh timbers, the galley embodied the power of Venice.

The King yawned. He had already seen too many galleys at the Arsenal. But he accepted graciously when invited to come aboard.

Doge Alvise Mocenigo did not lead King Henry to the quarterdeck, as his guest expected. Instead, the Doge took him down steep ladders to the dark hold, where yellow lantern light flickered in the encircling darkness. Mocenigo gestured without speaking, directing his guest's eyes to the mark on the heavy keel beam, which was lit by the bright circle cast by a hanging lantern: *H III*.

EVENING: JULY 19, 1574
VENICE: CA' CAPELLO ON THE GRAND CANAL

'A powerful state! A very powerful state!' Henry of France declared portentously. 'A good ally, but a bad enemy. Venice is not to be taken lightly.'

Her fingertips resting on his arm, Bianca Capello Buonaventura, called the Countess of Prato, smiled with affection and amusement.

The King was still very young in mind, although by the calendar only three years younger than her own twenty-six. Aware of his youth and inexperience, he sometimes assumed the heavy manner of a man twenty years older.

Bianca found it comical, such oracular sentences falling from the soft mouth of a young man whose fair beard was still wispy. The rulers of the Serene Republic would, however, have rejoiced had they heard his conclusions.

Henry of France had strolled happily into the gilded trap set by those rulers. He now believed Venice was still all-powerful on the seas, despite the humiliating treaty she had signed with the Turks thirteen months earlier. The weakened Republic badly needed powerful allies – and France had, for the time being at least, been won over by brilliant showmanship.

'I knew it when I saw that new galley,' Henry said. 'Six hours from keel to battle-ready warship . . . And others coming along the line. Who could stand up to the Arsenal's might?'

Despite the King's naïveté, that point was incisive. Marco liked to talk about 'the manufacturing strength' of the city. Yet he could not quite acknowledge that *La Serenissima*'s productive capacity was even more vital to her survival than her brave seamen. A senior commodore of war-galleys could hardly acknowledge that the Arsenalotti, rather than his crewmen, were the mainspring of Venetian power.

The King spoke his mind because he considered Bianca an outsider like himself. With youthful earnestness, he had declared that she was virtually his cousin, a member of the Medici family, even if outside the blanket. The French were great realists, and Henry observed: 'Whatever the priests say, you are my cousin Francesco's true consort.'

Warmed by royal approbation, Bianca curtsied low to begin the formal dance, and Henry III bowed as low. Artfully adapted, the old peasant melody swelled from the viola da gambas, the harpsichord, and the flutes. The caress of her silken skirts against her bare legs was pleasantly sensual. Heavy perfumes mingled with the fragrance of cakes baking below. All her senses were fulfilled, for the regal ballroom of the Ca' Capello on the Canalazzo delighted her eyes.

Opulently gilt against a pale blue background, circular plaques bearing the Capello arms alternated with plaques bearing the Wingèd Lion. Two nude Greek maidens in pale-yellow marble supported the mantelpiece, on which two pink-marble cherubs fluttered.

Initially grandiose, even domineering, on closer acquaintance, it was a harmonious room. But it was not restrained. Simplicity, much less austerity, Bianca mused, was no part of the era generally called *il periodo d'oro*, the golden age of Venice.

Twirling exuberantly, the King bumped into a buxom brunette who was draped with necklaces and bracelets. Bianca recognised Carla Grimani, who had been a favourite enemy of her girlhood. Now Carla Morosini, she was a second cousin by marriage. Turning to rebuke the gentleman who had jostled her, Carla saw the King and curtsied heavily.

As she sank down, the rope of Arabian pearls around her neck broke. The King dropped to his knees on the mosaic floor to collect them.

'Oh, Your Majesty!' Carla Morosini gasped. 'You mustn't kneel to me!'

For nobles who boasted that they were the equals of royalty, the patricians were behaving as if bewitched by the young King of France. Carla's husband, portly Aldo Morosini, Director of the Grain Trade, proved her point.

Reaching out to raise Henry from the floor, he drew back abashed at having almost committed the affront of touching the royal person. How, then, was he to prevail upon the King not to gather up spilt pearls? He planted his broad foot in its white-satin shoe on the three nearest pearls – and ground them into powder. Thus inspired, he searched eagerly for new pearls to crush, darting back and forth like a cockerel hungrily pecking at kernels of corn.

Henry of France, still squatting on the floor, looked on. He was obviously astonished again by Venetian profligacy.

'I beg Your Majesty, please desist!' Aldo Morosini declaimed. 'Before Your Majesty all else is dross. What do a few pearls matter, even all the gems of the Orient, beside Your Majesty's royal dignity?'

Aldo's two brothers rushed to join him in the new sport of pearl-crushing. Seeing that some guests were visibly pained by the vain-glorious performance, Bianca concluded that neither Venetian frugality nor Venetian reverence for material wealth had perished entirely. Suppressing a smile, she curtsied to the bemused King. He appeared to have forgotten not only the dance, but herself, in his fascination at Venetian prodigality.

A hand slipped under Bianca's elbow and drew her erect. She was surprised to see Marco smiling down at her. They had agreed not to be seen together tonight, largely to keep gossip-mongers from inventing a new scandal. While his wife was away, she had perhaps unwisely stayed at Ca' Capello with only his aged mother as chaperone. She was relieved to see his new wife's pastel-pretty face at his shoulder.

Angela Tron Capello's full lips opened over very white, very regular teeth that seemed like a row of doll's tombstones. In her blue eyes, where life should have flared, there remained a dead space.

Bianca wondered if Angela would ever bear up to the burdens of marriage. She wondered, too, about Angela's behaviour in bed. It would be in bed – and *only* in bed. Marco's wife would never make impromptu love in a forest glade or on a midnight beach.

Bianca gave her cousin by marriage an empty smile. They had exchanged meaningless greetings and small talk that morning, when Angela returned from her father's villa on the mainland. They would never exchange female confidences. Angela obviously disapproved of her – not least for her easy comradeship with Marco.

Bianca suspected that Angela had fled to the *terraferma* on the eve of the King's arrival to avoid being outshone in public by her notorious cousin by marriage. Why else should a socially ambitious bride absent herself from even a single moment of the most splendid festivities Venice had ever known?

Tonight was different. As châtelaine of Ca' Capello, the Lady Angela Tron Capello was the King's hostess and could ignore the unpalatable reality. Yet Ca' Capello on the Canalazzo had been charged to receive Henry III for the same reason as had the Palazzo Capello on Murano: Bianca Capello Buonaventura, *maîtresse en titre* of Francesco I, Grand Duke of Tuscany.

Bartolomeo Capello was, nonetheless, exultant. Glowing in black satin shot with gold, he was clearly not troubled at owing his new glory to the daughter for whose head he had once offered two thousand ducats. He and she had exchanged no intimate words. Nor was the predatory gleam wholly absent from his eye when he looked at her.

He had already astonished Bianca, who thought herself beyond being surprised by him. He had spoken with immense self-satisfaction of his success in bringing her up to be a 'perfect lady, fit to preside over any court in Europe'. Bartolomeo Capello as a tutor of young ladies!

Noting that she was gazing meditatively at her father, Marco winked at her. That familiar gesture amid the formality of a royal reception delighted Bianca. Angela beside him could not have seen him wink, but he drew both ladies aside, his hands cupping their elbows.

'I promised to clear up your mystery,' he said. 'And Angela's entitled to know. We have no secrets from each other, do we, my dear?'

Angela smiled dutifully, and said tartly: 'Of course not, my dear. Not on my side, anyway.'

Ignoring her jibe, Marco led them to a group of green velvet chairs standing before the windows that overlooked the rear courtyard with its pretentious Lepanto staircase. Handing them into their chairs, he slouched into the third and put his blue leather shoes on the fourth. The master of Ca' Capello thus signalled that he desired privacy.

'You want to know who did it?' he asked abruptly. 'The whole story?'

Bianca nodded. He would, regardless, tell her in his own time only what *he* thought she should know.

'Paolo Crespelle was in Constantinople five months ago,' Marco continued inconsequentially. 'It was better for the Tuscan Wild Boar to go than a staid Venetian. The treaty's not *that* stable. He found Joseph Nasi was very ill, perhaps dying. You know, the old Duke of Naxos.'

'I know very well . . .' Bianca began, but Angela's words overrode hers: 'The anti-Christ, the filthy Jew who sucked the blood of good Christians!'

Bianca wondered why a little bundle of unthinking, vehement prejudices like Angela was to hear these revelations. Marco rolled his eyes, but waited stoically for his wife to finish her ritual abuse.

'The old man appeared to be dying of a lung complaint,' he resumed. 'It was, he told Paolo, the fault of Venice, which had driven him into the wilderness . . . with all its hardships. Constantinople, the most luxurious city in Asia, a wilderness! Well, aside from that rhetoric, Paolo saw the Duke was also dying of a broken heart. His New Judea and Israel, the Hebrew Nation he founded in Galilee, had ended in impoverishment and quarrels. There, too, he said, Venice had failed him.'

'Venice failed *him*?' Bianca could not help interjecting. 'Why he plotted *against* . . .'

'Not as he told it. The old Duke said he'd always worked for a balance of power. The only way to ensure trade was to ensure that neither side was ever so powerful that it could do as it pleased . . . bear down the other. By failing to stand up to the Sultan, Venice had broken the mould.'

Bianca was fascinated to learn that the man she thought an enemy of Venice was in his own eyes a conciliator. Nonetheless, she raised her eyebrows. She did not want an analysis of recent history; she wanted to know who had killed her husband.

'All right, Bianca, I'll get to the point,' Marco responded to her impatience. 'Joseph Nasi said *he* had hired the assassins who killed Pietro. He said he had no choice. He had to clear his skirts with the Sultan, had to prove he wasn't plotting with the Christians, which he was, of course. Also, he had to re-establish his honour with his fellow Jews. He couldn't let the murder of his physician and the desecration of the Holy Torah go unpunished. So he took a life for the life that had been taken.'

'That simple!'

Biance was appalled, but, an instant later, she was also relieved. Pietro had made his own fate. His killing had nothing to do with the intrigues of Florence, and her lover Francesco had nothing to do with the killing. Indirectly, she herself could be considered partially responsible. She and Marco had sent Pietro to Constantinople. Yet he would have acted as he had no matter where he was, no matter what she did or did not do. His own nature had made his death inevitable.

'Thank you, Marco!' she finally said. 'My deepest thanks! When I tell this tale, bring out the truth at last, my name will be cleared. I can hardly wait to . . .'

'You'll *have* to wait a long time, maybe forever,' Marco interjected. 'Unless you want my blood on your head. If you tell the tale, you'll have to offer proof, some backing. If you don't say how you heard, you'll only make matters worse, revive old rumours with a tale that sounds false. If you do tell how, you'll implicate not only me, but yourself. Our enemies will use your evidence to discredit us, to discredit Venice herself, for our filthy spying. And the State Inquisition will assuredly . . . ah . . . remove us. To make sure we can say no more.'

Bianca glanced doubtfully at Angela. To have her fate rest in those plump, dimpled hands!

Since she could say nothing about Angela, she asked meditatively: 'Marco, do you ever wish you were out of it? It's not just a dirty business. It's a very dangerous business.'

'Out of it!' His surprise was genuine. 'How could I be out of it, Bianca? As a naval commander or a prosecutor, as an ambassador or a spy, a gentleman of Venice serves as the Republic directs.'

CHAPTER XXII

THE sun was a molten weight in the bleached blue sky, and the earth was parched ashen by three months of drought. The olive trees on the ridges of the Apennines shrank into themselves to save every drop of moisture for their bitter green fruit. Their arrowhead leaves were dusty in the arid heat of late August in the hamlet of Pratolino, some nine miles north of Florence.

On the slopes above the thread of a dry creek, the brown grass was without savour to the hungry sheep. The grapes on the vines that marched in files along the hillsides were stunted, yet plump with sugar. If rain came, just one downpour before the pressing, the vintage would still be meagre. But the wine would be vermilion, fragrant, and very strong.

The chestnut trees had months earlier lost their waxy spikes of pink and white flowers. But nuts lay thick on the gravel paths that wound through fresh green foliage watered from deep springs that never failed. Battalions of spear-straight Tuscan cypresses stood guard, their green needles so dark they looked black in the dusk.

The great house on the knoll was deep pink, just a shade lighter than the faded red of Venice. The five-storey façade, pierced by fifty-two windows, was approached by two flights of steps that linked terraces enclosed by stone walls. The last flight of steps, which divided into two curved sections to embrace a subterranean entrance, led to the entry court. The marble pediment above the brass-bound doors bore the Medici arms: six golden balls beneath a lion's head roaring. A plaque on the granite frame of the doorway displayed the Wingēd Lion of Venice above the silver-and-blue hat of the Capellos.

Francesco I of Tuscany had built the village for his *maîtresse en titre*, Lady Bianca Capello Buonaventura, sometimes Countess of Prato. All the Medicis had a passion for country houses, and Francesco already possessed six. But he loved best this villa, which was made for domestic joy, not public dignity. Even more deeply in love with Bianca after more than a decade, he had built it to please her. He was still adding to the house, for he would never stop building. He suffered from the 'sickness of the stones', an incurable malady that drove him to fill his domain with monumental structures.

The sloping red-tiled roofs of the villa were studded with thirty-two chimneys serving sixty-four fireplaces. The stoves and hearths of the kitchens were in a separate building, as were the fires that heated the water that ran through lead pipes to the heated bathrooms in the private quarters. Such amenities were almost unknown elsewhere in Europe.

Francesco was a pioneer of technology. Applying after a lapse of a thousand years the sophisticated methods of the comfort-loving Romans, his architects had created a luxurious villa of classical modernity.

Other man-made wonders were set through hundreds of acres of parkland. The Royal Villa was a realm of its own, remote alike from the tension of the city and the squalor of the countryside. Here the Grand Duke of Tuscany, who was primarily a philosopher and a scientist, could evade the demands of state, even though his ministers still sent him importunate messages.

A little after ten on the evening of August 29, 1576, the master of the Royal Villa, dressed in a plain linen shirt and cotton breeches, was conferring with his favourite architect, the sculptor Giambologna, in the small salon on the third floor of the east wing. The pink-and-amber decor, like the spindle-legged chairs with harp-shaped backs, were very feminine. The small salon was Bianca's favourite, her private domain.

A canvas square of half-completed *gros point* embroidery destined to cover a cushion was tucked behind the chair in which Francesco sat. On the beige leather top of Bianca's writing-table lay a sheaf of papers relating to the Uffizi Palace, which was now a gallery showing contemporary artists, as well as their recent forerunners like Raphael and Michelangelo. Francesco had transformed the Uffizi from an office building to please Bianca, who oversaw the gallery herself.

He could almost hear her husky voice saying: 'Franco, even a great artist works better for knowing the larder's full. Our painters and sculptors need regular incomes. We can keep them going by commissioning works for the Uffizi, as well as for houses and churches.'

Smiling at his memory of Bianca's enthusiasm, the Duke only half-heard Giambologna's monotonous voice, which contrasted with his flamboyant appearance: '. . . a pressure of ten atmospheres for the jets.'

'Ten?' the Duke asked. 'Enough to keep the fountain playing continuously? I want it to spurt a hundred feet high.'

'Just enough, Your Highness,' the architect replied. 'Too much pressure would starve the other water displays. Besides, the water supply is not absolutely certain.'

'I see.'

Francesco was annoyed at himself for having forgotten both the shortage of water and the needs of the twenty-two other fountains in the park. God knew he had reason to be distracted, but any imprecision or lapse, above all his own, disturbed him.

His regal discourtesy softened by a smile, he turned away abruptly and tinkled the crystal bell on the marquetry table beside his chair. He waited, not speaking, impatiently drumming his fingers on the mother-of-pearl inlay. Within thirty seconds, a red-cheeked footman in a long green-and-crimson coat scratched softly on the door.

'Go,' the Duke directed, 'and ask the women how your mistress does.'

Francesco de' Medici looked at the plan that lay on the table, tracing the network of pipes with a forefinger stained yellow by the acids he used in his chemical experiments. He nodded and clicked his tongue against the roof of his mouth, then frowned. Fearing his patron's nitpicking, Giambologna was anxious for the integrity of his grand design.

'This little pump?' the Duke asked. 'Wouldn't it be better here?'

'Ideally, Highness, yes. You've got a keen eye. But, as you see, the main pipe feeding it would then cross here. A straight run of pipe is more efficient than putting in four elbows.'

'I see!' said the Duke somewhat ominously.

'Your way looks shorter,' Giambologna maintained. 'But it's really not.'

With an effort, the absolute ruler nodded, but added: 'We could try the short way.'

'Of course, Your Highness, though you'll find it won't work. But I'll make a note.'

The architect marked the plan with red ink – and made a mental note to ignore that mark. If the Duke's alterations resulted in a malfunction, the Duke would forget making the proposal. That was the royal prerogative. Yet Giambologna was happy with his royal patron.

To no other ruler in Europe would he have dared speak as straightforwardly as he did to the tolerant and intelligent Francesco I.

A scratching on the door heralded the young footmen, who reported gravely: 'No change, Your Highness. The Countess is holding her own, but there are no further developments.'

'Let me know just as soon . . .'

'As you command, Your Highness.'

The footman closed the door, and the Duke stalked to the window. The wheel set with vertical blades, which hung from the ceiling, was driven rapidly by the sturdy legs of a footman in the tiny room next door. But Leonardo da Vinci, who had designed the device to move the air and create a cool breeze, had rarely endured such still and heavy weather in Florence. The salon reeked of stagnant heat.

Francesco normally enjoyed going over the plans for the villa and the park, a straightforward task beside the taxing experiments he performed alone. Usually that task helped him relax. But tonight he was as taut as a harpsichord string.

To divert his patron, Giambologna turned the conversation to sculpture. They exchanged animated opinions on Donatello and the della Robbias, as well as the immortal Michelangelo. Yet the Duke could not give the subject his full attention. An ear cocked for noises in the corridor, he kept glancing at the door. After almost an hour, it opened again.

'Your Highness, still little change,' the young footman reported. 'But they say it's going well.'

'She's not suffering?' Francesco was anxious. 'She isn't, is she?'

'Not greatly, Your Highness. The women say no.'

The footman's tone was affirmative, but his mobile Italian features expressed grave doubt.

'Go back! And wait! I don't want to see you again until you have something positive to report.'

Abandoning both the plans and the conversation, Francesco paced the small salon. He threw out remarks that, the architect judged wisely, required no answer. From time to time, he poured small glasses of colourless grappa, the potent *acqua vitae*, which was flavoured by a sprig of rosemary in the flask.

Although he detested grappa, Giambologna wisely allowed his glass to be refilled and expressed his gratitude for the honour the Duke did him by pouring with his own hand. It was not often necessary to flatter this sovereign, who wished to be treated as a fellow craftsman, though, of course, a *senior* craftsman. But the Duke's tension was tonight as solid a barrier as a brick wall.

Three hours later, the door opened without the usual deferential scratching. The apple-cheeked footman stood beaming in the doorway.

'Good news, Your Highness!' he announced. 'Wonderful news! The Countess has just been delivered of a robust infant . . . a boy. Both are very well.'

'I must go to her!'

Francesco's forehead was still creased by worry. But, as he spoke, the tension was smoothed from his face by joy.

'First, but very quickly . . . I must give her time to compose herself . . . a glass of wine, my friends.'

The Grand Duke with his own hands twisted the cork from a flask of Montepulciano. Ignoring the footman's protests, he poured the dark wine into crystal goblets. With Italian grace, half egalitarian and half paternalistic, he clapped the architect and the footman on the shoulder and lifted his glass in a toast: 'To Bianca! To my son! To the heir!'

SEPTEMBER 5, 1576
PRATOLINO: THE GROTTOES OF THE ROYAL VILLA

The grotto of the Great God Pan was dank even on the heat-raddled fifth day of September. Instead of using the subterranean doorway embraced by the divided steps outside, Bianca and Francesco had come down the hidden stairway from the first floor. Bianca did not wish to make a mystery of their visit, but neither did she want to call attention to it.

When Francesco uncovered his lantern, yellow light flickered on the hairy goat-legs and the wooden pipes of the Great God Pan. Illuminated from below, his satyr's grin was diabolical. Francesco smiled appreciatively at the fantasy realm he had created.

Then he turned to Bianca urgently, his features strained with worry above his broad white collar. She smiled, still wan a week after the birth of her son. Her yellow muslin dress, which left her ankles bare above strip-leather sandals, was simple even for a country afternoon.

'The boy's all right, isn't he?' the anxious father demanded. 'He's not sick? Not deformed? With all the swaddling clothes, I can't tell.'

'You mustn't worry, Franco my dear,' she replied. 'He's very well, a beautiful baby.'

'Then why all the mystery? I can't believe you're suddenly overcome with a longing to see Pan. Why bring me down here to this out of the way . . .'

'Because it's out of *everyone's* way. In the villa there's always someone listening . . . Franco, have you thought about the christening?'

'We'll call him Antonio Cosimo. After Bartolomeo for your father, if you'd like. Or Marco for Venice and your ancestor Marco Polo, *il Milion*. But there's plenty of time. I want to get powerful godparents and witnesses who will . . .'

'*Not* after my father, though Marco would be nice,' she answered. 'Franco, I'd like to baptise him tomorrow. Friar Giulio, the old Franciscan, can do it. Not secretly, though. I want everyone to know. And I want them to think we're trying to keep it secret.'

The Duke knew that strange whims afflicted pregnant women. Obviously, even stranger fancies afflicted mothers after giving birth. He replied indulgently: 'I like doing what you wish. But isn't it peculiar for the heir to . . .'

'Franco, he's *not* the heir. You forget!'

'That scrawny Filipo of Joanna's? Yes, of course, he's my son, but he'll never live to sit on the throne. He's far too sickly.'

'He *is* the heir though.'

'Yes . . . Just now.'

'Filipo must *remain* the visible heir, Franco. Your brother Ferdinando wouldn't dare interfere with the nephew of the Emperor. But he'd sweep aside the grandson of Bartolomeo Capello of Venice. If Antonio alone stood between him and the throne . . .'

'Bianca, my dear, I know how you felt about Nando, even before the attack on your palazzo. You're by no means wrong, I've realised. My little brother wants my throne. He's become a monster . . . maimed by jealousy. Not only that, but we're constantly watched by his hirelings . . . in Florence, even here in Pratolino . . .'

'That's why I wanted to come to the grotto. No one can eavesdrop on us here.'

'What's worrying you? . . . I've been too happy. Only thinking about our good fortune. But I can see you've been brooding. You should've been recovering from your ordeal.'

'Ordeal? Hardly! Peasant women are back in the fields two hours afterwards. But I have been thinking hard. Franco, I've decided

Antonio must be branded a fraud . . . no child of yours and mine. Then he must disappear.'

He looked at her in astonishment and finally said: 'This is madness. What's wrong with you, Bianca?'

She replied with asperity: 'Listen first, then judge me.'

'All right then! What've you got to say?'

'You said it yourself, Franco. Your brother Ferdinando will do *anything* to seize the throne . . . anything short of murdering you and poor little Filipo.'

'No need to murder poor Filipo. He's not long for this world.' Francesco declared grimly. 'But murder me? Nando could murder me easily enough. And what then?' He paused to reflect and then spoke his thoughts aloud: 'I know the people don't love me. But they do love him. He's a swashbuckler, a braggart, a bit of a mountebank. They love him for that, the way they loved my father.'

'So you do agree,' Bianca interjected. 'Ferdinando *could* kill you and take the throne.'

'Let me work it out myself,' he snapped. 'Don't drive me!'

He pondered for a time before saying decisively: 'No, Nando will not have me killed – at least not for some time. Anger at the assassination of a lawful sovereign could do him out of the succession. The people want order and legality. They've had too much strife, too much disorder.'

'Even so, Florentines are used to violent political change – not like Venice. Even if Ferdinando wouldn't murder you, what of Antonio? Suppose Antonio stood in your brother's way, Antonio, the son of the Venetian adventuress?'

'Ferdinando would flick the lad away with a single finger. Preferably *before* I make Antonio my heir, *before* poor Filipo passes away. My little brother Nando would remove the threat – and leave himself the sole heir.'

'We're agreed then, my dear.' Bianca felt no triumph at having brought Francesco to her way of thinking. 'We *must* . . . It hurts me, grates on my heart. Yet we *must* discredit . . . disown . . . Antonio for his own protection – even though it means discrediting me!'

'I don't like it, Bianca. I don't like your always taking the blame!'

'How else can we protect our son? So that he can, someday, take his rightful place on the throne. I shall know that he will in time be Grand Duke of Tuscany. What more consolation do I need?'

The next day, the child was baptised Antonio Cosimo Marco in the little round chapel that stood a hundred yards from the villa. Old Friar Giulio, who had seventy years earlier been an agile Pratolino lad, was now so old Francesco had to whisper those names to him twice. Although his hand shook and he doused the baby's head, instead of sprinkling a few drops of holy water, Bianca was pleased by the simplicity of his brown habit belted with a piece of rope. She had dreamed of her son's being baptised by the archbishop in the cathedral like Pellegrina ten years ago. Yet she was curiously content.

Antonio was just eight days old, but his mother's fond eye could already see in his eye the shrewdness he inherited from both Medicis and Capellos, two dynasties of traders and bankers. His father saw that the dome of his hairless head promised nobility and intellectual power. He would, both parents agreed, be a great man in his time.

Antonio's godfathers were the sculptor Giambologna and the Count of Abruzzo, the senior nobleman among the small court the Duke could not avoid bringing with him to the Royal Villa. His godmothers were the ladies-in-waiting, the Countess of Abruzzo and the young Baroness Adacci, who was the sister of Paolo Crespelle. Bianca had dreamed of reigning dukes, even king and queens, but she had to be content with the humble godparents who stood beside the font. Her plan would not allow her to seek more exalted sponsors, even if she had had the time.

No matter how loyal, the congregation would gossip volubly about this hurried baptism, which smacked of low conspiracy. All the courtiers and servants were dedicated gossips. How could they be otherwise, being mostly Florentines?

They would wonder aloud why the Grand Duke and his *maîtresse en titre* had been anxious to have the infant baptised without delay – and virtually in secret. What, they would ask, had the parents to hide?

Dukes and kings had for centuries proudly acknowledged offspring born out of wedlock. They had ostentatiously ennobled those natural children and their mothers. Yet Francesco had not made Bianca a marchioness or Antonio a count. He had not even confirmed the title Bianca sometimes used for convenience, Countess of Prato.

What fears stalked the noble parents? What were they concealing?

The noble parents provided the gossips with round answers to those sharp questions. They thus stoked the fires of rumour.

'Since we *must* do this,' Francesco had decided, 'let us enjoy it.'

Bianca, who had conceived the plan, could not pretend to be light-hearted. It was necessary, but painful, the deliberate destruction of the little reputation she still possessed among the Florentines. Her plan's success would be crowned by her being deprived of her child. Although she was torn between necessity and instinct, she knew she had not imagined the danger that made ruthlessness essential.

The danger was real – and immediate. She banished her tears, and she did what she knew was necessary.

She hurriedly sent away Giovanna Conti, who had attended the birth. The midwife took with her the leather lute-case that was her most prized possession. She liked to soothe her ladies' labour with music.

Giovanna Conti rode off in a donkey cart, sitting between the lute-case and the silk bag that held her fee. The bag was very heavy, a munificent reward even for a Medici.

In the lute-case was, simply, her lute. But Bianca's maid Lucia whispered in the servants' sitting-room that the case had not held a lute when it was brought into her lady's chamber. Pressed to reveal its contents, Lucia smirked meaningfully. Then the major domo and the woman who was chief keeper of the linens gave her more wine.

After her fifth beaker, Lucia asked conspiratorially: 'Have you ever heard a lute play itself? Have you ever heard a lute sound just like a day-old baby crying?'

Then, horrified and contrite, she swore the upper servants to secrecy. But she knew they would pass on the spicy titbit.

Only four women beside Bianca herself knew that she had truly given birth to Antonio. Besides the midwife and Lucia, they were the Countess of Abruzzo and the Baroness Adacci. As godmothers, the noblewomen had special responsibility for his well-being.

'Not much more to do,' Bianca told Francesco with forced composure. 'All that's left is finding the woman who was our benefactrix. We must find the "true" mother.'

CHAPTER XXIII

ANGELA TRON CAPELLO complacently touched the minute bulge under her heart with the tip of her long-nailed index finger. Although it was invisible under her winter skirt of quilted blue wool, she was intensely aware of that slight swelling. She smiled reminiscently. Her husband had reacted with typical masculine excess when she told him her hope of her condition. Marco had summoned not one but two professors of physic from the University of Padua.

Padua's physicians were the best in the world. Some of their practices were disgusting and, it was said, violated the tenets of Holy Church. Yet cutting up the corpses of paupers and criminals gave them intimate knowledge of the human body.

Angela shivered fastidiously. But, she reminded herself, she was an enlightened daughter of the enlightened late-sixteenth century. Though it was distasteful, she recognised that her body was much like the body of a woman strangled for theft. Marco had taught her to face facts, as, he said, her family did not.

The professors from Padua had been put out at being summoned for 'such a simple case'. Their diagnosis was, however, clear and simple. She was pregnant, and she would deliver a robust child after eight months. How they could be sure the child would be robust, she could not understand. But why question that cheerful prediction?

Angela looked out of the window of the sitting-room adjoining the bedchamber on the second floor and shivered again. Fog was sweeping up the Canalazzo. Curling in woolly grey tendrils in the west towards Cannareggio, it lay thick before Ca' Capello, portending snow. She could hardly see the square Palace of the Treasurers just across the canal, and the spire of the Frari was wholly obscured. Under a leaden sky, the candles in the shops on the Rialto Bridge were yellow pinpoints.

Angela loved early winter, when Venice drew into herself. She was now snug inside when all outside was bleak. The city was uniquely her own when the clouds lowered and the cold winds blew. No longer overrun by hordes of visitors, Venice belonged to the Venetians from November to March.

For a moment, she forgot the threat that hung over the city. At least, no one in Ca' Capello had been stricken. Not yet and, she would see to it, never. She had taken every precaution from garlic hung over doorways to asafoetida and whale's ambergris worn in little sachets around the neck. She could not risk her child's welfare. Any infected servant would be out of the palace two minutes after the first sign.

The professors from Padua had said the cold would slow the spread of the pestilence. But they had warned that Venice was again besieged by the plague, the Black Death that had three centuries earlier killed a third of Europe. Angela preferred to think of it as just another fever. A virulent fever accompanied by a severe rash, but a fever the cold weather would assuredly check.

The blessings of winter were mixed. The cold and its terrible ally, the bone-biting damp, would soon drive them into the cramped rooms below. No matter how high the fires were built, it was impossible to take the chill off the spacious, high-ceilinged, marble-floored rooms. Only piling on layer after layer of clothing would keep them from freezing, even below. Angela detested the discomfort and the smells after not bathing for weeks on end. Still, there were salves for the itching and perfumes against the smell. Also wine and, even better, grappa, far more warming than fires.

Astonishingly, the physicians had told her she must drink no grappa, none at all. As for wine, they said, not even a litre, no more than two goblets a day. Otherwise the infant could come to harm.

The infant! It was still hard to believe that her thoughts could so casually touch on the child she carried. Some three years after her wedding, she had finally conceived.

God knew she and Marco had tried hard for a long time. She had even learned to enjoy the trying a little. Well, perhaps not really enjoy, but at least tolerate it. She did love holding Marco in her arms, and she loved to see the excitement her body aroused. As for the final act, well it was no longer *too* terrible.

She had visited the wisest midwives and herbalists, even those said to be witches. All were surprised at her coming to them for help in *starting* a baby. They specialised in *stopping* babies. None had done her any good. But she had refused to see the professors from Padua who, Marco said, could help if anyone could. She would not have a man pawing her.

Three months after she gave up hope, resigning herself to childlessness, she had found herself pregnant. She had not then greatly minded the learned professors' examining her to make sure. In her triumph, that intrusion was trifling.

Angela looked up from her reverie to see her husband gazing down at her fondly. His black hair shone in the candlelight, and his face was ruddy from the chill wind outside.

'Filthy weather!' Marco extended his open hands towards the pink marble fireplace. 'God help poor sailors on a day like this.'

Angela smiled at that prayer, which he uttered whenever the weather was bad. Poor dear, he did hate not going to sea for so long, almost three years now. But vital matters kept him ashore, not the least, she reflected complacently, looking after herself. Now high in the Secret Service, Marco was often kept late in the hidden corridors of the Doge's Palace. He had, besides, been head of their branch of the Capello family since his father's death, and the family's demands were heavy.

At thirty-two, her husband was still a stripling in the service of a city whose great hero, Admiral Sebastiano Venier, the victor of Lepanto, was vigorous at eighty. Yet Marco sometimes complained, only half-joking, that he needed a juggler's dexterity. His own trade was the naval and the intelligence services, but the Capello business interests were diverse and widespread. Sadly, his sisters' husbands were untrustworthy, and he had no brothers to help oversee the Capello enterprises: the shops and the merchant vessels; the forests and the timber yards; the bank and the money-changers' stalls; also, more and more important nowadays, the manufactories that produced textiles and garments, paper and books, bricks and tiles.

'Some wine,' she urged. 'You've earned it!'

Marco poured from the pitcher of mulled wine keeping warm on the hob before the fireplace.

'Marco, I feel so . . . so well!' Angela said exuberantly. 'Like a new woman, a wonderful new woman.'

'You *are* wonderful! No doubt about it!' He smiled at her self-praise. 'You've never looked so well, so beautiful!'

'Not just outside, Marco, but wonderful inside too.'

'It is wonderful of you to start a baby. Even if I do miss the trying, which was also wonderful.'

'Now, Marco, you promised!'

He had agreed, albeit reluctantly, when she told him the physicians had advised her to refrain from love-making from this moment until three months after the baby's birth. Perhaps that was not *exactly* what they had told her. But it would do him good to restrain the animal side of his nature.

'You know, my dearest, I'm still surprised that we have to stop for so long. None of my friends' wives . . .'

'Every case is different . . . You know, Marco,' she changed the subject, 'I was thinking of Bianca. She can't have a child. But I can!'

Marco was hypersensitive about Bianca. But she could permit herself to flick the whip once, secure in her triumph. She sensed that his curious relationship with his cousin was anything but innocent politically. She suspected that it had not always been so innocent in other ways.

'I'm giving you a child, dear, all on my own,' Angela rejoiced: 'Not like Bianca. She had to fake it.'

'Not *entirely* on your own, dear. I helped.' He smiled tolerantly. 'As for Bianca, it certainly seems so.'

Marco wanted to say more, but could not allow himself to. The danger to Bianca, as well as to her son, would be mortal if the truth came out.

He confided in Angela on almost everything else, even the secret business of the state. But he could not talk candidly to his wife about Bianca, for whom she nursed an extraordinary dislike. Certainly she could not be jealous! Yet he could not trust Angela with the true story of the birth of Antonio Cosimo Marco Capello de' Medici, to give the infant the full name he would bear when his father legitimised him by decree.

'Wine from Crete?' he asked instead. 'With cloves, a touch of sugar, a sprinkle of ginger, and lots of cinnamon – if my taste buds don't lie.'

'All except the special sugar bought by Capello traders in the Orient – and brought to Venice by Capello ships.'

'Even the Cretan wine, of course. How much longer we can hold that island, I'm not sure. I ought to have a look. But I'll worry about Crete another day.'

'I know you hate being land-bound, but Paolo does well. He was doing brilliantly as commodore of our trading ships – until you sent him to Florence.'

'I had to, Angela,' he responded defensively. 'No one else can see so quickly how the land lies there. You know, I miss him. Not just his shrewdness in a deal, but his wit, his company.'

Angela wondered whether she also had to be jealous of Paolo. But Marco was not inclined that way. Many patricians were, so many the government was attacking that widespread taste for their own sex. The birthrate was falling. More than two thousand noblemen had sat in the Grand Council in 1651, but now only thirteen hundred did – and their number was still declining.

A perfunctory tap sounded on the door, and a tall footman in the silver-and-blue Capello livery came in. After his hurried entrance, he seemed loath to state his business. He stood silent, nervously twisting a silver button on his long-coat until Marco raised an impatient eyebrow.

'Forgive me for disturbing you, sir,' the footman finally said. 'There's a messenger below. Not from the Doge's Palace. The rascal doesn't even talk proper Venetian. Says he *must* see you. No one else but you.'

'I'll come,' Marco said. 'This happens from time to time.'

The messenger was waiting under the eye of a burly footman in the rear courtyard beside the staircase that displayed the Lepanto relics. He was dressed like a Venetian boatman in a brown smock and bell-bottomed canvas trousers. But his accent and his cocky self-assurance were Florentine.

Marco extended his palm and said curtly: 'Give it to me!'

'You're truly the nobleman, Marco Capello, sir? I've got to be sure.'

'As you know full well. Give it to me!'

With a crooked grin, the messenger handed Marco a small parcel sewn into an otter's skin for protection. Marco gave him a coin, and he vanished through the land-door.

Marco wandered meditatively into his private office on the first floor and drew out the chair before his cluttered desk. The stiff paper, compressed by the otter skin, sprang open when he cut the stitches. Recognising both Paolo's writing and Bianca's, he saw that he held two despatches in different ciphers. He began deciphering Paolo's first, occasionally consulting the cipher-key he took from his belt-pouch.

Paolo confirmed his previous report that Antonio was the true son of Bianca Capello Buonaventura and Francesco de' Medici. Bianca had summoned him and told him to pass that fact on to Marco, if he had not already done so. Paolo had naturally agreed to include a message from the Grand Duke and herself. After that prologue, his message summed up the tense situation in Tuscany.

'Bianca and Francesco can now depend upon few Tuscans and fewer Florentines. Cardinal Ferdinando's intrigues are virulent. He is spilling out so much gold it is exceedingly difficult for our friends to find anyone they can rely upon.

'The Duke's younger brother is determined to be Grand Duke himself – as soon as he possibly can. Only a remnant of family affection keeps him from assassinating his brother. He also fears the assassination would be brought home to him – and the Vatican would have to withdraw its support. Even the Florentines, who esteem him as a hearty carouser, a tireless womaniser, and a very good fellow, could turn away from him in fear if he were proved to be a murderer. To that extent morality still endures in Florence, although in their morality, as in all things, the Florentines are wholly self-serving.

'Nando they call him, as if he were a hard-drinking bully boy and no more. This Nando has bought three-quarters of his brother's courtiers – as well as half his brother's ministers. By promising princely payments he has convinced most of Tuscany's neighbours that neutrality will be the best policy if the brothers should clash openly. The College of Cardinals Nando already controls, and he is making good progress with King Philip of Spain, who dislikes his cousin Francesco's inclination towards Venice.

'But this filial younger brother does not plan to clash openly with his elder brother. He plans to push Francesco off the throne gradually, bloodlessly if possible. To that end he is also buying the goodwill and support of all the guilds and factions of Florence.

'Nando's rumour-mongers point out that Francesco has not given Tuscany a credible heir, only that sickly little half-Austrian scrap Filipo. They argue: "How desperate Francesco must be to give out falsely that his mistress has borne him a son. And that child really the son of a low woman and a woodcutter. Or a gypsy or an itinerant musician, depending on the speaker."

'All this is doing Francesco no good. A good man, but an awkward prince, he is losing stature in the eyes of his subjects. They do not understand his pleasure in locking himself up in laboratories or spending hours in artists' studios. They whisper – the tolerant, art-loving citizens of Florence – that their Duke is a secret homosexual, rollicking with artists who ape the loves of the deceased masters Michelangelo and Leonardo. They say he keeps a notorious foreign courtesan as his *maîtresse en titre* only to conceal his unnatural vice – and to provide a spurious heir to the throne.

'The carefully tended myth about Antonio's birth is, thus, working against his father's interests. Yet the myth is not firm enough to protect the heir presumptive. Antonio is, therefore, to be reported tomorrow to have died of an infant's fever – lest his loving uncle Nando's assassins kill him just to be sure. But how long, I wonder, can that expedient serve?

'I leave the parents' suggestion for your judgement.'

So, abruptly, ended the dispatch. The letter from Bianca proposed a solution.

'We did not want to put the burden on Paolo Crespelle without your approval. Francesco and I wish to send Antonio into the fastnesses of the hills, to vanish until times are better. My lady-in-waiting, Baroness Adacci, Paolo Crespelle's sister, has persuaded her father to give the infant shelter and protection. No one would expect the old Baron, the independent brigand of the hills, to help the Duke. It is well known that he hates the Medicis.

'With your permission, I propose to charge Paolo to take Antonio to his father's castle above Pistoia. Paolo Crespelle, son of our old enemy and officer in the navy of Venice, is one of the few Tuscans we can now trust.

'And only Paolo can do it. The appearance of my lady-in-waiting or her husband anywhere near the Castello Crespelle with an infant would give the game away before it started. When Paolo takes Antonio to his father, my son will appear just another of his by-blows.

In haste, with my love,
Bianca

After reading the dispatches, Marco called for his cloak and went back into the chilly evening. Impatient, he did not summon his gondola, which would have been slowed by the fog on the Canalazzo. Instead, he walked briskly through the winding alleys, reaching the Doge's Palace in twenty minutes. He hardly noticed the distance, for he was shaping his plans in his mind. Nothing for it, he decided, but to go to Florence himself. Angela would fret at his being away over Christmas. But he had been at home every Christmas now for four years.

One of the three State inquisitors was always on duty in the small wood-panelled office between the torture chamber and the cells. He asked only as a courtesy for there was no question about this operation. To Marco's astonishment, the Inquisitor shook his head decisively.

'Certainly not!' he declared. 'Your presence would only stir suspicion and unrest in Florence. And it would go even worse for the Lady Bianca. Commodore, you're too old to play at disguises.'

The Inquisitor yawned in the teeth of Marco's automatic protests and finally said: 'Even you don't believe what you're saying. I'm sorry, but I must overrule you. Let Paolo Crespelle handle it. Better a Tuscan for a Tuscan mess. Please draft your orders for him tonight.'

The Inquisitor smiled a gracious dismissal and turned to a desk heaped with reports. But he swung round as Marco touched the door-knob and spoke as if it were an afterthought: 'You might let me have a copy *before* it goes off. I know that's unusual for a senior man like you. I know you need my approval only for an operation that puts you in the field. After all, I'm only your superior administratively . . . not in skill or experience. But in this case . . .'

Marco smiled at the flattery, but he knew the Inquisitor was right. He was too eager to join the game being played in Florence, perhaps in part because he wanted to get away from Venice for a while. Yet both good manners and professional pride required him to concede gracefully.

'You're quite right,' he said a little stiffly. 'I should not have proposed it.'

'May I make another suggestion?' Ornate courtesy repaid Marco's concession. 'Do please remember this, Commodore, in everything you do: this affair should ideally end by the boy's being moved to Venice. The heir presumptive to Tuscany, what a hostage!'

EARLY MORNING: DECEMBER 25, 1576
FLORENCE: MOTHER EARTH'S TAVERN

Paolo Crespelle sipped the thin, sour wine and drew a sour face. His grimace was visible to none of the cutthroats, whores, and cutpurses in the one-room tavern tucked into the market behind San Lorenzo. The two candles made from melted butt-ends had burned out at half past one in the morning, and the wood-scrap fire on the open hearth in the centre of the room was dying.

This, Paolo reflected, was not his notion of Christmas.

Echoes of the chants he had earlier heard from San Lorenzo still lingered in his ears. The one service of the year he truly enjoyed was the mass at midnight that celebrated the birth of Our Lord. Of course, he attended mass regularly, as much to give an example to his subordinates as to ensure that no suspicion of irregularity fell on him. But he loved the Midnight Mass for the Nativity.

Yet it would have imperilled his neck to attend tonight. Any unusual action would invite suspicion that he was a spy. Since he was that, he dared not deviate from the normal behaviour of the rabble among whom he sat.

Although they sometimes furtively sketched the sign of the cross, none would enter a church. Not just to keep their henchmen from mocking their piety, but for fear of arrest. The Night Watch kept special guard on churches. Having forgotten Our Lord's love for the poor and His mercy to criminals, fat priests and fatter bishops no longer fought to keep churches beyond the reach of the temporal power. For the rogues and jades who surrounded Paolo, church was not a sanctuary, but a trap, even at Holy Christmastide.

He was a captain of war-galleys, Paolo reflected even more bitterly, a senior captain in the world's finest navy, lately often acting commodore. A man of substance as well, grown rich from trading in the Orient, where he exercised the full authority of a merchant-commodore of the House of Capello.

Yet here he sat and scratched his lice bites and dreamed of a tub of hot scented water and slave-girls to rub him down afterwards as they did in Constantinople. And why?

Because he fitted in, 'blended well into his native habitat', as Marco Capello had said in his latest placatory letter. Well, he supposed he did. He had acquired not only the hypocrisy of the courtiers, but the cant of the streets when he first came to Florence to learn swordsmanship in the *sala delle armi* of the Medicis' Pitti Palace and to unlearn his rough hillman's dialect.

The next Baron Crespelle was not surprised at what he had now learned by posing as an itinerant fencing master fallen on hard times through his love for low women, dishonest ducats, and cheap wine. After a week of loitering in the taverns, chop-houses and wine shops of the underworld, he knew that half the footpads and whores of Florence were taking the coppers of Ferdinando Cardinal de' Medici. Yet few knew for whom they peddled lies, spied, and, upon occasion, killed. The Cardinal's henchmen covered his tracks well.

Paolo Crespelle was well known in Florence as a Venetian naval officer and an associate of Marco Capello, cousin and intimate of the Grand Duke's mistress. Paolo Crespelle had, therefore, vanished. Instead, there was now Pinchio Stracciatelle, the name obviously false, a down-at-heels bodyguard for hire who was a fugitive from justice in the city of Lucca.

That rascal must now crown his work for Grand Duke Francesco I and for Venice by hiring murderers. Whether in his own person or in disguise, Paolo would not do that deed himself. Nothing in his understanding with Venice required him to kill in cold blood, though he gloried in killing in the heat of battle. Much better to have creatures of the Cardinal commit the crimes that would foil the Cardinal's plots. Pinchio Stracciatelle would already have vanished as abruptly as he had been born.

The difficulty did not lie in finding a murderer. He knew with certainty eight killers for hire among the thirty-odd men and women who were gnawing at rabbit bones, drinking wine from chipped cups, and squabbling in the Taverna di Madre Terra, the Tavern of Mother Earth. The spare, stooped landlady, called Mother Earth to mock her childless state, had died of the disease of bad air, *mal aria*, six months ago. The tavern was now in the hands of the *Impresa*, the Enterprise, which dominated crime – and much lawful business – in Tuscany. Paolo was waiting for *il Presidente*, the chief of the Enterprise.

Paolo's difficulty did not lie in finding a professional murderer in Florence in the year 1576. He could contract for the Pope's assassination for twenty-five ducats or the Grand Duke's for twenty. His difficulty was in finding a killer who would persist against obstacles – and remain silent afterwards.

Paolo stretched his legs, sketchily covered by patched hose grey with filth. He tugged down his doublet, which was too small, but bespoke past glories by its tarnished silver braid. He narrowed his eyes against the smoke that refused to spiral out through the hole in the plaster-and-lath ceiling.

He had not lain with a woman for three weeks, but was tempted by none of the sluts in grimy, low-cut blouses and full, stained skirts. If not cutpurses or cutthroats, their swains were pimps, forgers, burglars, or footpads who wore not gentlemanly hose but loose breeches cut off below the knee. He was happy to leave those women to their bravos, thus avoiding both quarrels and the Spanish disease from the New World, also the crabs they carried in their private hair.

Paolo's thoughts turned to Countess Abruzzo. The voluptuous Countess was the last woman he had lain with before becoming

Pinchio Stracciatelle. She needed consolation for the neglect of Count Abruzzo, who had recently developed a lust for gambling and for boys. The Count would certainly prattle to his new friends about the deception the Grand Duke had practised to protect his bastard son. Fortunately, Paolo had found not only pleasure, but an answer to that problem in the Countess's bed.

'Dearest Annabella, you must scream at him for letting out the Duke's secret,' he had told her. 'That'll ensure he keeps repeating the tale. You, too, must tell your friends the truth – in strictest confidence, of course. I'll see that my sister does the same.'

'I thought you were mad, Paolo,' she replied. 'Now I know you are. Have you forgotten? We've sworn to keep the secret.'

'Best way to keep it is by whispering the truth . . . whispering that Antonio is the true child of Bianca and Francesco. All Florence will then *know* you're lying to protect your lady. Who'll believe the truth from the lips of loyal ladies-in-waiting?'

'What of the midwife, Paolo? And the woodcutter's wife my lady picked to be the "true" mother?'

'What of them?'

'When they hear we've told the truth, they'll speak out themselves. Why should they keep an oath I've broken? But, I suppose, they'll be disbelieved too.'

'Never!' he replied. 'Everyone expects the nobility to lie. But simple women of the people, no. Everyone'll believe the midwife if she swears she saw Bianca give birth to Antonio. And the woodcutter's wife if she swears he's no child of hers.'

'What of your plan, then?'

'They could ruin it!'

The Countess hesitated an instant before confiding: 'Giovanna Conti, the midwife, I hear she's already telling her cronies. She's *so* proud of midwifing the Duke's son.'

The next morning, Paolo had taken the infant Antonio on his saddlebow for the long ride to Castello Crespelle in the crags above Pistoia. He had advised Bianca to send her trusted young footman, who also knew the truth, to the mountain village that Giovanna Conti was entertaining with dramatic tales of the 'birth of the little prince'.

The footman was to tell the midwife she must revert to her story of bringing the woodcutter's son into the Lady Bianca's chamber in her lute-case. Otherwise, she would die. Sadly, Paolo had concluded that she must, in any event, die to protect Antonio and his mother from Cardinal Ferdinando's assassins.

Old Baron Crespelle had given a gruff welcome to his first-born, who at thirty-eight showed no sign of coming home to oversee the family vineyards and grain fields. Still, better serve distant Venice than the rascally Medicis.

'So you're back, my son,' he said. 'What brings you into the wilderness?'

'To see you, Father, of course!' Paolo replied as gruffly. 'And to beg you to look after this boy. Son of a friend of mine who can't tell his wife.'

'Always a friend, Paolo? Never your own.'

'Father, to dream that I . . .'

The Baron, grinning, had declared: 'I'll call him Paolino anyway.'

Remembering their parting, Paolo smiled wryly into the smoke and stench of Mother Earth's Tavern. He saw himself, strangely reluctant to leave, riding off from the shadow of Castello Crespelle's square tower. Someday, he supposed, he would go home.

Paolo started when he felt a hand touch his shoulder, and his hand went to his dagger. Then he rose to follow the hunchback in the stained velvet doublet. The tavern, he now learned, possessed another room. Although small, it was hung with tapestries, warmed by a fireplace, and lit by wall-sconces holding tapered candles. The thin man wearing a blue-checked jester's mask, who sat at a walnut table, was still wrapped in a heavy cloak that bore a dusting of snowflakes.

Without a word, the host poured wine from a glass pitcher into a goblet and motioned Paolo to drink. True to his character as a disgraced fencing master, Paolo tossed the wine down. Then he smacked his lips to show that, having known better days, he could appreciate the vintage.

'Understand you've got a job for us.' *Il Presidente*'s voice was muffled by the mask. 'Who do you want done in?'

'A woman . . .' Paolo began.

'Cost you extra. Mostly we don't do women. Whores maybe, but who'd pay for a whore's life? Respectable women're a problem, though. My men don't like it.'

'I'll pay . . . pay well.' Paolo blurted like the amateur he wanted to appear. 'Actually, it's two . . . two women.'

He had chased the possibilities around his mind for hours. He hated condemning the woodcutter's wife who was the ostensible mother of the infant apparently brought in the lute-case. Why should she die for agreeing to assist the Lady Bianca in her deception? Yet, he had concluded sadly, she had to die.

If the midwife were killed, but the woodcutter's wife left alive, his plan would be exposed. Ferdinando would ask the obvious question: *Why kill one, yet leave the other alive to testify to putting her child into Bianca's bed?*

It must be obvious that both women who could, presumably, testify to the deception had been removed. Otherwise, Ferdinando would certainly conclude that he must trace and slay the child – on the off-chance that the boy was indeed his brother's son.

'A hundred ducats,' *il Presidente* said.

'Agreed!'

'. . . each,' the chief of the Enterprise added. 'Sorry, but that's the price. It's a lot of trouble . . . very costly for me. Like I said, the men don't like killing women.'

'A sad waste, brother,' Marco agreed heartily. 'But that's the way he wants it, the Cardin . . .'

An eyelid winked conspiratorially behind the mask's peephole, and *il Presidente* assured him: 'I never heard that, my friend. Never heard a word.'

CHAPTER XXIV

FOR the first time in three quarters of a century, the palazzo on the Grand Canal called Ca' Capello was deserted. Behind the malachite pillars that framed the windows no human being stirred. In the great ballroom, no shod foot trod the marble floors and no appreciative eye surveyed Tintoretto's allegorical – and erotic – painting, the Judgement of Paris on the ceiling. Not since the first piling was driven into the canal bottom in 1500 had the site been without any human presence: not even a watchman or a caretaker, since there was no need to guard against human predators. An outbreak of looting had been crushed without mercy late the previous year, and no Venetian would now steal his neighbour's goods. Thieves were deterred almost as much by shame from preying on their fellow unfortunates as by fear. Other predators were not deterred.

The rats had not yet come out. But Marco Capello knew they were waiting behind the walls to take possession of the abandoned palazzo and devour any food they could find. Not for some time would the rats begin gnawing at the leather objects, the fabrics and the candles. They were too sleek with good living. While the Black Death devoured men, women, children and infants, the rats grew fat.

But only for the moment. Twisting in the gondola for a last look at the palazzo, Marco swore he would return soon to rid Ca' Capello of the infernal animals.

He had resisted leaving, perhaps resisted too long, for the plague had been stalking Venice almost a year and a half now. Five months earlier, he had sent his pregnant wife to her widowed mother's villa at Stra on the Brenta. But he could neither abandon his duties in the secret corridors of the Doge's Palace nor turn his back on the trickle of commerce that still flowed through his warehouses. Not while Doge

Alvise Mocenigo and his family held out as bravely as a garrison under siege.

The Senate, too, remained in constant session, and Marco had his part to play in that executive body, whose number was still falling through deaths. He had been elected two years earlier, owing his elevation to Admiral Sebastiano Venier. Although now eighty-five, the victor of Lepanto was the most influential man in Venice.

Marco respected his obligations as a senator. A patrician of Venice was an important man by his very birth, but a senator could prove his worth by meritorious work. If the Senate did not carefully direct administration, anarchy would follow. No senator, Marco felt strongly, should leave Venice in her agony, lest chaos intervene and the common people grow disillusioned with the hereditary ruling class.

Yet he had now been ordered to leave, and even a senator of Venice was bound to lifelong obedience once he joined the Secret Service. Not only the renewed threat of the Black Death, but events elsewhere, had forced him to close Ca' Capello, sending his surviving servants and clerks to refuge on the *terraferma*.

The gondola, draped with black in the city's universal mourning for her plague dead, sculled down the lower reach of the Canalazzo towards the Basin of St Mark's. Only one out of every six palazzos on the banks was *not* shuttered and deserted. Pathetically few vessels moved on the maritime city's main artery: two gondolas, two cargo-wherries, and three coffin boats.

The pulse of Venice still beat, but with agonising slowness, thready and weak. The inns and hostelries that had catered to an ever-flowing stream of pleasure-bent visitors were closed when that stream dried up. For the first time in a century, the White Lion Hotel, which accommodated the substantial and the powerful, had shut its doors. The law courts had gone into indefinite recess when litigants, lawyers and judges alike fled to the *terraferma*. The few prisoners who still survived were dying, left unfed when the warders took the keys to the cells. Silence hung over the stricken metropolis, an unearthly silence that was, nonetheless, as oppressive as a pall of black clouds.

When the six-pronged blade on the gondola's prow thrust into the Basin of St Mark's, the single passenger saw an uncanny scene. Glowing honey pale under the robin's egg sky, the Doge's Palace looked over a virtually deserted bay. Just four bluff-bowed merchant vessels lay at the Mole feverishly discharging their cargoes of food; lavish bribes and dire threats kept the scant supplies coming. Just three war-galleys were anchored off St George's Island; the bulk of the

Navy had been sent to safety elsewhere, leaving the city defenceless. But who would attack a city that was dying of a virulent disease?

The other vessels in the bay flew not the crimson banner with the golden lion of Venice, but the yellow flag of the disease. The old lazarettos were crammed with the dying, and the improvised new ones with suspected cases. To accommodate and isolate the overflow of patients from the lazarettos, ten obsolete galleons had been towed into the bay loaded with food, fresh water, medicines, doctors, and priests. Few of those Good Samaritans would touch shore again – and almost none of their patients.

The setting was the same, Marco reflected, the immortal vista of Venice. But this was no longer the city whose splendour and power had three years ago overawed Henry of France. The splendour was now blurred as if a grey fungus had crept over a glowing seascape. The power was crippled, for there were neither surviving Arsenalotti enough to build and repair ships nor sailors to man them.

Half the men and women who had entertained the young King of France were stricken or already dead.

What use to Arnaldo Foscari, immured in the family vault, the gold and ruby belt Henry III had bestowed in gratitude for his hospitality?

What value now the 18,000 ducats, enough to hire a thousand men-at-arms for three years, Henry had paid the jeweller Cantarin for a sceptre? Bianca had laughed delightedly when Marco commented: 'Maybe Henry lost his old sceptre on the way here. You'd think a king would travel with a spare just as a lady carries an extra hairbrush.' But Cantarin had lain in the wet clay of his temporary grave on the Giudecca for sixteen months now.

What use the gold chains the King had given to the forty noblemen who attended him? What was it worth now the sapphire ring Marco had himself received after his reception for the King?

Not that those gifts had ever been much use to anyone. The *Proveditore di Pompe dello Stato*, the State Supervisor of Ostentation, had immediately sequestered those princely gifts. Their recipients could apply for permission to wear the baubles on any occasion when their display would benefit the state. Short of another – and most unlikely – visit by Henry III, Marco could think of no occasion that would satisfy those conditions.

Even the strategic and political advantages won by the extravagant entertainment of King Henry, Marco mused with some bitterness, were now almost beside the point. The visit had initially served Venice well, fostering sympathy between the bigoted Frenchman and the wily

Doge Alvise Mocenigo. That quasi-alliance had taken pressure off the Republic by splitting the ring of her enemies.

Smiling, Marco remembered the Doge's parting plea to the King to spare the beleaguered Protestants of France. Henry had looked in open amazement at his fellow Catholic who was pleading for mercy for the mortal enemies of church and state.

Henry held with his older brother, Charles IX, who had ordered the massacre of French Protestants on St Bartholomew's Eve in 1572. He had warmly congratulated Bartolomeo Capello on bearing such an auspicious name. His brother, he then recalled, had grown so passionate while watching the slaughter that he demanded: 'Bring me a Protestant to kill myself!'

The gondola bumped against the pier, jolting Marco from his reverie. He sprang ashore, marvelling at his unhampered passage through the empty Piazza, which had two years earlier been the busiest square in Europe. He marvelled, too, at his own good health. Hardly remarkable at his age, his vigour was almost miraculous in a city half of whose people had been afflicted with the rash, the swellings, and the black flux that gave the disease its name.

Marco realised as he slipped through a side-door of the Doge's Palace and threaded his way along the secret corridors to the chambers of the State Inquisitors that he was glad to be leaving with honour. The horrifying spectacle of the city he loved lying comatose was too much to bear any longer. Besides, he could serve neither Venice nor his family if he, too, were stricken.

'God speed, Commodore!' The duty officer was elaborately courteous. Marco Capello was his superior by five ranks, although he had been delegated to pass on the commands of the single surviving Inquisitor, who now lay in bed.

He added respectfully: 'Please always remember your directive: *Guard him as you would your own son! Guard him as you do your immortal soul and the honour of your family!'*

Marco realised that he was extremely irritated as he loosened his collar, untied the laces that kept his hose taut, and settled into the cushions in the roomy cabin of the eight-oar launch. He was not sure *why*. He had been treated with punctilious courtesy by the Service, and that did not happen often. Yet he was in a rage.

The voyage up the Brenta to Stra would take several hours. But the launch was comfortable, and the enforced relaxation would do him no harm.

He would not go hungry. The chicken keeping warm in an earthenware pot had been spiked with rosemary and sun-dried tomatoes, then stuffed with artichoke hearts and lemon before being moist-roasted in the bread oven. There were no shellfish. Some physicians had got it into their heads that the plague came out of the sea. Infected water creatures, they believed, passed on the Black Death. Ca' Capello had avoided all fish and seafood. But it had not made much difference. Cousins, servants and clerks had still sickened and died.

Fortunately, no one believed wine spread the plague. Quite the contrary. A little wine not only settled the stomach, the physicians said, but was a safeguard against disease.

That remedy really did not help much either. Marco knew two teetotallers, rare birds in Venice, who had survived unscathed. He knew dozens of heavy drinkers who were quite dead. Still, it was good to sip a full-bodied red from Asolo, even if it were not a specific against the plague.

He grimaced in sympathy with poor Angela, who could only have two glasses of wine a day until the child was born. He hated their long separation, which was even more painful because she was no great letter-writer. He would, at least, be in plenty of time for the birth. The midwife said early or mid-May, and it was not yet mid-April.

Having a son, even a daughter, he had been told repeatedly, would change his life. Thirty-three was a little old to become a father for the first time. Even Angela at twenty-four was several years beyond the age at which most ladies bore their first children. The professors from Padua had warned him that she was a little narrow in the hips, but had advised him not to tell her. With a skilful midwife, there should be no danger.

Marco Capello a father! It would be hard to get used to. He had not thought much about fatherhood before this journey gave him time for reflection.

Yet in a month he would be father to not just one child, but another as well. From a virtual bachelor living alone in the deserted city he was to be transformed into a patriarch in an instant.

Marco now knew precisely why he was angry. But he would think about it later.

The Inquisitors' clerk had given him the news he had been awaiting for several weeks. Within two days, Paolo Crespelle would arrive with Antonio, the son of Bianca and Francesco de' Medici. Marco's instructions from the State Inquisitors had been unequivocal from the beginning of the operation: *You will adopt this waif with full legal formality, giving out that he is the son of a distant cousin.*

Well, Bianca was a cousin, though hardly distant. She and Francesco had finally consented to that adoption in order to kick dust in the eyes of any agents Cardinal Ferdinando de' Medici might still have on the trail of the boy.

Ferdinando seemed convinced by reports of the death of the infant he believed Bianca had originally smuggled into her bedchamber. The unexplained appearance of a male infant in the household of Marco Capello, would, however, awaken his suspicion.

By adopting the child Marco would allay that suspicion. The Cardinal was too proud of his blood. He would not believe that his elder brother could, whatever the circumstances, allow an outsider to adopt a Medici – particularly a Medici who could soon be heir apparent to the throne of Tuscany.

Besides, Bianca had refused to entrust her son to anyone but her cousin Marco for what could be years. Although doubtful of Angela, she relied upon Marco. Since he could not keep the boy without adopting him, Bianca had reluctantly agreed and had persuaded the Grand Duke.

Marco expected Paolo to come to Stra from Chioggia at the southern tip of the lagoon, where a very distant relation, who was not noble, lived in humble circumstances. Their neighbours would confirm the birth of a son to Maria, wife of the boatman Angelo Capello and already the mother of twelve hungry children. Since Maria, the stout eternal mother, was always either pregnant or nursing, no one would doubt that birth.

Travelling as an apothecary's clerk bringing medicines to the plague-stricken city, Paolo would come to Chioggia by sea, carrying the infant, well drugged with poppy juice, in his bag of herbs. He would then buy passage to Stra from Angelo Capello. Upon arriving at the Villa Tron, Angelo Capello would beg his wealthy kinsman to adopt his son. It would, he was to say while weeping unashamedly before the servants, be burdensome – and court ill-fortune – to keep his thirteenth child at home.

Francesco de' Medici's signet ring, now concealed in the swaddling clothes, would prove Antonio's paternity when the time came for him to return to Tuscany. In turn, Paolo Crespelle would take Bianca the diamond-and-sapphire tiara looted from the secret hoard of Grand Admiral Ali Pasha after Lepanto. Although she disliked and feared

Bianca, Angela had agreed to give up her tiara. She was deeply touched by seven-month-old Antonio's romantic history, and her heart went out, if prematurely, to Bianca as a fellow mother.

When Francesco wanted his son back, he would send the tiara to Marco. Nothing else could convey the message and prove that the messenger came from the Grand Duke.

There were no seams in the plan to work loose. The boatman Angelo Capello, the only possible weak point, knew that confirming the story to all questioners would ensure his continuing to receive ten ducats a year. Knowing the commodore's power, Angelo also knew that betraying the secret would bring disaster on himself and his family.

The subterfuge was all the more necessary now. Filipo de' Medici, son of Joanna of Austria and heir apparent to the Grand Duchy of Tuscany, was clearly dying. Normally, the death of his ill-omened first-born son would have enabled Franceso I to produce Antonio and proclaim him the new heir. Normally, his relieved subjects would have greeted the robust new heir with an outpouring of loyalty. But Antonio, the son of Bianca Capello Buonaventura, could not be proclaimed heir apparent as long as Joanna of Austria was his father's legal consort. Regardless, Francesco would not put Joanna aside, although the Pope, who wished to please him, could assuredly be persuaded to declare the marriage void.

It was not Joanna's fault, her husband said, that she was a dull woman who could give him so little love. Nor was it Joanna's fault that he needed a sparkling, loving woman beside him. Having already given her much cause for sorrow, he would not compound her sorrow by casting her off. Nor would he offer a mortal insult to Joanna's brother, the Emperor, or offend her cousin who sat on the throne of Spain. Tuscany had no need of new enemies.

That, Marco reflected as the sail of the launch caught a fresh breeze, was the end of the tale. That dilemma had forced the Grand Duke and his *maîtresse en titre* to ask the help of Marco Capello and the Venetian Secret Service.

Well, not *quite* the end of the tale. Even in the midst of the plague, the bureaucrats were knifing each other. His informants within the Service reported a struggle among factions regarding how best to use the heir presumptive to the Tuscan throne for the benefit of Venice. Much greater power would be the automatic reward of the faction whose viewpoint won.

Marco resolved that no one would win. He would never surrender

Antonio to the State Inquisition, not to the Council of Ten or the Senate itself. When the tiara was put into his hands, he would send Antonio back to his parents. Meanwhile, no one else would touch the boy, regardless of the presumed interests of *La Serenissima*. It would have to be enough for the government that the lad was in Venice.

Marco Capello's anger grew. For the first time since entering the Secret Service, he was deeply disturbed by its acts. Ironically, his closest friend, his lieutenant and confidant Paolo Crespelle, was responsible.

Marco had seen many men and quite a few women die violently in open or secret battle. He had seen some die simply because they got in the way. But he had never killed the innocent, not as Paolo had murdered the midwife Giovanna Conti and the woodcutter's wife chosen to play the mother of Bianca's child. Those deaths weighed on Marco as no death had in the past.

True, Giovanna Conti had blabbered that the birth in the Royal Villa was real. True, the woodcutter's wife might be discovered not to have been pregnant during the time she had been isolated in the hills while her husband cut timber.

But renewed warnings to the two had been all that was really needed. It was not *necessary* for them to die to make the tale and the faked birth just a shade more plausible.

A nobleman of Venice was taught that he must always put the state first. A nobleman of Venice who entered the Secret Service pledged again to put the interests of the state before all else. Yet there was one demand the State Inquisition could not make upon him. A nobleman of Venice put the interests of the state before all else *except* his personal honour.

The past was gone. But he could ensure that such infamies did not occur again under his aegis. He would have a few words with Paolo Crespelle when his lieutenant arrived at the Villa Tron.

He would ask: 'Was it necessary, *absolutely* necessary, to murder the women?'

Paolo would colour at the rebuke, but would hold his temper, shrug, and reply equably: 'Marco, *you* ordered the deaths. You instructed me: *At all costs, get the boy for Venice!*'

And he would retort: 'So I did. But to my mind these murders were *not* necessary.'

Shrugging again, Paolo would say: 'To my mind, they *were*. You know, I was regretting that I hadn't contracted for the woodcutter's death, too, when he got in the way and was killed. That relieved my mind – and saved Venice a few ducats.'

Hating that cynicism, Marco would add: 'Well, next time, make sure what you do is *absolutely* necessary.'

They would then drink a glass of wine together and renew their friendship. But there would be coolness between Paolo and himself for a time.

That dialogue never took place, though the written rebuke Marco later sent Paolo was to arouse not just coolness, but bitterness, between them. The dialogue never took place because Paolo was not eager to see his superior. When Marco arrived at the Villa Tron just before midnight on April 11, 1577, the Tuscan had already appeared, left the infant, and gone off with the tiara for Bianca.

No more than glancing at Antonio, who looked well to his untutored eye, Marco forgot his anger – and forgot Paolo. Donna Angela, the aged butler told him, had begun her labour ten hours ago, but the end appeared nowhere in sight. Yet Marco's dour mother-in-law, Flavia Tron, was calm, her seamed face serene above the big white ruff she wore with a dove-grey afternoon gown. It was, she said, not unusual for a first birth to take many hours, even a day.

Rushing up the Y-shaped marble staircase to Angela's bedroom, Marco found that the midwife, who knew better than Flavia Tron, was worried. Seeing Angela pale and clammy between the linen sheets on the big bed, tears forced from her eyes by pain, Marco was horrified. He was also alarmed.

Pausing only to kiss her blue-veined forehead and murmur an endearment, he called for the butler. The old servant's bald head, Marco noted incongruously, looked like an egg on the platter of the old-fashioned six-inch ruff of the Trons' green-and-gold livery.

The most reliable footman, he directed, was to ride to the University in Padua immediately. He was to find Professor Giuseppe Ortolan, either at the dissecting theatre or at his rooms opposite the Palazzo del Bo, and bring him back to the Villa Tron. A bag containing fifteen ducats in gold would persuade the learned physician.

The next ten hours, weighted with pain and fear, passed slowly.

The midwife muttered something about a blockage. Clearly unable to help, she scrabbled under the linen sheets and tugged at the obstacle between Angela's thighs. Marco was glad he had sent for the physician without delay.

Angela writhed on the bed, drenching the embroidered sheets with her perspiration and her blood. Soaked through, they had to be changed repeatedly. Marco spent the first two hours holding her hand and murmuring encouragement. Her nails left bloody semi-circles on his palm each time she strained to expel the intruder in her body.

'It's tearing me in half!' she screamed. 'Help me! Help me, Marco!'

Tears prickling his eyelids, Marco could only tell her help was on the way. Between spasms, she remembered Professor Ortolan and was grateful. But, after one violent spasm, which stained the bed with urine as well as blood, she stared at him with terrible accusation. In the flickering light of the candles, her dark-blue eyes looked black, almost starting from their bony sockets.

'With respect, sir,' the midwife finally said. 'Most gentlemen can't take it. Too hard on 'em. Sir, ladies're tougher th'n they look. But gentlemen, no. Better go out for a while.'

Feeling a traitor, Marco accepted that advice with some relief. He also accepted with appreciation half a duck and a carafe of wine from the butler.

Fear drove him back to the bedchamber within a quarter of an hour. He left after five minutes, having found Angela dozing and her mother seated beside the bed. The stench of blood, urine and faeces struck Marco in the face like a fist, and the bile rose in his throat. He gagged, but gulped it down. Flavia Tron did not speak. But she looked at him with contempt, accusation even more scathing than Angela's in her eyes.

Marco fled from his mother-in-law's baleful stare. There was, in truth, no one more useless at a delivery than the father. Although his wife's torment was his fault, he could only help her by keeping out of the way. Yet he repeatedly returned to find Angela writhing in pain. Drained of blood, her face was tallow-pale when the dawn's bleak light peeped into the room.

The clip-clop of hooves in the cobblestone courtyard finally sounded above the arrogant crowing of the cocks. Marco listened anxiously. But he did not hear the hooves of a second horse.

'I tried, sir,' the footman told him. 'I tried my damnedest. I jollied him and begged him. Then I showed him the gold. But 'twas no good. Too busy with the Black Death, he said. Couldn't possibly come.

Damned patricians, he said, think they can order everyone around.'

'We'll see,' said Marco. 'Are my pistols still with my saddle?'

Professor Giuseppe Ortolan came without a pistol being drawn. He complained and carped. He said the illustrious commodore should be in quarantine, should never have left the city. Even he himself should not go into the plague-free zone along the Brenta, having been exposed to the plague in the city only yesterday. It was, he whined, midwives' work attending a birth, not a task for a distinguished professor of physic. Yet he finally agreed to come for double the fifteen ducats Marco had originally offered.

That immense fee, Ortolan knew, was an assertion of manhood – and a mute declaration of a husband's love. Knowing he could have had more, he commended himself on his moderation in taking only as much as would maintain five men-at-arms for a year.

The physician preened the villainous moustache that was at odds with his soft, pallid face and his soft, pudgy hands. He thrust into his leather valise a device like a pair of wooden platters mounted on a big scissors frame. He clapped on the physician's mask with the twelve-inch nose filled with juniper and other herbs against the plague. He then declared himself ready.

Surprisingly, the professor rode well, untroubled by the sledge-hammer blows of the sun. A little past two in the afternoon, they pounded into the courtyard of the Villa Tron.

The midwife was waiting outside on the landing where the inverted V of the double entrance stairways met. Now herself as pale as her patient had been that morning, she was no longer spiritedly defending the sacred female mystery of birth. Her resentment of male interlopers vanished, she extended her bloodstained hands to the physician, half-welcoming and half-imploring.

'Thank God you've come, Professor,' she said. 'My lady started labour a whole day ago. Now she's bleeding, bleeding bad. I can't do nothing.'

Professor Giuseppe Ortolan stripped off his riding gloves, scooped up his leather valise, and took the stairs two at a time. In his relief that Angela would now have the best treatment, Marco allowed himself a taut smile. Rushing up the stairs, his ridiculous proboscis like a long beak going before him, his bony legs flashing in yellow tights, the physician looked like a harried stork.

Ortolan emerged within five minutes to demand hot water, towels, and grappa. He no longer wore the protective mask. His hands were as bloodstained as the midwife's, the half-circles of grit under their nails black. He gulped from the big bottle of grappa before vanishing again into the bedchamber.

Neither physician nor midwife emerged again for an interminable time. Twice, shrieks made Marco's knees tremble, and he leaned against the wall. He had not eaten since the midnight of another day, but he wanted nothing except a sip of grappa. Determined not to leave his post outside Angela's door, he shrugged off the old butler's paternal hand on his sleeve.

Almost two hours later, the professor emerged. His face, naturally pallid, was now a dirty grey-white. But his moustache bristled triumphantly, and a smug smile lit his doughy features.

'Only Ortolan could've done it!' he announced. 'Who else knows the secrets to control haemorrhaging? Nothing to fear now. All's well!'

'The child?' Marco demanded. 'Also well?'

'Oh, the infant's not out yet,' the professor said coolly. 'That's another matter.'

'And . . . and my wife? You said all was well?'

'So it is . . . for the moment. She was on the point of bleeding to death. But that danger is now past, thanks to my skill. I've given her opium to relax. As for the infant, we'll see?'

'See?' Marco demanded.

'Sit down, Ser Marco,' the physician directed. 'You're weak from exhaustion and emotion. When did you last eat?'

'Sometime last night. It's not important. What is there to see?'

'I shall see whether I can save the infant. If I cannot, no one can. Then I'll take out the child to save the mother.'

'Why wait?' Marco demanded. 'Save my wife now! Forget the baby!'

'We shall see. Holy Church instructs us: *Always save the new life!* Only when there is no hope for the child may I sacrifice it to save the mother.'

Marco fought down a nightmare image of an infant's being chopped up, first an arm, then a leg, even a tiny sundered head grinning toothless. But he pleaded: 'Now, Professor, save my wife.'

'You were eager enough to put yourself in my hands, Ser Marco. Now you must abide by my judgement. Perhaps, after a while, she'll be strong enough to try again one more time and . . .'

'You're torturing her. You *must* stop.'

'By no means. As Holy Writ tells, woman is condemned to bring forth in travail and pain for Eve's sin. A little pain is normal, beneficial.'

'A *little* pain!' Marco interjected. 'God!'

'We must have nourishing broth for her, made with the herbs I've given your butler. Then one more try with the forceps.'

Through the flow of words, Marco asked: 'Forceps? Those wooden platters?'

'Precisely. Forceps to extract the child undamaged. Naturally, midwives hate it. But, for shoulder dystosia, forceps can do wonders. Only in supremely skilled hands . . . that is, my hands.'

'Shoulder dystosia?'

'Ser Marco, the shoulder is stuck in the birth canal. The midwife struggled to turn it. In vain. However, with my forceps . . .

While Angela lay half-drugged, her husband, despite himself, slept in snatches in a chair before her door. The night passed like a disjointed dream, interspersed with moments of waking, mouthfuls of tasteless food, and burning gulps of grappa.

Shortly after midnight, at the beginning of the 13th of April, the bloody figure of the physician popped out of the door. To Marco's exhausted eyes, he was a demon out of a puppet show: powder-white face, forearms red with gore, and the diabolical forceps.

'Congratulations, Ser Marco!' The normally ebullient professor's voice was weak. 'Congratulations on securing the finest physician in Europe. Only I could have done it.'

'Tell me!'

'I have given you a fine, healthy daughter. Both noble ladies are very tired, but both will be well. I say that, I, Professor Giuseppe Ortolan, master anatomist . . . No, don't go in. They must sleep.'

Almost thirty-eight hours after Angela Tron Capello's exhausting labour had begun, the Villa Tron was blessed with joy. Shouting for wine, Marco Capello forced the physician to sit on the staircase beside himself. Within two minutes, the butler and three footmen appeared, followed by six smiling maids carrying a dozen crystal goblets. Marco waved an invitation to them all to share the *prosecco*.

Pale and drawn in her rumpled grey gown, as gaunt as her daughter, Flavia Tron lifted her goblet to her son-in-law, to the physician, and to her servants. There was no condescension in her misty eyes or her relieved smile. Why should a noblewoman of Venice not drink a toast with her household at a time of such joy?

'To my granddaughter!' Donna Flavia said. 'And, equally, to her new brother who sleeps below!'

Marco lifted his goblet. He had forgotten Antonio.

By mid-June of 1577, relief had come to a Venice brutally depleted by the Black Death – relief so vast it brought great joy. The epidemic had not yet been declared at an end, in part to avoid provoking fate. Yet it was all but over after two terrible years.

The Statistical Office had taken a careful census whose devastating results would never be published. Nearly one out of every three Venetians living two years earlier was now dead and buried. Some 175,000 in mid-1575, the population had two years later been scythed to 124,000. Yet relief at their deliverance was so overwhelming that the survivors faced the immense tasks of restoration with uplifted hearts.

It was truly a time of joy for the family once more living in Ca' Capello on the Canalazzo. Above all, Angela was fully recovered from the illness that had gripped her after the harrowing birth.

Marco grimaced when he remembered the months of anxiety, when it seemed that her fever would never fall nor the foul discharge from her womb ever stop. Part of the placenta had been left in her womb. That was, Professor Giuseppe Ortolan had said, a regrettable oversight, though understandable in his exhaustion. But, thanks to his genius, Ortolan now said, his patient had fully recovered to rejoice in her robust daughter. And the purple marks left by the forceps were slowly fading from the infant's forehead.

The tiny dark-haired girl with the dark-blue eyes had been christened Helena after Marco's maternal grandmother. Antonio, the son of Bianca Capello Buonaventura and Francesco de' Medici, now Antonio Capello by adoption, had dark-red hair, but his eyes were his father's dark brown. Despite the repeated disruptions of his brief life, he was sunny-tempered.

To celebrate those domestic joys and the end of the pestilence, Marco had commissioned a new mural for the ballroom. Sadly, he could not employ the master Titian, who had died during the plague. Marco had outbid other eager patrons to obtain Tintoretto who, although arrogant and difficult, was almost as great a painter as Titian. Some said greater.

Marco was saddened when he looked round the enormous Hall of the Great Council, which occupied the entire third floor of the east wing of the Doge's Palace. Before the plague, some thirteen hundred had sat in the Hall for sessions of the Great Council, which included every noblemen over twenty-five. Today, all the surviving members present for the election of a new Doge numbered less than eleven hundred.

After bringing his city through the pestilence, Doge Alvise Mocenigo had died, not of the plague, but, it appeared, of exhaustion. The funeral rites had concluded when an effigy with the late Doge's features was raised over the heads of the throng in the cathedral of St Mark. The seamen who were his pallbearers had appealed lustily nine times: '*Misericordia!* . . . Mercy for his soul!'

The bass melody of male greetings and male gossip echoed through the Great Hall and lightened Marco's mood. Although the occasion was solemn, the noblemen were animated, even merry. Few hid their glee at having lived through the carnage. Grieving for those they had lost, as they grieved for the late Doge, the patricians of Venice, who were gathered to choose the next Doge, nonetheless rejoiced for family and friends who survived – and for themselves.

Yet the atmosphere in the Great Hall, while light with relief at the end of the ordeal, was heavy with concern for the future. For some reason, Marco remembered the first gathering of his class in the Palazzo del Bo of the University of Padua. Elated at their new maturity, the young men had, nonetheless, been nervous before the challenge of the future. Guffawing at the crude jokes that eased the tension, the hereditary legislators of the Most Serene Republic were today not greatly different from the adolescents who had been entering the university.

Few chambers in Europe could match the grandeur of the Hall of the Great Council, which was designed to accommodate every adult nobleman of Venice, more than two thousand at one time.

Today, the Doge's throne was vacant between its golden pillars, as were the lesser thrones of the six Ducal Councillors on either side. Instead, a page wearing a crimson tunic of medieval cut stood beside a golden vessel filled with metal balls. Each nobleman over the age of thirty was to receive a ball. Those who drew brass were to leave; those who drew gold were to remain.

Marco closed his fist over his ballot. He held it up to the teller, who cried out: 'Nobleman Marco Capello draws gold. All his connection to withdraw.' Bartolomeo Capello lead half a dozen Capellos from the Great Hall.

After half an hour, only the thirty nobleman who had drawn gold remained. This time, they drew their ballots from a golden basin set on a pillar. Marco shrugged at drawing brass and withdrew.

Yet he could not leave the Palace, for he might be called back. The nine noblemen left in the Great Hall would vote for forty electors, who would in turn be reduced to twelve by drawing lots. Those twelve would then elect forty-five electors, who would be cut by lot to eleven. Finally, those eleven electors would vote for the forty-one noblemen who would then directly elect the next Doge.

Marco's name did not turn up again, and he was not unhappy. The process was as tedious as it was necessary to prevent chicanery. Since no one knew at the beginning who would elect the Doge, the forty-one final electors could not be suborned. Since chance played a greater role than votes, no one could stuff the ballot boxes.

The ritual was, however, hardly necessary today. Admiral Sebastiano Venier was virtually certain of election. The most honoured and most influential man in Venice, he would, at eighty-six, obviously be an interim Doge.

Some ambitious men preferred to wait a few years before seeking the office, letting Sebastiano Venier bear the burden – and the opprobrium – of the recovery from the plague. Others swore they would do anything legal to avoid the onerous and largely ceremonial office. But, once elected, no one could refuse to serve as Doge for his entire life.

Early the next morning Sebastiano Venier was proclaimed Doge. The victor of Lepanto then began his ordeal by honours.

Walking in the procession behind the new Doge, Marco Capello wore the black cloak edged with black fur and the silver stole of a nobleman who held no administrative office. His own work was secret.

He wondered what he might be wearing tomorrow, for the new Doge had drawn him aside after the election to say: 'Come see me before the banquet. I have work for you.'

Venier, tall and imposing, was clad in a scarlet robe worked with gold lace and caped with royal ermine. The golden *cornu* on his head suited his long, lined face with its long white beard. His natural authority was overwhelming.

A man to follow to the ends of the earth, Marco told himself emotionally when Sebastiano Venier stood before the great altar of St Mark's Cathedral. After the mass of thanksgiving, fifty Arsenalotti carried him in an immense chair around the Piazza of St Mark's while he tossed coins to the people.

Venice made her son royal, but curbed him first. The Admiral-Doge had already signed his *promissione*, a pledge that defined his responsibilities and limited his actions. He might neither increase his powers nor surrender them. He might see no one in private, but only in the presence of his advisers, with whom he must agree beforehand on every word he said to a foreign ambassador. No one might kiss his hand or kneel before him. He might not indulge in trade or go to the theatre or call upon a friend. Moreover, neither his sons nor his brothers might vote in any council or accept any rank in the Church.

The arduous office could, moreover, bankrupt its holder by its demands on his private purse. On his death a committee would examine his every act in office. If the committee found, as it almost invariably did, that the Doge had used state funds improperly, his heirs would be required to reimburse the Treasury.

Yet those restrictions could crumble before a strong-willed Doge who enjoyed wide support from the nobility and the people. Such a Doge could rule like the reigning duke he was by title. Sebastiano Venier, Marco believed, would be such a Doge.

Marco learned that he was right when he was summoned to the private apartment where the new Doge was dressing for the banquet that would begin three days of feasting and celebration. His old commanding officer embraced him formally, as any superior would a valued subordinate. But the Admiral's hand gripped Marco's arm hard in personal affection. No one else was present. The new Doge was already bending the rules that hedged him.

'Marco my son,' he said, 'tomorrow every nobleman who fought at Lepanto will put on a red cloak – and wear it for a full week. Venice must remember who saved her from the infidels.'

Marco smiled with delight. He did not normally see much point in parading martial glory or shaming the lily-livered who had stayed at home. But Venice had begun to forget her saviours.

'Afterwards, you will change your black cloak for a scarlet robe with wide sleeves like mine. I am making you Ducal Councillor from the district of St Mark's. Thus one of the Minor Council, the cabinet of my closest advisers.'

The Doge smiled, showing yellowed teeth in the white depths of his beard, when Marco raised sceptical eyebrows.

'The Senate will confirm you, never fear. You are to be the man the people call *il Rosso*, the Red One, for his scarlet robe. You will sit with the two State Inquisitors in black from the Council of Ten. You will also advise me on all matters concerning the Secret Service – at home and abroad. And you will see that the Service follows my wishes.'

Speechless, Marco bowed in obedience. His admiral had just crowned his career in the State Inquisition with its highest office – and had made him one of the six most powerful men in the Republic.

CHAPTER XXV

'I CALLED you back because of the Grand Duchess's death,' Marco Capello told Paolo Crespelle. 'We've got to move at once to meet the crisis. And who's better equipped to . . .'

'I thank you for the compliment,' Paolo replied negligently. 'But I'd prefer to go back to sea. I need the money. So do you, my friend.'

'I'm not supposed to trade with . . . ah . . . contacts. You know that.'

'Naturally. That goes with your red robe! You're too straight . . . won't use the job to feather your own nest. But you can't eat honour. It's past time for me to go back to sea, back to the Orient to trade. To get some money – for both of us.'

'You're right in a way,' Marco mused aloud. 'Business is bad . . . terrible. And I've got no time to look after it. You know . . .'

The State Inquisitor called *il Rosso*, the Red One, checked himself. He had not summoned the Tuscan to chat familiarly. Instead, he said severely: 'After this assignment, *perhaps* you can go to sea.'

Paolo ignored the coolness that had lain between himself and his closest friend and ranking superior since the death of the midwife and the woodcutter's wife sixteen months earlier. They had not seen each other since Paolo went south to help Bianca in September 1576, almost two years earlier. He had repeatedly proposed that he return to Venice for consultation, but had, instead, been sent further south to Sicily for a time.

Paolo had replied strongly, indeed abusively, to the letter that conveyed Marco's carefully tempered rebuke – and had received a heated reply. After that, the two men had written formally, discussing only their joint business ventures and the business of the Secret Service. Too closely bound to part without tearing each other gravely, they had chosen not to strain the ties that continued to bind them.

Marco still considered Paolo a brilliant agent who was superb in an emergency, although inclined to brutality and to flout orders. Paolo considered Marco a superlative naval officer and a first-class spy-master, who needed protection against his own soft streak.

Logically enough, Paolo was staying at the White Lion Hotel, not, as in the past, with Marco and Angela at Ca' Capello. Marco had been one person as a commodore and merchant whose work for the State Inquisition was secret. He was now a public figure as the red-robed chief of the State Inquisition and its Secret Service. Paolo might as well have put up posters announcing that he was a secret agent as stay at Ca' Capello.

The Tuscan was too well known to use disguise in Venice. The owners of the White Lion thought him a wealthy Florentine merchant and soldier of fortune, once in the Venetian naval service, who had quarrelled over business matters with his friend, the Ducal Councillor and State Inquisitor Marco Capello. That was true enough, depending on your definition of business.

But the Tuscan was anonymous, virtually invisible, among the dozens of foreigners who came to the Doge's Palace in their colourful native costumes: Turks and English, Neapolitans and Germans. Marco had received him in the formal Chamber of the State Inquisition, rather than his private office, in order to underline their differences. Paolo was furious at that slight, but would have preferred the rack in the nearby torture chamber to showing his anger.

Marco was bemused by his subordinate's casual manner. He knew well that old trick of Paolo's, appearing as if nothing in the world could trouble him. He was, nonetheless, put off his anger. He found himself smiling and agreeable when he had meant to be stern and brusque. *Too soft again*, Paolo would be thinking. Well, they had to discuss the problem, and they could not do so in anger.

The Tuscan Wild Boar, the crew of the *Angels* had called Paolo. He was now a sleek and prosperous wild boar. His red bristles had been allowed to grow into smooth waves, and his motley clothes had given way to a cerulean-blue cloak worn over a silver-embroidered doublet that a dandy would not disdain. Just forty, he had put a little weight on his shoulders and his face. But he had always been too thin, almost gaunt.

Paolo saw little change in the man who had climbed to the top of the Venetian power structure at the age of thirty-four. A little fuller around the red lips, a little slower in movement, a little more inclined to deliberate before speaking, a little slower to let a smile touch his eyes. But those were the marks of the responsibility he bore with his new power.

Underneath, Paolo saw the same decisive, often impetuous galley captain. Even the grey sprinkling on Marco's black hair emphasised his youthfulness by its contrast. The few extra pounds would come off after a few days' campaigning – if they ever campaigned together again.

'You're very cheerful, Paolo,' Marco said. 'But don't become *too* relaxed. And don't forget what I wrote you about the women's deaths. No need to talk about that any more. You know my wishes. I need you badly now. But one more trick like that – and I'll see you burned.'

Taken off guard, the Tuscan was, nonetheless, cheered by that flash of Marco's old steel.

'I understand your message,' he grinned. 'Whatever *burned* means.'

'You'll find out if . . . Just don't make it necessary. Now, can we talk?'

The Doge's Palace still reeked of smoke, charred wood and damp four months after a conflagration had swept it. Every corridor was filled with the musty smell of fresh plaster. Paolo had been led past scaffolding, ladders, and enormous rubbish bins to the Inquisitors' Chamber. He had been jostled by hurried workmen and fended off by stern foremen. The Venetians were restoring their Doge's Palace at a frantic pace.

'The job'll be done by the end of the summer.' Marco could, disconcertingly, still see into his mind. 'No more than eight or nine months. Thank God they turned Palladio down. He wanted to demolish the whole palace and build a kind of Greek temple.'

'You're very comfortable here.'

'This room was untouched. Exactly as you see it now, it was before the fire.'

'Handsome, but chilly.'

'That's the intention. But you get used to it, working here.'

In his scarlet robe, Marco Capello sat alone in a red velvet chair behind a polished oak table strewn with files and scrolls. That slight disorder made the room appear more human to the Tuscan, who lounged in a leather chair opposite the Red Inquisitor.

'You get used to it,' Marco repeated. 'Only thing is there's no one to talk to. My two colleagues in black from the Council of Ten? They're almost enemies, certainly rivals.' He allowed himself that calculated indiscretion to lighten the atmosphere. 'You know, I sometimes wonder whether fate isn't taunting me.'

'Fate? How do you mean?'

'Luck, I suppose. The priests say there's no such thing. What we call a run of luck, good or bad. They say good luck is God rewarding our virtuous deeds and our devotion to Himself.'

'And bad luck?'

'They say He's trying us, as He tried Job. To test us and make us better, the Patriarch insists. But I'm not convinced. Maybe the devil sends a run of misfortune. You know, I'm by no means sure I'll be sitting in this chair a week from today, not to speak of a month.'

'As serious as that?'

'After our old Admiral's death, yes. It was very strange. Venier survived the great fire, though he refused to leave the Doge's Palace till it was put out. Then to die in bed only a few months later. What irony!'

'And your position?'

'Obviously, I owed it to the Admiral. For the moment, they're afraid to put me out. The new Doge doesn't want to juggle senior posts just yet. But how long?'

'It's that precious . . . that vital to you . . . this position and this power?'

'Paolo, you're as close to being a Venetian nobleman as an outsider can be.' Marco realised that he was not keeping his old friend at a distance, as he had planned, but he no longer cared. 'Yet even you can't fully understand. Position and power, they're very attractive. I worked all my life towards those goals, and I'd hate to lose them now. Above all, though, I don't want to be known as one who failed the ultimate test. It's wonderful to reach your goal. It's diabolical, cuts much deeper, to lose what you've won.'

'What signs are there that you could lose it?'

'You're right, of course.' Marco grinned. 'I should know, if anyone does. No! No signs at all! But why keep me on?'

'Because you're very good at your job – superb.'

Confiding in his old friend, the Red Inquisitor realised how he had missed their frank talks. Paolo Crespelle was the only man in the world to whom he could talk without pretence. He could, of course, talk as straightforwardly with Bianca or Angela. But some things you could only say to a man – and some things it was not wise to say to a wife.

'Fate was malignant!' he said. 'Losing the children hurt worst. Both of them, Helena and Antonio! Why in the name of God were they stricken *after* the plague was over? An infant fever, Giuseppe Ortolan said. Nothing could be done. Paolo, it was less than a year we had them with us. But it was like having my arms torn off when they both died . . . within just three days . . . Did Bianca know when you last saw her?'

'My God, Marco! I am sorry . . . so very sorry. It'll be agony for Bianca. No, she didn't know.'

'I've written. Better if I could tell her myself. But I've written, as best I could.'

'And Angela?' Paolo asked. 'She must've been devastated. Has she started to get over it?'

'After ten days? Hardly! Anyway, she . . . You don't know, do you?'

'When I walked through that door, I knew hardly anything you're telling me.'

'Paolo, it's uncanny . . . unbearable,' Marco said softly. 'Last year, only ten months ago, we were rejoicing. The plague was over! We had the two babies! Venier was elected Doge! I had my new posts! Even trade was looking up . . . And now *everything's* gone bad. You asked after Angela. She's barren, Paolo, barren after the infection that followed Helena's birth. We'll never have another child.'

Relentlessly practical and happily unmarried, Paolo almost asked the obvious question: *Why not adopt an heir?* He caught himself in time. His friend would not welcome that suggestion just now.

'I probably shouldn't tell you, but I will,' Paolo instead said. 'After all, you've got to know Bianca's state of mind. She was furious at the women's death. Wouldn't speak to me for a year.'

'You've now learned Capellos don't like underhand deaths.'

'She got over that. But she's becoming morbid. Her conscience is badly bruised. I wish I never . . . but that's another story.'

'Same story, Paolo. Go on.'

'Duchess Joanna's dying so suddenly set Bianca off again. She says she's surrounded by death . . . she's an angel of death. Everyone around her: Pietro Buonaventura, the two women, little Filipo, Francesco's legal heir, though that was no surprise. And now Joanna, whom she never wished dead.'

'She never did? Never?'

'Never!' As always, Paolo championed Bianca. 'You don't know what a good woman she is, your cousin. But now the Florentines'll say she arranged Joanna's death, even though Joanna died in childbirth. Also that she poisoned Filipo.'

'Filipo? Everyone knows he was sickly. And Joanna? You know

they sent for Ortolan before Joanna was brought to bed. Later, the professor told me it was unavoidable. She'd had only eight children in thirteen years, but Joanna was worn out. Ortolan pointed out she'd also had four miscarriages. Worse, only two of her children survived: Eleanora and Maria. Joanna just gave up. And Ortolan could do nothing to save her or her new daughter.'

'So he told me, too.'

'Paolo, *when* did you talk to Ortolan? Before or after Joanna's death?'

'Why . . . before *and* after.'

'You didn't, did you? You didn't bribe Ortolan? You didn't tell him not to be too zealous in keeping Joanna alive?'

'How could I?' Paolo shrugged. 'Those were not my orders. But I didn't precisely weep when I heard the news.'

'She was a dreary creature, but that's hardly reason enough to get rid of her.'

'Let's just say I didn't weep. Would you've ordered it if you'd had the chance?'

'I don't think so, but . . . Poor Joanna, she didn't have a very pleasant life . . . or death. But it *is* convenient, *very convenient*.'

'If Antonio were alive, it would be marvellous,' Paolo said. 'He was an embarrassment when Joanna lived. But now he'd be . . .'

'God, I wish I could be there when Bianca learns of . . . that he's gone,' Marco mused. 'She'll need someone. But, still, she's got Francesco.'

'Does she? I'm not sure.'

'What does that mean?'

'Francesco's making a tour of his territories, looking for answers to his dilemma.'

'What dilemma? It can't be . . . not after all this time. He's not dithering about whether to marry Bianca?'

'Exactly! And he's being pushed. Chiefly, of course, by Ferdinando de Medici, who hates Venice . . . hates you and me because we're behind Bianca, his arch-enemy. Obviously, Ferdinando's been heir apparent since little Filipo's death. He gives out that Bianca is barren. But, naturally, he doesn't want to chance her producing a legitimate heir. Ferdinando's gold is breeding all sorts of moral questions. Anyway, Francesco's courtiers don't want a grand duchess who's cleverer than they are.'

'So?' Marco asked.

'So courtiers are asking questions. *How could the Grand Duke marry a woman who lived in sin, notoriously in sin, for so long? How could Tuscany hold up her head among the other states if the Duke married such a woman?* Not, of course, that anyone asks *who* made her such a woman!'

'And Francesco?'

'As I said, he's gone travelling, looking for an answer in the hills. How, he's asking God, can he stand before the Holy Altar beside a woman who lived in sin so long?'

'Can we let Bianca deal with it?' Marco asked. 'Must we get involved?'

'Normally Bianca can handle anything. But not when she herself is the heart of the problem. But, in my own way, I've tried to see that Francesco gets the right answers.'

'Who from?'

'A soothsayer I know and a gypsy herb woman I know.'

Marco smiled at the jargon. In the language of the Secret Service 'a person I know' meant a paid agent.

'And these two, you just happened to run into them, eh, Paolo?'

'Exactly! And they just happen to say the right thing. The sooth-sayer says the stars, the moon and the stars, presage the happiest union ever known: Francesco with Bianca. The herb woman's given him a potion to test Bianca's love, to see if it's true and deep. Not that she wouldn't pass the test anyway.'

'Of course. My cousin is a woman of immense virtue.'

'She is certainly that, almost a saint.'

'Quite!' Marco responded, knowing there was no point in his irony. Paolo had fallen in love with Bianca at their first meeting. His devotion, now virtually adoration, had sprung full-fledged after ten minutes – and could never be shaken.

Marco tinkled the crystal bell that stood beside the glass tray holding his cut goose-quills, his inkwells, and the fine sand for blotting his words. A black page wearing a long Oriental tunic and a turban knocked cursorily and entered the Inquisitors' Chamber. Without con-sulting Paolo, the Red Inquisitor directed: 'Two long ones.'

The page raised his hand to his turban and then swept it across his body, bowing profoundly. Paolo chortled with laughter after he had left.

'He's to remind me who's the real enemy: the Turk!' Marco's smile acknowledged the absurdity. 'No reason, though, to scorn their coffee. Best thing we've taken from them.'

'Except for mathematics, astronomy, and metallurgy.'

'Those were just improvements, not original discoveries. Now, shouldn't we give the Grand Duke spiritual counsel?'

'I didn't want to bring the Church in until I spoke to you,' Paolo replied. 'Too tricky.'

'I, we both, know a Franciscan friar in Pratolino. Friar Giulio'll soothe the Duke's conscience . . . counsel him well. Friar Giulio'll tell Francesco that his soul will be in dire peril *until* he marries Bianca. How the Florentine dog thinks he can debauch an honest lady of Venice and then . . .'

'Any other instructions for me?' Paolo ignored the Venetian's prejudices. 'What to advise Bianca?'

'Yes, of course. Suggest to Bianca that she tell her Duke she is on the point of leaving for home. She *will* leave if he does not marry her within a month. That ought to do it.'

'Who really understands Francesco? Sometimes, I think, not even Bianca. But, with her talent, it should work.'

'You and I, Paolo, will now make Bianca Grand Duchess of Tuscany. Without a doubt, we will.'

'Obviously, you still enjoy your work.'

'Sometimes,' Marco conceded.

'Also, it'll save your job,' Paolo observed. 'Cousin to the Grand Duchess of Tuscany, thus cousin-in-law to half the royalty of Europe. Who better to run the Venetian Secret Service?'

'You know, the thought did occur to me. But only just now. Anyway, here's our coffee.'

CHAPTER XXVI

THE morning sun, streaming through the windows of the minstrels' gallery high behind the twin thrones, touched the golden biretta of the Patriarch of Venice. Laying aside his pastoral staff, the Cardinal-Archbishop raised the crown above his head with both hands.

Rubies, emeralds, sapphires, and diamonds entrapped the sunlight, tossing the brilliant rays back and forth. Cascades of colour dazzled the upturned eyes of the woman whose hands were joined in prayer before her.

'*Nunc proclamus urbi et orbis* . . .' the Patriarch intoned in Church Latin. 'We now proclaim to this city and to the entire globe the marriage of Francesco de' Medici, Sovereign of the Grand Duchy of Tuscany, to Bianca Capello Buonaventura, Noblewoman of Venice, subsequently a widow of the city of Florence. We proclaim and affirm the Holy Sacrament of Matrimony entered into by Francesco and Bianca at the Royal Villa near the hamlet of Pratolino in June of the year of Our Lord preceding.'

The sunlight flamed on the yellow-silk vestments of the Patriarch, who was second only to the Bishop of Rome, the Pope himself, in the hierarchy of the Holy Catholic and Apostolic Church. Bianca Capello de' Medici lowered her eyes.

'*Duxessa Grandissima et Meritorissima Tuscanis te Biancam incoronamus* . . .' The old man's reedy voice rustled through the Great Hall of the Council in the Old Palace: 'We now crown thee, Bianca, Most Grand and Meritorious Duchess of Tuscany to reign beside thy Husband and Lord, Francesco, first of that name to hold this Throne.'

He set the crown, blazing with light, on Bianca's flame-bright hair. Her neck was bowed for an instant by its unexpected weight, and she knew that she had taken up a burden, as well as attaining the highest

(300)

possible distinction. No airy symbol, her crown was a substantial mass. Never had she imagined that she would at the supreme moment of her life be preoccupied with the weight of the crown she had sometimes despaired of ever wearing.

She was now twice royal, royal in her own right, as well as royal by her marriage, now affirmed by her coronation. As Marco Capello promised years ago, the Doge and Senate had four months earlier bestowed upon her the quasi-royal title and rank: *True and Loyal Daughter of the Most Serene Republic of Venice*.

Bianca was now vindicated and transformed: from noblewoman of Venice to the consort of a ruling sovereign and virtually royal in her own right. She could now by right call King Henry of France cousin, as she had by his courtesy five years earlier.

This Bianca was a new being, a royal being. To her vast surprise, she was transformed in her innermost self, as well as the eyes of others. She had not expected to feel herself wholly altered, despite her profound reverence for the rites and forms of Mother Church: the Holy Oil that annointed her forehead; the liturgy that consecrated her as a royal vessel of the will of God; the prayers raised by four cardinals and six archbishops for her well-being; and the homage of the illustrious assembly that glittered in the Great Hall of the Council this mild October morning in this blessed era one thousand five hundred and seventy-nine years after the birth of our Lord Jesus Christ.

The female choir in the gallery behind her was singing the *Salve Regina*, praising the most royal female ever known, the Blessed Virgin Mary. Intensely aware of herself as a royal female, Bianca gave thanks for the physical beauty and the acute mind with which God had endowed her.

Her hand, extended to receive the golden orb from the Patriarch, brushed the pearls sewn on the skirt of her white gown. She smiled to herself, mocking that ostentatious garment. Her smile widened in fond exasperation with her husband, who had insisted that she dress like a bride for her coronation.

She had wanted the gown to be striking, but not overdone. Yet Francesco, whose taste was usually good, had repeatedly demanded further embellishment.

He did not, he had said, begrudge the three hundred thousand ducats he was pouring out for her coronation. To mark the onset of a glorious new phase of his reign, it was not too much to spend enough to hire fifty thousand men-at-arms for a year or, by another measure, an entire year's revenue of the old Republic of Florence, which the

Medicis had supplanted. But he insisted that her coronation gown, which took the place of the wedding gown she had been unable to wear, should be the most splendid garment seen in Italy for three centuries.

Well, splendour had been muddled with excess – and there had been nothing she could do about it. The design was not extreme, except for the ten-foot train of white satin heavily embroidered with the fleur de lys of Florence picked out with seed pearls and borne by six pages. The flowing skirt which flared over horse-hair petticoats just revealed the tips of her white-satin pumps embroidered with the Medici coat of arms in semi-precious stones. The long vee-shaped bodice that compressed her waist was cut square across to show the swell of her powdered breasts.

Even at thirty, well *almost* thirty-one, Bianca reflected complacently, she still had the most beautiful bosom in Florence. Irritatingly, her nipples were chafed by the heavy silk required to carry the profuse embroidery, the lace inserts, the pearl and diamond appliqués, and the gold wire that now elaborated the classic model she had originally chosen. The chafing was irritating, but, in truth, exciting as well.

She was engulfed by sensation: the musky incense rising from swaying gold censers; the bass rumble of the monks' Gregorian chant; the candle flames; the heavy fragrance of perfumes; and the light gleaming on the gilt that framed the paintings on the ceiling thirty feet above her head.

Biance felt a sudden welling of desire. Her body grew heavy with wanting the bearded Duke who sat beside her dressed in cloth of gold with diamonds. Glancing at Francesco's muscled legs, she caught his deep brown eyes fixed on her face. She smiled crookedly, the tip of her tongue touching her upper lip for an instant, a sensual signal under five hundred pairs of eyes. His left hand moved, so slightly none but she could catch the gesture. Yet she felt her hips move minutely in response. The gesture was his own private sign, as if he were cupping her breast.

She had sometimes wondered whether she would have loved Francesco as deeply if he had been an ordinary count or baron, even a merchant, in short a nobody. She had also read that question in the envious looks other women gave her. She had told herself that she would undoubtedly have loved Francesco whatever his way of life.

She now realised that she could never know whether she would have loved Francesco as deeply if he had not been the heir to Tuscany. His rank was integral to himself, and he would have been totally different, another person entirely, without it. She could only know that she loved this Francesco de' Medici who held that rank.

Such were women's fancies. When they were not discussing the pleasures of the flesh so frankly they would shock naïve men, such speculation filled the lazy afternoons of ladies with little else to occupy them. Bianca was not accustomed to that kind of talk, never having had intimate female friends, except in her girlhood.

Nor did she now. The only women she could trust were her maid Lucia, with whom she would certainly not gossip idly, and her ladies-in-waiting, the Countess Abruzzo and the Baroness Adacci. She could make neither her confidante, certainly not now. Nor could either be her friend, for neither was her equal.

Loneliness was the handmaiden of power. She had to forgo the pleasure and the comfort of intimacy between equals. From this day, she would be the superior of every woman she met, except queens and princesses, whose self-importance made true friendship impossible.

She had chosen that fate – and she would choose it again. She was, in her own way, as dedicated as a nun. Instead of a coarse black habit, she wore glossy silks and glowing jewels. But she was as closely bound by her love of Francesco and her duty to Florence, as well as to Venice, as nuns were by their love of Jesus and their duty to God.

She had almost missed the glory – and the pain. It had been very close whether she were to become Grand Duchess of Tuscany or return to Venice in disgrace to be bustled into a nunnery herself. Her fate had rested in the hands of one man. Though brilliant, able, courageous, and sensitive, he was also moody and temperamental.

She had staked everything on one throw, as if it were only gold or jewels she was hazarding, not her entire life. In her mind's eye she could see herself walking with Francesco in the park of the Royal Villa, and in her mind's ear she could hear their tense exchange, as clear as if they were actors on stage.

Bianca loved the Villa Royal more than any other place on earth. Francesco had taken her advice on almost every stone. He had even built her a refuge for sick animals behind the stables, which some days treated more than thirty dogs, cats, and birds. An avid hunter, he felt, like his peasants, that dogs and cats were work animals and not to be pampered. But he was always ready to indulge her. For her part, Bianca could not bear the enclosures where he kept wild animals in cages: lions, tigers, buffalo, reindeer, even a white rhinoceros.

That day in late May the previous year, Francesco had just returned from Pistoia, where he had been hunting with his former antagonist

Paolo Crespelle's father, the old Baron. He had come back only after Bianca wrote to him imploringly three times.

The Duke still wore his leather hunting jerkin, stained with the blood of wild boars and stags. Bianca was airy and light in cream muslin embroidered with tiny blue fleur de lys. The time was late afternoon, and the setting was the gravel paths meandering among the dark cypresses, against which glowed the waxy white tapers of the chestnut trees.

Two hundred jets of water sparkled iridescent in the sunlight, rising more than a hundred feet to arch over the main drive. Nearby, a waterfall played a Corelli toccata in deep organ tones; the ingenious artificer Buontalenti had made it possible to change the melody at will. A twice-life-size bronze statue of the Great God Pan piped a rustic dance before a grotto where mechanical figures of nymphs and satyrs played risqué little scenes.

The couple paused before the pond where hundreds of fish sported under the eye of a guardian spirit so skilfully carved it seemed to emerge from the living rock. Some were trout or carp for the table. Others, brilliant orange or silver with diaphanous fins and tails, were called Far Orientals because they originated in Cathay.

When Francesco and Bianca came to the lake covered with the broad leaves of water-lilies and lotuses, she waved away the attendants following them. Fearing her displeasure they all scuttled behind box-hedges trimmed into pyramids, balls, peacocks, and elephants. Out of sight, they nudged each other gleefully.

Ever since a page had stumbled on Bianca and Francesco making love under the chestnuts, the attendants assumed that their master and mistress wanted privacy for just one reason. That had almost been true – until the past few months were clouded by the death of Joanna of Austria. Now Francesco was too preoccupied with his conscience and the advice of his councillors.

Bianca did not look directly at him, but at the enormous figure representing the Apennines, which the sculptor Giambologna had set on the far side of the lake. The granite colossus, more than fifty feet high, was seated on a knoll and bowed as if supporting the weight of the mountains. He looked as if he had always been there and would always be there.

'I sometimes envy his serenity,' she said.

'Serenity?' Francesco replied. 'He's not serene. He's agonised, as if he's got the whole world on his shoulders.'

'Sometimes I feel like that, too.'

'What's the matter, my dear? What's troubling you?'

'You, Francesco! You're troubling me. I'm very worried.'

'I know I've been away a lot. Had to straighten some things out in my mind. But I love you just as much as ever . . . even more. Everything can go on just as before.'

'Francesco, that's the problem. If you really loved me, some things would change.'

'Oh?'

'You'd marry me. It's time.'

'Why can't we just go on as we have for the past fourteen years? For a while at least?'

'I can't bear it any longer. I really think I'd rather go home . . . go into a nunnery. It was one thing when she, Joanna, was alive. I loved you, and I wanted to be with you – and nothing else mattered. I still want to be with you always. But it's different now.'

'Bianca, I'm under enormous pressure. Some say the Pope would forbid our marrying because . . . because of the past, our past. Others say I'd look ridiculous if we married now. The common people would laugh at me – and no ruler can let himself be ridiculous. Many argue that I must serve the state, make a state marriage.'

'You made one state marriage. And look how that left you! Francesco, you're a man of flesh and blood and feeling, as I know so well. A man, as well as a prince. You have a duty to yourself – to that man. Anyway, an unhappy prince cannot rule well.'

'You know I want to. I'd do it in a second if all this pressure . . .'

'If he . . . Antonio . . . had lived, would it be different?'

'Of course, it would, my dearest. I'd have an heir. Giving my people an heir would make up for everything else. But, now, the pressure! If I married you, there'd be riots in Florence.'

'And later?'

'Then, too, but maybe not as violent. After all, it's only a few months since Joanna . . . the pressure from my brother Nando and the Pope . . .'

'Neither wishing you well. And who'll help you bear that pressure when I'm gone?'

'Gone? What are you saying?'

'Francesco, I do love you – deeply. But I did warn you. Now I've made up my mind. If you and I are not married within the week, I will go back to Venice.'

'You can't mean it! You're just threatening!'

'Am I? Wait and see!'

'You can't do this to me, Bianca. Or to yourself. You'd be miserable.'

'Of course, I'd be miserable. But I'm miserable now. Francesco, I love you so and I've given up so much: my good name, my family, normal friendships. But I can't bear it any longer. The humiliation is too great. Just going on as before, it would *prove* I'm no more than your whore. And if you marry another princess . . .'

'Not that in a hurry.'

'Either I'm worthy of you or I'm not,' Bianca said passionately. 'My blood is as good as your own, my lineage older.'

'Just as soon as things've blown over, I'll . . .'

'No, Francesco, *not* later, *not* just as soon. If we're not married within the week, I will go back to Venice.'

The Holy Sacrament had been performed in private three days later, June 2, 1578. So soon after the death of his first wife, there could be no public ceremony. Friar Giulio, the old Fransiscan, had presided; the only witnesses had been Francesco's *aide de camp* and Bianca's ladies-in-waiting. But the commitment was as strong as if they had been married in San Lorenzo by a cardinal flanked by ten bishops.

Bianca had staked everything – and had won. She had sworn she would throw away the love that was the centre of her life if her lover refused her. She had no other choice, perhaps, but the risk had been colossal.

What, she wondered, would she have done if he had refused? Suddenly she knew with certainty that she would indeed have left him, torn herself away with a shattered heart. The next moment, she was again not so sure.

Bianca Capello de' Medici, the anointed Grand Duchess of Tuscany, broke out of her reverie. The Patriarch of Venice had just picked up his pastoral staff with its double-barred cross. Raising his hand, he gave her his blessing in sonorous Latin. She smiled when the Cardinal-Archbishop added in plain Venetian: 'Never forget, Bianca, that *La Serenissima* is your true mother. You played among her canals when you were small. Never forget that you are a True and Loyal Daughter of Venice.'

As if to underscore that admonition, the Venetian Ambassadors rose. Antonio Tiepolo wore the gold-and-crimson robes of the highest office below the Doge, a Guardian of St Mark's. Marco Capello wore the red robe of a Ducal Counsellor and State Inquisitor, the positions he had lost shortly after the death of his patron, the Admiral-Doge Sebastiano Venier – and regained when her own secret marriage was made public. Her father Bartolomeo Capello wore a nobleman's black robe. All three also wore the golden sash of the Knight of St Mark, the honour bestowed upon her father and her cousin to demonstrate further the Republic's delight at this coronation.

Swollen with pride, Bartolomeo Capello placed a father's kiss on her forehead, and she realised that she was no longer afraid of him. The past was past. The man whose violent temper had almost shattered her life was no more than her ageing father, grey where he was not bald, hesitant in his movements, and reconciled at last to his wayward daughter.

Marco Capello bowed to her – and winked. Flushing in surprise, she smiled at the man who was, next to Francesco himself, chiefly responsible for her present state. The next man, the Ambassador Antonio Tiepolo, Bianca knew only as the head of a great family who was, with the Patriarch, joint leader of the Venetian delegation to her coronation. Tall and very thin, he showed his dog-teeth when he smiled and bowed.

Behind Antonio Tiepolo, four pages in yellow tights and green doublets bore damascened caskets on green velvet cushions with gold tassels. The Ambassador opened the first and presented her with a belt fashioned entirely of gold. Her father took from the next casket a golden crown set with gems, the homage of Venice to her twice-royal daughter. Last, Marco kneeled to offer a ring of gold set with a ruby as big as the top joint of his thumb.

Moved even more by the affection of Venice, albeit belated, than by the value of those gifts, Bianca began to speak of her gratitude. But Antonio Tiepolo motioned her to wait.

The necklace he took from the fourth casket threw out a fountain of light. After a moment of stunned admiration, Bianca clasped around her throat the string of forty diamonds, each one larger than the nail of her index finger. This was the 'ten thousand ducat surprise' at which Marco had hinted.

Venice could be terribly mean-spirited, but she could also be incomparably lavish when she chose. As Grand Duchess of Tuscany, Bianca had just sworn to put the interests of her realm and its chief city, Florence, before all else. But she would never feel about Florence as she did about Venice.

Francesco had decreed that she was to be crowned in the Hall of the Great Council of the old Republic of Florence in the Old Palace, as he himself had been. The Hall was undeniably splendid with its murals, its gilt woodwork, its tall arched windows, and its royal dais. It was also called the Chamber of the Five Hundred, the largest number it could accommodate. The Hall of the Great Council in the Doge's Palace could seat more than two thousand – and was four hundred years older.

Nor were the murals by Vasari as awe-inspiring as the murals in that other Great Hall, above all Tintoretto's Paradise, which she had last seen at the banquet for Henry of France. The scenes of Florence extending her sway over neighbouring Tuscany were pastel-pretty and, somehow, feeble beside the robust portrayal of Venetian triumphs in distant lands. In almost every mural there appeared Cosimo de' Medici, as if the state were one man. That was not the Venetian way.

Venice was a far broader canvas. Venice looked outward to the world, while Florence had, until recently, looked hardly farther than Tuscany, certainly not beyond Italy. Even Pisa and Genoa, sea-powers themselves, had always looked as much inland as overseas. But Venice was cut off from the mainland by the lagoon and the swamps that had made her an ideal refuge against persecution since the sixth century. Perhaps Venice *had* to look outward. Regardless, Venetian audacity and Venetian intelligence had conquered and illuminated a world far greater than provincial Tuscans knew.

Yet she must never give the mobs any excuse to denounce her for favouring Venice. They were already saying in the streets that only love potions had made Francesco marry her. As if the devotion of fifteen years were all a trick!

Eagerly encouraged by her brother-in-law, Ferdinando de' Medici, her enemies also blamed her for the death of Joanna of Austria. While Joanna lived, the Florentines had scorned her as a crude German woman, suited to be a priest's housekeeper, but no more. Now, Joanna was endowed with a multitude of virtues, superior in every respect to the 'Venetian whore'.

Bianca tried to put the deaths of the midwife and the woodcutter's wife out of her mind. Those murders, done for her benefit, she would never have ordered. Those deaths would always weigh on her soul, as would the murder of Pietro, her first husband. Yet she was, at most, only indirectly responsible. She had endowed perpetual masses for their souls, as she had, of course, for the soul of poor little Antonio, her son.

Antonio! She must not think about Antonio today. God knew that she thought about Antonio at mass every day of her life.

Bianca Capello de' Medici, Grand Duchess of Tuscany, heard the female and the male choirs singing the Te Deum in concert. The solemn stage of her coronation was over.

The receptions and banquets, the processions and spectacles, would go on for another five days. She was looking forward to the entertainments as eagerly as a child, although she hated the golden chariot drawn by two lions heavily drugged with poppy juice, their spirits already broken by systematic ill-treatment. Some horrors she could not prevent. Instead, she thought about the grandeur to come, so much greater than the grandeur already displayed – and all for her this magnificent week.

The Venetian delegation, which numbered two hundred, including sixty Capellos, had been received by the entire court of the Grand Duke, riding in gilt coaches lined with silk. Spectacular fireworks had preceded a mock war staged by young gallants, which was followed by a verse drama with music telling the tale of Three Slaves of Love.

That had been the beginning. The bridal party, more than a thousand strong, was now to journey to the Royal Villa to hear music composed for the occasion and verses in praise of the bride written by the poet-laureate Torquato Tasso and by the Grand Duke himself.

Praise of the bride would be followed by praise of her native city in the pageants still to come.

A 'divine messenger from the old gods of Greece and Rome' would the following day arrive at the enormous stage set before the Pitti Palace in the golden chariot pulled by the two tormented lions. The messenger would vie with an actor playing Apollo, the Sun God, in reciting paeans extolling the bride's beauty and her virtue. The spirits of the air, the sun, the moon, and the night would judge the contest, contributing their own praise as well.

Neptune and dolphins and the Adriatic and Tyrrhenian Seas and whales and sea nymphs would then appear, sporting in vast tanks of water. Finally, a tableau of Venice triumphant over the Turks at Lepanto would lead a multitude of banners bearing the Wingēd Lion of Saint Mark and the Capellos' blue-and-silver hat.

Troupes of supporters had been assigned to cheer and shout and applaud at appropriate moments. No use, Francesco had said, leaving that to chance, although Bianca's charms would spontaneously evoke wild enthusiasm – as would the feasts he gave the common people and the coins he threw among them.

Rising as the Te Deum ended, Bianca placed her gloved fingers on the shimmering cloth-of-gold forearm her husband the Grand Duke offered. She turned slightly, looked up at him, and smiled.

Before power, before public glory, before all else, their love bound them eternally. Love was supreme: constant, unchanging, yet always new and always exhilarating.

One thing was, however, greater even than love, though never as splendid: the responsibilities that were intrinsic to their power and their grandeur. Even more than she had in the past, Bianca silently pledged, she would work with Francesco for the welfare of their people, all their people, for amity between states, and for the glory of Christendom, above all Florence and Venice.

There could never be another day like this. Her triumph and her dedication were perfect. Yet, almost perfect. If she could only give Francesco an heir to the throne of Tuscany, she would be gloriously happy, in truth ecstatic, forever.

CHAPTER XXVII

IL periodo d'oro! Even the official scribes sometimes lapsed from their starchy formality to call the era they chronicled the Golden Age. The people did so spontaneously in the year 1587.

Bianca, Grand Duchess of Tuscany, looked out on the park of her Royal Villa on the last day of April, 1587. But she did not see the springtime green expanse with its statues and fountains. She saw instead in her mind's eye the achievements of her co-reign with Francesco I. Next year it would be almost a decade, but it was not too soon to take stock, starting with Venice, her native city.

Trade had greatly improved, despite challenges from Northern Europe, and Venice was prospering. The Republic had largely recovered from these twin catastrophes, the Black Death and the conflagration in the Doge's Palace.

Marco Capello, raised to the additional dignity of a Guardian of St Mark's, was content at the age of forty-three, despite his sorrow at his wife Angela's inability to bear a child. Like his city, he was prosperous. More prosperous, he joked, because he did not manage his enterprises himself. He had placed all his ventures – from printing to shipping – under the direction of his lifelong lieutenant, Paolo Crespelle. The Republic decreed that two of its servants might not engage in trade, the Doge and the Red Inquisitor.

Marco was ruthless and unrelenting in promoting the Republic's interests abroad through the Secret Service, which he controlled. But he was tolerant of harmless dissent at home.

When challenged by conservatives, he pointed out that Venice had never imposed intellectual conformity. She had always benefited from encouraging diverse approaches to manufacturing and science, as well as philosophy, which also meant theology. She had benefited as much from giving a home to such diverse people as Jews and Greeks.

Opinions could, therefore, be freely expressed – as long as they did not challenge the benevolent sway of the hereditary nobility.

Tuscany, too, was tranquil under the rule of a Grand Duke whose second marriage had made him more attractive to the common people. Francesco I still immured himself in his laboratories to experiment with rock crystal, with smelting, and with explosives, as well as with more abstruse alchemical problems. But he was no longer so shy. With his wife Bianca by his side, he even appeared to enjoy receiving his people, merchants and workers as well as the nobility.

The people were no longer as hostile to the 'foreign adventuress' who had married their sovereign. Market-wives and ox-drovers even had an occasional word of praise for the Grand Duchess. She knew, of course, that they would revert to slander and abuse if times got hard. But times were good, very good, eight years after her coronation had begun a new era. Francesco and she had worked hard for that great progress, and the people were grudgingly appreciative.

No longer the scapegoat of the Florentines, Bianca was not only a heroine to Venice, but a favourite in the Vatican. The Pope had astonished her three years earlier by sending her the Golden Rose, the accolade he bestowed only on the outstanding figures of the age.

Most kings and princes had *not* received the Golden Rose, which was awarded no more than two or three times a decade. Admiral Sebastiano Venier was one of the few Doges whom the Pope had thus distinguished, largely for his role at Lepanto.

Bianca was delighted with that hard-headed approbation of the power she exercised in conjunction with Francesco. She was as proud of the other accomplishments the Pope cited: her work for the poor, her fostering of trade, agriculture, and manufacturing, her contribution to Venetian-Florentine amity, and her patronage of the arts.

Even her brother-in-law, Ferdinando Cardinal de' Medici, was not stirring up the people and the court against her as virulently. For the moment he was quiescent.

She had no illusions about Ferdinando. Intent on succeeding Francesco as Grand Duke of Tuscany, he would shrink from no evil, except, it appeared, murdering his brother.

Ferdinando had virtually bankrupted himself trying to depose them, chiefly by blackening Bianca's name. He called her 'the witch', charging that she had cast a spell on Francesco with her body and her potions. The Grand Duke, his younger brother argued, was, therefore, not fit to rule Tuscany. He was the puppet of an alien hand, not an independent sovereign.

Few took Ferdinando's absurdities to heart. Yet Bianca believed his silence worth buying. She had persuaded her reluctant husband to pay his brother's debts, hoping that kindness would dilute Ferdinando's venom.

It was an irony worthy of the mischievous old Greek gods: Bianca placated her vicious brother-in-law by repaying the large sums he had spent trying to destroy her. But it was worthwhile. Apparently convinced that he had no hope of deposing Bianca, much less Francesco, at the moment, the Cardinal had returned to his conspiracies in Rome. Bianca was reasonably safe until her brother-in-law suspected that she was likely to produce a son, who would, naturally, have a prior claim to the throne.

No fond uncle, Ferdinando simply ignored Francesco's two surviving daughters born of Joanna of Austria. Eleanora or Maria could, presumably, succeed to the throne if Francesco died without fathering a male heir. But there was no likelihood of a woman's legal rights prevailing over a warrior-cardinal. The Medicis, proud of their sophistication, believed they had created a new style of government based as much on intelligence, finance, and law as on force. But, even in the enlightened High Renaissance, a strong sword arm, a total lack of scruples, and abundant cash – or plausible promises – to hire large numbers of men-at-arms counted for more than justice or statecraft.

It all came down, thus, to a male heir whom Ferdinando could not sweep aside. Francesco was forty-six, still young enough to train an heir to defend himself and his realm. At thirty-nine, Bianca was past the best age for motherhood. Yet, having already given birth twice, she would not face the danger attached to a first pregnancy at her age. Since both prospective parents were fertile, there seemed to reason why they should not beget, by God's Grace, a boy.

But time was against them. This was their last chance.

The Grand Duchess looked out and saw the park from the balcony of her bedchamber on the second floor of the Royal Villa. The pink and white flowerets of the chestnuts were in full bloom and the peacocks were screaming in the shrubbery. A cock-pheasant trundled into flight after a long run, his wings whirring loudly. His orange-and-green feathers shone lustrous in the morning sun.

Bianca yawned, and her head drooped. She straightened her neck, feeling guilty at such drowsiness in the morning. She would normally have been busy since dawn. But she was letting things go. The Uffizi Gallery was collapsing into chaos because she was not giving it proper attention. Francesco wanted her opinion on a proposal to reduce farmers' taxes, but she had not found the energy to read the file.

Lucia, her maid, had left a goblet full of a dark herbal mixture beside her. Grimacing, she lifted the goblet to her lips. She set it down undrunk, repelled by its stench.

Resolutely, Bianca lifted the goblet again and gulped down the mixture. She suppressed a shiver of disgust. Yet, were it necessary to drink the revolting mixture twenty times a day, she would do so without complaining.

After the struggle and the pain that had brought her to this sheltered balcony amid the heavenly peace of her Royal Villa, she could hardly object to minor discomfort. Very little was required of her now. All she had to do was sit in the sun and think pleasant thoughts.

So Professor Giuseppe Ortolan of Padua University had said, and the professor was a miracle-worker. All she need do, he had said, was be comfortable and content, like a broody hen. All she need do was incubate her new life within her.

To her surprise, Bianca was enjoying her idleness. Although her waist was only a little distended, she felt as if she were already enormously swollen – and still swelling. She delighted in that sensation. She had never before been able to relax into the mindless torpor of untroubled pregnancy.

She had not really wanted Pellegrina, Pietro Buonaventura's daughter, now herself married to a nobleman of Milan. When Pellegrina was born, Bianca had already learned that she was married to a scoundrel, a philanderer, and a liar.

Carrying Antonio, her first child by Francesco, had been exciting and gratifying. But how could she have relaxed? However royal, her child would be a bastard. Besides, she had then lived in fear of Cardinal Ferdinando's assassins.

But everything was different this time. Even her fear of Ferdinando was muted. Not because she believed he had reformed his ways or abandoned his ambition. Because he did not know of her pregnancy – and would not know until after the birth.

Thinking back on it, the hardest part of all had been persuading Francesco. He had adamantly refused to allow a male physician to examine her – and there were no female physicians. The old midwife, Sister Barbara of the Oblate Sisters, was dead, and the Abbess, Lady Chiara, said regretfully that none of her present midwives possessed the skill the Grand Duchess required. When her cousin, Marco Capello, grew worried enough a year before to flout protocol and offered to send Professor Giuseppe Ortolan to see Bianca, the Grand Duke had declared: 'I won't have my wife pawed by a mountebank in a funny mask.'

Conceiving had not really been the problem, almost the contrary. She had suffered three miscarriages since her marriage. The last, only eighteen months ago, had been mocked by the irrepressible Cardinal Ferdinando. She had, he said, 'planned another false birth, but had failed to fool even her gullible husband'.

Finally Francesco had recognised that he could, as the exasperated Marco wrote, kill his wife by his stubbornness. He had recognised that she could be broken physically and emotionally if she went on as she was: first great hope, then black despair. Not to speak of the injury the failed pregnancies were doing to her womb.

Francesco had finally agreed to allow a male physician to examine her. No more false modesty! They lived in the late sixteenth century and medical science was making great strides, particularly at the University of Padua.

The examination itself was more uncomfortable than painful. At the beginning, she was rigid with embarrassment. She clamped her legs together when the Professor cast a great black cloak over her bed. Thus, he explained, he could examine her with her maid and her ladies-in-waiting present for propriety's sake, but without their seeing the examination.

'It's seeing that makes ladies worry,' he said. 'Take away the seeing, and ladies aren't so worried.'

'Maybe other ladies aren't worried. But I am – horribly.'

'A few years ago, I was too grand to practise gyneopathy,' he chatted. 'Leave it to the midwives, I said. They know what they're doing. Even treating the Commodore's wife, I did under protest. But now . . .'

Cold fingers parted the lips of her sex, and Bianca gasped at the shock. She stiffened in revulsion. But the gentle voice went on unperturbed in broad Venetian.

'That's it, m'dear,' he soothed the Grand Duchess. 'Just open up and let me do it. Easy now. Over in a minute or two. As I was saying, I changed my mind completely. If we couldn't help women, the women who bore us all, what good were physicians? I now believe the *highest* calling is helping new life into this beautiful world . . . Sorry, afraid that hurt.'

It had hurt, that wrench deep within her. Yet the worst was not the pain, but the indignity. At least, it was nothing like making love, as she had feared. Her embarrassment receded. Still, it was a strange experience this gyneopathical examination.

Bianca could not feel the Professor's hand deep within her, except as a distant pressure. But she detested having those parts of herself under strenuous scrutiny. Well, if prim little Angela could stand it, so could she.

'That's that, m'love,' Professor Ortolan finally said. 'All over now. Not so bad, was it?'

The physician reverted to formality when he emerged from under the cloak. With a little bow, ludicrous in the shiny grey medical robe draping his pudgy figure, he declared: 'Your Royal Highness, I am happy to report that it can be put right. Riding and walking've given you excellent muscle tone. All in all, you have a beautiful pelvis.'

Still shaken, Bianca could only smile in response to the strangest compliment she had ever received.

'You also have what we call an incontinent cervix,' he said. 'Press ahead . . . get yourself pregnant again. Enjoy it, Your Highness. Then, after two months or so, I'll pop back and put in a little stitch. That'll keep the heir where he belongs till he's ready to come out.'

Ever curious, Bianca asked the Professor to draw her a diagram. After recovering from his irrational jealousy at another man touching his woman, Francesco, the scientist, was fascinated by the way the Professor proposed to strengthen the neck of her womb. That drawing renewed the hope he held most dearly – and most desperately.

EVENING: SEPTEMBER 16, 1587
PRATOLINO: THE ROYAL VILLA

Remembering the hours his son Antonio had taken to come into the world, Grand Duke Francesco I settled down with a sheaf of state documents in his wife's small salon to await news. Having spent most of the past three months in bed, Bianca was eager to have it over. Arriving from Padua two days earlier, Professor Guiseppe Ortolan

(316)

had assured the Duke that the birth would be easy and, he hoped, quick.

Nevertheless prepared for a long siege, the Duke had asked two of his cronies, a mediocre painter of great conviviality and a brilliant chemist of little charm, to join him that evening. For the moment, he was content to sit alone and give his fantasy free rein. All his visions, all his hopes, came down to one small being: a son and heir.

Within a few hours, a day at the utmost, he would know. It was sooner than expected, though he had, fortunately, insisted that Ortolan return when the birth was apparently still a month away. Hard to believe Bianca had not miscounted, for she was enormous.

They had intended to move to the Pitti Palace for the birth. In that most public of Grand Ducal residences, Bianca had planned to command a dozen noblewomen, among them her known enemies, to be present at her lying-in to see that no fraud occurred. Ferdinando's creatures would then have been hard put to foment rumours that this pregnancy, too, was faked and the child a foundling.

Only his brother Ferdinando would keep pounding on that same old theme. Who else but Ferdinando would believe Bianca and he himself were so stupid they would use the same ruse over and over again, expecting it to be believed?

Ferdinando did think they were stupid. After Bianca's last miscarriage he had spread the old tale: she had attempted to deceive her husband, who, on discovering the fraud, had repudiated the false heir. Ferdinando's mental processes were a mystery, but one had to guard against his malice.

When the Professor, that little Venetian mountebank, said Bianca could not be moved to the Pitti Palace, she had suggested that several respectable matrons of Pratolino, perhaps a pair of nuns as well, be invited to witness the birth. She got that idea from a book.

In her idleness Bianca was reading again the historical works she had loved as a girl in the face of her father's contempt for female learning. In one old history book she had discovered a precedent. Unexpectedly going into labour in a little Italian town in the year 1194, the Empress Constance had put up a tent in the piazza and invited the local matrons to attest to the birth of her son, who became the great Holy Roman Emperor Frederick II.

Repelled at the thought of his wife's making a spectacle of herself for the wives of merchants and artisans, Francesco had, nonetheless, finally agreed to her suggestion. Even Ferdinando would not assert that a dozen honest women, nuns among them, had been bribed to lie about the birth.

The Professor had brusquely vetoed the plan, saying: 'I can't have a flock of women milling around disturbing my patient, not to speak of myself. I'm not worried about this delivery. But it can't be a simple matter for a mother of thirty-nine after so many miscarriages . . . They're not going to say I brought the baby in my little leather bag, are they?'

'That's precisely what they *will* say,' the Duke had replied. But the Professor was adamant, and all their hopes hung on him.

The Duke initialled a report warning that the Arno was becoming so fouled with the waste of dye works and tanneries that the oxen would no longer drink from it. The recommendation that all these manufactories be closed while a solution was found he vetoed with a single black stroke of his goose quill.

'Let it be set to rights,' he scrawled. 'But not at such great cost to my subjects and my treasury.'

He was scanning again the long-deferred proposal to reduce the taxes of those farmers who produced more than twelve and a half hundredweight of grain an acre, when the Professor himself flung open the door of the small salon. His normal fidgety dignity vanished, the Professor was highly excited.

'Congratulations, Your Royal Highness, a thousand congratulations!' he cried. 'You are a father again, twice a father. Her Royal Highness has given you a boy and a girl, as I suspected. Easy as shelling peas, it was. Because I was there, of course.'

'My wife . . . she's all right?' Francesco asked the perennial father's question. 'And the child . . . the children? Both whole and well?'

'Under my care, Her Royal Highness is well, though it has been an ordeal. Carrying two infants, a tremendous strain at her age.'

The Professor accepted a glass of grappa from his host's hand with a nod of thanks.

'The royal infants, Your Highness, *will* be well,' he said. 'But they are premature. At least a month, though I suspect even as much as five to six weeks early. They'll need special care. But there's nothing to worry about!'

CHAPTER XXVIII

'WHY,' Ferdinando, Cardinal de' Medici asked portentously, 'does God make all things die?'

It was a most unpriestly question, a question any youthful seminarian could answer halfway through his first course in apologetics. But Ferdinando was no theologian. He was not even a priest, although his father had bought him a cardinal's red hat when he was fourteen.

Ferdinando de' Medici was more comfortable in the saddle of a war-horse than a cathedral stall. In the confessional box, he would have been disastrous. His milieu was the battlefield, the tournament, and, above all, the small backroom, whether of tavern or palace, where the shrewdest intriguers of a nation of intriguers wove their plots. Tutored by Niccolo Machiavelli, whose works they often misinterpreted, Italians had become as addicted to conspiracy as Cathayans. Ferdinando de' Medici was a natural conspirator, and the common people loved him.

Nando, the people called him, Nando the Amiable. He was hearty and generous with them, hail-fellow-well-met with blacksmiths and drovers, with men-at-arms and camp followers, with merchants, manufacturers, and vintners. Like his father, Grand Duke Cosimo I, Ferdinando understood instinctively that a prince of the High Renaissance must command the enthusiastic loyalty of *all* his people, not just bishops, barons, and bankers, but herdsmen, craftsmen, and innkeepers as well. No more than Cosimo did Ferdinando play a false role. In the depths of his being, even to his slightly enlarged liver, he was truly Nando the Amiable, at thirty-eight the high-living, plain-spoken, lecherous, wine-quaffing sensualist he appeared.

Tonight Ferdinando was all in black: tights and trunk hose of fine black wool and a black doublet fastened with shiny jet frogs, even a black velvet cap with a black plume.

Lolling in a leather chair in Francesco's laboratory in the cellar of the Pitti Palace, he was uncannily like his introverted, intellectual brother. The same large brown eyes looked out under the same heavy black brows, and the same straight nose sprang from the same high, sloping forehead. Even his gestures were similar: the same confidential cupping of the hand to draw the listener in and the same aggressive thrust of the beard. Ferdinando was an inflated, coarsened version of the reserved, fastidious Francesco.

The tall, heavy-set, florid Cardinal was all but identical to his father, who had died at fifty-five after a series of strokes brought on by intemperance in all things, from power, battle and intrigue to food, wine and women. Ferdinando's face was broad, massive across the cheekbones; his brown eyes were cold as a swamp in January; and his full lips were habitually clenched tight.

Those lips curled in an ironic smile as he assessed the three men perched on the tables and benches of Francesco's laboratory, which gave them the total privacy no other room in the palace offered. When the Prince spoke, they were as attentive as schoolboys. Yet their deference was tinged with familiarity, and their posture was casual.

One was a plump priest; he wore the purple sash of a bishop over his black moiré cassock and smacked his purpling lips over the wine in the rock-crystal goblet he had found on a shelf. Another was very tall, some six foot five, and very thin; a cavalry officer in a sword-dented breastplate, his spurred boots rested on a dented helmet with plumes of Medici gold and blue. The last squinted through thick spectacles with heavy metal rims, which were tied round his ears with black laces and rested uneasily on his blunt nose; his grey academic robe was splotched with dried blood from anatomical dissection and pinholed with acid burns.

'It's sad, very sad, you know,' Nando the Amiable said. 'God never meant my brother to be a ruler. God made him to be a school teacher, a professor of alchemy, maybe, with his retorts and test-tubes. My father could never understand Franco.'

He drew a face that was meant to be pitying, but, somehow, looked gloating, and added: 'If my esteemed brother'd had five or six mistresses, the old Duke would've been happy. A chip off the old block. But he couldn't understand why Franco had only one mistress . . . and was so boringly faithful to her. Sure, Bianca's a fine piece, frisky as a filly on the mattress. But *only* Bianca! My father gave Franco hell's fire for his immorality.'

The priest, the soldier, and the anatomist gave those reflections the attention the speaker's power demanded. He had made them all, and he could break them almost as easily. They were, however, surprised at both the intimacy of Ferdinando's confidences and their length. Not normally garrulous, he was rambling tonight.

'With all his chances, I can't fathom it,' the Prince-Cardinal resumed. 'He could've conquered Perugia easily, taken a big bite out've Bologna. Instead, he sat here building villas and blowing up laboratories.'

'Surely not so simple, Eminence . . . ah . . . Highness,' the bishop remonstrated. 'Francesco I has made Florence famous for art, *the* centre of art in Italy. That adds up to gold in the long run. And he's created the Academy . . .'

'What earthly use is an academy?' Ferdinando demanded. 'A talking shop full of pompous fools in academic gowns and scribblers with the seats out of their breeches.'

'The Academy will make Florence *the* centre of culture,' the bishop replied. 'Make the speech of Tuscany the standard for all Italy. That means ducats – and influence over men's minds.'

'Also the Venetian alliance, Highness,' the cavalryman said. 'It's served us well, kept us from attack.'

'And will go when my brother goes. Or his whore-witch goes.'

'Not necessarily, Highness, not if we strive . . .' the bishop observed.

'You lot have all the answers.' Ferdinando veered away from the issue. 'But you haven't told me: *Why* does *God let every living thing die*? Can't He make an immortal being?'

The bishop responded. 'Immortality He reserves to Himself. We cannot fathom His design.'

'That's no explanation,' Ferdinando snapped. 'It's only clear that the old die so that the new can take their place.'

'The only explanation,' said the anatomist, 'that's scientifically demonstrable.'

The cavalryman said: 'His Highness has got hold of precisely the right end of the stick.'

'What do you mean, precisely?' the anatomist asked.

'The old's got to make way for the new,' the cavalryman answered. 'That's happening right now, thanks to God.'

'Wounded, the message said, only wounded, though severely,' Ferdinando interposed anxiously. 'That's right, isn't it?'

'Far as it goes,' the anatomist replied. 'But he won't last till morning.'

'Extraordinary, isn't it?' Ferdinando mused. 'I've been patient all these years while the whore-witch queened it over all of us. And now a spear goes astray. Not the boar, but Franco is speared. Of course, I grieve for him. I'd never *let* it happen, would I?'

The cavalryman and the anatomist glanced at each other and shrugged. The bishop raised his eyebrows and then raised his eyes to Heaven.

'Of course not, Highness,' he said emolliently. 'To raise your hand against your brother! Another Cain! Never, Your Highness. But you're absolutely right to assume the Regency immediately with the Grand Duke disabled.'

'And the girls?' Ferdinando asked. 'You're sure they can't . . .'

'With whose support, Highness? Who'd rally to two weak young women? They're perfect for marrying off to kings. Assets, not a problem.'

'So, Highness,' the anatomist said, 'you're as good as crowned. No one to oppose you.'

'And no nonsense about a legitimate heir? This pregnancy? I've heard whispers, though they've tried to keep it quiet. Another fake, of course. Who'd be stupid enough to fall for that old trick?'

'No one, Highness,' the cavalryman agreed. 'But why not take the Venetian witch out of play as well?'

The abstract discussion he had carelessly initiated now over, the newly-proclaimed Prince Regent of Tuscany was relieved and decisive. He directed the cavalryman: 'Giulio, take a troop to Pratolino and bring the witch back. Treat her gently for now. But, above all, bring her back!'

LATE EVENING: OCTOBER 20, 1587
PRATOLINO: THE ROYAL VILLA

Paolo Crespelle clattered up to the entrance court of the Royal Villa at eleven in the evening, some ten minutes before the cavalry colonel called Giulio was ordered to ride to Pratolino. The Grand Duchess's Household Guard had passed Paolo through the gates, wondering why the mad baron was riding in the pelting rain. The iron-shod hooves of his escort set the wet gravel flying and awakened the servants.

Paolo usually approached the Villa quietly. Decades in the Secret

(322)

Service had made stealth on land as instinctive to him as was daring at sea. But he had tonight ridden from his aged father's castle above Pistoia to Pratolino with twenty-eight troopers behind the Crespelle banner. Since urgency ruled out his normal secrecy, audacity must get him through.

Riding east across country on mountain trails, the troop had finally reached the main north-south road from Florence to Bologna. Their bright gonfalons drenched by the rain, they had clattered past villages whose people peered at them through closed shutters, fearful that the wars had come again to Tuscany. They had ridden twenty-five miles across the ridges of the Apennines when they reached Pratolino. Time was very short.

Having seen him from her balcony, Bianca was waiting in the small salon, a woollen robe wrapped around her in the chill October night. Paolo looked at her in obvious surprise. Why should she not be dressed for bed so close to midnight?

'I've come for the babies, Bianca . . . Highness,' he said without preamble. 'Ferdinando's men will be here within the hour. They must not find the babies. Send to get them ready. I must leave within twenty minutes.'

Bianca stared at him, mute in astonishment for an instant. She began to speak, but he overrode her.

'I have a friend, a widow who owns the Osteria in Borgo San Lorenzo. She'll keep them safe. No one'll know them. They could be guests' brats or her daughter's. She'll know you, of course, when you can fetch them. But give me Angela's tiara to mark them.'

'Paolo, *what* is all this? Why must I send my babies away? Why are Ferdinando's men . . .'

'My God, Bianca, I am sorry. They haven't reached you yet, have they? Not sent to tell you?'

Bianca shook her head and sank onto the couch. Fear clamped her throat shut. She shook her head again.

'They haven't? Bianca, there's no time to soften it. Francesco, the Duke, is hurt, desperately hurt. He'll survive, *if* he gets the best treatment, and . . .'

'I must go to him.' Knowing the disaster, which was almost the worst she could imagine, Bianca was firm. 'Tell me all you know. I'll leave the door ajar while I dress.'

She darted into the adjoining dressing-room, where her maid Lucia waited, already holding a riding habit with long leather hose beneath the skirt.

'Where's Ortolan?' Paolo demanded. 'Still looking after the babies? Good! Take him with you. If anyone can, he can save the Duke.'

'What happened, Paolo?' Bianca's voice was muffled by the folds of the dress she was pulling over her head. 'How could Francesco . . .'

'An accident, they say. A long spear tossed into the air by a wild boar impaled the Duke. So they say! My sources suspect otherwise. Anyway they've taken him to the infirmary of the Little Sisters of Mercy in Prato.'

EARLY MORNING: OCTOBER 21, 1587
BORGO SAN LORENZO

Twenty minutes later, two cavalcades clattered down the gravel paths and onto the high road. Riding fresh horses from the Royal Villa's stables, Paolo and his troopers, with the infants and a nursemaid, turned north-east towards Borgo San Lorenzo. Escorted by sixty men of her Household Guard, Bianca, with her maid Lucia and the physician Giuseppe Ortolan, rode south towards the junction above Florence where she would turn west for Prato.

Again Paolo and his men cut through the forests that cloaked the Apennines. The pine branches, heavy with rainwater, whipped across their faces, almost unseating them, and the undergrowth threw out tentacles to hobble their horses. Shortly after one in the morning, they approached the hamlet called Borgo San Lorenzo.

Leaving his men in the forest, Paolo took the infants and their nursemaid to the Osteria. They might have been only late travellers, though Tuscany was not so serene that a woman and two infants escorted by a single armed man would ride confidently through the night. Fortunately, they were not seen entering the town.

Paolo thrust the infants into the arms of his astonished mistress, handed her the diamond-and-sapphire tiara with a word of explanation, kissed her, and was gone. His troop rode back towards the high road, striking it a short distance north of Pratolino. There he split his escort, needing speed more than that paltry force. He sent twenty men back to Pistoia, advising them to sleep in the woods, above all to avoid the Royal Villa. Taking eight men with him, Paolo rode south towards the side road to Prato, where the wounded Grand Duke lay in the nunnery.

An hour earlier, just before Paulo arrived at the Osteria, the Grand Duchess and her sixty cavalrymen had approached the turning to Prato. Bianca rode astride at the head of the cavalcade, as light in the saddle as any cavalrymen. The troopers always said: 'When you ride with our Duchess, you ride hard!'

She was outdoing herself today, her flame-bright hair, which had been let down for the night, streaming in the moonlight that had succeeded the rain. Beside her rode the fresh-faced Captain of the Troop, a twenty-two-year-old son of a petty noble house who looked eighteen. On her other side, Professor Giuseppe Ortolan, to her surprise, easily maintained the hard pace.

At the tail of the cavalcade, two troopers rode protectively beside the maid Lucia, who sat in her saddle like a bundle of old clothes. Her skirts kilted up around her thighs, she too rode astride. From time to time, she groaned, but she would not desert her lady.

The unpaved road, pounded into stone-studded solidity by the impact of feet and hooves over the centuries, had also been deeply rutted by the wooden wheels of ox-carts. The clanking of steel bits and steel weapons, above all the thudding of iron horseshoes, deafened the riders to the barking of foxes and the hooting of owls in the woods. The ammonia stench of sweating horses and sweating men overcame the astringent scent of the pines. There had been no rain this far south, and white dust rose thick from the road, choking the riders in the rear. The light was spasmodic, obscured by the billowing dust, failing entirely when the half-moon was hidden by clouds.

Preternaturally alert because of her raging fear for Francesco, Bianca was first to see the dust cloud in the south. Her troop was ascending a rise in the road. When they came to the top, the troopers saw the blue banners with the six golden circles of the Medici like their own. Only the Household Guard carried those banners and flaunted blue-and-gold plumes on their helmets.

Drawing closer, Bianca counted a full squadron of Household Cavalry, twice their own number, riding north at a gallop. Her heart thawed a little. Francesco's aides, stricken by the tragedy, might have failed to send a messenger to her immediately. But they had now dispatched a squadron to escort her to him. This meeting was a good omen. She smiled for the first time since Paolo had told her of Francesco's wounds.

An instant later, her heart plummeted. The leading banner, well ahead of the dust billows, was now clearly visible in the moonlight. The Medici coat of arms was not crowned with the coronet of a reigning Grand Duke. She recognised the immensely tall, stick-thin figure riding before the banner. Colonel Giulio Arseno was Ferdinando's assassin man, a bully who savaged and killed at his master's command.

Still, it was good of her brother-in-law to send an escort for her. A gallant gesture! Emergencies drew families together. Yet instinct warned her: so uncharacteristic a gesture could not bode well. Bianca shivered beneath her heavy cloak, but shut her mind to that small dissenting voice.

Colonel Giulio Arseno rode forward with four troopers who wore full body armour that sheathed their shoulders and arms. Her guards wore only ceremonial breastplates. Halting half a dozen paces from the Grand Duchess, the colonel lifted his battered helmet from his grizzled head and bowed in the saddle.

'Welcome, Colonel.' Bianca took the offensive. 'My gratitude for coming to take me to the Duke.'

'Honoured, Your Royal Highness,' he replied. 'And my deepest sympathy. I am instructed to crave an audience for His Highness, the Prince Regent Ferdinando de' Medici.'

'Afterwards, of course.' She kept the anger from her voice; Ferdinando had been very quick to assume the Regency that was properly hers. 'I always have time for my brother-in-law. But, first, the Duke. Let me pass, Colonel.'

The tall man did not reply, but rode straight at Bianca and the two men who flanked her, the physician and the captain of her troop. She wheeled her mare to ride around the colonel, and the captain drew his broadsword. One armoured trooper whirled a spiked ball on a chain against the captain's unprotected throat, and he slid from his saddle.

On the back swing, the spikes dug into Bianca's ribs. A few seconds later, she felt blood flow down her side. The colonel snatched the mare's reins from her weakened hands and spurred back to his own men.

The ranks opened to admit them, but the colonel's men did not pause in their charge. Pressing their surprise, the squadron hurtled at the Duchess's astonished troopers.

Clutching her side, feeling the blood drip between her fingers, Bianca watched in horror that numbed the pain in her side. Billows of dust concealed the shock as the two forces met. But she could see the tips of the flagstaffs above the dust.

Her own banners, marked by the coronet, split, joined again, wavered, and retreated. The colonel's banners without the coronet surged forward. The sound of clashing weapons proved that her men were fighting hard. But they were outnumbered two to one.

The end came quickly. Within four minutes, the din of clashing steel ceased. Only horses screamed in pain, and men groaned.

The dust-curtain lifted to show the appalled Grand Duchess that two thirds of her men were wounded or slain. Swords and daggers drawn, Ferdinando's troopers were stalking among her lightly-armoured men. As she watched, a trooper thrust a dagger into a sergeant's throat. The next man the trooper approached nodded vigorously, and the trooper shook his hand. The pantomime was clear: either her guardsmen joined her enemies or they died.

But all humanity was not flown. The seriously wounded they left alone.

Horrified, almost despairing, Bianca saw all she had built crashing to earth. If Ferdinando dared use force against her, why should he not take the helpless Francesco by force?

She became aware that someone was helping her alight. A cloak was thrown around her.

'Not now, doctor,' the colonel directed Giuseppe Ortolan. 'You can treat her later. Now, she's to mount and ride.'

'If I don't treat her now, there'll be *no* later,' the physician replied stolidly. 'Are your orders to bring the Grand Duchess to your master dead?'

The colonel watched, silent and impatient, while the physician, sheltering Bianca under his black cloak, examined her wounds. After fifteen minutes, Ortolan felt he could delay no longer. Besides, where was rescue to come from, the sky?

'She can ride now, Colonel,' he said. 'But slowly, very slowly.'

'Mount!' A bugle shrilled the command. 'Mount and ride!'

All except the dead and the severely wounded leaped or struggled into their saddles. For the first time, the resolute physician was indecisive. He looked from the wounded lying in the road to Bianca, who was his first responsibility.

The colonel made up his mind for him.

'Mount!' he directed. 'You'll look after her, not them.'

The main force, which now included twenty of the Grand Duchess's Guard, rode south towards Florence. But forty armoured troopers turned north towards the Royal Villa on the colonel's command.

An hour later, Paolo Crespelle and his eight troopers heard the clanking of armour and the thud of cantering hooves. Five minutes later, the early dawn light flashed on Ferdinando's troopers. Prudently withdrawing into the woods, Paolo watched them clatter past.

'Ride!' he shouted at his men after they had passed. 'Ride like the Devil.'

Half an hour later, Paolo heard the groaning of the wounded, who had been abandoned in the road. Lucia, the maidservant, lay among them, her skirts pulled up to show her scrawny legs and ample buttocks.

Swearing to himself, Paolo knelt beside a wounded corporal with a gaping chest wound, who pleaded for water. After drinking, the corporal babbled an account of the clash. Paolo let him sip again from the water-bottle before laying him gently back in the dust to die.

'Mount!' he directed his men. 'Ride back on our trail and catch your comrades! Petty officers are to ride to every castello of every ally of the Grand Duke . . . every enemy of the Cardinal. Bring me a thousand men, this evening at the north gate – and we'll free Florence from the usurper.'

He would be better alone in Florence. Amid the turmoil that must be welling in the streets, a bumpkin from the hills would pass unnoticed. There was not much hope, even if his father could rally a thousand men-at-arms. All depended on how badly Francesco was wounded.

Would Ferdinando, Paolo wondered, help his brother live or help him die?

Yet Ferdinando might do neither. He could simply do nothing. Denying Francesco skilled medical treatment could kill him almost as fast as slipping a knife between his ribs.

Monumental and imposing, the Pitti Palace was, nonetheless, a noon-time edifice. The ridged stone walls were soft yellow in the sunlight; the acres of gardens were bright with flowers and flashed with fountains in the daylight. But dusk had fallen on all that splendour, some twenty-four hours after the first report that the Grand Duke had been severely wounded in the chase.

The laboratory in the cellar built for Francesco I was a night-time place. Small and secretive, it was, nonetheless, richly decorated, as the Duke liked his refuges from the affairs of state. The barrel roof rested on gilded eaves. The original hewn-stone walls were covered with walnut panelling picked out with gold. On the walls hung six of Leonardo da Vinci's anatomical drawings in red crayon.

Most prized by the prince who loved art and science were two paintings by the lesser Venetian master Giaccomino. One was lit by the glow radiating from a golden stone held high by a bearded man. It was called *The Alchemist*. Against the sombre background of the other painting, a man's corpse lay on a high table shining sickly white. A masked figure in a blood-stained robe was slitting the belly to reveal the yellow fat beneath the skin. Called *The Anatomist*, that painting hung over the hidden door to the tunnel from the mansion in the Via Maggio where Bianca had lived before her marriage to the Duke.

Exhausted, hungry, and depressed, Paolo Crespelle stood behind the door in the tunnel, his eye to the peephole concealed in the painting as one of the bolts that held together the dissecting table. Paolo had been waiting since five that evening, shortly after Ferdinando de' Medici proclaimed himself Grand Duke of Tuscany.

His beloved elder brother, Francesco I, the new Grand Duke announced, had died the preceding day from a sudden attack of *mal aria*, the disease of evil air. To ensure that his own reign was not corroded by acid suspicion, Ferdinando further announced, an autopsy would be performed this evening in the late Duke's own laboratory by independent anatomists.

Paolo Crespelle savagely condemned his own mistakes. He had let Bianca go into the monster's lair, when he should have insisted that she come with him. But how could he have kept her from riding to her wounded husband?

The dying corporal of her Household Guard had said she was

wounded. Ferdinando, who loathed Bianca as a witch, might allow Ortolan to save her so that he could burn her at the stake – if he dared so affront Venice.

All his vigilance, Paolo told himself, could not have averted the accident to Francesco, which he now believed deliberate. Had Ferdinando known? He had always refused to take advantage of Francesco's vulnerability to kill him.

Yet Ferdinando's henchmen, alarmed by Bianca's reported pregnancy, Paolo concluded, must have arranged the accident. By neither announcing nor denying the birth of the twins, Francesco and Bianca had thought to confuse Ferdinando and to stay his hand until they could present the heir apparent to their subjects. To show a sickly baby to the people would have been folly. Only two weeks more and the premature prince would have been sturdy enough for the ceremony.

Ferdinando they had, perhaps, confused. But his underlings had evidently struck down the Grand Duke Francesco, not knowing whether his consort had finally given him an heir. Against such ruthless stupidity there was no defence.

Francesco's death was a catastrophic defeat for the Venetian Secret Service. The foreign policy that had served Venice so well for a decade would have to be changed totally if the new Grand Duke jumped the other way. Even if Ferdinando maintained friendship with Venice, the intimacy that had centred on Bianca could not be preserved.

Francesco's death, Paolo reflected, was also a catastrophe for himself and Marco. The prince they had supported and the policy they had built around him were equally dead. Whatever policy came next would be planned and executed by others – after they had sucked the background knowledge from Marco's files.

Paolo Crespelle himself was bound to be highly unpopular under the new reign in Tuscany. When he had gathered the last shreds of information, he would be off to Venice to report. He himself would take Bianca's babies to safety in Venice. With two delicate infants, there could be no repetition of his rough and ready packing of the robust seven-month-old Antonio into a leather satchel. But he would find a way, and Venice would at least be pleased to have two royal hostages.

So much for hard-headed professional planning.

Quite unprofessionally, he abruptly decided he would not go until he had saved Bianca. Although he feared there was nothing he could do short of storming the Pitti Palace, he would find a way. Yet he thanked God that he had sent a messenger to his father retracting his order for troops to assemble at the north gate. An attack could only lead to civil war – and her certain death.

If he were the complete professional agent, he would set off for Venice immediately with the infants and his report. But he had loved Bianca since their first meeting – and had learned to love her even more afterwards for the charm and the intelligence with which she used her power. Now she lay wounded, at the mercy of her enemies. With Francesco dead and Marco far away, he was the only man who could save her.

He did not know how. Not yet. But nothing would stop him. What was good for Venice, good for himself, his own safety, even his life – nothing mattered beside Bianca, the only love of his forty-nine years on earth. Hereafter, he would serve only her, wherever that pledge led him.

Paolo Crespelle, the agent, was finished. Paolo Crespelle, the man, was now all.

His entire body shuddered uncontrollably as he finally yielded to the racking emotion he had been resisting for almost twenty-four hours. But his eye did not leave the peephole.

Paolo saw three men enter the laboratory. The first was a shabby fellow in a soiled academic robe with heavy spectacles tied round his ears with black laces. Strutting like a cock in a farmyard, he was obviously the superior of the scrawny young man in a similar academic robe similarly stained. The third man was Professor Giuseppe Ortolan, for once deflated. His habitual jauntiness had deserted him; his moustache drooped; his yellow tights were torn; and his crimson doublet was spotted with mud. He looked dispirited, and, above all, frightened.

The anatomist and his assistant pushed a table covered with a black cloth into the brilliant yellow circle cast by the lantern hanging from the gilded eaves. The assistant drew the black cloth down to reveal the bearded face, the arched chest, the heavy penis, and the muscled legs of Francesco de' Medici, late Grand Duke of Tuscany. The corpse was waxy yellow, and a six-inch wound gaped pale red in the black-furred belly just above the groin.

To Paolo it appeared clear beyond question what had killed Francesco. But the anatomists were not satisfied. The bespectacled Florentine lifted a scalpel and made an incision around the throat. Deftly, delicately as a man peeling an orange, he rolled the skin back from the incision, covering the face.

Paolo looked away. Violent death he had seen hundreds of times. Violent death he had himself inflicted scores of times. He was fully prepared, indeed expected, to meet a violent death himself. But this cold-blooded carving of a corpse like a pig he could not watch.

The door through which the three had come opened, and Paolo heard faint music from the ballroom above, strange in this house of mourning. When he recognised the melody, the hair on his neck bristled.

The macabre song had been a favourite of Lorenzo de' Medici, who was called the Magnificent: 'Carro della Morte . . . Carriage of Death', which could mean the tumbril that carried the condemned to execution or the corpse-wagon that carried away victims of the plague. When that snatch ended, drums and trumpets introduced a baritone singing another favourite of Lorenzo and the bellicose Florentines, the rousing 'A la Battaglia . . . Into Battle'. The door, held by a patient page who was obviously awaiting a personage, remained open.

Above the song, Paolo heard the brisk clicking of heels on the flagstones of the corridor and also the clanking of spurs. Two men were approaching the laboratory from opposite directions, the spurs from the outer door, the heels from the upper floor.

The two met and halted for a time just out of sight. The Grand Duke Ferdinando I then entered, wearing the black of deep mourning. He spoke over his shoulder to Colonel Giulio Arseno, who wore a battered breastplate with the blue-and-gold uniform of the Household Guard and carried his helmet under his arm.

'. . . two, not one?' Ferdinando said. 'You're sure?'

'After my men found the nursery, Highness, I went to see for myself. There's no doubt about it: *two* brats, boy and girl from the blue and pink shawls.'

'So, *this* time, the witch wasn't pretending. Or was she? How in the name of God you let them . . .'

The colonel remained silent.

'Find them, Giulio!' Ferdinando de' Medici exploded. 'I want them in my hand. Guard every pass and every port. Search every town, every mountain hamlet, every castello, even if you have to force your way in. Don't start a war, but do anything else. *Just find them!* I want the witch's brats in my hand!'

The colonel bowed and strode out, his spurs jangling. Glancing impassively at the flayed corpse on the high table, the Duke asked the anatomist: 'All done, then? All set out, signed, and sealed? Let me see the papers.'

'Your Highness, we are not quite ready. A little while yet.'

'What's holding you up? I need the papers.'

'Highness, we had to find the independent expert. May I present Professor Giuseppe Ortolan of the University of Padua? Then, Highness, we had to . . . ah . . . persuade Professor Ortolan to . . . ah . . . assist us.'

'All persuaded now, is he? Or shall I . . .'

'No, Highness. Not necessary. He's totally persuaded.'

'Then get on with it. I want the papers within the hour.'

The new Grand Duke swept out of the laboratory, pausing only momentarily to eye the corpse of the late Grand Duke and shake his head. Paolo Crespelle wondered what that gesture meant. Triumph? Sympathy? Indifference? Contrition? He would never know.

The anatomist resumed his peeling of Francesco's head. His assistant cut into the chest over the sternum and wrenched back the skin from the massive ribs. Paolo turned away, but kept his head close to the peephole. He could hear the grating of a saw on bone, and a sickly squishing like something soft and damp dropping into a bucket.

'Isn't this a bit, a bit extreme?' Professor Giuseppe Ortolan enunciated with great care, as if reasoning with dull children. 'Holy Church . . . the people . . . will be furious at our desecrating the body of the . . .'

'The people don't give a fart about Francesco,' the bespectacled anatomist replied curtly. 'And *our* bishop says it's all right. He's in Nando's pocket, just like you and me.'

'But why bother?' Ortolan protested. 'If it were *mal aria*, there would be no question. The state of the body alone. Anyway it's obvious how this man died. Why this lunatic charade?'

'Nando wants it,' the Florentine replied. 'And Nando gets what he wants from me – always. I don't want my neck stretched. Do *you* want to end up like him there on the table?'

'But, as scientists, we . . .'

'Science be buggered! This is politics. And look at the pay. I'm happy with a hundred ducats. You ought to be very happy getting away with your life.'

Paolo Crespelle leaned his forehead against the rough stone framing the door. The cold and the pressure would keep him awake, exhausted as he was. From time to time, he looked through the peephole. Each time, he turned away in pity and in horror from the poor, naked, bony, bloody thing that had been a mighty prince.

'That'll do,' the anatomist finally told his assistant. 'No need to go on any longer. Give me the papers and sew him up.'

'You had the papers ready all the time?' Ortolan asked.

'Of course. Now sign here and here.'

'It doesn't matter what I sign.' Ortolan consoled himself aloud. 'It's ludicrous, totally unscientific, completely implausible. No one could possibly believe we really found *mal aria* was the cause.'

'There's thousands that will, Professor. And they're the ones that count.'

Paolo Crespelle looked through the peephole again. He saw the assistant anatomist crudely sewing up with black tarred twine the wounds the scalpels had inflicted on the body of Francesco I.

Outwardly, Paolo had liked Francesco in a casual, distant way. Inwardly, he had hated Francesco for possessing Bianca. But he detested this final indignity. The Grand Duke was being stitched up like a roast for the oven.

Yet Paolo waited still. The impatient Ferdinando would assuredly return for the autopsy report falsely attesting that his brother had died of *mal aria*. Ferdinando might then drop some hint regarding Bianca's whereabouts. Breathing shallowly to stop himself from falling asleep, Paolo waited and watched.

Yet his eyes closed of their own accord, and he began to slip down the rough wooden face of the hidden door. He was jerked back to consciousness by a grating noise, which sounded in his waking muzziness like table-legs moving on flagstones. Assuming they were moving the Grand Duke's body back, he looked to make sure.

The table stood under the lamp, the black cloth spread again over its grisly occupant. The assistant anatomist twitched the cloth aside with a single motion – and only pain kept Paolo Crespelle from fainting.

His clenched hands drove his finger-nails into his palms so hard they bled. Rage hammered in the blood flowing in his temples, and he choked back the bile that rose into his mouth. His trembling hand grasped his wrist so hard he felt the bones creak. Otherwise, he would have hurled himself through the door with his broadsword drawn and butchered the defilers.

In the circle of golden light lay the naked body of a woman. Her eyes were closed, but a faint smile curled the perfect mouth in the oval face, as if they had killed her with drugs. Her skin was still fair, not yet waxen, and the hair streaming over her shoulders was flaming auburn. The triangle between her thighs was the same vibrant colour, and her breasts, even as she lay on her back, rose proudly to pink nipples. She was as perfect as he had always imagined her, unmarred except for the jagged wound in her left side, a blemish that set off her beauty.

How often had he dreamed of seeing her thus! God was cruel

beyond imagining to inflict this final indignity upon her – and this torment upon him.

Paolo Crespelle let go of his wrist and slipped his broadsword from his belt. He would not allow them to carve her, too, like a pig for their amusement.

'You let her die!' He heard Ortolan cry out in anguish. 'You filthy animals, you just let her die.'

Paolo drew back his boot to crash the door open. He did not know what he would do after he had killed the obscene anatomists. Perhaps carry her away through the tunnel. Something would suggest itself, some voice would tell him what to do. He cocked his foot to drive the door open.

He checked himself so suddenly his entire body grew rigid. Ferdinando was entering from the corridor followed by four men-at-arms and a plump priest wearing a bishop's purple sash over a shiny black moiré cassock.

The Grand Duke eyed the body of his enemy and licked his lips. Behind him, the men-at-arms gawked until he turned on them menacingly.

'No need to cut her up, too,' Ferdinando directed the anatomists. 'The witch'll never be seen again. Just sign the papers and wrap her up. *Mal aria*, too. Later, you're to spread the tale, whisper in confidence that she poisoned herself. Remorse for poisoning my brother and his true wife Joanna before that. But *mal aria* officially.'

Anointing Bianca's forehead with Holy Oil, the Bishop said a short prayer, concluding '. . . *in nomine Patris et Filii et Spiritu Sancti!*'

The Duke glared at the men-at-arms, who were shifting uneasily from foot to foot, their swords creaking in their scabbards. He turned to speak softly to the bishop. Finally, he confronted Professor Giuseppe Ortolan, who had shrunk into a dark corner, hoping to go unnoticed.

'You're free, Professor,' he said. 'But never forget who gave you your life – and can as easily reclaim it. I'll be frank. If you died or disappeared, the death certificates would look odd. So I'm letting you go.'

Despite his terror, the professor looked the Grand Duke in the eye. But he did not speak.

'Obviously, you're not to talk about this,' the Duke added. 'If you play the fool and do, who'll believe you? And what'll conniving at lies do to your reputation as an objective scientist? Or your life expectancy? Talk and you're worth nothing to me alive.'

Turning again to the men-at-arms, the Duke directed: 'After midnight, say two or three, the city'll be quiet. Who'll be wandering around tonight? Bury the witch under the Bridge of the Holy Trinity.'

EARLY MORNING: OCTOBER 22, 1587
FLORENCE: THE BRIDGE OF THE HOLY TRINITY

At one that morning, Paolo Crespelle waited in the shadows under the Bridge of the Holy Trinity, which connected the Via Turnabuoni with the Via Maggio. He was alone, having sent his men to watch Professor Giuseppe Ortolan along the high road north and see that he was not killed. The mercurial Ferdinando could change his mind.

Besides, only one pair of eyes was needed now. All the mailed hosts of Christendom, led by the Archangel Michael with his flaming sword, could do no more than one man alone. All anyone could do was watch prudently.

Paolo shivered in the cold October night. He wanted only to sleep for days. Yet he owed this last service to Bianca. Not for Venice, not for Marco, but for himself, who had loved her in silence.

Near the retaining wall of rough stone blocks, the low water exposed patches of black mud littered with refuse. When the rains came in a week or so, when the spring floods came, those patches would be covered with water. Above him, the most graceful bridge in Florence caught the moonlight in its arches.

Paolo shivered again. The tattered garments of a rubbish scavenger, the lowest of men, were a sure disguise for the dashing Baron Paolo Crespelle. Ferdinando would be after him, too, before long. But those rags were little protection against the wind that whined through the canyon between the embankments of the Arno.

They came at two when the city was silent, Ferdinando's three men-at-arms. One pulled the short shafts of a handcart like those the market porters used for moving lengthy and heavy goods. The flat bed of the handcart bore a slight body wrapped in a black shroud caked with dried blood. Two men-at-arms clambered down to the river bed on the footholds in the hewn-stone walls, and the mud squelched beneath their boots.

The third lowered Bianca's body on a rope. When they slung her onto the river bed, the soft mud sucked at her eagerly.

Paolo shuddered at the obscene sound. He clenched his hands together to keep them from his sword and dagger.

'All them Venetians love water,' said one of the grave-diggers. 'Now she's got all she needs forever . . . for eternity.'

'She wanted Tuscan earth,' said another. 'And she's got that too.'

The first kicked an abandoned sandal onto the grave and said: 'Nando's wiping her out. Wherever her coat of arms, the funny hat, is next to Francesco's, the Medici golden balls, it'll be chiselled away. They're going to put Joanna's back, as if she was his only wife.'

'Venetian whore!' The third spat on the hidden grave. 'Nando says she was a witch.'

'She can throw a spell on this,' said the first. 'She'd have grabbed it quick enough before!'

Hidden in the shadows, Paolo saw them urinating on the new grave. A storm of fury bore away his resolution to do no more than watch prudently.

He jerked his broadsword and his dagger from the belt under his rags and leaped at the men-at-arms, shouting the old battle cry: '*St Mark and Venice!*'

All three were dead within forty seconds, dead on the grave they had desecrated.

Paolo wiped his sword on the leader's cloak. He kicked and shoved the bodies into the deep shadow under the embankment, where they would slowly sink into the mud. Turning reverently to the new grave, he went down on his knees and dug with his sword and his hands.

Within three minutes he had freed her from the clutch of the stinking mud. He lifted her tenderly. The slight form was no burden, even in death, until he came to the retaining wall. But he tied two of the men-at-arms' cloaks into a sling and worked her up slowly. Laying her gently on the handcart, he knelt to pray.

Four minutes later, Paolo Crespelle rose to his feet, and stepped between the shafts of the cart. His ragpicker's tatters flapping, he trudged wearily beside the Arno. The wheels of the cart wailed disconsolately, and its boards grated against each other.

The Tuscan Baron slowly bore the remains of the last Grand Duchess of Tuscany out of her city of Florence. His body, hunched like an ox between the shafts, and the cart's long bed, and the pitiful mound that had been Bianca Capello de' Medici, all cast grotesque, shifting shadows on the cobblestones in the feeble moonlight.

No longer caring whom he might meet, Paolo trudged eastward, his broadsword lying at Bianca's head like a cross. He knew his actions were a little mad. Perhaps he was a little mad himself. But what did it matter?

EPILOGUE

THE Red Inquisitor was normally not permitted to leave Venice, for he carried a treasure-chest of state secrets in his head. The Doge in Council had, however, sent *il Rosso* to Florence after reading Paolo Crespelle's half-coherent report of the deaths of Grand Duke Francesco and Grand Duchess Bianca, as well as the near-miraculous survival of their twin infants. Only Marco could wring the truth from his grief-paralysed agent, and only Marco would Paolo trust with Bianca's babies. The Executive Council wanted the entire truth regarding the death of the lady who bore the quasi-royal title, True and Loyal Daughter of the Serene Republic. The Council further wanted her twins brought to Venice, reckoning they could some day be of use to the state.

Marco had not gone to Tuscany furtively, but publicly, indeed ostentatiously. He had been designated Ambassador Extraordinary, charged to express to the new Grand Duke the sorrow of the Republic over his deprivation and, if possible, to forge new ties between Venice and Tuscany. Marco's entourage, which included a hundred men-at-arms, would protect him from the Florentines. The responsibility to keep the peace imposed by a diplomatic mission would presumably protect him from himself and his fury at Bianca's foul murder.

The Red Inquisitor's loyalty to Venice was severely tested. Years earlier, when he reprimanded Paolo Crespelle for the deaths of the midwife and the woodcutter's wife and forbade such casual violence, it was an act of personal honour whose consequences for the state were slight. Regardless of how Marco might cover his tracks, slaying Ferdinando de' Medici would be an act of personal vengeance that could have a disastrous effect on the state. Wearing the gold-embroidered crimson robe of a Ducal Councillor and a Guardian of St Mark's, Ambassador Extraordinary Missier Marco Capello therefore smiled and bowed to the usurper Grand Duke of Tuscany, Ferdinando I.

He was always to remember that audience with shame. It was the most galling act of his life, relieved slightly by his sensing that Ferdinando de' Medici was intimidated by his presence. Knowing the Ambassador's love for his cousin Bianca and the immense power of the Red Inquisitor, the criminal on the throne wondered fearfully what revenge the wily Venetian was planning. So Marco later learned from an intercepted letter warning the Grand Duke's allies in Rome that the Venetian Secret Service would be responsible if he met an unexplained death.

The evening after that audience, Marco rode to Pistoia, casually incognito as a merchant from Dalmatia. He did not care if he were recognised, indeed preferred to be recognised. Diplomatic protocol required him not to kill his official host, the Grand Duke. Protocol did not require him to refrain from worrying his host by visiting the Baron Paolo Crespelle.

Duke Ferdinando knew that Paolo was his implacable enemy. He also knew that he could not attack Paolo, who had gone to ground in his castello. Any frontal attack would rouse a wasp's nest of Crespelle adherents, joined by all Ferdinando's enemies. He was not so firmly seated on the throne that he could risk a revolt of feudal-minded barons. He was still living down general unease at the brutal way in which he had seized the throne. Marco knew Ferdinando would, therefore, worry frantically about what was passing between his two fervent enemies.

Actually, the old friends spoke little of the Duke. They were already in complete, though virtually unspoken, agreement that Ferdinando would – some day, somehow – suffer grievously. Finding Paolo's passion for revenge as fiery as his own, Marco would have liked to talk about manoeuvring Ferdinando into destroying himself – without showing their hand. But Paolo was almost incapable of reasoned discussion.

'I buried her, Marco,' he said. 'With my hands and my sword, I buried her. With my bare hand and my blade . . . the same way I took her from an unhallowed grave under the Arno's water. A secret grave . . . a whore's grave . . . they put her in.'

Marco looked anxiously at his closest friend, whom the sailors had called the Tuscan Wild Boar. Paolo's face was ruddy in the leaping light of the tree trunks burning in the fireplace in the early dusk of early December. Though dry, his hazel eyes glittered hecticly.

Though his squirrel-red hair was fashionably long, it was bristled and streaked with grey. His voice was steady, but strangely hoarse, like a suppressed sob.

Marco had known for two decades that Paolo was hopelessly in love with Bianca, having never loved another woman completely. He had expected his lieutenant to be frantic, for it was hardly more than a month after her brutal murder. He had expected, perhaps, tears, certainly vehement grief and rage. Paolo was a Tuscan, not a self-controlled Venetian. There were no tears and no curses.

Yet Marco realised that he had underestimated Paolo's devotion to Bianca: how she had dominated his existence.

Marco had not expected this flat calm, the apparent absence of all feeling, which he knew was false and fragile. Nor had he expected his lieutenant to be so disoriented by sorrow that his sentences trailed off into near nonsense.

'I . . . I buried her . . .' Paolo paused for an interminable moment, as if seeing the scene again. 'That is, you see, Friar Giulio buried her . . . with me, Marco. You understand . . . I was there. He . . . we . . . buried her behind the little round chapel where the chestnuts fall on the . . . on her. It's a mound, only a little mound. No cross . . . or anything. We were afraid the Duke's men would find . . . otherwise . . .'

That rambling account would have been embarrassing from anyone. From the lips of Paolo Crespelle, the man of iron-and-oak, his companion in a score of battles, it was for Marco as agonising as a lash across his back.

'If they . . . anyone . . . comes looking, they'll never connect it with my Lady Bi . . . with her.' Paolo stumbled, but concluded with forced briskness. 'Some day I'll put up a plain stone cross there.'

'The children, Paolo!' Marco spoke curtly to ensnare his lieutenant's wandering attention. 'Where do I find them? I'll be taking them back to Venice.'

'Naturally!' Suddenly, it was the old Paolo speaking, galvanised by the need to perform one last service for the women he had so loved. 'I expected nothing less. But it won't be simple or easy. Now . . .'

The twins who were barely two months old, Paolo explained, could not be left with his occasional bed-partner who owned the Osteria of Borgo San Lorenzo. Not when the usurper Ferdinando's troops, police, and secret agents were scouring Tuscany for two infants of that age. They had, therefore, been separated and given temporarily to two unlikely guardians.

'I should've claimed them and brought them to Venice the day after . . . after I . . . after she went to her rest,' Paolo said, shamefaced. 'But I couldn't . . . too broken up. And now every move I make is watched. But I got Angela's tiara back.'

The girl baby had been placed in the Orphanage of San Rocco in Lucca, which cared for deformed children. She did not stand out among a dozen other brown-eyed infants, all very slow in their minds; a few drops of poppy juice a day subdued her normal animation and made her bright eyes dull.

That refuge could serve for only a few weeks, at most a month. Not only because Ferdinando's search was implacable, doubling back on itself to inspect again places already inspected, but because the dose of poppy juice had to be increased constantly. If the dose kept rising for another five or six weeks, she would become an irredeemable dullard, totally dependent on the drug.

The infant who was the rightful Grand Duke of Tuscany was sheltered by the Count of Abruzzo, whose wife had been Bianca's senior lady-in-waiting. The Count was now repentant, trying to atone for deserting his wife for debauchery for several years. She could, therefore, ask him what she would – and Annabella, Countess of Abruzzi, wanted protection for the son of Bianca, once Grand Duchess of Tuscany.

The Count had entrusted the boy to shepherds, a man and wife who did not come down from the high pastures with the winter. He was not likely to be discovered among the crags of the Apennines, where no one ventured at this season. With food enough to last till spring, the infant prince was safe from harm, barring illness or accident.

But the Count of Abruzzo was restive. His guilty conscience struggled against his sense of self-preservation. He feared Ferdinando's vengeance if his role were uncovered, which was not at all unlikely in the long run.

Not only the shepherds, but the two men-at-arms who had seen to their provisions, knew that a boy child was in hiding in the hills. It needed no great wit to guess that he might be the missing Medici, nor any great greed to covet the three thousand ducats Ferdinando offered for information about the infants. Besides, the Count saw no possible advantage in keeping the boy safe. How could a minute waif, with only the problematical backing of notoriously cautious Venice, possibly depose his ruthless uncle and take the throne?

'We've got a week's grace, maybe two, but no more,' Paolo summed up, now brisk. 'Thank God you came. I can do nothing . . . too many spies. But you, with the tiara to prove your bona fides, you can claim them. Though how you'll get them out of Tuscany, I simply don't . . .'

'I'm beginning to see a way.' Marco's confidence in the fledgling plan increased as he spoke. 'It's still a little fuzzy, but I've got an idea. You will definitely be able to do something: the hardest part.'

Before he left the next morning to return to Florence, Marco outlined the operation to his lieutenant. Conveniently, it required no further open contact between them.

Neither Paolo's servants nor Marco's entourage could miss hearing their voices raised in anger an instant later, though their words were unintelligible. The next morning they said their good-byes stiffly, as if pretending to amity. Ferdinando's spies might suspect that the quarrel had been staged and, therefore, intensify their surveillance. They might wonder whether disagreement on tactics had caused the rift. Either way, Marco would have gained what he wanted: greater vigilance on the part of his enemies.

Before leaving, the Ambassador Extraordinary wrote to the Baroness Adacci, Bianca's former junior lady-in-waiting, who was Paolo Crespelle's younger sister, Cecilia. Since it was vital that he and she should not be seen together, Cecilia's old nursemaid carried the message. Marco asked for no reply to his explicit instructions. He knew the Baroness would be glad to play the role he had assigned her in the drama he was staging.

Upon returning to the Venetian Embassy in Florence, he sent for a cooper, a drover, and a farmer, who came in by the tradesmen's door. Sitting behind a screen, he pruned all Venetian intonations from his speech, so that they did not know with whom they spoke. All readily agreed to carry out his commissions, for he paid generously.

Six days later, Marco sent for a physician, who entered by the front door and was ushered into the presence of the Ambassador Extraordinary by obsequious attendants. Professor Giuseppe Ortolan had praised the man's professional skill, but had warned that he was constitutionally indiscreet and an incorrigible snob. The medical man was certain to gossip about his illustrious patient, who was suffering from an ear ache and a wrenched back.

The ear was red, and the surrounding skin was hot. In no doubt

'I should've claimed them and brought them to Venice the day after . . . after I . . . after she went to her rest,' Paolo said, shamefaced. 'But I couldn't . . . too broken up. And now every move I make is watched. But I got Angela's tiara back.'

The girl baby had been placed in the Orphanage of San Rocco in Lucca, which cared for deformed children. She did not stand out among a dozen other brown-eyed infants, all very slow in their minds; a few drops of poppy juice a day subdued her normal animation and made her bright eyes dull.

That refuge could serve for only a few weeks, at most a month. Not only because Ferdinando's search was implacable, doubling back on itself to inspect again places already inspected, but because the dose of poppy juice had to be increased constantly. If the dose kept rising for another five or six weeks, she would become an irredeemable dullard, totally dependent on the drug.

The infant who was the rightful Grand Duke of Tuscany was sheltered by the Count of Abruzzo, whose wife had been Bianca's senior lady-in-waiting. The Count was now repentant, trying to atone for deserting his wife for debauchery for several years. She could, therefore, ask him what she would – and Annabella, Countess of Abruzzi, wanted protection for the son of Bianca, once Grand Duchess of Tuscany.

The Count had entrusted the boy to shepherds, a man and wife who did not come down from the high pastures with the winter. He was not likely to be discovered among the crags of the Apennines, where no one ventured at this season. With food enough to last till spring, the infant prince was safe from harm, barring illness or accident.

But the Count of Abruzzo was restive. His guilty conscience struggled against his sense of self-preservation. He feared Ferdinando's vengeance if his role were uncovered, which was not at all unlikely in the long run.

Not only the shepherds, but the two men-at-arms who had seen to their provisions, knew that a boy child was in hiding in the hills. It needed no great wit to guess that he might be the missing Medici, nor any great greed to covet the three thousand ducats Ferdinando offered for information about the infants. Besides, the Count saw no possible advantage in keeping the boy safe. How could a minute waif, with only the problematical backing of notoriously cautious Venice, possibly depose his ruthless uncle and take the throne?

'We've got a week's grace, maybe two, but no more,' Paolo summed

Passing Pistoia the next day, he did not turn off the high road. But, at the crossroads leading to Castello Crespelle, he repeatedly cracked his whip over the stolid oxen.

Saying he expected guests, Paolo Crespelle had sent a scullery boy to watch for a carriage showing a red pennant. The only red he had seen, the boy reported, was the cloak of a young woman sitting beside an older man in an ox-cart. The peasant was impatient, kept whipping the oxen.

But the scullery boy had seen no carriage. That was not remarkable, since Paolo was expecting no guests.

Had he, Paolo asked, seen a child? When the boy said he had not, Paolo gave his orders.

Escorted by the same men-at-arms who had ridden with him to the Royal Villa some two months earlier, he clattered out of the cobble-stone courtyard at dusk. The small detachment carried no banners, and the gleam of its armour was concealed by heavy cloaks.

Nonetheless, Ferdinando's spies in the trees along the trail noted the departure – and sent an urgent message to their chief in Pistoia. It looked ordinary, a routine foray to keep the men and horses fit, perhaps by mock skirmishing. But the officer in the lead, whose face was muffled against the cold, rode with the same awkwardness the younger Baron Crespelle exhibited in the saddle after so many years at sea.

When his rearguard reported that they were being followed, Paolo smiled in satisfaction and turned his horse's head towards Lucca. He had a rendezvous at the Orphanage of San Rocco.

The detachment arrived just before dawn, an hour after the departure of the farmer and the young woman in the red cloak. After seeing her mother, she had decided to go on with the peasant to Livorno to see her aunt. The hay had been delivered to the orphanage, and the four wine-casks were now checked and roped in place. There was no sign of an infant.

While the oxen plodded towards Livorno, a hundred and ten miles away to the south-west on the roundabout route that skirted Pisa, Paolo Crespelle and his men slept in the hay in the barn of the orphanage. An hour after dusk on the third day since Marco's departure from Florence, they set out again, turning north-east toward the Apennines and the border of Emilia and Tuscany. Generously provisioned by the nuns, each trooper now carried a bulging sack behind his saddle. Two troopers appeared nervous, for they were constantly checking their saddle-bags.

Paolo's forward scouts soon reported that fifty men of Duke Ferdinando's Household Guard were riding ahead of them. A few miles behind rode a full squadron of a hundred and twenty-five led by Colonel Giulio Arseno. When Crespelle, that renegade in the service of Venice, made his break for the frontier, the two units would grip him in a pincer.

Some seventy miles to the east, the cavalcade of the Venetian Ambassador Extraordinary inched along the high road to Bologna. In three days it had made only thirty miles, held to the pace of the slowest of the porters carrying His Excellency's gilded litter and further delayed by frequent stops to let the Ambassador rest. The Tuscan troopers escorting the cavalcade cursed the boring duty. At this rate, they would not get back to Florence for Christmas.

Their commander was a lieutenant colonel, newly promoted for his devotion to the new Grand Duke. Already satisfied that not one infant, much less two, was hidden in the cavalcade, he, too, was eager to return home. But he had been ordered to accompany the Ambassador to the frontier of the Venetian *terraferma*.

On the fourth day, a courier on an exhausted horse overtook the cavalcade. The lieutenant colonel read the dispatch and frowned.

Apologetic, almost sheepish, he told the commander of the Venetian escort that he had been ordered to search the cavalcade. Unscrupulous officials, it had been learned, were attempting to smuggle contraband goods. If the contraband were discovered by any of the states they must cross, it would be mortally embarrassing for both Tuscany and Venice. He did not say what the contraband was.

The search yielded some fine examples of Florentine pornography in the officers' baggage and many cruder examples in the troopers' saddle-bags. Also, of course, the usual Florentine worked leather, embroidered silk undergarments, and fashion jewellery, which soldiers and courtiers were taking back to their women. But no contraband – and no infants.

The lieutenant colonel apologised again. He had to search the Ambassador's litter, as well. Although His Excellency was above suspicion, something could have been sewn into its cushions. The Venetian commander protested icily at that gross violation of diplomatic immunity, but he could not, short of violence, prevent the intrusion.

The Ambassador did not protest, but watched in dignified silence as the troopers rummaged through his litter. They did not dream of tearing the bandage from his face. They were not looking for an imposter in his mid-forties, but for a pair of two-month-old children.

When the Ambassador's cavalcade began moving again, Paolo Crespelle's troop was threading the tangled trails north of Pistoia. The troopers knew every turning and every tree of that maze, where they hunted wild boar and deer. For a critical hour, the detachment shook off the Grand Duke's men.

They had, it appeared, truly come out to practise skirmishing. The troopers wheeled and charged, tearing up the ground, trampling shrubs, and breaking branches of the trees surrounding a clearing. Broken arrows and spears were left where they fell. Then, while Colonel Giulio Arseno raged at his scouts for losing the unit, Paolo Crespelle took leave of his troopers.

'Ride for the border as fast as you can,' he directed. 'First, trail your coats and let Arseno's men find you again. Then, lose them and get across the border. Make for the Etruscan tombs south of Bologna. I'll find you there.'

They left him in the clearing, the two infants who had been carried in the saddle-bags of the nervous troopers now snug at his feet in their blankets and swaddling clothes. Baron Paolo Crespelle then bent to the most dire act of his life. It was necessary, the last offering he could make to Bianca. It was necessary, but it was very hard.

Allowing himself no time to reflect, he picked up the whimpering boy child by the feet and dashed his head against a tree. The thin skull cracked open like a nut.

Dropping the boy, Paolo took up the girl and slid his dagger between her frail ribs. The point had penetrated no more than an inch when her soft breathing stopped.

Leaving the little corpses where they lay, Paolo mounted his horse and rode after his troopers. He did not know whether he could catch up with them; he only knew he had to escape the Duke's men. If they could not capture him, they could not question him – and the two mute forms would tell their own story of an ambush by bandits and the weak perishing.

His guilt was somewhat lessened by his knowledge that the two infants would have died within a few years anyway. They were both severely afflicted, physically as well as mentally, the nuns had told him, praising his charity in assuming the care of the little creatures. But, as yet, they bore no outward mark of their afflictions, none, at least, that would persist in death.

Riding northwards through the frost-rimed trees, Paolo Crespelle wondered again if he were wholly sane. If he were a little mad, it was a strange madness, for it touched only Bianca. For her he had twice done grave crimes, killing innocents, as he would for no other. But the time of his madness, if it were madness, was now over.

While her brother rode north, the Baroness Adacci yawned and huddled into her red cloak. At five in the afternoon, darkness was falling, and her perch in the ox-cart was hard. Since they could not stay at an inn, it was time to make camp.

It was past time for her to see to the two infants hidden in the wine-casks. She was not happy about keeping them drugged with poppy juice. Nor did she trust the ingenious hiding places in which they lay. All four casks would gush wine if their bungs were hammered out. But smaller casks were concealed within two, well cushioned for comfort. The baroness feared that the copper tubes that supplied air might be twisted or that wine might seep into the inner barrels and drown the twins.

Marco Capello had repeatedly assured her that could not happen. But did he really *know*?

She was, however, glad she had agreed to accompany him on this slow journey towards refuge for the babies. She loved her brother, and she cherished the memory of Bianca Capello de' Medici. For those two, she would do far more than making this fantastic journey as nursemaid to the fugitive prince and princess.

'Cecilia, it's almost over,' Marco said. 'Tomorrow we'll be in Livorno.'

'And they'll be safe,' she replied. 'I'm sure of it.'

Those words signalled the end of the adventure. Marco knew instinctively that she was right, and the tension flowed out of his bones. Somehow, he also knew that the two feints, Paolo's and the mock ambassador's, had wholly diverted Ferdinando's attention.

That evening, when they camped and Cecilia Adacci looked after the infants, he knew the road to Livorno lay open before them. Two days later, the weary oxen plodded unhindered down to the wharves of the port that had been built by the infants' grandfather, Cosimo I, and expanded by their father, Francesco I.

Marco approached the master of the Genoese merchantman *Dove*, which was sailing that evening for Bari on the east coast of Italy. Had the *Dove* not been in port, he would have drawn from his memory of the encyclopaedic files of the Venetian Secret Service a dozen other ships that would have served as well – largely because of their captains' inclination to larceny.

The captain of the *Dove* asked no other questions after Marco answered his first: 'Is passage worth twenty ducats to you?'

He obviously believed they were smuggling jewels or spices. Why else would they insist that their two casks of rough country wine be crammed into their already cramped cabin?

A few hours later, the *Dove* was sighted by two Venetian galleys. They were part of a full squadron sent to patrol the coast of Tuscany off Livorno and carry the Red Inquisitor and his two adopted children home to Venice.